A BATTLE OF WILLS

Shayna's head was thrown back, her hands raised high, raised to strike.

"Shayna," Corwyn's voice was frozen steel.

She turned to Jaimah and spoke in a frightened voice. "Let me draw upon your powers, Jaimah."

Jaimah stared at her. It was a request that even in her wildest imaginings Jaimah hadn't expected to hear from Shayna's lips. All these years Shayna thought that she had nothing and was worthless.

"Quickly, Jaimah. Stand with me, girl. We will defeat him together."

Her words were like splinters of ice tearing into Jaimah's flesh. Shayna would use her in the next moment whether she agreed or not. Yet, this woman had raised her, had almost been a mother...

It was an effort to wrench her eyes from that contact.

Along the arch of the sky flashed a jagged sword of purple lightning...

THE
APPRENTICE

Deborah Talmadge-Bickmore

A Del Rey Book

BALLANTINE BOOKS • NEW YORK

To Sting, for the inspiration
    that led to the writing of this book,
To Karol, for her help in bringing
    the vision to fruition,
And to Steven, who was a great part
    of the writing, after the fact.

To Mother, for all her love and encouragement.

Sometimes words meant for one purpose
    can mean something else, ie.,
WRAPPED AROUND YOUR FINGER
—The Police, SYNCHRONICITY 1983

Chapter One

Hᴉꜱ ʜᴀɴᴅ ᴄᴀᴍᴇ ᴡɪᴛʜ ᴀ ʜᴀʀᴅ ᴛʜᴜᴅ ᴀɢᴀɪɴꜱᴛ ᴛʜᴇ ᴅᴏᴏʀ ᴀꜱ Jaimah tried to push it closed. Her heart lurched in sudden fear.

"Go away," she said. "Shayna sees no one."

"She'll see me."

His midnight blue eyes seemed to conceal ominous depths that she sensed with rising alarm. "I have been many days getting to this place." His voice shivered like ice through her. "I will not leave until she sees me."

Jaimah's heart beat with jarring strokes. "I can't disturb her," she said. "You'll have to go away." She pushed at the heavy wooden door again, but his weight was on it.

"Tell her I'm here."

Jaimah stared at him in fear.

He was weather-beaten, the hood of his gray travel-worn cloak thrown back to reveal blond hair falling across his neck.

Never had she seen anyone like him. In all the years that she had served Shayna in the tower, never had anyone ventured up the mountain and requested entrance. Not even Hagoth, the merchant who came twice a year, would come inside. He was always eager to leave, unable to put aside his plainsman's fear and abhorance of Shayna and the mountain any longer than it took to deliver his merchandise and receive his silver.

Now this stranger came, demanding to be let into the tower

to see Shayna. And Shayna was locked in her rooms.

"Go away," Jaimah said again. "She will not see you."

"I will not be turned away." He reached up and gripped her arm.

Jaimah flinched, her breath catching in terror. She sensed, in that contact, an indescribable power that radiated from him, something so dangerous and forceful she panicked. She tried to tear herself from his grasp. But he held her firmly and would not let her retreat.

His dark blue gaze smoldered down into hers, and suddenly it seemed that the world narrowed abruptly to his eyes and she was yanked into their depths. They were blue, midnight blue, like a dangerous storm. And somehow it was as if he knew her—very well.

She gasped at the intensity of that impression.

"What's going on down here?" another voice demanded. Shayna!

Jaimah spun around, twisting her arm out of the stranger's hand, and looked up to the dark figure descending the shadowed stairs. Her stomach clenched.

"Speak up, girl!" Shayna reached the bottom of the steps and came forward. She was tall and fair, wearing black robes that were long of sleeve and high of collar. Black hair, thick and shining, hung down her back. She had delicate features that could be either gentle or cruel, long slender hands, and eyes as black as a moonless night.

She came to a stop where the light from the door stretched across the stone floor. She looked past Jaimah to the stranger.

"I tried to make him leave . . ."

"Be still, Jaimah."

Jaimah bit her lip, casting a furtive glance to the stranger.

"I have traveled a long distance to see you," he said.

Shayna nodded. "I knew that one day someone would come." She stepped back to let him enter. "Come with me." She moved to the stairs, then paused to look over her shoulder. "Close the door, Jaimah."

Jaimah hastened to push the heavy door shut and then followed Shayna and the stranger up the two flights of curving stairs to where Shayna's chambers were.

That the Lady had not sent the stranger away both surprised and frightened Jaimah. She did not understand why Shayna had let him into the tower. He was obviously from the plain, and the people of the plain shunned the tower. Fear and hatred of Shayna and her powers kept the plainsmen away from the mountain where the tower stood. And Shayna seemed to prefer it that way. She even seemed to foster the ill feeling toward her and her tower.

But now this stranger had entered into its dark walls. He had come to where vapors and fires filled the air as Shayna wove together her words and her powders. He had entered into where even Jaimah cringed in the corner at the things that came out of the smoke. And the stranger entered Shayna's rooms without fear, his dark eyes smoldering in a way that made Jaimah shiver.

"Wait here," the Lady told her, and Jaimah was left alone in the gloom. So she sat down on the stone floor with her back against the clammy stone wall and hugged her knees to her chest. She chewed anxiously on her thumbnail and watched the heavy wooden door in the dark. Time passed. Her feet ached with the cold, but she ignored them. She put her brow to her knees, closed her eyes, and waited.

"Jaimah," a soft voice brought her head up. The heavy door had opened and Shayna stood within the chamber, her black robe swirling to a rest at her feet. Jaimah rose, looked past the Lady to the stranger who was standing in front of the window at the other end of the room. His cloak had been removed and a red tunic made his figure appear to blaze.

"Lady?" Jaimah said weakly.

"Come in, girl. Don't stand there like a dolt." Shayna stepped aside and let Jaimah come hesitatingly into the room.

The brazier glowed with ruby heat from recent use, and the air was heavy with spicy perfume. Jaimah looked uncertainly from the brazier to the stranger as the door swung closed behind her with a quiet thud.

Shayna came around her with a whisper of robe and stood beside the brazier. "Jaimah, this is Corwyn."

Jaimah looked at him from lowered eyes. He was silhouetted against the window, afternoon light falling past his shoulders to the floor at his feet. He was looking steadily at her, his face expressionless, but his eyes were alive with an alertness that caused Jaimah's insides to quake.

"Corwyn is going to be my apprentice. I want you to take him to the chambers directly below mine. See that they are made ready for him." Shayna turned her dark eyes on Jaimah. "Anything that he needs, see that it is provided. Is that clear?" There was a hint of threat in Shayna's tone.

Jaimah quickly murmured, "Yes, Shayna."

She knew the unspoken meaning to Shayna's words, heard the veiled hint in the Lady's voice. Nothing was to be done for this Corwyn without Shayna's knowledge. She was to serve him only as long as his wishes were in accordance with Shayna's will. Jaimah darted another nervous look at him and saw that he was still watching her. For an instant, she felt that he knew her thoughts, but she shook off the feeling.

"Be quick about it, Jaimah," Shayna was saying. "There is much that yet needs to be done before the midnight hour."

"Yes, Shayna," Jaimah said.

"Quickly, girl!" Shayna's voice was quiet, but impatient, demanding instant compliance.

Jaimah moved to the door, looking back to see that this new apprentice was following her. She led him into the cold, dark corridor. The door closed, leaving them in semidarkness. "This way," she murmured as her bare feet padded softly along the stone floor, then down the dark stairs that curved along the wall. The new apprentice came wordlessly behind, his boots echoing hollowly against the stone walls. At the end of the stairs, Jaimah hurried along another corridor to a large wooden door much like the one that barred Shayna's rooms. She pushed it open revealing a large, dimly lit chamber.

"These are your rooms," Jaimah said softly, almost afraid to speak to him as he came to stand beside her. The stranger's eyes wandered through the room, lingered briefly in each dark recess and then moved on again.

"The sleeping chamber is beyond," Jaimah said, indicating another closed door within the shadows of the room. "I will bring sleeping furs and will dust and sweep."

The stranger looked down at her in silent appraisal, his face in shadow. Jaimah shivered under his dark gaze, feeling again that somehow he knew her. She dismissed it and hurried across the shadowed room to escape his scrutiny. She pulled aside the heavy drape that covered the large window, stepping out of the cascading dust that fell from the deep folds.

Yellow sunlight came through the window and Jaimah looked about the room, her nose wrinkled in a frown. The room was large and empty. It was a duplicate of Shayna's, except in reverse; the door to the sleeping chamber was on the northern side, the fire hearth directly opposite. The stone wall that held the large windows was curved, being the outside wall of the tower. Jaimah shivered as she felt the cold that crept in through the stone from the mountain. Thick dust lay on the floor, undisturbed except for her footprints and the eddied swirling patterns caused by her hurry to get away from the new apprentice.

Corwyn crossed the room and opened the door to the sleeping chamber, revealing a shadowed room beyond. There was an empty bookcase standing against the wall, not fitting exactly, because the wall there was curved also. A table stood next to the bookcase, only the corner showing. Both pieces of furniture were covered with thick dust.

Corwyn disappeared into the darkness of the room, his footsteps muffled by the dust. Jaimah heard him pull at the drapery, and light fell across the dust on the floor.

She went to the door, looked in, and saw a sleeping cot covered with dust against the wall, the head at the curved wall next to the window. A heavy, musty odor met her nostrils and her fingers unconsciously found the cold support of the stone wall as she watched Corwyn inspect the room and then the view from the window.

"I will go get the sleeping furs," she finally said when he didn't turn from the window. He nodded, and Jaimah waited for him to speak. But, when he didn't, she turned from the door uncertainly and crossed the room, letting herself out into the corridor.

Descending the spiral staircase, she went past the large entrance door, down to the cooking and washing room. She drew a bucket of water, got a broom, some rags, and some bedding furs. Turning to leave, she hesitated with one foot on the stair.

Looking over her shoulder, she searched the shadows of the room for the presence that suddenly she could feel was there.

"Encheon?" she queried softly. "Encheon, is that you?" She turned and was met by silence. She looked about the room, waiting for the presence to show himself. But the gloom of the shadows remained undisturbed. "Encheon?"

She saw that the thin plank door to her room stood open, resting against a large washing bin. "Are you in there?" She walked across to her room and peered into the darkness. Nothing moved. "Encheon?"

No one answered her.

Finally, reluctantly, she went back to the stairs and climbed slowly up to Corwyn's rooms. She hesitated at the door, dreading to go in.

Corwyn's back was to her in the large room, his attention out the window when she finally opened the door. He glanced at her over his shoulder, his hair shining like polished gold against the flame of his tunic. "Come here," he said in a quiet voice.

Jaimah put down the bucket and broom, draped the furs over her arm, and went to him, clutching the rags tightly in her hands.

"Tell me what I am seeing," he said.

She took a quick look at his angular profile, thinking that his face could have been carved out of stone, he looked so stern and arrogant. She swallowed nervously. "There," he said, indicating with his chin. "Where does that lead?"

Jaimah looked at the trail he meant, leading from the tower, twisting and winding up into the bare crags of the distant peaks—Shayna's trail. "It goes to the Peak," she said.

"And there?" He turned his head to look at the deep ravine that fell away from the foot of the tower.

Jaimah peered past him. "That is where we grow our herbs." she murmured.

She let her eyes return to the lonely peaks that surrounded them on all sides, bare, jagged, rough and harsh. Life of any kind was scarce out there. The winds were cold, the nights icy, the winters eternally long. Only below, in the ravine, was the mountain hospitable enough to grow the plants and herbs that Shayna used for her spells and powders. It was there where Jaimah also grew some of the food that they ate.

Corwyn turned away from the window and went to where she had left the bucket and broom. "Come," he said. "I will help you."

"Oh, no!" Jaimah said in alarm. "You must not." She started toward him. "Shayna would never allow it." A brief sardonic smile eased the tightness of his mouth. Jaimah stopped short when she saw it. "You don't understand," she said. "She would be very angry."

Corwyn stepped to the door; very deliberately he pushed it until it closed with a soft thud. "She'll never know."

Jaimah stared at him uncertainly, knowing that she should object. But she didn't know what to say. Corwyn picked up the broom. "You dust."

Her eyes followed him as he went to the other room, her

fingers gripping the rags in a death hold. The sound of the broom sweeping across the floor, steady and rythmic, came to her through the door. Reluctantly, she went to the bucket of water, picked it up and stood undecided at where to begin. She wanted very much to leave the rooms completely.

Corwyn's voice came to her, "Start with the shelves."

Jaimah hesitated uneasily.

Only the knowledge that Shayna was waiting for her moved her through the door to the bookcase. She began wiping the thick, heavy, cloying dust from the shelves, apprehension prickling her scalp. She could feel his presence in the room like a tangible thing, a presence that was something other than his physical body, something much more powerful. It reached beyond him and around him, filling the room, touching everything. He spoke in her ear, "It's not so bad, is it? My helping?"

Jaimah spun around, startled.

His face was close to hers, amusement at the corners of his dark blue eyes. Her hands tightened on the shelves behind her, the edges pressing painfully into her back. "It is not the way things are done here," she said pointedly, not knowing why she spoke so harshly. The abruptness brought a flicker of a frown to Corwyn's eyes. Jaimah regretted it at once.

He seemed to assess her eyes before he said, "Indeed." There was something in his tone, or on his face, that was almost a challenge, and Jaimah was suddenly cautious. She could not turn away from him, held prisoner by the bookshelves behind her and the scrutinizing gaze of his eyes. He was looking at her as if he knew her, but was seeing her for the first time. Jaimah felt her breath still in her throat. After a moment, he stepped back. "If we don't get busy we'll never get finished. Shayna did say that she wanted this done quickly."

He went back to where he had been sweeping and, with one hand, pulled the straw mattress off the sleeping cot and shook it. Dust flew everywhere. They were back on familiar ground, if there could be a familiar ground after so short a time. Jaimah opened her mouth to speak, to say that Shayna wanted her to do the work. Corwyn's look cut her off, saving her the effort that she knew was futile.

Sometime later, she stood in the center of the large room, leaning on the broom, her chin resting on her clasped hands. She could hear Corwyn replacing the bucket by the door. Both rooms had been swept and dusted and the windows washed. She was tired; her body ached, and she longed to go to her room where she could sink into the oblivion of sleep. But she knew Shayna was waiting for her upstairs. She would have to run for herbs and powders and bottles while Shayna struggled with some obscure spell that had been occupying her for several months. Tired as she was, there would not be much sleep for her this night.

Jaimah roused herself. "I have to go now." She moved across to the bucket, bent to pick it up, and rose to find Corwyn watching her. She flushed.

He reached out and took the bucket from her. "I will go with you."

Jaimah swallowed, looked down at the bucket, then back up again. "I don't know if Shayna will allow you . . ."

Corwyn turned, opened the door, and stood aside for her. "Come, Jaimah," he said. "Let's dispose of this first."

She hesitated, with misgivings, but went reluctantly into the hall. He followed her, closed the door behind them, and went with her downstairs in silence. There he dumped the water where she showed him. Then she placed the rags into the washing bin.

"Now," Corwyn said, taking hold of her arm before she could escape. "Let us go find Shayna." Jaimah flinched at his touch, but his grip was strong and unyielding. "I am, after all, the new apprentice," he added. "Should I not be there to see what the Lady does?" There was that in his voice which made her stop and look at him apprehensively. His eyes looked darkly down at her and she wondered wildly for a moment if Shayna had let a menace into the tower. It was a long moment before he said, "I do not think the Lady will wait patiently for long."

Jaimah nodded her head slightly, admitting that he was right. Shayna would soon come. Corwyn smiled triumphantly. "Shall we go?"

He propelled her, gently but resolutely, up the winding stairs, past the entrance, past his chambers, and up again and into the dark hall before Shayna's door. Jaimah shrank back once there, suddenly loath to go in. There was danger inside, more than ever before. She could feel it, like an actual presence. An aversion that was close to panic took hold of her as she faced that wooden door, pulled back at Corwyn's unrelenting grasp, trying to escape. But he drew her closer, almost in front of him.

"Come now," he said, his voice so low that the words were nearly a whisper against her ear. "It won't do to be afraid." Then he added. "Knock on the door."

Jaimah swallowed and put out her hand, but the door came open. Shayna stood silhouetted against an orange sunset that streamed into the dark hall from the large windows.

"I have been waiting," she said coldly.

"I'm sorry, Shayna," Jaimah murmured. Corwyn released her, and she felt strangely alone.

Shayna looked over Jaimah's head to Corwyn. "Did you find your rooms satisfactory?"

"Yes. I shall be very comfortable there. Thank you, my Lady."

Jaimah, surprised at the deference she heard in his voice, shot a glance at him over her shoulder and saw that his expression was masked in respect and submission.

"The girl made them ready?"

"Everything has been done."

"Good." Shayna swung her gaze to Jaimah. Then she looked back to Corwyn. "Come in." She turned and went across the room.

Jaimah slipped to the chair that was her accustomed place in the far corner and huddled there as Corwyn closed the door. His eyes sought her in the shadow and rested on her a moment. Then he turned to Shayna.

The Lady was staring absently at an open book on the table beside her. The index finger of her left hand traced small designs on the page; her thoughts were obviously on something other than the book.

Jaimah brought her knees up to her chin and wrapped her arms tightly around them. She lowered her forehead to her knees and closed her aching eyes. She did not like it when Shayna was preoccupied. Unpleasant things usually began to happen. She rubbed her eyes, glad that her chair was in the shadows behind the large book-laden table. She wanted to be forgotten for the moment.

Shayna tapped her fingernail on the table several times and, coming to some sort of decision, turned to Corwyn. "I have been thinking," she said, "about your duties. I had intended once before to take an apprentice..." She looked meaningfully at Jaimah. "But I was deceived, and she is inept." There was a moment of strained silence before Shayna turned her eyes back to Corwyn. "Consequently I had put all such considerations out of my mind."

Jaimah kept her eyes lowered and leaned against the cold wall, humiliated by Shayna's revelation. The heat of embarrassment burned her face, and she tried to make herself unnoticeable.

"I am inclined to think," Shayna continued, "that, though you have talent, which you demonstrated so ably earlier, you are largely undisciplined and practically untrainable. I think that you are impetuous and are expecting a great deal—very soon. But too soon." She turned to the window and looked out at the dying sunset. "It would be unwise to allow you to delve into any of my secrets until we see how far your talents extend." She looked at him over her shoulder.

"Whatever you think best," Corwyn replied.

Jaimah thought she could detect disappointment in his voice. She looked at Shayna from her lowered eyelashes, for she also had heard the words that the Lady had left unspoken, and she shuddered. By the time Shayna was through with him, he'd have no talent left.

Jaimah glanced at him bleakly, a glance that warned, a glance that he did not see.

He faced Shayna, an almost aggressive air about the way he stood, his hands clasped behind him, his head erect, his eyes steadily on the Lady.

But Shayna did not see. She was looking again at the open book on the table.

Corwyn turned his head a fraction and fixed Jaimah with a dark gaze that was both secretive and calculating. She stared back with foreboding. She was concerned for him, for she knew what Shayna was capable of; yet, at the same time, she was afraid of him.

"To begin with, then . . ." Shayna said. The mask of submissiveness rose again on Corwyn's face. "I will have Jaimah teach you the care of our herbs."

Jaimah sat up with a start, taken by surprise. "No!" The exclamation was out of her mouth before she could stop it. Instantly she regretted it and would have given anything to take it back. She knew that Shayna would not be patient with her outburst.

"You object, Jaimah?"

"Well," Jaimah looked at her fingers uncertainly. "No.

But..." She glanced quickly at Corwyn. He was watching her but his expression was unreadable. "Surely not the care of herbs?"

"Why not?" Shayna's voice was cold.

"I thought...I mean..." Jaimah stopped, wishing she hadn't said anything at all.

"Speak up, girl!"

Jaimah blinked as she watched her fingers twist together. "Taking care of herbs is servant's work," she finally said.

Shayna snorted in derision. "Don't be stupid! How else is he to learn?"

Jaimah kept her eyes lowered, not daring to say anything more and give Shayna reason to humiliate her further. She wanted to run from the room. She did not see Shayna turn and pull the heavy drapes over the window, shutting out the last purple of the fading sunset. She looked up at Corwyn from the gloom of her corner. He was watching Shayna with such intentness she feared the Lady would notice. But she didn't or, at least, didn't seem to.

Shayna went to the brazier, treading softly across the stone floor. From a small dish that was a part of the brass she threw a pinch of yellow powder onto the hot coals. Long twisting and writhing tendrils of smoke rose into the air, saffron-colored, entwining, until a heavy cloud was hanging over-head. A heady fragrance slowly filled the room. Heavy and intoxicating fingers of amber reached out and entered Jaimah's head, rippling and curling.

She watched, through the haze that was gathering before and behind her eyes, as Shayna moved around the brazier to stand in front of Corwyn. She could hear Shayna speak in low tones, but she could not distinguish the words. And yet she could feel the power that came from them.

Then Shayna raised her right hand, and on her index finger a ring began to glow with a golden light.

Jaimah peered through the growing smoke, not sure at first what she was seeing. She thought that maybe she was seeing wrong. Surely Shayna was not using the ring. Then she tried to move with a sudden desperation when she realized that what she saw was real. Shayna threw her a look that clearly said, *Don't interfere.* But Jaimah struggled with all her might against the stupor that was coming over her. She had to warn Corwyn about the ring, tell him about the pain it held—and the terror. She fought to stand.

Corwyn turned, looked at her briefly, and in that moment she sensed a power in him so strong it tore the breath from her. The force of it was so concentrated and so intense that it seared through her like surging fire. She gasped for air, staring at him through the growing mists.

Then, just as suddenly as it had come, it was gone and Corwyn turned away. A numbness began to spread throughout her body. She could only watch through the thickening vapor as Corwyn reached out to touch Shayna's hand. Then the mists behind her eyes congealed and blackness came over her.

When she opened her eyes, a piercing light stabbed through her head. She raised a hand to cover her face. Soft footsteps and the whispering of robes came to her ears. She heard Shayna's voice, quiet and low, "It is over, Jaimah."

Jaimah peered through her fingers, winced at the bright light. She blinked several times before she could see. The light was coming from the brazier, actually only a soft glow. But it seemed to, be a glaring brightness too harsh for her eyes. She lowered her hand, squinting and blinking at the tears caused by the light. Corwyn was gone.

She looked at Shayna appalled. "You used the ring." Her voice that was filled with accusation was barely above a whisper.

Shayna's eyes narrowed. "Take care of what you say, Jaimah. These are matters that do not concern you."

"What did you do to him?"

Shayna looked steadily at Jaimah without answering, her eyes hard and cold. She seemed to be evaluating something that had suddenly occured to her, then she dismissed whatever it was with an impatient turn of her head. "Ask no more questions of me, Jaimah."

The girl covered her aching eyes with her hand, shutting the light out to ease the painful throbbing within her head. She wanted to cry but couldn't. Long ago. . . . When had it been? It seemed like yesterday when she, too, had felt the power of the ring. The terror of that experience was still within her memory. No matter how self-possessed Corwyn was, he wouldn't ever be able to withstand the ring. In time there would be nothing left but an empty shell of a man, completely enslaved to it and to Shayna.

Jaimah swallowed the nausea that was starting to rise in her stomach. She had to get away from this room.

She stood up shakily and leaned on the table for support. The walls spun around her, and she closed her eyes. "Shayna," she said weakly. "I think I'm going to be sick."

Shayna put an arm around her and made her sit down again. "Here," she said reaching for a goblet that was sitting on the table. "Drink this."

The edge was pressed to Jaimah's lips, and she sipped cautiously. The warm liquid was bitter, horrible. She pulled away from the cup.

"No," Shayna said. "Drink it all."

Obediently Jaimah reached for the goblet and quickly drained the contents, holding her breath against the biting odor. Almost immediately the dizziness left her. The pounding in her head was still there, but she could at least move without the room swimming in front of her.

"Can you walk now?" Shayna asked.

Jaimah rose hesitantly to her feet, then nodded. She moved slowly across the room and reached for the door. Shayna was there first and opened it for her. Her black eyes turned to Jaimah, fierce and caustic. "Tomorrow, you take Corwyn to the ravine."

Jaimah nodded weakly, her strength already lessening. She turned to leave, but Shayna laid a hand on her arm to stop her. "Don't ever cross me, Jaimah. This is a warning. It would not bear well for you. Remember that." Jaimah returned her gaze unable to understand what she was talking about. "Go to bed, Jaimah," the Lady said at last.

"Yes, Shayna." She turned into the hall and the door closed, leaving her in darkness.

Jaimah groped for the wall, found it, and leaned against it. What little strength she had received from the goblet ebbed away. She stood with her head bowed trying to find the will to walk away from the door. Finally she followed the wall, one hand supporting her, until she reached the staircase. She started down it, certain that she'd never make it to the bottom.

When she finally reached the last step of the first flight, she could go no farther. She lowered herself to the step, put her forehead to her knees, weariness covering her like a thickness of dust. "Encheon, where are you?" she whispered. She leaned against the wall, the cold from the stonework slowly seeping into her body and into her bones. The minutes dragged by, icy and deadly. She let the chill claim her, unable to resist.

After a time the door down the hall opened, and quiet footsteps came toward her. Strong arms picked her up, cradled her, and carried her through a door that was closed softly. Then she was aware of thick furs around her. A moment later, strong hands were massaging the life back into her limbs, slowly, deliberately. Warmth and strength spread from the touch, easing the grip of ice in her muscles and bones. After a while, she slept.

Chapter Two

JAIMAH WOKE TO FIND HERSELF LOOKING OUT A WINDOW AT dark sky and at the mountain that was just beginning to be discernible in the predawn. She lay still, reluctant to move, trying to remember. The bed was warm, enveloping, and she longed to stay in it forever. But it was not her cot. Slowly, she let her eyes study the dark room. Against one wall stood a familiar black shape that she knew to be Corwyn's bookshelves. She could barely make out the table next to it. A faint line of light came from under the closed door, dim enough to suggest candlelight.

She sat up, shivered, and pulled the covering from the bed to wrap tightly around her. Her feet shrank from the icy floor, but she stood and went silently across the room. Running the fingers of one hand through her hair, she cautiously opened the door.

Corwyn was sitting at a table that Jaimah had never seen before, reading from a large leather-bound book by the light of two candles. The flickering flame reflected a dusky yellow from his hair and cast the lines of his face into dark shadow. The confidence and the arrogance that Jaimah had seen the day before was back, unhidden by the mask that he had shown to Shayna.

He looked up from the book with shadowed eyes. A faint smile touched his lips, and he stood, leaving the open book on

15

the table. "I see you are recovered." Although he spoke quietly, his voice was distinct.

She did not answer, but looked at him, recalling the scene of the night before. Shayna had used her ring . . . she remembered this vividly. But he was not hurt! Confusion held her without words. Corwyn's eyes caught the perplexity on her face, and he laughed softly as he came around and leaned on the table. "What is wrong, Jaimah?"

She hesitated, not knowing what to say, then answered, "I was expecting to see you . . ." She stopped, seeing something she couldn't identify flicker across his face. "I thought . . ."

"What did you think?"

"That Shayna . . . her ring . . ."

Amusement danced in Corwyn's eyes and played around his lips. Jaimah was unsettled by it. She turned her attention to the table on which he sat, one leg slung over a corner. There were intricate carvings all along the edge, and the massive legs ended in clawed talons on the floor. "Where did you get that?"

Corwyn looked at it with a shrug. "Oh, I just conjured it up." His eyes turned on her again. His words had sounded playful, but his gaze was serious. Jaimah wondered suddenly if he had indeed plucked it out of thin air, created it out of nothing. She looked at him suspiciously.

"Did you sleep well?" Corwyn asked.

"Yes," she said softly. Suddenly she wanted to flee. There was a dangerous aura about him, and it made her afraid. "I have to go now," she said. "I have to prepare Shayna's breakfast."

"It has already been done." Corwyn leaned back and picked up the book he had been reading. Closing it he stood and came to her.

"You took Shayna her breakfast?" Jaimah was aghast. Her mind immediately whirled through the repercussions that that would bring; a clear memory of Shayna saying, *Don't ever cross me*, leaped at her.

Corwyn walked past her into the shadowed sleeping chamber and slid the book into the bookcase. Jaimah saw in the dim candlelight that an entire shelf was filled with books. She barely had the presence of mind to wonder where they had come from. But she returned to what Corwyn had said. "Shayna will be angry," she murmured.

"She will not be angry." Corwyn came to her and looked

down into her eyes. Jaimah shrank back against the door.
"You don't understand," she whispered.

"What don't I understand?"

"Shayna will be angry that I have let you do my work."

"You have not let me."

"That makes no difference. She will think that I have."
Jaimah was feeling very uncomfortable with him standing so
close to her.

"Does that frighten you?"

"Yes." She nodded, thinking of the ring and how it had
once been used on her. She had to clench her hands to keep
from trembling.

"Don't worry." He turned to walk back to the table, and
Jaimah followed him with her eyes. "Shayna's breakfast is
downstairs waiting for you to take it up to her." Corwyn
looked at her over his shoulder. "I have been keeping it warm
for you."

Jaimah studied him, feeling both foolish and grateful,
wondering how he had known about the morning routine. She
recalled the moment when she had felt that indomitable power
emanating from him the night before. She searched for it now,
but only got a hint of menace that seemed to be hidden behind
his eyes.

Corwyn turned to her as if he knew what she was thinking.
She lowered her eyes and went to the other door. As her hand
touched the latch, he asked, "Aren't you forgetting something?"

"What?"

"The herbs."

"Oh." Jaimah's heart thudded with dismay. She had forgotten and had thought to escape to her own room after taking
Shayna her meal.

"It *is* the Lady's wish." There was a hint of mockery in his
voice.

"Yes," Jaimah said. "Of course." She pulled the door open.
"I will be ready in a few minutes." Before Corwyn could
reply, she slipped out into the hall; she stood just outside the
door for a moment trembling . . . or shivering. She didn't
know which. She pulled the fur tighter around her, then went
down the stairs to the cooking area.

The food was there just as Corwyn had said it was: cheese,
honey tea, heavy slices of meal bread with melted butter drip-

ping from them, all setting neatly on a tray close to the hot brick hearth. Rich steam rose from a pot of bubbling stew over the coals. Everything was ready.

Jaimah dished up a bowl of the stew, put it on the tray, and carried it up to Shayna's room. Balancing the tray on her hip, she knocked softly. The door swung open, and she stepped in, closing the door quietly with her foot.

Jaimah gaped at the room in astonishment, not quite believing what she was seeing. Shayna was leaning over the table, engrossed in the measuring of several powders into a small bowl. All around her—piled in the corners, mounded in the open spaces—stood the jumbled mess of her possessions: boxes, trunks, books, bottles, all hastily gone through and then discarded. The shelves along the walls were nearly empty, the tables completely covered with articles that Shayna normally kept hidden from sight. Jaimah stood looking at it all, speechless.

"Well, what is it, girl?" Shayna's impatient voice came from her bowed head.

Jaimah found her voice. "I brought your breakfast."

Shayna picked up another bottle of powder and pulled out the cork. "Yes, yes. Put it down."

Jaimah looked around for a place that wasn't covered with open books or randomly placed bottles. Then with one hand she began to move bottles aside from the corner of a small table standing close to the door. Setting the tray down she asked, "Is there anything you want me to do?"

Shayna measured a small amount of powder into the bowl. "No. I have no need of you today."

Jaimah turned to the door to leave, hesitated uncertainly. Shayna looked up impatiently. "What now?"

"Don't you want me to put any of this away?"

Shayna looked around at the mess and scowled. "No. I want you to take Corwyn to the ravine. Teach him how to grow herbs."

Jaimah nodded and slipped out. A feeling of foreboding followed her as she padded down the hall.

She went down the stairs, past Corwyn's floor, past the entrance, and into the cooking area. She went into her small room behind the washing bins. There she changed her shiftlike dress for one that was warmer, ran a comb through her shoulder-length dark hair, and tied it back with a string. Splashing cold water on her face, she peered at her gray eyes and small face in a broken piece of mirror she had.

Steeling herself for the ordeal of taking Corwyn to the ravine and wishing fervently that she didn't have to, she turned to leave, then saw in the shadowed corner of the small room a shimmering of air that brought an exclamation of relief from her.

"*Encheon!*"

The lacy phosphorescence grew swiftly in size, like a ghostly fire catching and flaring on dry wood. The wall and the small wooden chest of Jaimah's belongings could be seen through the rippling iridescence, as if seen through a glittery veil. It congealed until it had gained enough substance to appear like a quicksilver cobweb of light, and it rose and fell in slow motion like the fire it resembled. But it was something very different indeed.

"Encheon, I am so glad you are here." Jaimah moved to the center of the room. She wanted to ask him where he had been, but she knew he would not tell her. He had been away for four days. She had called but he hadn't come, and that was unusual. It wasn't very often that he stayed away for more than a day, then never said where he had been, even when she asked.

"Favored One, I am pleased to be here, also." The quiet voice came out of the slow-moving flame and was hollow, as if coming from some other place. "But I have come only to bid you farewell."

Jaimah's heart thudded. "Farewell?"

"My time here has come to an end. I must return to my place."

"What do you mean? You're going away?"

"I am sent away."

"Sent away? Who is sending you away?" Jaimah stared at the shimmering flame in confusion. Somewhere her stunned thoughts told her he was joking, that he was having fun at her expense, and in a few moments he would laugh and bring it all to an end. But deep down inside, a cold realization knew that he was not. He was truly being sent away. And a sudden thought came to her "Shayna! She is sending you away!" Something very near panic raced through her. Somehow Shayna had found out about him.

"No, Protected One. It is not your mistress who sends me away. But another." His voice was soothing, intending to comfort as was his way, but Jaimah was not touched by it.

"Who then? I don't understand," she cried.

"Please, Beloved One. Do not fear so. Everything will be all right."

But she did not believe him. He was her long-time companion and friend, the only other besides Shayna that she knew. And although he was a disembodied entity, without shape or form, she had come to depend on him as her sole source of solace, waiting every day for him to appear as he did most of the time. She had shared her thoughts with him, had shared her troubles with him; and he, in return, had given her comfort. His only requirement was that Shayna not know of him. And he never said where he had come from, nor why he had started to appear in her room at night.

He showed her things that she had never seen; rivers, oceans, deserts, mountains with trees and flowers. He showed her animals and fish, birds tiny and large. And he showed her the Watchers, great beasts of silver and gray and white, slope-shouldered, large of paw and mouth—watchers of the mountain, roaming its crags and cliffs in silent, unseen presence, a tangible weight on the senses if one reached out to search for them.

Encheon talked to her of knowledge, of magic, and of many things that Shayna did not. He came sometimes when she called, and sometimes he came when she hadn't called. He came when Shayna was angry and had banished her to her room. He came when she was lonely and afraid. Always, always he was there when she needed him.

But now he was telling her farewell. He was leaving her, never to return. She felt as if the very foundation of her soul was being ripped from her.

"Encheon, please say this is not so. Please say you'll stay."

"There is nothing for you to fear, Revered One. All is as it should be."

"What do you mean?"

"Another has come to the tower."

"Corwyn?" Jaimah tried to understand what he meant. "Shayna has taken him as apprentice."

"You have no need for me now. This is as it was always meant to be."

"No!" she cried, a new horror coming to her.

The ghostly flame rose and fell, the shimmering intensifying briefly, like the rippling of quicksilver across a table. "You have nothing to fear."

"But I do! I felt from him . . . a power . . ." Her voice fell to a whisper. "I'm certain of it."

"Good." The voice seemed pleased. "Maybe you are feeling true. And if you are, you can learn from him. He is one of your kind. He can teach you."

"You can teach me."

"No, Precious One. My time here has come to an end. It was always to be thus. I can't stay."

Tears slid down Jaimah's face, unchecked. "What am I to do? Without you, I have no one."

"Not true, Beloved One. You are not as alone as you think. The way is inside yourself. I have always taught you thus. You only have to reach inside to find it."

"But without you, I am nothing."

The flame blazed brighter than she had ever seen it, almost as if Encheon were angry with her. "Not so, Honored One! Who you are is not what you see, true. But in time you will learn. Who you are is what you make yourself to be. This, also, I have taught you. This you must never forget. Promise me!" The flame reached out as if to touch her. Jaimah flinched from the anger of that reaching. "Promise me! You will remember I have taught you this!"

"I promise." she choked and crossed her arms tightly in front of herself unable to restrain a sob.

The tendril withdrew and wrapped around itself.

"Don't leave me."

"Go, Little One. He waits for you."

"Who? Corwyn?" she asked in horror.

"Go. He is waiting for you." The shimmering fire rose, slowly stretching.

"Encheon! Please don't leave," Jaimah cried.

"Farewell, Jaimah."

The flame grew thinner and thinner, rising almost higher, it seemed, than the room. And then, without further word, it faded and disappeared. Jaimah faced the empty room with tears streaming down her face. Slowly she sat on her cot and lost herself into the pain of her grief.

How long she sat there she did not know. Time lost all meaning. Even thought lost meaning. But after a space, she drew herself up, washed her face, and combed her hair again.

When she left her room, she found Corwyn leaning against the wall, eating a slice of the meal bread. Numbly she picked up a piece of bread herself but forgot to eat it. She stood looking at him, the first stirrings of some emotion akin to hate moving within her.

His doeskin breeches had been replaced with black ones, and he wore a white tunic and short boots. "Was Shayna pleased with her breakfast?" he asked, his eyes alight with sly amusement.

Jaimah shrugged with barely concealed resentment. "I don't know. She was busy when I took the tray to her."

"Still trying to work her spell?"

"How did you know..." Surprise stopped her, and she looked at him angrily, the mocking tone of his voice echoing through her head.

"I know a lot of things," he said.

"Yes," Jaimah thought. "I just bet you do." She looked away, unable to meet his eyes. "Let's go," she murmured, moving in front of him, evading his hand as he reached to take her arm. She picked up a hoe, a spade, and a rake from a cranny behind the ovens. Then she went up the stairs to the entrance hall without looking to see if he was following.

Juggling the garden tools, Jaimah tried to open the massive doors that led outside. Corwyn took hold of her arm. "Let me," he said, and took the tools from her grasp. "All right. Lead the way."

Exasperated, Jaimah pulled at the monstrous door with all her might. She had been carrying the garden tools all by herself for years now; there was no need for Corwyn to take them from her. Angrily, she waited for him to step through, and then she struggled to get the door closed again. When she turned around he was watching her with a faint smile.

"What are you laughing at?" she snapped as she strode past him to where the path led away from the tower.

It started toward the plain and then branched off and zigzagged into the ravine. Jaimah marched along the edge, surefooted, where she had walked hundreds of times before. Her feet knew every inch of path, and now they carried her, while her thoughts whirled with a confusion of anger and grief over Encheon.

"Jaimah," Corwyn's command brought her head up. "Look."

Jaimah stopped and looked out across the ravine. The space opened out and away from the rock in every direction, a huge cleaving space that she had looked at many times before, but now, somehow, saw through other eyes. It was an impossible, breathtaking gap in the face of the earth through which the far distant plain could be seen. And up from this void shone a soft, luminous light of early dawn that penetrated every corner of the mountain. It seemed even to penetrate the distant cliffs and hanging terraces, all sculptured in colors neither white, gray, brown, nor beige, but a fusion. And in the far distance, above the plain, a bit of lonely cloud drifted across a pale dawn sky.

Then she heard the silence and felt it like something solid, face-to-face, a silence so profound that the whole colossal chaos of rock and space seemed to sink under it and pull her into it. For a little while the grief she felt at Encheon's leaving was far, far away.

She felt Corwyn break the spell and come close behind her, his breath stirring her hair. A sudden compulsion came across her to lean back against him for just a moment, but she shied away angrily and hurried down the path. A soft chuckle followed her.

The trail fell steeply. As she walked, dust spurted from under her feet like jets of water. The dust hung suspended for a moment, then drifted away. She walked on downward. The trail twisted around an immense rock buttress, cut under an overhang, and swung sharply left. By the time they came down to the floor of the ravine, the sky was a bright blue. As soon as the slope leveled off, they came to the garden, a large patch of ground cleared of brush and grass to hold neat rows of strong, healthy plants. Across the narrow valley, the mountain rose again in stark stone.

Jaimah paused to look at the straight rows and the growing plants of the garden, trying to feel a glow of satisfied pride. The working of the soil was the one enjoyment she had, and she usually liked to look at what she had done. But today that pleasure was gone.

Corwyn came to stand beside her, resting the tools on the ground in front of him. His eyes took in the garden with a measured study. Finally, he nodded and said, "Very nice." She looked up at him and frowned. There was no effort to mask the look in his midnight-blue eyes, showing that he had knowledgeably assessed her skill and was favorably impressed.

Jaimah murmured a tight "thank-you" and reached for the hoe. "I'll go over there," she said, and then escaped to the farthest row of the garden, where she always started, and began hoeing at the newly sprouted weeds, loosening the soil and starting a furrow for water. She dug her toes into the soft soil, trying to forget about Corwyn, hoping that he'd follow her example and start turning the soil in a row somewhere else. She pressed her feet into the cool dirt, deliberately keeping her back turned. After several minutes she glanced at him and saw that he was still where she had left him, watching her with an intentness that frightened her. She stood up straight as her eyes met his. A shiver she did not understand ran through her.

He walked slowly over to the beginning of the row in which she stood and laid down the spade and rake. There was something about the way he looked at her or the way he walked that made Jaimah apprehensive. She stepped back as he came down the row toward her. She glanced at the trail on the other side of the garden, measuring the distance in her mind, unsure whether to run or not.

Corwyn stopped to pick a blossom from the row of herbs that she had been hoeing and lifted it briefly to his nose. He then closed the short distance between them, twirling the flower between his fingers. Jaimah's grip tightened on the hoe until her fingers hurt.

"What do you call this?" he asked, holding up the blossom so that she could see it. Tiny white petals clustered at the top of the stem, and a dusty-yellow center was thick with pollen; an aromatic fragrance wafted up from it.

Jaimah looked from the blossoms to Corwyn's eyes, swallowing to find the strength to speak. "Loveroot," she finally said.

"Oh?" He looked down at the row. "What do you make with it?"

"Love potions," Jaimah answered huskily, suddenly feeling, but not knowing why, that he already knew the answer.

He looked at her sideways, his eyes starting to dance with a kind of mischief. "Does it work?"

"I don't know."

"You mean you've never seen it used?"

"No," she said inaudibly.

Corwyn stepped closer so that he was looking down on her. The shadow of a veiled smile crossed his face. "Do you suppose," he said, brushing the flower along the line of her jaw so that she flinched, "that it would work if you just tasted the pollen?" His blue eyes sparked with mischief and something else more dangerous, and his hand closed around her arm.

Jaimah stared up at him. For a moment she was too stunned to think. Then she suddenly knew, as she had never known anything before, that the flower Corwyn held up to her was indeed that potent and that Corwyn knew it. He had always known it. She tore her arm from his grasp, recoiling from him and the flower with a strangled cry and stumbled backward. She turned to flee toward the trail.

"Jaimah!" Corwyn's voice whipped out around her, pulled her to a stop. She stood still a moment, trembling, then turned to face him. Her tongue touched dry lips.

"Don't go," he said. He tossed the flower away. Jaimah's eyes followed it. "Come," he said. "We have work to do." He turned to retrieve the shovel and rake. Jaimah followed him, picking up the hoe with trembling fingers.

She watched as Corwyn bent to the raking, holding down a shudder as he smoothed the soil with firm strokes. He was directly between herself and the trail, and she knew she would never reach it before he did. She turned and began to hoe at the row again. She could feel Corwyn's nearness and had to grip the hoe tightly to keep it moving. Then she heard the rake stop.

"Jaimah."

The hoe in her hand paused for only a moment, then worked feverishly until Corwyn's hand came around her and grasped the handle. "Jaimah! Look at what you're doing." She saw suddenly that she had chopped up a large section of the row. The plants lay in a tangled mess at her feet.

"Oh, no!" she whispered, and dropped to her knees to pick them up. Loose dirt fell from the roots, and she shook them gently. She almost laughed at the irony when she realized that it had been the loveroot she had mercilessly destroyed. If Shayna saw them. . . . Jaimah shivered, not wanting to think about it.

Corwyn knelt beside her. "Let me," he said, and took the plants from her cold hands.

His sure fingers separated the tangled leaves and stems, and he laid each plant, one by one, on the ground. They were already beginning to wilt. Jaimah looked at them with a sinking heart.

Corwyn dug a shallow hole with his hand and picked up a plant, arranged the roots into the hole, then swept the soil to the base of the plant, pressing it firmly with his fingers. He brushed the dirt from each leaf until the plant was standing as it had been before. Continuing with each plant, he planted them where they belonged, taking care over each one. Each plant seemed to be stronger and healthier than before when he finished.

Jaimah watched him with a frown. The ghost of a memory tugged at her—a cold darkness, strong arms, the closing of a door, soft, warm furs, and strong hands touching and stroking slowly, intimately, their touch sending strength and energy into her own limbs, just as they now sent life back into the plants. She stared at Corwyn and at his hands—long-fingered, strong, confident—mesmerized by their movements. An unexplained tremor stirred in her.

Finally, Corwyn sat back, his blue eyes turned on her, dark and fathomless, his blond hair shining in the morning sun that had finally come up over the mountain.

"Who are you?" Jaimah asked in a whisper.

"Who do you think I am, Jaimah?"

"I don't know." She glanced at the plants now seeming more vigorous than the rest of the row. Corwyn also looked at them, then back to Jaimah.

"I am who you see."

"An apprentice could not do this," she said, gesturing to the loveroot.

"I have a little talent," Corwyn said with a shrug. "Shayna thinks I have a little, anyway. That's why I have come here— to train what I have."

Jaimah looked at the plants again, doubtfully. His talent didn't appear untrained to her. She thought of the night before when they had been in Shayna's room. He had faced the ring and seemed untouched by it. That alone spoke of more than just a little talent. Her heart thudded painfully as she thought on that. If she was right, he was in far more control of his powers than he had led Shayna to believe. And if so, what was he trying to hide?

Then, moved by something she did not understand, she said, "You'll have to be careful, Corwyn."

A frown touched the lines of his face.

"Shayna will strip you of everything you have." She spoke the truth; the Lady would not allow a power such as his to escape her. But why Jaimah felt impelled to warn him she did not know.

The frown eased from Corwyn's face and he smiled. "You

do not need to worry, Jaimah. No one can trap me." He sounded so certain that she believed him and was relieved.

He reached out and took her hand. "Come. Show me what you are growing." He stood and pulled her to her feet. "Tell me what this is." His foot nudged a bushy plant in the next row that was mostly a bluish green fuzz.

"Marshwart."

"What is it for?"

Jaimah looked at him, disquiet stirring within her. She felt somehow that he was testing her, that he already knew what it was for. Without knowing why, she was certain that he knew everything there was to know about her garden. "You tell me," she said, suddenly not wanting to answer.

"No, Jaimah," he said firmly. "You are to tell me."

Feeling uneasy she said, "When ground, it makes a sleeping powder."

Corwyn regarded her silently for a moment with a calculating assessment. Then he turned, stepping over the row of marshwart, and touched a tall plant that came almost to his shoulder. "What is this?"

"Monkshood."

Corwyn picked one of the hood-shaped blossoms and handed it to her. "What's it for?"

Jaimah stared at the deep-purple flower, unsettled by an encroaching sense of dread, the feeling that he was about to upset her perception of things and that everything was going to be forever changed. Again, she did not want to answer. "It summons the creatures of the night."

"How do you prepare it?"

"It is dried and then burned as it is. The smoke brings the creatures."

"Why?"

Jaimah frowned, puzzled that he would ask. "Because there's a spell in the smoke." One did not need to ask why a spell worked. It just did because it was a spell. It was as simple as that. But Corwyn was shaking his head, slowly, firmly.

He said, "Smoke is not a spell, nor does it have power." He took the purple blossom from her and crushed it in his fingers. Then he held it for her to smell. A musky fragrance rose from it. "It's irresistible to the poor creatures," he said. "I'm sure they'd follow it anywhere. A useful thing at times."

He tossed the bruised flower away. Jaimah looked to where it landed, confused.

Corwyn stepped around her and, with a hand on her back, gently guided her down to the end of the row. Jaimah pulled back with instant reluctance when she saw where he was taking her.

There, at the end of the row, grew the spiney, white plants that she loathed to be near. She had always left them until the last to work with because the feeling of revulsion was so over-powering whenever she was near them. It took all of her will even to tend them. And now, as Corwyn determinedly propelled her toward them, she found that she wasn't the least bit surprised that he was taking her there.

As they approached the first short plant, Corwyn slipped his arm around her to keep her from backing away. Before he could ask her the herb's name, she whispered, "Hazel," and a shudder ran through her.

"What's it for?" he asked.

"I don't know." Her voice sounded dead to her ears, and she wanted desperately to pull away. Corwyn bent to pluck one of the small white leaves. He straightened up, holding it in the palm of his hand. As he looked at the chalky barbs, Jaimah watched his face. The mask was gone. His eyes smoldered, and in them was knowledge and danger. When he looked at her, she flinched as if he had assaulted her and she tried to look away. But she couldn't.

"You know what it's for, don't you, Corwyn?" It was more a statement than a question, and Jaimah found that she dreaded the answer.

"That is not the point, Jaimah."

"What is the point?"

"The Lady wants you to teach me."

"Teach you something you already know?"

Corwyn flexed his hand, turning the barbed leaf over. "You could tell me how often Shayna uses this."

"Not often," Jaimah said hesitantly and then added, "Although quite a bit lately. We don't usually grow this much. But Shayna insisted that I plant more. I hate it."

And when he looked at her for further explanation, "It's evil," she said.

"You are careful, aren't you?" he asked. "You don't touch it, or let it scratch you?"

"No," she whispered, unsure why she was becoming frightened.

"Good." He dropped the leaf and pushed it under the plant with the toe of his boot.

"What does Shayna do with it?" Jaimah asked. "Why does she need more of it now?"

Corwyn dropped his arm from around her and stepped away. "The Lady has not said?"

Jaimah felt suddenly cold. "No."

He was silent for a moment, then said, "Let us go back and finish the hoeing."

"Aren't you going to tell me?"

He stopped and seemed to be choosing his words. "You know more about Shayna than I do." Then he changed the subject. "What should we be doing now?"

Jaimah frowned. "Running water down the rows."

"Then let's be doing it."

Corwyn moved past her and went back to the first row, to the loveroot, stepping easily over the marshwart. He picked up the hoe and held it out to her. "This time," he said when she reached him, "be more careful with the loveroot. I may need it sometime."

Jaimah took the hoe and went down the row away from him, dismay and fear at his words disturbing her. She turned to look at him uncertainly and was shaken more to see him smiling with mischief after her.

Chapter Three

THE WATER RAN SWIFTLY IN THE DITCH, CLEAR AT FIRST, BE-
coming cloudy, and finally rounding a bend and disappearing
under a layer of brown scum.

Jaimah sat with her feet in the water that was coming clear
out of the spring as she was accustomed to do each time she
irrigated the garden. But now she found no pleasure in it.

The late afternoon sun was shining brightly on the gray
crags of mountain in front of her. Soon the shadow of the peak
behind her would begin its slow climb up the white cliff face.

She lay back and looked up into the sky, the aching pain of
grief and the thoughts of Encheon too close to the surface for
her to successfully push them away.

She heard Corwyn drop the gardening tools by the path and
then come quietly toward her. She closed her eyes, hoping
he'd think she was sleeping. There was movement that told
her he had settled beside her. She peered at him through her
eyelashes. He sat with his arms around his knees, his chin on
his arm. The sunlight shone on his head like burnished gold,
and his back was straight with a touch of arrogance, as if he
were accustomed to having his word obeyed. She studied him
for a long time before he turned his head and looked at her.

"Why so quiet?"

Jaimah put her hands under her head and shrugged.

"You're not quite sure of me." There was a twinkle of
amusement in his eyes as he answered for her. "I can under-

stand that." He turned and rubbed his chin on his arm thoughtfully. Jaimah watched him, uneasiness beginning to creep over her. "How long have you lived here?" he finally asked.

She waited a moment before she answered. "I don't know. I think a long time. It seems a long time."

Corwyn stretched out and leaned on his elbow facing her. He picked a blade of grass and began twisting it around his fingers. From the shadow of her lashes she watched the movements of his hands, fascinated by them without exactly knowing why.

"Why don't you leave?"

"Leave?" She looked up at him in amazement. "Why would I leave? Where would I go?"

"There's a whole world out there."

Jaimah's eyes widened. "Oh, I couldn't. This is where I've always been. This is where I belong. This is where I . . ."

"Serve Shayna?" he asked dryly. "Don't you want something more?"

"What more is there?"

There was a long moment of silence.

"Tell me, Jaimah," Corwyn's voice was quiet. "You have felt the power of Shayna's ring?"

Jaimah looked up to the sky with a shudder. She did not want to answer. Finally she said, "Once. Long ago." Memories of that time flooded over her—the pain, the terror, the begging and the pleading for it to stop, and finally the willingness to do *anything* so that it would.

The moments lengthened into minutes, and Corwyn did not speak. She watched him pick another blade of grass and begin to weave it around his fingers. His eyes were downcast, thoughtful, his mouth in a firm line. He rolled the blade of grass into a little ball and tossed it away with a flick of his fingers. "The Lady is delving into something that she cannot control."

Jaimah frowned at him. "What do you mean?"

"This spell she is trying to control. It is dangerous." Jaimah looked at him, slowly took in his meaning. "With it she hopes to bind the Master."

"The Master?" Jaimah echoed. Cold went through her.

She closed her eyes as memory came of Encheon coming to her room and spiriting her away to the desert.

Such a vast emptiness spread as far as her mind's eye could see—golden and brown sands, small brush in the sheltered crevices of brown and gray rocks, and lizards and sand beetles scuttling about, leaving serpentine tracks over the sand. Never had she seen anything like it.

Encheon took her on the wind over the barrenness of the sand and rocks, skimming just a few feet off the ground. Rising hundreds of feet to the crest of one dune, they'd sweep down and up to the crest of the next. She had smelled the sand and the dusty aroma of the windflowers and had felt the fierce heat of the sun, so different from the eternal cold of the mountain.

And in the distance she had seen it. While standing in her spirit self on a dune, she saw in the far distance a fortress abutted up against the crags of an orange and brown cliff.

"What is it, Encheon?" she had asked. "Whose dwelling place is that?"

But instead of answering her, he took her high above the desert so that the horizons fell back until they stopped at the mountains. And swiftly they approached the fortress, flying over a balcony and through open doors into a large spacious room, larger than any room Jaimah had ever seen before. It was filled with tables and tall bookshelves holding thousands of books, old and bound with ancient leathers. Then he took her along a warm hallway lit with firebrands set in sconces on the walls.

"This is the fortress of the Master," Encheon's voice had intoned in her mind. "It is here where he rules over all things powerful. Here he watches and waits." And when she would have asked him what this Master watched and waited for, Encheon stopped her. "Ask no questions, Little One. Only look and learn. No one is as strong as the Master, though many have tried to be his equal. And some have even tried to be greater. But no one has or ever will succeed."

As Jaimah listened, her attention centered on a door at the end of the corridor. It was of dark wood and was intricately carved with designs all around its borders. But it was not the door that drew her attention. It was what she could feel waiting on the other side.

Suddenly she knew that this Master that Encheon spoke of was behind that door, and he was waiting for her. She could feel him like a tangible presence that she could put out her hand and touch. And he was very much aware of her.

This was why Encheon had brought her here, why he had taken her to the desert—so that she would go beyond that door . . .

Then she felt something reach out to her, a power so great and so overwhelming it frightened her. The indescribable strength of it threatened to spin her off into oblivion. She was suddenly terrified that, if it were allowed to touch her, she would be lost in it forever.

Gasping and crying out in her mind, she flung herself away and jerked her mind back to her body that sat trembling violently in the darkness of her room. And she thought she heard an echoing cry following her through the void. But it held such a note of disappointment that she knew it was not her own. Nor was it Encheon. She had listened to that echo and shivered.

After that Encheon never talked to her of the Master, nor did he ever take her back to that desert that stretched out before the fortress, though sometimes at night, she thought she could hear the echo of that cry and feel the power of it reaching out to her to draw her back beyond the door in that torchlit hall.

She opened her eyes and looked at Corwyn. His gaze was still downcast.

"His name is Mordrin Morangus," he said. "Some call him Morgus. He has powers that Shayna hasn't even conceived of . . . yet. She'll never succeed. Morgus is not one that anyone can fool. He will destroy her before he is ever trapped by her."

"How do you know all of this?"

"I saw it." He pulled up another blade of grass and rolled it into a ball.

Jaimah sat up and pulled her feet out of the water. "I don't believe you. Why would Shayna want to go against this Master?" Yet she knew why even as she said it.

Corwyn also sat up. "Believe what you wish." His tone was suddenly cold and distant, and Jaimah instantly regretted the lack of warmth in his voice.

She looked out across the garden and saw that the furrows were nearly full. Soon they'd be returning to the tower. She stood, half-expecting Corwyn to stop her, but he didn't. She did not look down at him as she walked away, her bare feet following the bank of the ditch.

She threaded her way through the small maze of furrows,

drawn for some reason to the short row of hazel.

The sun was settling lower in the west. On another day Jaimah would have been just opening the gate to the spring, following the water, making sure that all the furrows stayed free of obstruction. Then she would have to climb the trail back to the tower in the dark.

But now she stood looking at the chalky white plants, wondering why they so repelled her and yet, at this particular moment, drew her.

She had for so very long been with Shayna in the tower, with nothing to relieve the sameness of her days, except for Encheon. On a thousand previous days, she had watched water fill little ditches, waiting to climb back to the tower where she would have to help Shayna. She knew that Shayna was trying to control a new spell. She had been doing so for some time.

Jaimah looked over to Corwyn. He was watching her, studying her, waiting.

On a thousand previous days, she had longed for someone other than Encheon to talk to, someone of her own kind to change the pattern of her existence. Now she wished he'd go away.

She looked at the hazel again, the muscles in her stomach so taut they hurt. She knelt, almost forgetting to breathe as she looked closely at the white plant. She understood that somehow this plant was important. She reached out to touch it but stopped, remembering Corwyn's warning.

She drew in a deep breath, sat back on her heels, and began uneasily to take account of this new state of affairs. Corwyn knew more about Shayna's doings than she did, after only two—no, not even two days. Whether she liked it or not, he was apprentice where she was only servant.

After a time, a step sounded to her left. For an instant, she ignored it, then looked up. Corwyn reached out a hand to her. "Come," he said. "We are finished here. I have already closed the water gate."

Wordlessly, Jaimah let him help her to her feet and lead her away from the hazel.

Then he stopped. Jaimah looked up at him questioningly. He was staring intently up at the tower, and she turned to look at it apprehensively.

At first she couldn't tell what had caught his attention. Then she heard it, too—a sound like that of rushing wind, or the roar of a mountain lion. A burst of fire suddenly exploded from the tower and lit their faces, hissing down into the ravine toward them. Jaimah shielded her eyes with a startled cry. Corwyn seized her and pulled her back, running toward the hazel, and beyond, past the edge of the garden. He pushed her downslope, to a shelter under an overhang on the opposite side of the ravine.

Jaimah crawled in and huddled at the back of the little cavelike impression, trembling with fear. The world that she could see beyond Corwyn's shoulder was lit in fires of white and red, swirled in mists and steam and smoke and clouds of dust. She saw the face of Corwyn in the light, set in a silent rage that terrified her even more than the raging fires outside. She heaved with a cough from the reek in the air and tried to smother it. The air was thick and choking.

The fire died quickly, and Jaimah saw that the ravine had been left untouched. Incredibly, the inferno had destroyed nothing. She twisted in the confined space to get a better look, but could not understand what she saw.

"Corwyn . . ." she said, but he motioned her to silence. Her heart chilled within her. Whatever was happening was not over. A low rumble had begun in the rock of the mountain and grew into a tremendous roar. Jaimah put her hands to her ears to shut out the sound, but it was useless.

An explosion heaved the earth, throwing Corwyn back against her. Jaimah cried out in panic, fearing that where they lay was about to become their tomb.

A white light lit the ravine and grew until it blinded her so that all was white. The cliffs howled and screamed as the stones of the mountain grated and moved against each other. Large boulders crashed down from the heights. Jaimah tried to move, to roll out into the open before the mountain came down. The white blew over them and became red.

A wind came, fierce, hot, burning them where they lay hidden. Corwyn moved, took Jaimah's hand and pulled her out from under the overhang as he stood to face the ugly red. Jaimah shut her eyes, then opened them to see through the flame until the tears poured down her face. The tower still stood intact, even though the rock upon which it sat heaved and reeled and shook.

And while she watched, the cliff seemed to slide, crashing down, dust and smoke skirling and boiling up into a mon-

strous cloud that rolled out from the deafening noise. Jaimah
stared in horror. And then the sound stopped.

It was eerie, incredible. For a moment, Jaimah thought that
she had gone deaf, so absolute was the silence—not a sound,
not a whisper.

Corwyn's arms were tight about her; at that moment, he
was the only thing that was real to her. But then he uttered a
word that chilled her beyond belief. "Shayna." His voice was
low and angry and sent a shiver over her skin. She stood
utterly still, not daring even to breathe. She longed to flee, but
some compulsion kept her from moving.

Corwyn's hand slid down her arm and took her hand in his.
"As soon as the dust settles, we climb," he said.

Jaimah looked up at him with frightened eyes. She was
about to protest, then thought better of it; and when Corwyn
decided to move, she went silently where she was compelled
to go. She clung to his hand as they picked their way across
the rubble that covered part of the garden to where the beginning of the crumbled slope was. Jaimah looked up fearfully at
where the tower now stood several yards closer to the edge.
The path had been obliterated by the ledge that had broken
away and slid down into ruin.

Corwyn climbed up onto a boulder and paused long enough
for Jaimah to scramble up beside him. The boulder rocked
under their combined weight, and Jaimah gasped, grabbing
Corwyn for support. He eased off the boulder and climbed up
a pile of loose rubble, pulling Jaimah behind him. She cried
out in shock as the rocks stabbed and cut her feet. Corwyn
took her elbow and helped her over them.

Then he hurried her, though she stumbled at times and
struggled over rocks and boulders. They toiled slowly up the
crumbled slope until Jaimah gasped, "Stop," and sat down
against a boulder to catch her breath.

For a moment she sat with her eyes closed, her body heaving with the effort of suppressing a cough. She was loath for
some reason to show any more weakness than she had to. A
small shower of stones rattled past her as Corwyn came to sit
beside her.

"It will be dark soon," he said. Jaimah thought on that,
understanding his urgency. Her need to cough eased after a
few moments, and she stared at the ravine below, exhausted.

Corwyn stood up and drew her to her feet and waited until
he was certain she had her balance. She bit her lip to hold

back the cry of pain when she put her weight on her swollen and bleeding feet.

"We must reach the top before dark," he said quietly.

Jaimah turned and looked up; without protest, she began climbing ahead of him.

The slope became steeper and harder to negotiate. Boulders rolled easily and dirt and rubble slid underneath them. Jaimah stumbled, slid and landed hard on her feet with nothing more than a hoarse sob of shock. Corwyn seized her and held her up while she stood gasping for air.

He kept an arm around her thereafter, preserving her against another fall.

Twilight came, purple and gray, and the boulders of the slide merged into each other. Corwyn's breath was strong in Jaimah's ear, and the movement of his climbing from one boulder to the next was slow and even. Still, it was torture for her to keep up with him.

Finally, they were no longer climbing but were stumbling forward to the base of the tower. Jaimah, no longer forced to walk, simply slumped to her knees and leaned against the cold stone of the tower.

"Let me get the door open and then we can do something about your feet." Corwyn moved away into the darkness. Jaimah closed her eyes, trembling. Soon Corwyn was back, a dark shadow in the night.

"The door won't budge. I think it's been sealed."

"Sealed?" Jaimah asked hoarsely.

"A spell."

"Shayna wouldn't seal the door against us."

"Not knowingly, perhaps." He folded his arms and stared out into the night.

Jaimah turned slowly and sat against the tower. She shivered violently in the cold breeze and watched the icy moon creep up over a distant peak.

"What are we to do?" Jaimah asked. She sat waiting, huddling against the cold.

"We'll have to find another way in." His voice seemed to come from far away.

"There *is* another way," Jaimah said, a memory suddenly coming to her of a time in the past when Shayna had used another door. "I'd forgotten. There's a tunnel. Around on the other side. It's been closed for years."

"Could you find it again?" he urged. And he stooped down, helped her up.

"I will try."

She began slowly to walk, picking her way with care. Corwyn's arm came tightly around her, taking most of her weight; then, reaching down, he picked her up and carried her easily in his arms.

They came at last to a sheltered place that was on the other side of the tower, close to the trail that came up from the plain below—a shelter hidden from easy notice, withdrawn beneath a granite overhang.

Jaimah sat on the rock where Corwyn placed her and bent her head against her knees. This was all she could do, all she had strength for.

Corwyn stepped forward searching in the dark for the door that was there. After a moment a catch spring *twang*ed and he pushed the door with all his weight. It slowly opened with a groan.

Snapping his fingers, a small green globe sprang into being over his head. He disappeared inside for a time and then returned, the green globe floating above him.

"Are you ready?" he asked.

Jaimah wordlessly attempted to stand, but Corwyn forestalled her and picked her up. He carried her into the black passageway. The light moved with him, bathing them both in a soft green glow.

After several yards, the chill from outside could no longer be felt, and the difference in the temperature was a relief.

"Here we will rest," Corwyn told her. He put her down, trying to spare her undue pain. But she landed hard on an unseen protrusion in the floor.

"Oh!" Jaimah whimpered and sank to the floor in agony.

"Still," Corwyn said quietly. "Still. Lie still." And Jaimah lay quietly then, shuddering as Corwyn knelt and examined her feet in the green light. His fingers gently searched the wounds, and Jaimah bit her lip to hold back a strangled cry. She closed her eyes tightly and tried to will the pain out of her feet and legs where it was lancing up and down like lightening. Then gradually the pain eased, and she could feel the gentle touch of Corwyn's hands, seeming to pull the pain out of her flesh. His fingers moved slowly from heel to toe, leaving warmth and strength where they had been.

"Now stand," Corwyn said.

Jaimah got to her feet, Corwyn sitting back to watch. She felt only a ghost of pain remaining and walked shakily to the wall where she put out a hand for support.

"Are you all right now?" Corwyn's voice echoed off the walls and rang hollow. Jaimah looked at him, bathed in the green light, and for once was glad that he was there. She stepped away from the wall and tried not to listen to the questions that rose again in her mind about him.

"They feel much better," she said. "I think that I can go on now."

"We will rest first."

"I am well enough to go on." Jaimah at once regretted her words, thinking that perhaps Corwyn needed the rest, unsure about him again.

"Come on," he said then. "Watch your step."

Jaimah walked at the slow pace her still-tender feet enforced upon her, Corwyn walking beside her. He had been right in saying that they needed rest; her strength flagged quickly. When she drifted over to the wall to use it for support, Corwyn did not.

"We shall go cautiously," Corwyn said. "We do not know what has taken place inside. Shayna may have opened doors that would have been better left closed."

Jaimah looked at him uneasily, but asked no questions. Their footsteps echoed strangely off the walls and down the tunnel.

It was a place of spirits, of powers that were silent. Jaimah looked up at the walls and the ceiling that held the rock of the mountain over them. They hid secrets that only Shayna knew about. It seemed an empty world, an empty mountain. She could feel the rocks and crags of great age towering over them and around them, some accessible, some not. She knew there were a few places where only Shayna went, where no other person was welcome—places of mystery where no one ever ventured.

That is, until Corwyn.

Prescience struck Jaimah as she looked over at him, seeming to be more than he claimed and yet not claiming more—dangerous and yet not.

This, too, was added to the mystery of the mountain.

The tunnel could not have been very long, with the entrance only a short distance behind the tower, but Jaimah had to walk slowly, and the walls crept by, and the tunnel inched out behind them at a snail's pace.

The walls soon began to close in about them as the way narrowed. Jaimah sought for some familiarity, but found little. Reluctant to break the silence that had come between them, she did not say anything to Corwyn.

And eventually, there stood before them the door to the tower; it seemed absurd that one should be there, a small door in the bulking rock that was a part of the mountain—a small wound in that world of massiveness.

Jaimah paused. It occured to her that what was behind that door might be far worse than anything they had seen outside. Perhaps they would be better off not going in, after all. They could just walk away without looking back and leave the mountain and its cold, barren peaks and crags behind. But it would be impossible to walk away not knowing . . . not ever knowing what had happened. Her years with Shayna demanded a measure of loyalty and dictated that she walk through that door to discover if the Lady was alive.

"Stand aside," Corwyn said and put out his hand to examine the door. Jaimah leaned against the wood. After a moment of pushing, the door grated open, a gaping hole of cold black in the wall. Corwyn led the way through the door, and Jaimah saw in the green light that still shone down on them the cooking ovens and washing bins that were in the area outside her room. All looked as it should be.

Blackness stood at the foot of the stairs, thick and tangible. Through it they climbed, the green globe casting an eerie glow on the steps and walls. All seemed as it should be, dark, cold, and silent. The entrance hall and beyond were quiet, the hall to Corwyn's door was dark, and the stairs to Shayna's rooms were empty. But Shayna's door stood open, red light spilling out onto the floor.

Corwyn snapped his fingers and the green light winked out, leaving them in the ruddy twilight. He strode forward to look into the room. He whispered something that Jaimah did not understand. The sound grated on her ears, and she went to him, staring in shock at the fire-gutted chamber. The red glow came from the brazier that still stood in the center of the room. Jaimah looked for Shayna but did not see her.

"Don't touch anything," Corwyn said, and Jaimah recalled that he had said similar words about the hazel, a chilling echo that brought the same dread.

She tried to shake off the chill of fear and stepped closer to Corwyn. She searched what she could see of the room with her eyes for unseen dangers, knowing that, if any existed, she would never be able to tell. She could step into them with no forewarning nor premonition. And yet she felt that there was something, some feel to the room that was not quite right, something other than what they could see.

Inwardly she shrank back from going into the room to search for Shayna, but she was very reluctant to remain outside alone in the hall when Corwyn went in. He did not seem afraid. "Come," he ordered. His voice echoed weirdly in the burned-out room. Jaimah stepped forward uncertainly through the doorway and took his hand when he held it out to her. She drew a careful breath then and surveyed the ruin about them.

Everything was destroyed utterly—tables, chairs, books, bottles, and shelves; all were completely gone, except for the brazier that still burned with glowing embers. She had not known what they'd find, had imagined a hundred nightmarish things, but had not expected such silence, such isolated emptiness.

And Shayna gone.

Foreboding recurred in her and the remembrance of Corwyn saying that Shayna was attempting what she could not control, that she'd be destroyed in the trying.

Now the room was fire gutted, with no trace of victory. The spell that Shayna had so frantically tried to understand now seemed to have been just as Corwyn said—a thing she could not control. It suddenly seemed sinister and threatening —a weapon, perhaps, set by this Morgus for just such as Shayna to trigger. It had turned out wrong, just as Corwyn said it would.

And it had all centered here - *here*, in the heart of the tower that was reduced now to ashes. Jaimah turned and searched the recesses where the red glow was complete, thereby leaving little chance for anything or anyone to be recovered.

She saw all there was to see, all she cared to see. She withdrew her hand from Corwyn's and returned to the door. She stopped, taking in the room with a last glance, as if hoping to find things different from a moment before.

"Corwyn?" she said, suddenly wanting to get away from there.

He turned abruptly and came to her, taking her hand with a deep intake of air as if he were glad to draw a breath outside the room. His angular, grave face seemed suddenly of another, safer world.

"Let's go," he said. "There's nothing here."

Jaimah was surprised to see that the sky was already beginning to show a touch of gray when they started down the stairs. Time must have flown with unnatural speed while they had been in the tunnel and in Shayna's room. She could see the sky out of the tiny window at the top of the stairs. Dawn would come swiftly as it always did on the mountain.

"Are we going to leave the mountain?" Jaimah asked.

Corwyn shook his head. "No. We have not yet found Shayna."

Jaimah frowned to herself. She had supposed that Shayna was dead and that there was nothing left in the tower for her. She had thought that Corwyn would leave and that she would have to leave, also. Shivering in the biting air that moved up the winding stairs, she began to think longingly of a warm fire, something hot to eat, and a warm bed in which to sleep.

Corwyn started down the stairs first, his footsteps echoing from the walls and down the corridor below. Suddenly he stopped.

Jaimah heard the door at the same instant, a groaning of hinges that grew louder and ended with a hollow thud that only the massive entrance door made. Jaimah moved down beside Corwyn, looking at him. He looked back, his eyes unreadable in the dim light.

"Maybe the spell has worn off," she said.

She moved still closer to him, clenched her hands, and nervously crossed her arms in front of her. She wondered how he could always remain so calm, but she was glad because of it.

"Come," Corwyn said to her.

There was no more sound from below while they climbed down the stairs. They advanced slowly, practically inching down each step. Jaimah clung to Corwyn's arm, trying to feel forward with her senses to discover what awaited them; cold numbed her feet. She groped for each step, stumbled when the steps ended, and fell against Corwyn. He put out a steadying arm and drew her close. She took a breath and walked beside him, trying with difficulty to keep her feet moving without faltering. She wondered that the familiar stairs should feel so strange.

There was one more flight before they came to the entrance hall where they would confront whatever was waiting for them there. She found Corwyn's protecting arm a comfort, even though she shivered from the cold and her feet were painful from the icy stone. She felt a terrible, isolated feeling as she descended the shadowy stairs. This place that had been her home was now a strange, frightening place that she did not recognize.

And there was nothing to do, no retreat, no turning back to find another exit. Corwyn took her down to the light.

They came to the end of the stairs and stopped. Jaimah blinked into the harsh light. Shayna looked up from a floating orange flame that hung in the air before her. Jaimah's heart lurched, thinking it was Encheon. Then she saw that it was not. Cold rushed through her in reaction, and she clung to Corwyn for support.

"Are you all right, Shayna?" Corwyn asked. The tone of his voice was carefully guarded.

Shayna's dark eyes flickered over his face, to Jaimah, to his arm about her. "I thought that both of you were dead. Sit down. Things got out of hand here for a moment . . ."

The orange flame hung in the air between them, resembling a dying hearthfire. Jaimah could feel that it was potentially dangerous.

She felt Corwyn's muscles tense at Shayna's words, and she knew without looking that he was keeping his anger hidden behind a mask of subservience. She had great misgivings when he sat down on the step, leaving room for her beside him. She sank down next to him, and Shayna nodded her approval, looked back to the orange flame.

"There is danger here," Corwyn murmured softly. Jaimah understood his meaning. Shayna was still trying to control the spell, and they were caught in the middle of it. She shivered.

They two were helpless, servant and apprentice, one conditioned to obey, one sworn to obey.

And Shayna was holding them—Shayna whose obsession drove her against all caution and wisdom.

Jaimah touched Corwyn's arm wanting to ask him for an escape, wanting to warn him of things that only she knew Shayna was capable of.

Corwyn looked at her, his eyes unreadable. And Jaimah recalled with a jolt her doubts about him. This awoke a new fear in her, that she was alone against the two of them, that *she* was the one caught in the middle.

Shayna stood as if hypnotized, staring into the orange flame, her face bathed in orange light, her eyes black. And even though nothing seemed to be happening, Jaimah's skin prickled with apprehension and nervousness. She tried inwardly to reason away her uneasiness, to tell herself that Corwyn was wrong about what was happening. This was only another spell in the long line of spells that she had witnessed.

She could not convince herself. They were alone with Shayna, and Shayna was playing with their lives.

She watched Shayna and saw that there was a small change in the orange flame, a slight difference in color. She stared at it. Her hand sought Corwyn's, seeking a reassurance that she hoped he would give, even though she was certain that she had reason to fear him, also.

Corwyn's fingers closed around hers, but when Jaimah looked at him, his attention was on Shayna and the flame of light that was still changing in subtle tones by slow degrees.

"What is it? What is happening?" Jaimah asked in a whisper.

"Sh," said Corwyn. "Nothing yet. She does not yet know what to do."

Jaimah looked back to Shayna, who still stared at the flame that was now glowing pink. Something was happening, despite what Corwyn said.

"Apprentice," Shayna said in a hollow voice. "Come here."

"Yes, Shayna," Corwyn said with deference. And with an ease that was painful for Jaimah to watch—seeing her only ally, such as he was, go to Shayna without hesitation—he rose and strode to the Lady without a backward glance.

"Please," said Shayna. "Hold out your hand, Corwyn."

"As you wish."

He spoke to her in tones of obedience and reverence, and Jaimah was shaken by it. He held out his hand to Shayna confidently, not flinching nor hesitating. She grasped hold of his hand, almost possessively. She turned her eyes on him.

"I require your aid," she said. "With your talent I will be able to see beyond this light and will be able to do what I need to do."

Corwyn looked doubtful, like a student unsure of his instructions. Then finally with a nod of agreement he closed his eyes in concentration.

Shayna turned to the burning fire of pink, stretching her hand out to it, muttering words under her breath, staring intently into the light.

Jaimah stood and moved around so that she could see Corwyn's and Shayna's faces, fearful in the electric power that she could feel writhing in the room. "Shayna?" she asked. Corwyn's eyes opened and flashed a warning at her. The flame blazed up suddenly and disappeared. At that moment Shayna sagged, as if the power had been sucked from her the moment Corwyn had looked away. He caught her.

Jaimah found herself shaking, and she looked at Corwyn for answers.

"What happened?" she asked, her voice a note too high.

"We had better get her upstairs," Corwyn said. "We'll put her in my room."

Jaimah stared at him, then turned her attention to Shayna, as he picked her up to carry her up the stairs.

"Open the door," Corwyn said once they were in the dim hall that led to his rooms. Jaimah ran ahead and flung it open. Corwyn carried Shayna into the sleeping room and quietly put her on the cot. Then he covered her and pulled the heavy drapes to shut out the bright morning. He paused to close the door before turning to Jaimah.

Jaimah felt she should have objected for some reason. She did not. She turned and found a large chair close to the table to sit in. Her jaw was tight; her hands clenched under her crossed arms with such force that, when she realized it long after her shaking had subsided to a tremor, her fingers were numb and there were four marks where the fingernails had dug into each palm.

"She failed," Corwyn said to her. "A second time."

Jaimah looked at him. There was the arrogance again, the self-possessed confidence that he always kept hidden from Shayna. He was frightening. Jaimah watched him closely.

"She will try again," Corwyn told her. "I do not think she will be stopped so easily."

He was right, Jaimah knew, having seen Shayna try again and again until she attained the results that she wanted. Doubtless, she would be driven even harder and would more desperately seek Corwyn's talents. She would try to wrest them from him until they were her own, all so that she could control the power of this new spell.

"We must be careful," Corwyn said quietly. "You must be exhausted." He came around the table and stood looking down at her. He bent, took hold of her arm, and pulled her to her feet, moving her gently to the door. He went with her down the stairs to the cooking area where he set about building a fire in the hearth and cutting some meal bread and cheese. Jaimah huddled close to the fire and ate with a relief so great she felt like crying.

Corwyn sat close by, eating in silence, staring into the flames of the fire, intent on some inner thought.

Jaimah got up after several minutes to make some honey tea. "No," Corwyn said quietly, as if he knew her intentions. For once, she agreed with him. She was too tired to do anything.

She sat back down, numb in mind and body, and let the warmth of the fire envelop her. She felt Corwyn's eyes on her and looked at him in the flickering firelight. Drawing up her knees, she wrapped her arms around them, ignoring the ache in her muscles. When Corwyn did not look away, she got up the courage to ask, "What happened to Shayna?"

Corwyn hesitated, then shrugged. "It was too much for her." He poked at the fire with a metal rod. Sparks flared and died.

"Will she be all right?"

"In time, she'll be as good as ever."

Jaimah looked into the fire after that, resting her cheek on her knees. She thought longingly of her cot but could not summon up the energy to go to it. At least she was warm and didn't have to move. There was time enough later to worry about Shayna. Then she was brought out of what seemed like a moment of blank thought when Corwyn put an arm around her, lifted her to her feet, and guided her to her room, where he left her to a dreamless sleep.

Chapter Four

JAIMAH LAY AWAKE IN HER COT FOR A LONG WHILE, STARING at the dark ceiling. She could tell it was night, because the darkness was thicker in her room, which was always gloomy, anyway. There was no light from the fire in the cooking area, so it must have gone out. The tower had a ghostly quality, a silence that seemed to whisper up and down the winding stairs, far different from the silence that had before been in the halls.

She thought about Encheon then. Grief at his going rushed over her, and she wept. Long minutes she lay grieving, until she forced it away and sat up.

She found the prospect of getting up and climbing the stairs to find Shayna and Corwyn not in the least bit appealing. Even hunger was not enough to make her want to leave the warmth of her bed. But somehow curiosity, the uneasy desire to know what was happening, what was going to happen next, drove her from the furs and into the cold of the cooking area.

She did not know how late the hour was, nor whether she would find Corwyn awake or asleep in his room. She ran up the winding stairs that rarely knew the difference between night and day, because they were always shrouded in darkness, except for the tiny window that let a small amount of light into the hall to Shayna's door. There was now not even the faintest glow from that source or any other.

There was no response to her quiet knock on Corwyn's

door. She knocked again a little louder, hoping that he was not sleeping.

The door opened, seemingly on its own. Jaimah drew a deep breath before she stepped into the room. The light from two candles on the table flickered in the draft from the door. She advanced slowly, wondering where Corwyn was. The door to the other room was open.

"Corwyn," she whispered, then aloud, "Corwyn."

The silence continued, and yet Jaimah could feel a presence in the dark beyond the door. She stepped to the door and listened intently, but there was nothing, not even breathing. She went to the table and got a candle, returned to the door.

"Corwyn. It's me, Jaimah. Are you in there?"

"Jaimah?" The voice was Shayna's. Jaimah entered the room and saw Shayna on the cot. Her voice was without strength, her chest heaving from exertion, as if she had just climbed the slide from the ravine. "Find Corwyn," she ordered.

Jaimah went to her and knelt down, shaken to see her this way. Shayna looked utterly confused. Jaimah held her hand, an ache constricting her throat.

Slowly, slowly, Shayna seemed to get control of herself. "Go find Corwyn."

"Yes, Shayna," Jaimah said miserably.

The eyes began to lose their focus again, the confusion coming back. "Corwyn," Shayna whimpered. "Where . . ." Her voice trailed off into whispers that Jaimah could not hear.

"I'll find him." Jaimah stood looking down on her, watched her slip into her dream. Shayna's breathing was rapid. Her head turned from side to side in delirium. Her mouth worked and mumbled words that froze Jaimah in her tracks. "Mordrin . . . Morgus."

Jaimah withdrew, her heart beating painfully against her ribs, walking slowly at first, then more rapidly until she had to slow to keep the candle from being extinguished. The episode frightened her.

She went to the stairs to stand and look first up and then down, wondering where Corwyn was. She decided to look for him upstairs, because she had not seen him below. Perhaps he had gone back to Shayna's rooms.

Jaimah started up the stairs, going slowly to let the candle burn as brightly as it could, nursing it so that it would not die. It did, anyway.

She slipped the candle into a pocket and reached out for the wall at the side of the steps to use as a guide and a support, having done this countless times. The chill of the air was even more biting than before, and Jaimah began to wish that she had brought a fur. She shivered, hurried along the hall toward Shayna's rooms, and found them empty. Going back to the stairs, she decided to continue to the next floor and finally to the roof. Her head hurt; she had not realized it before, and now she took her time.

She did not go above Shayna's rooms very often. The stairs and the hall were the same as below, with the exception that the door to these rooms was locked. Above that was the roof. If Corwyn wasn't there, she didn't know where he was; she would have to conclude then that he had left the tower. A chill that was not born of the night air settled on her at that thought.

The soft padding of her bare feet whispered on the stairs and off the walls, the only sound. She reached the door to the roof and stopped to gather her courage before she pushed it open. This was the only place where Corwyn could be, if he had remained in the tower. She stepped through the door and scanned the whole horizon, the glittering stars, and the dark shape of the peaks against their light.

Something else was there, a presence—no, two—watching from somewhere out there in the dark. The Watchers! A chill fear shivered through her. They had never come so close before. She went to the parapet and looked out into the night. Somehow, she knew that if she were able to see through the darkness, she would see them on the path that led to Shayna's Peak where it cut along the base of the cliff. She stared in that direction and wondered if they could see her.

There was a footstep, just one! The sound seized her and held her still. She heard it again, spun toward the sound, and saw a dark, cloaked shape a yard or two away.

The figure approached easily, not at all bothered by the darkness, and stopped in front of her. Although Jaimah could see only a black form in the near-total darkness, she knew it was Corwyn.

"What's the matter?" he asked.

"It's Shayna." Jaimah stood still, heart pounding. "She is asking for you." A cold gust of wind blew into her face, lifted her hair, then fell silent, heavy and chill. "She is not well."

Corwyn touched her cheek, brushing his fingertips toward her mouth. "All right, I'll come." He turned, holding out a hand for her to come by his side. Jaimah breathed a thankful sigh, then squinted over her shoulder and looked far into the night, wondering if Corwyn had felt the Watchers, also.

A strange silence followed them as they made their way down the stairs and into Corwyn's rooms.

"Corwyn."

The stir, the whisper from within the dark sleeping chamber, caught Jaimah by surprise; she'd thought that Shayna would still be lying down. She looked now and saw a shadowy figure in the doorway. Shayna came into the room as far as the table. The candlelight cast shadows over her face and lighted her eyes with a dancing flame.

"You shouldn't be up," Jaimah told her, for she was not sure that Shayna yet had the strength to be moving around. She recalled how weak and confused the Lady had been just minutes before. She watched Shayna's face closely, saw the confusion in the Lady's eyes, and held her breath, looking uneasily to Corwyn.

"I see you brought him," Shayna said. "That is good."

"I found him as quickly as I could," Jaimah replied, struck to the heart, remembering Shayna as she had always known her, strong, demanding, and decisive. Now she was much less than that. "He came right away."

"I had not thought that you had gone yet," she said. And then, with a trace of weariness, "I had supposed that I had been dreaming." She reaching out, groping blindly for the table.

Jaimah went to her and caught her with an arm around, found her trembling uncontrollably. "Come," she said. "You must lie down." She began to guide Shayna back to the sleeping chamber. Corwyn stepped forward, lending his strength. Shayna grew calm.

Jaimah stepped back and watched as Corwyn settled Shayna back onto the cot, covering her with the furs.

"What is the matter with her?" Jaimah asked. "Why is she like this?"

"She will recover," he said. He looked up at her. "Believe me."

Jaimah did not answer. She moved to where she could see Shayna better in the dim candlelight that came from the other room. "It's just that I've never seen her like this."

"It won't last." Corwyn knelt beside the cot, his hand taking Shayna's, calming her. Jaimah sensed what he was doing and somehow felt the calming effects herself.

He was a comfort to be with just then. But Jaimah did not let herself forget that there had been other moments when she had been afraid of him.

"Jaimah?" Shayna's voice was high-pitched and unnatural. "Where are you?"

"I am here."

There was a flutter of the Lady's eyelids, barely discernible in the dark. Jaimah went to Corwyn's side so that Shayna could see her.

"Go to sleep," Corwyn said. "Everything will be all right."

Shayna made to rise again, but Corwyn gently restrained her until she gave it up. Jaimah sighed inwardly as the Lady seemed to drop off to sleep. Corwyn motioned her back to the other room, and she followed him wordlessly.

Corwyn seated himself behind the table and Jaimah noticed that there was now another chair in the room. It was standing unobtrusively in the shadows close to the draped window. It was a heavy chair with bulbous legs, a high back, and curving arms. She looked questioningly to Corwyn, asking him wordlessly where it had come from. He shrugged almost wearily and motioned her to sit. She did, hesitatingly, glad that it was in the shadows so that she could study Corwyn without his scrutiny in return.

Leaning back, she ran her hand along the curved arm confirming to herself that the chair was real, a product of some power that Corwyn possessed. For some reason of his own, he was willing to show it to her, but kept it hidden from Shayna.

She withdrew her hand, suddenly loath to touch the satin-smooth wood, and trembled, thinking about the things she had seen Corwyn do, all of it done with such ease, where Shayna had to measure, recite, and conjure to produce anything of the like.

She looked at Corwyn, fear flooding her. He was not what he appeared to be, of this she was certain.

"Jaimah?" Corwyn asked, bringing her out of her thoughts. "What's behind the locked door upstairs?"

Jaimah looked at him confused. "I don't know."

Corwyn strode to the door, opened it, and looked at her. His eyes were dark in the shadow where the candlelight faded, his face expressionless except for a trace of weariness around his mouth.

"Come. Let's go find out." There was a fine sweat on his brow in spite of the cold.

"We can't," Jaimah said standing up. Corwyn's smile was tired.

"Yes," he said. "We can."

And thereafter Jaimah answered nothing, but went with him up the dark stairs and stood by as he put his hand to the latch. There was an audible click and the door swung open.

"Corwyn?" Jaimah said at last, stepping between him and the door. "Must we go in there?"

"Yes." He edged past her and walked into the room, his footsteps becoming muffled in the dark. A green light snapped on; Jaimah peered hesitantly through the door. Dust covered the floor; in the recesses of the room loomed the black shapes of furniture. Corwyn was standing in the center.

She was not aware that her feet had moved, carrying her of their own accord to where Corwyn was standing, illumined in the glow of green light. She was uneasy in the shadowed room, feeling that they were intruding where they were not wanted.

"Why has this been locked?" Corwyn asked her.

"It's always been locked. Shayna has never opened it. She's . . . I don't know," Jaimah finished lamely.

Corwyn looked about critically. "I will need another room," he said. "Shayna cannot go back to her rooms. At least not for a while."

"You're going to stay in here?"

"Yes."

"I don't know if Shayna will approve," she said. "This room has always been forbidden. It was locked up before I ever came here."

She was shaking from the cold. He put his arms around her, drawing her close. The warmth he gave her was a relief. "There is no other place," he said. "I cannot very well go down to your room, now can I?"

Jaimah shook her head. She looked about the room. Dust was everywhere; she'd have to clean it. But she hoped that it could wait until morning.

Corwyn turned away without a word and went to the hearth in the distant wall, the green globe following him. Jaimah watched as he bent. A fire sprang to life.

An empty hearth and fire feeding on nothing but dust!

But there was heat, bright and radiating, heat that was inviting, compelling, strangely hypnotizing, and yet terrifying. In some ways it reminded her of Encheon. She swallowed at an ache in her throat and stepped forward, drawn by the warmth.

She stopped in front of the fire and let the warmth curl around her. She held her thoughts far away from Encheon and far from what would follow once Shayna discovered that the rooms had been unlocked.

She stared into the leaping flames of orange and yellow, barely aware that there was no sound from them. The absence of wood deprived the fire of the crackling and popping that was part of the comfort. She stared, to keep herself from thinking.

She heard Corwyn behind her, shaking a heavy fur and then coming toward her. He spread the fur on the floor by the hearth, covering the dust, the pelt side up. Putting his hands on Jaimah's shoulders, he gently pushed her down onto the fur.

"Sit," he said. "It is warmer here."

Jaimah did not question him, already feeling the difference. He brought back a couple of more furs that he had found within the shadows of the adjoining room, handing one to her and wrapping the other about himself. He suddenly looked tired, very tired. It surprised her.

She woke the next morning and found that the fire had gone out.

Chapter Five

SHAYNA, SEATED AT THE TABLE WITHIN CORWYN'S ROOMS, with a fur wrapped around, looked as if she had not slept. Her hands lay clasped in her lap, not from ease, but from an obvious attempt to keep them from trembling, an effort to appear stronger than she really was.

Jaimah saw, and knew that Shayna was not as she should be. She still had not shaken off the effects of the backlash—Corwyn's words—of the spell she had tried and could not control. She was still weak and struggling to get back on her feet, determined that this small setback was not going to stop her.

"Sit down," Shayna said.

Jaimah did so, subjected to the scrutiny of Shayna's dark eyes on a level with her own. She could not avoid the gaze, although she greatly wished to. She knew that Shayna was about to question her, long and hard, about the things that had occurred since she had left with Corwyn to work in the herb garden. That seemed so long ago, days, weeks, years. It was hard to remember that Corwyn had arrived at the tower only three days earlier.

"I was surprised to see you last night . . ." Shayna's voice trailed off, uncertain. "Yesterday? . . ." She shook her head. "I had thought you and Corwyn dead. The spell is much more complicated than I suspected and much more powerful. It's full of traps and dangers. I couldn't grab hold of it. The explosion . . ." Her eyes became unfocused, as if she were seeing it all again. "Do you know I couldn't even find Corwyn's talent to use it?"

Jaimah sat up surprised. "What do you mean?"

"It was as if he had none, as empty of power as a rock. Nothing. I couldn't have been wrong about him. I did see something there, I know I did. And yet, when I reached out to him to use what he had to help me, I found nothing, not even a glimmer. He was an empty shell. I couldn't have been wrong about him. I know what I saw when he first arrived here. I know what I saw. He has talent—repressed, but I *did* see it. I couldn't have been wrong."

"Do you think you were? Wrong, I mean."

"I don't know. I honestly don't know," Shayna said wearily. "I could have been. But how? I think that perhaps I just had nothing left of myself to use in reaching out to him. He couldn't have hidden it from me. I don't think so, anyway. That would take a great discipline, which he doesn't have." She eyed Jaimah narrowly. "This is not for Corwyn to know; you are not to discuss this with him. Now tell me, what happened out there, how did you and Corwyn survive?"

"Fire came, and earthquake—"

"This much I know."

"I'm sorry."

"I'm sure that you handled all that well enough," Shayna said, a slight frown on her face. "The fact that you're here means something. It seems to indicate that there is a possible way to grab ahold of this thing and be its master. If you hadn't made it back here, it would have shown that it would have been impossible, even for me."

"Yes, ma'am."

"Since the flash fire didn't kill you, perhaps I can deal with it, but I can't until I know more about the spell, know where it came from. I must know who created it. That would help, yes. And why the traps—then I could avoid them, maybe."

"Maybe?"

"Why do you suppose there are so many traps? Why did the creator risk his life to build something so complicated and so difficult to control?"

Jaimah shrugged vaguely, not knowing how to answer her. "To protect it, perhaps . . ."

"It doesn't make sense. I don't understand. All spells can be dangerous, if you don't know what you are doing, but I *should* be able to control this one. I have been preparing for this for a very long time. Why is it so difficult?"

"Someone doesn't want you to use it?" She was helpless to say anything else. Shayna seemed confused still, unable to come to terms with what had happened. She would not let it go; Jaimah knew her well enough to know that this was only the beginning.

"You're right," Shayna said, as if she suddenly understood something that she didn't before. "Of course someone doesn't want me to use it. That's why the traps. He's protecting himself."

It shook Jaimah. She still had some hope that Corwyn had been wrong about what Shayna was doing—that she was doing something that his untrained eyes had mistaken for something else. But again he was right, right in what he had no business knowing, apprentice or not. Just how he was able to find out what Shayna was doing, she wasn't able to figure. Shayna certainly wouldn't tell him, a stranger at their door.

"What do you mean?" Jaimah asked, dreading the answer. "Who is protecting himself? What are you trying to do?"

"Do? What am I trying to do?" Her voice sounded confused, as if she didn't understand the question. "Why, I'm trying to free myself." She waved a hand in the air and let it fall back to her lap. "I'm trying to remove an obstacle that has been standing in my way for years—a lifetime." Her eyes narrowed and a glint sparked there. "No longer will I be stopped at every turn, held prisoner, while he holds what is rightfully mine. I am going to free myself, Jaimah, rid myself of him once and for all, forever. And nothing is going to stop me, not traps that he sets, not a spell that goes wrong—nothing. I will have what is mine, and it does not matter how long it takes; I will have what is rightfully, morally mine, whether he stands in my way or not."

"Who is *he*?"

"Mordrin—Morangus—Morgus. Call him anything that you wish. When I am finished with him, he will be nothing. No name, then, can help him."

Jaimah sat silently a moment. In her limited knowledge, only one thing suggested itself. "He could destroy you," she said at last, because Shayna waited, determined to have an answer, and Corwyn had said it.

"Never. He does not know what I am capable of, nor of the resourses that I have in my reach, some that have come providently into my grasp, resourses that he would never suspect."

Jaimah sat and considered the several possibilities, few of them pleasant to contemplate.

"This brings up the point," Shayna said, "of your survival, yours and Corwyn's, and how you both were able to escape and in such remarkable condition. As I have said, I thought you both dead—you should have been dead." She leaned forward, her eyes burning fiercely. "What happened out there? How did you escape the flash fire? Tell me."

Jaimah studied it, trying to determine what it was that Shayna wanted to know. She would have to be careful with what she said and not give away too much about Corwyn before she had a chance to think about it.

"The fire came," she began, "rushing down the cliff at us from the tower. We ran and crawled under a ledge. For some reason the fire didn't reach us there. It just went by, burning nothing. But the earthquake came, and the trail to the tower was destroyed. We spent the rest of the time climbing the rock slide back to the tower." She shrugged, wondering how to continue. "That took a lot of time. We searched the tower from the bottom to the top for you. We thought you were dead and, after we saw that your room had been completely consumed by fire, we were certain that you had not survived." She hesitated before saying, "That's when we heard you downstairs."

"How did you get inside?"

"Through the door." She met Shayna's eyes without flinching, the only defense she could make, feeling for some reason that she could not tell her the truth, that she and Corwyn had come through the tunnel. She did not know why she lied and was greatly disturbed that she had done so.

"How did you get it open?"

"I—I don't know what you mean."

"The door was sealed. You should not have been able to open it."

"I don't think it was sealed. We had no trouble." Inwardly, Jaimah was quaking. It would have been better just to tell Shayna the truth; now she was caught, and she could not change what she had said; she had to ride if out if she could.

"Possibly it could have been sealed from the inside only. But that's very unlikely. If a door is sealed, it is sealed—from inside and out. I don't understand this, something about it doesn't ring true."

Cold settled into Jaimah's stomach. "Yes, ma'am." she said softly. "but we had no trouble getting it open." She had to ride it out.

"I suppose it is a possibility."

"Yes."

"You think it's possible?"

"I don't know, Shayna. I only know that we got in and found you gone."

"Yes," Shayna said thoughtfully. "I had taken the spell off the door by then. I went outside to find you and to see what had happened. I suppose you could have gotten in then, although I don't understand why I didn't see you." Hands trembling, Shayna pulled the fur tighter around her and folded her arms. "And Corwyn—what did he do during all of this?"

The question set Jaimah aback. "I don't know what you mean."

"You told me what you did, that together you made it back to the tower, somehow got in a door that was sealed, found me gone, then later found me. But you have not said one word about Corwyn himself and what he did, what his part was."

"What his part was?" She looked at Shayna, found that the caution that had caused her to lie was with her again. She swallowed before she spoke. "What is it you want to know?"

"What he did, what he said—how well you know him."

"I don't know him very well at all."

"But you spent all that time with him."

She looked at Shayna, unease stirring within her.

"True?" Shayna asked.

"If you say so."

"The first day in his rooms, the next in the garden—climbing the rock slide, you said, the next taking care of me."

"I had no control over the time that I had to be with him. You know that. You told me to go with him."

"That is rather well what I am talking about here, isn't it?"

Jaimah found nothing to say for several moments.

"I have been with him a lot," Jaimah conceded finally. "What is it you're really asking?"

"What is he like? When he is unguarded, does he show sides to himself that he does not want revealed? Does he appear different to you than to me?"

Jaimah felt herself pale and her fingers go cold. She leaned back, her eyes avoiding Shayna's and drew several slow breaths. Shayna was guessing too close!

"You do not answer?" Shayna asked.

"I don't know how to answer. What do you want me to say? That Corwyn is different with me than with you?"

"I'm asking you if you have seen anything about him that suggests he is something other than what he says?"

"In what way?"

"That maybe he does not have any powers at all, or maybe more than he has led me to believe. Or maybe he is exactly what he says he is and is truly here to learn."

Jaimah folded her arms against the chill that was coming upon her, wondering if Shayna was beginning to suspect something, knowing full well that there was deception involved. She looked Shayna in the eyes and was sure of it. "I don't know what to look for, Shayna." She shrugged. "He seems all right to me." The need for caution dragged another lie out of her, shaking her almost visibly.

They had lived closely and had seen much together; although she was only servant, Jaimah counted on that closeness desperately. She saw disbelief and then a slow yielding in Shayna's expression. "All right," Shayna said.

Jaimah sighed inwardly.

Shayna frowned, a tremor of strain around her lips. "I had thought, had hoped that I found the source of my failure, that Corwyn had somehow caused what happened to me, that the reason I couldn't reach his power was because he had none and had tricked me into believing that he had talent. But you wouldn't know about those things, would you? I guess . . ." She bit her lip, then went on. "I guess I'll have to start over. All that time!" She shook her head. "All lost, all that time. But you'll help me . . . and Corwyn. It shouldn't take as long, not with us all working together. We can do it. I'll have to have my books, my powders . . ."

"They're gone, Shayna," Jaimah said hesitantly.

"What?" Shayna asked, coming out of her thoughts.

"Everything that was in your rooms is gone, destroyed by the fire."

Shayna blinked in confusion and then comprehension lit her eyes. "Oh, yes. I remember. But that is no matter. You can go back to the garden and get the herbs I need. It is a simple matter to make more powders."

Jaimah let out her breath slowly. "Go back to the garden?"

"Why, of course. How else do you expect to get the herbs I will need? I want to begin as soon as possible." Shayna took a long breath, resting her hands back in her lap, betraying the tremble in her fingers. "I'll need some of everything: monkshood, marshwart, blue evening stalk, chalomine, terhound, cherille. You might as well bring loveroot also. And hazel. I want you to bring me some hazel this time. I think it's time to see what it will do to this spell."

"Hazel?" Jaimah asked, a chill going down her back and her hands becoming clammy. "I've never picked it before. You've always done it."

"I can't very well do it myself right now, can I? And I must get started as soon as possible. What happened to me can't go unchallenged. I must strike back as soon as I can, and I can't do anything without my herbs. Hazel's very easy to handle if you know what you're doing. It's just a matter of taking extreme care. You don't touch it with your hands; that is very dangerous. Never touch it with your bare hands or let it touch you anywhere that you're not protected. If you remember that, you'll do just fine. I must have some. I'm going to win this time, no matter what it takes."

"And if I can't?"

"Can't! What are you talking about, girl?" Then Shayna looked at Jaimah closely. "Why are you afraid of the hazel? You should not be. I have never told you about it, never said anything to indicate that it was any different from any other plant in that garden of yours. What has made you afraid? Was it Corwyn?"

Jaimah swallowed, fear seized her heart and constricted it. "It just feels dangerous," she choked.

Shayna was not convinced. Jaimah looked into her eyes, fully aware that Shayna's suspicions had been aroused. She had to do something to allay them.

"I'll get the herbs," Jaimah said. "But it may take some time. The trail to the ravine is gone. I'll have to climb down the rock slide."

"A simple matter," Shayna said.

"I'll have to wait until morning," she continued, talking fast, hoping to take the Lady's mind off Corwyn. "I'll need a full day, and I may not be back until late tomorrow night."

"Speed here is very important."

"I'll do my best, Shayna."

"Take Corwyn."

Jaimah nodded slowly and released a long breath. "All right," she said, and that was all. She didn't know, and didn't dare ask why Shayna wanted Corwyn to go.

She arose and walked across the room to the door, looking back once. Shayna said nothing, and Jaimah left with fear and resentment equally mixed.

There was the midday meal to prepare before she could think about tomorrow. She had lived all her life like this, doing as Shayna told her, no matter how unreasonable or impossible. This was no different.

The walls whispered the echo of her feet as she walked down the stairs to the cooking area and as she went about the business of cooking meal bread, vegetable stew, honey tea, cheese; the fare was always the same, day after day, the sameness of it somehow a reassurance.

Shayna stared at her when she set the tray on the table in front of her, and she thought that the Lady was still trying to put the puzzle of Corwyn together.

And she thought of Corwyn, trying to piece the same puzzle herself, hoping she could before Shayna did.

"Thank you, Jaimah," Shayna said to her. Jaimah nodded absently, knowing that it was not from real gratitude that Shayna thanked her.

There was a moment of uncertainty as she was walking back to the stairs. She paused to look upstairs, with the premonition that a battle of wills was about to begin.

She didn't know why she had lied to Shayna, nor why she had kept to herself the things that she had seen Corwyn do. It was as if she suddenly had felt that her very life depended on Shayna's ignorance and on her being able to stand between Shayna and her apprentice.

She folded her arms against the cold and walked quickly down the stairs back to the fire in the cooking hearth. She ate, deciding to wait a little before taking his meal up to him. She had to think. She cleaned almost aimlessly, feeling unfamiliar only because she had never felt displaced before. She was torn between her loyalties to Shayna and what she perceived as a threat to the life that she had known within the tower. There was a danger to her very existence, not only from Shayna, but from Corwyn as well.

She set about preparing a tray for Corwyn, wondering what he would say when she told him that Shayna wanted more herbs. She also wondered if she should tell him about the Lady's growing suspicions and what he'd do, if she did.

She balanced the tray on her hip and went up the stairs to his room.

Chapter Six

THE ROOM WAS DIFFERENT, CLEAN AND BRIGHT, WITH THE midday sun coming in through the window. The furniture had been rearranged.

And strangest of all, the room felt familiar, with far more familiarity than could be expected from just having seen it for the first time the night before.

She went in through the door, placed the tray on the large table in the center of the room, and looked around.

"How is Shayna?" Corwyn asked her, turning from the window, where he had been standing. Jaimah shrugged and drew in a deep breath, her own questions echoing in her ears. She was still unsure how the Lady was.

"She's still weak," she answered. "Shaky."

Corwyn came to the table and looked at the food that she had brought. Wiping a drop of gravy from the side of the bowl with his finger, he lifted it to his mouth before turning his gaze on her.

Jaimah avoided him by going to the window where he had been and looked out.

This window faced south, instead of west like all the others in the tower.

She put out her hand and touched the cold glass, looking up at the gray, jagged mountain that loomed up over the tower. She could see, by looking down to where the trail from the distant plain and the cliff met, the rock behind which was the door to the tunnel.

A movement caught her eyes. Something was on the trail. She squinted as she tried to make out the blur caused by distance. Suddenly she knew, without yet making out the figures. It was the merchant who came to the tower twice a year with provisions.

"We have company," she said, turning to look at Corwyn. She was glad that she could postpone telling him about the forthcoming trip to the ravine. "The merchant who brings our supplies is on the trail."

Corwyn sat down and took a bite of meal bread. "Yes, I saw him."

Jaimah watched him eat for a moment, then turned back to the window.

"I'll go and meet him. That way Shayna need not know that he is here. I know where she keeps the silver she pays him. I'll tell her after he's gone. She'll want to talk to him otherwise." She drew a deep breath and went to the table. "I'll go as soon as you are finished."

Corwyn picked up the mug of honey tea and drank it slowly; he almost seemed to be deliberately drinking it slowly. She watched him, unaware that she was staring; her scalp prickled and the blood in her veins ran cold.

She saw it, or felt it—the danger, the threat that he held hidden behind his dark blue eyes. And she knew, for a certainty, that she was in the middle, between him and Shayna, and the one in the most danger.

"I'll come back," she said, backing away and going around him, suddenly anxious to get out of the room. He stayed silent. She clenched her fists at her sides, uncertain what to do. "Shayna wants us to go to the ravine and gather more herbs for her. We were to go after you ate, although I told her we'd have to wait until tomorrow. But it will have to wait even longer, now that the merchant has come. She's become suspicious of you. She asked me if I've seen anything about you that she should know. I lied. I said I hadn't seen anything." Jaimah wanted to shut off the words. She was appalled that they were coming so freely of their own accord, not knowing why she was blurting it all out.

She looked at him in horror, but he said nothing. Pushing the tray away, he motioned for her to come and sit in the chair adjacent to him. She complied with misgivings, though she was somewhat relieved.

"Jaimah," he said, and the tone of his voice was quiet and even. "You do not need to lie to Shayna about me."

She made a noncommittal sound. She knew what would happen if Shayna learned the truth about Corwyn. If she even suspected that he had powers far greater than he had let on . . . She didn't even want to think about it.

"There is nothing for you to lie about," he said.

Jaimah frowned and shook her head. "You don't know Shayna the way I do. If she thought that you had powers of any kind other than those of a novice, she'd stop at nothing to strip them away from you. She'd use her ring. She's done it before." And she had. Encheon had told her of several instances. He had even shown her the remains of one unfortunate man that she had sucked dry, but who had somehow lived. He had dragged himself off the mountain and lived alone at the edge of the plain, a broken-down husk of a man, with little mind and body left. Jaimah shuddered at that memory.

"If she thought that you were anything but an apprentice, nothing could stop her—nothing."

"I don't doubt it," Corwyn said. "But all I am is what you see, an apprentice."

"But I've seen you do things that no apprentice could do."

"It's just a small talent—untrained."

Jaimah shook her head again. "What I saw was not untrained. What I saw was true power—the way Shayna wants it." And that revelation, new to herself even as she spoke it, caused her to shiver with fright.

Corwyn did not answer her this time, and she looked at him, afraid of him . . . and for herself.

"Come," he said, standing up, clearly bringing the subject to a close. "Let's go meet this merchant of yours."

She rose and followed him with a quick backward glance at the tray that remained on the table. She decided to leave it and come for it later when Corwyn was occupied with other things.

But Corwyn rarely seemed to be occupied with other things. At least, it seemed so to her. She could count on her fingers with some amazement that this was only the fourth day that Corwyn had been in the tower. Already it felt like a lifetime.

She followed him wordlessly down the stairs to the entrance door. Her stomach was knotting in dread; somehow she knew that this new element—the coming of the merchant—was going to cause trouble. At least she was afraid it would. Fervently she hoped that it would not. She looked sidelong at Corwyn as he pulled open the heavy door. He almost seemed malevolent in the black tunic top and breeches that he wore, and yet, at the same time, he didn't. This man was an enigma. And how she was to solve the puzzle of him, she did not know.

She forced her apprehensions aside.

Corwyn stopped to look at the jagged edge where the ledge had crumbled away, erasing any sign of a path or trail to the ravine. Jaimah also stared at the new edge, now much closer to the tower. A cold weakness settled in her limbs as the memory of the moment that had created that new ledge came back to her, but she determined not to yield to it. She thrust the memory away.

The air was remarkably fresh, with a clean, though chill, feel to it. It hinted that a storm was on its way. There was an absence of any breeze or stir that was uncharacteristic. But Jaimah didn't doubt that, before long, the clouds would be gathering on the peaks, and the gloom of early dark would be upon them. Retrieving the herbs for Shayna might have to be postponed even further until the storm was gone. Jaimah hoped that the storm would come; at the same time, she hoped that it would stay away. On the one hand, she really didn't want to go after the herbs, having to climb back down the slide and up again. But then, telling Shayna that she'd have to wait for the herbs was something that she didn't want to do, either.

It was the fearful respect that Jaimah had for Shayna's temper and a strong sense of loyalty to the Lady that made her hope a little more strongly that the storm would stay away, even though she was certain that it wouldn't.

Jaimah turned from the ravine and her thoughts and saw that Corwyn was watching her, his blue eyes unreadable. He stood facing the ravine and the break in the mountain through which the plain could be seen, but his head was turned. Jaimah once again had the distinct impression that he knew her thoughts. It was as if he had heard them or felt them, somehow. She shivered, but not from the cold.

She turned on her heel and went around the tower to where

the trail from the plain ended and peered down it, but could not yet see the merchant. Corwyn came up silently from behind and stood with his arms folded and his face expressionless. Jaimah was reminded of that first day when he had stood looking through the window in his rooms at the ravine. How long ago that seemed.

She sat down on a nearby boulder and rubbed her chilled arms. She couldn't remember ever being very warm. The cold of the mountain seeped into her bones and stayed there. She shivered. There was no sound at all, not even a stir of air, nor the soft intake or exhale of breath.

She was glad that Corwyn's thoughts seemed to be elsewhere just then. She could see him out of the corner of her eye, standing still like a statue, his blond hair gleaming in the sun. At that moment, she wanted nothing more than for him to go back down the trail to the plain or wherever he had come from and leave things the way they were before he had arrived.

All I am is what you see, Corwyn had said to her.

Jaimah wondered that he would not admit to being more than an apprentice, always claiming to be untrained. She could see that he was something more. She looked over to him and back again before he could notice. Perhaps she should tell Shayna after all, warn her that all was not as it seemed, that something was wrong, and that Corwyn was a danger.

Neither she nor Shayna could afford not to be on their guard. After all, they didn't know Corwyn nor where he had come from. They didn't know why he had come to the tower nor why he had sought out Shayna instead of . . . Morgus. In all the long years that Jaimah had been in the tower, no one— *no one*—had asked admittance, not even the merchant for whom they now waited. Fear and hatred of Shayna and her power had kept them isolated on the mountain and in the tower, away from the people of the plain. Why would he, ignoring the hatred of the plainspeople, come and demand to be taken within the tower walls?

Jaimah sat frowning, deep in thought, trying to decide what to do—protect Shayna or protect Corwyn. She found herself suddenly aware that Corwyn was again looking at her, pointedly, intently. And this time, she was sure he knew her thoughts! Whether he heard or felt them didn't matter—he knew what she was thinking. His blue eyes were steady on her; and she could not see behind them to judge what *he* was thinking.

The shock overwhelmed her.

She drew back suddenly, panicked; and this Corwyn did not like. He frowned and stepped away. The sudden coldness in that withdrawal was like a slap across the face. It shook her to the very center of her being, and she could not bring the resulting shivering under control. He stood and regarded her, the expressionless mask over his face.

Self-awareness flooded over her.

He had come to the tower; whatever his reasons, he had come. Shayna had given him access. Jaimah feared him; yet, at times, she didn't.

She stood and moved around the boulder, putting it between Corwyn and herself, shaking and tense when she looked up at him. She looked away. He was still regarding her, wordlessly, motionlessly.

She half turned to flee, as if he were about to strike her, found the cliff behind her, and stopped. It was not rational, this fear. He had not done anything to harm her.

In fact, he had not done anything to harm Shayna, either. The only thing that he had done was to hide the full extent of his powers from her. And his powers weren't all that stupendous. In fact, they were rather minor. Jaimah stopped in mid-thought, wondering where this new train of thinking had come from. Suddenly she began to suspect a new variable to Corwyn's abilities.

But she could not leave. Some will other than her own seemed to hold her still—not a forcing, but a gentle persuasion.

Her thoughts wound in upon themselves, suspicion vying with reassurance, gut-deep certainty of something wrong struggling with the desire that she was mistaken. Suddenly not trusting her own thoughts, she did not know what to think or what to believe. She realized that she could hear the merchant and his pack animals coming up the trail and absently turned to greet him, but he was not yet close enough.

She enfolded herself in her private turmoil and crossed her arms, hands clenched until they ached.

Confound it, Jaimah, she thought violently, and wondered if she were sane for the mere suspicion she entertained. Corwyn, whatever he was, not only knew her thoughts but could influence them. He could turn her suspicions into trust, could make her moments of uncertainty seem inconsequential and unimportant. But if that were so, she would not have the doubts that she now had. She shook her head. Her imagination was getting the better of her, and she had better put it to an end.

She took hold of the fact that Corwyn had not hurt anyone yet and clung to it, forcing all her doubts away.

Perhaps he never would.

Jaimah made herself walk around the boulder so that she could see down the trail, which put her close to Corwyn. With a sigh, she let her arms drop from the tight clench she had about herself. Smiling faintly, she looked up at him.

The mask that had been over Corwyn's face lifted, his eyes sparked with a hint of pleasure, and his bearing became less distant.

It felt very good to please him; it was threatening to annoy him.

And that by itself started another little niggling of suspicion at the back of Jaimah's mind.

Chapter Seven

THERE WAS NOTHING UNUSUAL ABOUT WAITING FOR THE MER-
chant at the head of the trail; at least there should not have
been. Jaimah had been doing it for as long as she could remember. But this time, Shayna was not there, full of questions
about the plain and the goings on there. This time it was
Corwyn—apprentice—who waited with her. Shayna was upstairs, unaware that the merchant had even come.

The merchant was a short, fat man, covered with heavy
furs. Only his eyes could be seen of his swarthy face, because
a dark, scrubby beard hid the rest. Jaimah was uneasy about
greeting him. She didn't know what to expect from him when
he saw that Shayna had not come to meet him. She wasn't
sure whether he'd demand to see the Lady or not.

His face was clouded with a frown when he came to a halt
before them, but the frown seemed to be from exertion rather
than from seeing a stranger waiting for him. He nodded with a
swift duck of his head, and his eyes darted to Corwyn and
then back to her again.

"Where be the Lady Shayna?" The accent was lower plain
and the voice harsh and guttural, difficult to listen to. Jaimah
was always glad when he had gone.

"She is ill," she said, looking quickly to Corwyn.

"I have all as usual," the merchant said. "Cheese, honey,
beast, grain, furs, and dress goods. Will the Lady inspect?"
His dark eyes slid back to Corwyn, unvoiced questions obvi-

ous in their glimmer. "Lady Shayna should see that all is as she wanted. Will be pleased. Have brought good things, good quality. Worth much silver." A hint of greed was there, wanting to get more silver than was usual. Jaimah caught it clearly. "Lady Shayna too ill to come and inspect?" He was going to try to take advantage of her absence, but Jaimah wasn't going to be trapped and counted on Corwyn's presence to throw the man off balance.

"I am sorry," she said. "Shayna will not be here. But we can handle this. I know what she wants and what she expected to pay. Corwyn here is her apprentice and, in Shayna's absence, has the same authority as she does."

The merchant frowned, and this time it was not from exertion. "All that the Lady expected is here." He looked long at the apprentice.

And Jaimah saw Corwyn as if looking through the merchant's eyes. The arrogance that seemed to ride easily on him like a cloak was there, and she saw him as a stranger in more than one sense. Here was an unlooked for power equal to that of Shayna. Not the same authority as Shayna, to be sure, save in this instance where it regarded the merchant and the supplies that he brought. The fact that the merchant had to deal with a stranger and would not be able to talk up the price rankled him. Jaimah could see that it did not sit well with him.

He did not look like a man who was accustomed to accepting a set price for anything without trying to dicker it up, though, in Shayna's case, Jaimah had never seen him try, probably because of fear more than anything. But this time . . . Jaimah could see it on his face. It was an opportunity thwarted.

"Let's see what you have," Corwyn said softly.

"Best we take the things inside, sir," the merchant said hesitantly, indicating the sky. "Rain soon and supplies be ruined. And have to pay silver anyway. Be shame to pay silver and have ruined supplies."

"Rain?" Jaimah looked up and saw that the storm had indeed come over them in heavy, gray clouds.

It didn't happen often, but sometimes it did, the clouds moving over the mountains without a breath of wind touching the ground. She had watched storms such as this, sometimes dangerous, sometimes not, wondering where they had come from. And she wondered now what kind of storm this would be—one that would be over before the morning of the next day or one that would last for days and bring snow and high winds, trapping them inside the tower for even longer than the storm would last.

Being confined within the tower for days on end normally was not an occurrence that caused Jaimah much concern. Her life, as a whole, was centered in the tower. But now the thought of being unable to leave the tower had terrifying connotations to it. Being locked up with Corwyn and Shayna was a frightening prospect. Jaimah immediately slammed the thought out of her mind. Why was she constantly plagued with the notion that Corwyn and Shayna were going to be at each other like two wild beasts?

Because she knew Shayna.

And with considerable reservations, she thought she was beginning to know Corwyn.

Then there was the matter of the herbs. Snow would not only make it difficult, if not impossible, to retrieve the herbs that Shayna wanted, but it would also make them useless.

With those thoughts on her mind, Jaimah fell in behind Corwyn, who was guiding the merchant around the tower to the large entrance door. She paused briefly to look up at the clouds that were becoming closer and thicker and willed with all her might that they would be only rain clouds.

If only she, too, could have a little talent!

Inside the tower, Jaimah found herself watching as Corwyn seemingly took charge and directed where the bundles and barrels were to be placed. They were to be gone through and inspected thoroughly before any monies exchanged hands.

Jaimah had been surprised that Hagoth, the merchant, ventured within the tower walls. She knew how the plainspeople loathed anything to do with the kind of talent that Shayna had. Encheon had shown her the mobs and the fanatical executions that were done in the name of purity. The images were emblazoned on her mind—horrible, brutal killings, done in mindless hatred. No plea for mercy was heeded, no cry for clemency ever granted. Why Encheon had shown her these things, she wasn't quite sure, but she knew that she would never be able to walk among those people. Even though she didn't have any talent of her own, she had lived with it, was familiar with it, and accepted it. It was all that she knew.

The sound of Hagoth's voice brought her thoughts back to the counting and the inspecting of the supplies.

The merchant was protesting. "The Lady Shayna never held back the silver until everything was counted. I don't cheat Shayna. She looks, but never counts. My merchandise is good."

"The Lady Shayna is not recently from the plain as I am, Hagoth," Corwyn said.

The merchant's head came up with a snap and his eyes narrowed. "You know me?"

Corwyn smiled sardonically. "I know of you. Your dealings can be, shall we say, less than honest at times. I don't intend to give you any opportunity to . . . take advantage of Shayna's absence. So, the sooner we can get started with this, the sooner you can get your money and be on your way."

Hagoth accepted the inevitable with a shrug. Jaimah wondered if Corwyn expected to find anything out of the ordinary.

They went through all the barrels, opened every bundle, and counted everything, relying on her say-so that it all was there. Hagoth grinned smuggly through his beard as container after container was examined and found to be just as it should be, the count right, and the quality good, just as it always had been. His eyes snapped with derision as he looked at Corwyn and laughed in mockery. "All here, eh?"

"This time." Corwyn's dark blue eyes found Jaimah and he nodded for her to go get the silver. Hagoth looked at her with a self-satisfied chuckle; but when he glanced back at Corwyn, the mirth died in his throat. The glint of steel that Jaimah had glimpsed from time to time behind Corwyn's eyes was smoldering in plain view now. The sight of this quiet, controlled fury shook her to the core and she froze, mesmerized, staring.

There was quiet. Corwyn looked back to Jaimah. "Go get the silver." His voice was almost a whisper, but it seemed to thunder around them. Jaimah swallowed, frightened, and ducked out of the hall and into the stairwell.

She ran as quickly as she could up the winding stairs to Shayna's fire-gutted room. She stopped at the door, suddenly anxious about the silver. Had it been destroyed with everything else? She hadn't even thought of it before. She went quickly into the adjoining room that had been Shayna's sleeping chamber. It, also, had been ruined by fire. Her hands sought the hidden spring in the wall and pushed it. A small door opened next to it, empty. The silver was gone.

She bit her thumbnail as she considered. She'd have to

go to Shayna after all. Reluctantly, Jaimah went down to the room where she was.

"My apologies," Jaimah said nervously when Shayna looked up from the book she was staring at. "The merchant has come and the silver is not in the hiding place. Did you put it someplace else, or is it gone?" She entwined her fingers together as she watched the incomprehension on Shayna's face turn swiftly into understanding and then anger.

"We did not wish to disturb you," Jaimah added quickly. "You seemed to need the rest, and we checked everything. All is as it should be, but the silver is not where it usually is. I thought that maybe you had moved it. If you have, I can still get it and take it to the merchant so that you can remain here and rest more." Her voice trailed off in uncertainty and she looked down to the floor, avoiding Shayna's eyes. "It was my idea, Shayna," she said. "I told Corwyn that you were too ill to come down."

She knew that she was focusing Shayna's anger on herself, but she didn't want the Lady to begin having doubts about Corwyn again. Shayna could be unpredictable at times and Jaimah didn't want this to be one of those times. She had to stand between them, keeping them apart, even though she knew it was probably impossible.

"You decided that I needn't be told that the merchant had come with our supplies, and you took it upon yourself to keep this knowledge from me? Now . . . do I have that right?" Shayna's voice was low.

"Yes, ma'am."

Shayna closed the book and slid it back away from her on the table. Her fingers drummed quietly for a moment before her clenched fist came down hard on the book with a thud. "I don't know what I'm going to do with you, Jaimah. Sometimes I think you're a curse sent to plague me. Never before in all the years that I've known has anyone so completely disregarded the things that have gone on before. Where is your loyalty? Are you such a complete dolt that these things don't enter your head? Or are you trying to provoke me? Is this a new game?"

"No," Jaimah murmured. She stood still, staring at the book on the table where Shayna's fist still rested, wishing that she could go downstairs to her room and hide until the merchant was gone and all had been forgotten and maybe . . . forgiven.

She did not know why she just stood there. Perhaps it was something as simple as hope that Shayna's anger would be appeased or simply waiting for new instruction, like the mindless creature that Shayna thought she was. It didn't matter, really.

Shayna stood up shakily. "Come here, girl. I want to talk to the merchant. There are things I have need to ask him—what news he can tell me of the plain."

Jaimah put her arm around Shayna and was dismayed at how thin she was, a thinness that wasn't visible, except around the face and hands, now that she looked for it. The voluminous robe that Shayna wore hid the rest. Shayna put a trembling hand on Jaimah's arm, which did nothing to reassure her.

"Are you all right?" Jaimah asked and did not believe her when Shayna nodded once weakly, her breathing coming in gasps.

It was the hardest thing Jaimah ever had to do, taking Shayna down those stairs, feeling how weak she was, knowing how angry she was, and remembering the look in Corwyn's eyes when she had left him. She wondered what was going to happen when they met, both angry.

"Find me a place to sit down," Shayna said as they neared the bottom of the steps.

Corwyn's face was touched with a frown when he saw them. Jaimah averted her eyes, unwilling to see what was in his.

"Find me a chair."

Jaimah led Shayna to one that was close by against the wall.

Shayna sat down weakly.

"Now," she said, catching her breath, "tell me what's going on here."

"They were waiting for me to bring back the silver, Shayna," Jaimah said, disturbed that she felt compelled to answer, instead of Corwyn. It was as if she could not stop the dread that weighed on her whenever she thought of the two of them together. She suffered the scrutiny of Corwyn's eyes for a moment guiltily, as if she were betraying him. And she did not know whose power would claim her, his or Shayna's. When the clash came, she did not know if she'd be able to pull herself free.

She smiled sadly at him, a mask that covered other feelings.

"Forgive me, Lady," Corwyn said. "I should have insisted that we inform you of the arrival of the merchant. Jaimah would have if I let her. I was remiss, anxious as I was to spare you unnecessary trouble."

Jaimah was touched by this, seeing that he was shifting the blame to himself. It surprised her, not having expected it of him. And she silently convicted herself of uncharity because of the suspicious accusations that had been going on in her mind ever since he had arrived. It was a long moment before she could pull her eyes away from his.

"I will let it go, this time," Shayna was saying. "But remember your place from now on." Shayna then turned to the merchant. "Jaimah informs me that you have brought everything as agreed?"

"Yes, Lady Shayna." Hagoth's head bobbed and he rubbed his hands together in a fawning way that disgusted Jaimah.

"Then you shall be paid." She looked at Corwyn pointedly as she continued. "Those around me did not stop to consider that you don't cheat me because of what I would do to you if you did." Corwyn looked back at her, all the arrogance gone, and only the anxious student hoping for forgiveness remained. Jaimah saw it with a troubled frown.

She leaned against the window and watched the snowflakes coming down. A moment before there hadn't been any. Corwyn came to her and stood beside her until she looked up at him.

"Shayna wants us to put Hagoth's horses into the tunnel to shelter from the storm." At Jaimah's surprised start he continued, "No, I didn't tell her that we already knew it was there. Come, before the storm grows worse." He turned away.

Shayna was counting the silver coins that Jaimah had retrieved from another hidden compartment in the fire-blasted room and was counting them into Hagoth's hand. The merchant's eyes were glittering with pleasure as he watched the coins drop one by one into his outstretched palm. Jaimah took a fur from the supplies and wrapped it around her shoulders before she followed Corwyn to the door.

He pulled it open and let her go through ahead of him. Rain and snow blew into her face with a stiff iciness that took her breath. The animals—four of them—stood with their backs to the wind, heads lowered. Taking two of them by the lead ropes, Corwyn motioned her to do the same. Together they struggled against the increasing wind to the tunnel entrance around on the other side of the tower.

Jaimah held all four animals while Corwyn opened the tunnel door. Then she led them into the dark. The green globe sprang into place as before, and Jaimah turned to see Corwyn removing the gear and trappings from the animals' wet backs. He then used the dry side of the pack-saddle blankets to rub them down.

Jaimah said, "They will need something to eat."

Corwyn stopped. "Look in the bags and see what's there."

They were full of a grain that Jaimah couldn't identify.

"Good," Corwyn said. "That'll hold them until morning."

"But then what will we give them?"

"I don't know. We'll have to wait and see."

Jaimah went to the door and looked at the snow that was coming down even faster now in the gloom. Night would be upon them before long. Dread filled her as she watched the flakes catch on the ground and stick. That only meant one thing—the storm would last for days. Corwyn finished what he was doing and came to the door.

At that moment, Jaimah shivered. "It's going to snow us in," she said.

He looked out for a moment, then asked. "You don't want that?"

She shook her head.

There was a pause before he said, "Don't worry. We won't be."

Jaimah glanced up at his face in the gloom. She had seen many storms that had begun like this. They all lasted for days on end. And yet, as she scrutinized the confidence on his face, she felt sure, somehow, that he knew what he was talking about. And she wasn't surprised to see the number of snowflakes begin to lessen until there was only a soft rain falling. She suspected, without knowing why, that it had been done for her. She looked up to find Corwyn watching her.

For the first time ever, she felt that she could trust him, maybe a little—could really trust him in a way that she had never been able to trust Shayna.

"Sit," Shayna told them when they returned. They had come through the rain to the entrance door so that Shayna would not know that they had discovered earlier where the tunnel led. Jaimah sat in the shadowed corner to the side of Shayna, apart from the others, knowing her place as servant and not as equal with mistress and apprentice.

The wall behind her was cold and she could feel the iciness reaching out to her. Behind that was the narrow entrance hall where Shayna had struggled with the glowing orange fire and had lost. In front of her was the receiving hall, a large empty room except for a few chairs, and a pile of provisions lined against the opposite wall. In spite of the chairs that were there, Jaimah sat on the floor, the fur wrapped tightly around her.

"Hagoth," Shayna addressed the short, fat man. "Tell me now of the plain and what is happening there."

There was a long pause while the merchant considered. Corwyn turned from the chair behind which he had been standing and moved over to the window out of Shayna's line of sight. Jaimah could see his face clearly as he waited for Hagoth to speak.

"Things are quiet mostly," the merchant said finally. "But trouble is brewing between the Warlords again. Some dispute over boundaries. But that's nothing new. Happens all the time."

"Tell me about it," Shayna said. The merchant riffled the coins in his hand, chinking them against each other, considering. Then, leaning forward, he began, talking in the harsh, guttural voice that Jaimah found so difficult to listen to. But Shayna listened wordlessly, with close attention to the stories he wove of the strifes and discontents on the plain. Jaimah stopped paying attention after the first few words.

She was lost in a blank thought when a sudden quiet, the absence of Hagoth's irritating voice brought her back with a start. Cold, followed by heat, washed over her as she tried to comprehend what had happened. Shayna was leaning forward, her eyes boring into Hagoth, while the merchant stammered in confusion. Corwyn still stood by the window, silent, but in a watching, waiting sort of way. His eyes, which were dark in the gloom, were intent on Shayna and Hagoth, as if he were assessing and calculating and making plans—or watching one unfold.

"Say that again!" Shayna said.

"Forgive me, my Lady?" Hagoth clearly was in a state of fluster.

"About Morgus. What did you just say?"

"Oh . . . that he's gone?" Hagoth shrugged in confusion. "It is not important. As far as I'm concerned, he should have left long ago."

"Tell me anyway." Her voice became a whisper and she looked as if she were about to throw a spell at him for delaying.

"He's disappeared. Left his place on the edge of the desert. Took everything with him. All that is left is the fortress. And if he never comes back it'll . . ."

"Gone?" Shayna gripped his arm so tightly her knuckles turned white.

"Yes, my Lady." Hagoth pulled his arm out of her grasp, cringing and looking confusedly and questioningly to Corwyn and Jaimah.

"Where did he go?"

"I don't know. Nobody knows. He's just gone."

Shayna sat back, a deepening frown lining her face. "Gone," she whispered. She clasped her hands together to stop their visible trembling. "Into hiding? Is he hiding?"

"I don't understand," Hagoth said, standing up. "Did I say something wrong?"

Shayna came out of her thoughts. "Oh, no, Hagoth. You just told me something that is of great importance to me." She looked for Jaimah and found her. "I wish to retire, Jaimah. I have to think."

"Yes, Shayna." She went to Shayna and helped her to her feet. She heard the Lady tell Corwyn to take care of Hagoth before guiding her to the stairs and up to her room. But Jaimah's mind wasn't on Shayna, nor on the import of the news she had heard. She was troubled by what she had seen, which neither Shayna nor the merchant had noticed, so absorbed were they in their own drama.

Corwyn, whose face she could clearly see, did not react to Hagoth's words with surprise as Shayna did, nor with the surprise that she herself felt. But he seemed to be waiting for the news to be revealed, as if he had already known it. And then his eyes had sought her out in the dark corner where she sat, and he looked at her long, as if he were trying to tell her something of great importance before he turned to the window. All the command and the self-possessed arrogance that she had ever seen him carry was there—in the way he stood. A sudden cold had flooded over her.

Jaimah helped Shayna sit down at the table. "Did you hear

what he said?" Shayna asked. "Morgus is gone. Maybe he is hiding. Maybe he's afraid. That must mean I'm getting close."

"Yes, Shayna," Jaimah said absently. "I hope so." She turned and left, but stopped in the dark hall just outside the door. She was more disturbed than ever before. She recalled when she was with Corwyn in the tunnel. She had felt that she could trust him then, more than she ever had trusted Shayna. But now she didn't know. He was hiding something. She could feel it in her bones. He was not what he seemed to be—and she knew where her loyalties must be. She turned back to the room, fully intending to tell Shayna everything. But the Lady was thumbing furiously through the book that she had been reading earlier, and Jaimah knew better than to disturb her.

She'd tell her tomorrow.

Chapter Eight

JAIMAH WAKENED, AS AT SO MANY OTHER WAKINGS, WITH A great reluctance on her. Her eyes rested first upon the wall, dark with shadow, but it was the shadow of early morning, very early morning, almost dawn. Jaimah grew uneasy, disturbed at a vague memory.

"Morgus," she whispered. "Morgus has disappeared."

She reached forth a hand and removed the furs that covered her, shivering in the sudden cold. She tried to sit up, but the effort was beyond her for the moment. "Time to get up, Jaimah," she scolded herself. "Have to!"

She tried again, knowing that she'd have to hurry so that she wouldn't run into Corwyn before she got to Shayna's room. She wouldn't feel safe until she had told Shayna everything she had seen him do—everything: heal the herbs that she had hoed up, heal her feet, produce that mysterious green light, cause a fire to burn in an empty hearth, and especially the different way he bore himself when he was alone with her.

She looked at the wall, her thoughts straying to the countless times when Encheon had appeared to her in front of it. The pain that the memory caused was like a knife thrust. How he could help her now, if he'd only come! But she didn't dare call. There was no one to hear. She thrust that thought forcefully from her mind with the sudden pain. He was gone. That's all there was. He was gone. She swallowed the ache in her throat.

Sitting up, she swung her legs over the side of the cot, shrinking from putting her feet on the cold stone floor. But urgency pushed her up and into the kitchen. She had stopped long enough to grab a fur off the cot and wrapped it around herself as she ran up the stairs.

She got to the top of the first flight and heard her name spoken low. "Jaimah." It was the voice that she feared—his voice—on the stairs above her. She turned to flee toward Shayna's door that suddenly seemed so far away down the hall. Cold slid to her stomach and lay there trembling.

"Jaimah," This time she heard him tread on the step and she hesitated, unsure for the moment whether to run to Shayna for safety or to stay and face him. She was certain that he had been waiting for her. And he was going to stop her. He would not allow her to go to Shayna now, no matter what. In her mouth, unpleasant and acrid, was the taste of fear.

She could move her feet. She found this a wonder. Turning slowly, as Corwyn came down out of the dark to her, she wondered at the guilt that assaulted her.

She remembered fire and pain and Corwyn, who—had she forgotten?—had protected her.

She stood now before him like a guilty child, condemned for what she had thought to do. She was devoid of any excuse and bereft of anything except remorse. And there was nothing to say in her own defense.

He had been waiting for her and had known what she was planning.

But there was dimly in her mind a belief that she must be wary, that somehow her thoughts were not right.

How did she know this? She could not remember.

She tried to flee, but succeeded only in turning partially to the wall before she stopped, unable to move. Corwyn's hand touched her shoulder where the fur lay and fell away.

Jaimah closed her eyes and wished that he'd go away and forget that she even existed. But he did not go. His hands closed on her arms and turned her to face him.

"It is early," he said. His hands slid slowly down her arms, over the fur, sending a chill through her. Then he let go. "I had not expected to find you here. Is anything wrong?"

"No," she lied, hoping that he didn't know that she had lied. "I could not sleep."

He looked at her steadily. "The storm has let up. And Hagoth has already gone on his way. That leaves the matter of the herbs that we have yet to gather for Shayna." Jaimah felt the soothing effect his voice had on her and became cautious. "I had thought to wait until it was light enough to see. A descent into the ravine will not be easy—even more difficult, now that it has rained."

Jaimah returned the gaze that she could not see in the gloom. He spoke as if nothing was amiss. He talked of going on with things as they were, as if nothing had changed, as if he didn't know why she had come up the stairs at all. He intended to keep on as if she hadn't seen what she had seen.

She stepped back. He stood motionless—threatening.

Disturbed, Jaimah turned away again, pulling the fur tighter around her like a shield. Corwyn gave a weary sigh; this perplexed Jaimah and put her off balance.

Visions crossed her mind, memory she did not want, of fire falling and Corwyn pushing her into shelter and shielding her with his own body.

"Jaimah," he said, the quiet sound of his voice bringing her around to focus on his shadowed face. "Let it go." A chill of fear raced through her. He knew. "It is not what you think. Let it go." He stepped closer, taking her arms in his hands again, a grip over the fur that was unyielding. She could see his eyes now, dark, bottomless. Her heart pounded with an emotion she did not recognize. "Let it go," he whispered. "Let it go."

"I can't." Her voice was almost a sob. The strength of his hands was making her tremble in a way that she did not like. Fear of him was in her—not fear for her safety, but fear for her soul. "I don't know you." She looked into those eyes that had no end and fell into them. "I don't know who you are." Her head was spinning, and the touch she had with reality was peeling away.

"You must believe I am only an apprentice. Nothing more." He paused and looked away briefly, jerking her back to herself. "For now—nothing more."

Jaimah dared not blink nor close her eyes, lest tears flow from them, shaming her. She stared at Corwyn and clenched her fingers tightly, the stab of her fingernails a hot and comforting pain.

His grip on her eased. "The light is growing outside," he said carefully, distinctly, as one would talk to persuade, "and you did say that Shayna wanted more herbs from the ravine. I do not know how long it will take us to climb down the slide. The sooner we start, the better."

This had the simple sound of reason in it. There was now nothing hidden in Corwyn's eyes. Jaimah capitulated and, bewildered as she was, began at once to think of the slide and of the rocks and boulders and of the treacherous footing.

But then there was Corwyn, on whom all things seemed to rest, who could with a look or a word cause such turmoil within her. His mere presence changed things that had always been.

Confused, she sighed, and then shrugged her shoulders, letting go of her previous intention. She felt the resistance of Corwyn's hands on her arms, their weight restricting her movements. One dropped away, and the other guided her beside him as he led her down the stairs and into the receiving hall. The early morning light shone softly in through the windows.

"I found," Corwyn said, "among the dress goods, some shoes that will protect your feet." He picked them up from a chair. "I want you to wear them."

Jaimah took them, slipped them on her feet, feeling the strangeness of them. She had not owned many shoes in her life, and it had been long since she had a pair. She couldn't even remember what they had looked like. These were of soft leather, with a hard sole, good for climbing. They were warm, and the relief to her feet was comforting. She did not let herself think about the fact that there had been no shoes among the provisions the day before when everything was being inspected, nor that Shayna had not asked for any to be sent.

Corwyn returned from downstairs. In his hand he bore a small bundle of cloth that he gave to Jaimah.

"To carry the herbs in," he said. "It will be much easier to bring them back in this than in the buckets you have."

Corwyn led the way to the door, pulling it open. Closing it behind them, he looked grimly at the jagged ledge in front of them. He strode to the edge and looked down the slide with a measuring gaze. "Care must be taken," he said, "to pick the right place to climb down. Some place that has settled more than the rest."

He took Jaimah's hand and also took the cloth from her, so that she could hold the fur wrapped around her shoulders. "Come," he said, pulling her gently with him, and then, "Here." He stopped. "You go first, I'll hold you."

Jaimah hesitated, unwilling to try the first step. But, taking a deep breath, she climbed cautiously off the firm ledge. The loose soil sank under her weight and she slid in the mud. She let out a startled cry but Corwyn's grip on her was strong and held her back. Thereafter she went slowly from boulder to boulder and stayed away from the mud.

All the while Corwyn held her hand.

Once she heard him say, "Shayna expects too much," which was the truth. Many times Shayna's demands were beyond reason, irrational, but Jaimah obeyed—always—no matter how difficult. She looked up at Corwyn with regret. He was only beginning to learn what Shayna was about. And her ring was at the center of it, and against that no one could stand. She wondered if his lack of concern was from ignorance or some other thing that would prove ill for Shayna.

"A new trail is going to have to be made," she said hoarsely. "Shayna will expect the garden to go on as usual. She will not consider all the damage that has been done and will not accept it as an excuse, if she runs out of what she wants after today."

She stopped to catch her breath. She stared down to the bottom of the ravine, trying to judge how far away it was and how long it would take to reach it at the pace they were going.

"Are you all right?"

"Yes—just tired." Corwyn came to stand beside her and, for a moment, let go of her hand. Jaimah flexed her fingers, feeling how light they suddenly were without the weight of his hand around them. She brought her hand up to look at it as if it had betrayed her.

She dropped it again and let go a carefully controlled breath, reminding herself that it was necessary to go down the slide this way. Without his strength, she'd surely slip or stumble and fall, perhaps to her death.

"You want to wait here while I go on?"

Jaimah considered the matter, staring at the steep slope of rock below her. It would be easier to stay behind, and she almost accepted the offer. But she knew that Shayna would question her on how the picking was done.

"No," Jaimah said, making an effort to relax. "I'll go on."

"As you wish," Corwyn said. "But take care. The way is more difficult from here on."

Jaimah glanced uneasily up at him and found his eyes on her. They were clear in the morning light, with nothing shielding their depth. They had been that way all morning, hiding nothing. She wondered about it.

"I think that way," he said, indicating that she should go to the right. "It appears more stable."

"All right," Jaimah answered. She turned and was about to step down, when Corwyn took her hand, bringing her up short. She resisted the compulsion to look at him again and took the moment to draw a deep breath.

She steadied herself and again began the climb down, though her insides shook from the grip of his hand.

The way was much harder, Jaimah found just as Corwyn had said it would be. The rocks slid and rolled, and the mud was slick as grease. If Corwyn hadn't had a firm grip on her hand, she would have lost her footing many times. Once a rock rolled under her weight and she fell, but Corwyn quickly pulled her to her feet, saving her from injury. Slowly, inch by inch they made their way down the rock slide until at last they reached the bottom and stood looking at the garden.

It was in shambles and half-buried under rock and dirt. Jaimah shuddered as she recalled the earthquake that had caused that devastation.

"Where do we begin?" Corwyn asked, letting go her hand and shaking out the cloth. Jaimah pulled the fur tighter around her, thinking that the days were growing chill and that winter must be coming for it to be cold, even though the sun was high in the sky. "Shayna wants a little of everything."

She heard him step away from her and cross the rubble. She shut her eyes to listen for the familiar sounds of the ravine. But it was silent, as if all that was native to the mountain had fled.

Afraid? she wondered desperately. Of Shayna and her spell? She looked at the destruction the spell had caused and had to hold down new anxieties. It was necessary to remind herself why she and Corwyn were there.

She followed Corwyn into the garden after a time, where he was already putting plants onto the cloth that he had spread out on the ground. She watched as his sure hands deftly snapped a monkshood blossom off in the exact place where it should have been picked. He dropped it onto the growing pile of herbs. Again he broke off a blossom in the correct way.

Jaimah said nothing, only noted that he pinched off the stem on the growing plant so that none of the juices would be lost, in just the way that Shayna had taught her.

"I should have known," she said after a moment, feeling the fool for letting Corwyn calm all of her suspicions about him. "You are no apprentice! You are deceiving Shayna—and you are making me a part of that deceit."

Corwyn paused in his work and turned to look at her, a long measuring gaze. "Is that what you really think?" She stared back at him for a moment, then turned, going across the garden, to gather plants alone where she could think and consider.

And then the sound of Corwyn's footsteps caused her to look up. He stepped over the marshwart and knelt at the loveroot. She saw that he picked several blossoms, more than he needed to, and put them in a pile beside him. Then he picked off exactly ten leaves, placing them with the blossoms. He gathered them all up, carried them to the cloth where he put them with the rest. He turned with deliberateness, walked down the row, stepped over a large boulder, and stopped at the hazel. Fear prickled Jaimah's scalp. She couldn't pull her eyes off him as he bent over, reached under a plant and pulled it from the ground, roots and all. He shook the dirt from it and strode back to the cloth, stepping back over the boulder.

He put the plant on the pile and looked at Jaimah. She recoiled, his gaze a physical assault.

Time passed. Several minutes, more or less, it seemed. Time ceased to have meaning as she stared into his gaze. It was measured only by the beat of her heart and the intake of her breath, shallow and frightened, with moments—minutes—hours between each one.

Corwyn turned, throwing her back to herself, gathered up the corners of the cloth, and tied them together. He then slipped it over his head and put an arm through, so that the bundle was on his back and the knot was at his side.

He strode across the garden to her and stopped to pick up the few plants that lay on the ground at her feet. Straightening up, he slid the bundle around just enough to put the herbs through the opening. Then his night-blue eyes rested on her. "Let's go," he said, holding out his hand for her.

She stood, avoiding him and his outstretched hand. Walking around him she started across the garden to the slide. A calm came over her, the quiet that comes when uncertainty is gone. She knew what she had to do, what she had wanted to do earlier, and that knowledge—determination—settled on her like a protection. She felt that she was in control for the first time in several days. Nothing was going to stop her this time.

She could hear Corwyn climbing the boulders behind her.

She stopped after a few minutes to rest, her legs burning and her lungs heaving. Corwyn stopped beside her. When she had caught her breath, she studied the slide to determine the best route and went forward, climbing slowly, holding the fur around her with one hand.

The slide was alien to what she was used to. The very look of it was harsh and unfamiliar, adding to an already hostile environment another unpleasant thing to endure. It was hard to breathe, and the thin air held a chill that hurt her lungs. She halted as she groped for firm footing. Ahead of her, rising up to the tower, the slide seemed to stretch out steeper and higher until it was impossibly high, looking higher than it had looked just moments before.

Then in the next breath she knew! Suddenly she knew with a clarity that startled her who he was and where he had come from.

She stopped, stunned.

She had felt it once before long ago. At Encheon's behest, she had tried reaching out with her mind—an experiment to see if she could do so. And what she had touched so terrified her . . . She wouldn't try again. She refused. Encheon had tried to explain.

She looked over her shoulder, half-turning. Corwyn met her shocked gaze with a puzzled look which quickly changed to comprehension. He saw what was on her face, and the confirmation of it was on his. He regarded her with a mixture of admiration and intense regret. Jaimah knew that he could not let that knowledge remain. He'd have to wrest it from her, and she saw the certainty of it in his eyes. Jaimah spun around to run from him . . .

Sudden disorientation fell upon her and she slid. Fear swelled up in her so that, for a moment, she could not see, and her foot missed a boulder and twisted under her with a painful wrench. She fell forward to her knees.

She thrust out her hands to prevent herself from tumbling back down the slide. A strangled cry tore from her throat as the boulders and rocks gave way and she was sliding uncontrollably toward Corwyn. In the next moment, she was in his arms.

She stared in bewilderment into his eyes. Dazed, she

touched him to see whether he was a dream or not, to be certain that she was still alive.

"Are you all right?" he asked.

"Yes. I think so," she said, trembling with reaction and shuddering inwardly at what might have happened if Corwyn hadn't caught her. It all rested on him again, on him who was becoming the center of everything.

His arms around her were a comfort, a place to remain, and yet . . . She pulled back, breaking his hold on her. She saw the steady, clear look in his eyes, and this was not the look of threat. She looked at him, puzzled. He was looking at her strangely for some reason, as if he were searching for something. Apparently he didn't find it.

"I am all right, now," she told him uncertainly.

Corwyn retrieved the fur that had gone a little farther down the rubble. Jaimah climbed ahead of him, as before, but Corwyn stayed close to her this time, his nearness a warmth at her back. They moved slowly from boulder to boulder. She tested each step carefully, not proceeding until she was absolutely certain that it was safe, knowing in some curious way that this was the last time she'd ever have to climb the dangerous ascent.

She was vaguely disturbed because the giddiness that had caused her to stumble was gone. She tried to clear her mind and wondered why her thoughts were so muddled. It took effort just to concentrate on moving her feet.

At last they came to the top of the slide, just to the left of the tower.

Jaimah moved away from Corwyn and allowed him to go ahead of her. Then she followed him through the tower's entrance door and up the winding stairs to the room he occupied. He spread the cloth on the table so that the herbs lay in a heap in the center. He gathered the ten leaves from the loveroot, and three extra loveroot blossoms to the side, and then quickly snapped the root system off the hazel. He turned to face her, picking up the loveroot and leaves.

"Shayna will want the herbs right away," Jaimah reminded him with apprehension as she realized that he planned on keeping what he held.

"She does not yet know that we've returned."

Jaimah felt fear, close and heavy, but she did not give way to it. This time she couldn't—not this time.

Jaimah shook her head, rebuking herself, pulling her

thoughts out of that single-minded and paralyzing fixation. She shifted to look at him better and the feeling lifted. "Corwyn," she said then, as directly as she could bring herself to speak, "what are you gong to do with those herbs? You have no business taking them for yourself."

Corwyn looked down at what he held and then raised his eyes to meet hers. His face was expressionless, but he looked like a man long accustomed to doing as he wished, whenever he wished, and not being questioned.

"I meant," Corwyn said, "to protect us."

"You mean," she said, taunting him, "you, a mere apprentice, think you can create something out of those herbs that would protect us from all the power that Shayna controls?"

Corwyn did not rise to the sarcasm. His expression remained emotionless, and his eyes remained steady. "I am not completely unlearned, Jaimah. There are some things I do know. I have never denied that. But I will point out that Shayna is not concerned for our welfare. We—you—are not safe here as long as she is determined to continue with this obsession of hers. I think we should do whatever is in our power to protect ourselves from her."

Jaimah frowned. This had the unexpected sound of reasoning to it. She stared at Corwyn, knowing that what he said was true, but she still had some doubt. She could go to Shayna now; she could bring about his end with a single word . . . But what was it that she was going to tell Shayna? For a moment, she couldn't remember. Oh yes, the things that she had seen Corwyn do. Yet, the thing that Corwyn said did have a ring of validity to it. As long as Shayna was fixed on this one purpose, neither of them were safe.

"What do we do?" Jaimah asked.

"It will take a little time," Corwyn said. "Come with me and I will show you."

The loveroot rested in a large bowl of earthenware on the stone table next to the hearth in the cooking area, a wilted mass of blossoms, aromatic and pungent. In a smaller bowl, right next to it, a dusty yellow powder covered the bottom— the pollen from the dying flowers, shaken carefully from each and set aside.

Jaimah held her breath as memory came to her, the memory of Corwyn holding a blossom close to her and wondering if a person only had a taste the pollen for it to work.

The roots of the hazel were put into another bowl and crushed into a smooth paste. An acrid odor wafted up and reached Jaimah where she stood watching Corwyn add the loveroot blossoms, one at a time, to be ground into the mixture.

Then each leaf was added and mixed in, changing the white to a pale green.

But the pollen remained apart, unused, waiting in the small bowl that had been set aside.

Jaimah turned away, taking a deep breath to keep from betraying herself to Corwyn. She would have left, had she the courage, but she hadn't and she could only turn away so that she wasn't staring at the bowl that held the pollen. She heard Corwyn moving around behind her, heard the sounds of bowls touching and of water being poured. Finally she looked around to see Corwyn bending at the hearth, ladeling stew out of the hanging pot. He came to her with the steaming bowl. Reaching over to pull a chair forward for her to sit on, he put the bowl on the counter and handed her a spoon.

"Eat this," he said. "You haven't had a thing all day. It is not good that you don't take care of yourself."

"I'm not hungry. I don't think I could even keep it down."

Corwyn put down the spoon next to the bowl of stew and, reaching out, took her hand. Gently pulling her to the chair and placing his hands on her shoulders, he slowly and deliberately made her sit.

"Do as I say, Jaimah. You are going to need your strength." He picked up the spoon and held it out once again for her to take. "Please don't make me force you."

"All right," Jaimah said, taking the spoon.

"It would not do well for you to become ill."

Jaimah ate, then drank the honey tea that Corwyn gave her.

"That's good," Corwyn said, taking the bowl from her when she was finished and placing it in the water basin. "Now it is time to continue with what we were doing."

"It is not finished?" Jaimah asked. And when Corwyn did not answer, she went on, "I don't know what you're doing anyway. Shayna always made mixtures and powders out of the herbs, but I never knew what she was doing. She never told me—not much anyway." She stopped and looked at the bowl that Corwyn picked up. "But I *do* know that she has never used the root from the hazel."

"It's just a simple variation," said Corwyn. "Nothing to be alarmed about."

"So you say," Jaimah said, forcing herself to voice the skepticism in her mind. The uncertainties just wouldn't go away no matter how many times she banished them. Weakness from the climb was on her again, a graying of senses and a shudder in muscles that were exhausted. She clenched her hand in her lap, drew a deep breath, let it go, and brought focus to her vision again. "I do not know why I need to be here," she said. "I do not understand any of what you are doing."

"I see," Corwyn said, after placing the bowl down in front of her where she could see the pale green liquid. "Perhaps I am mistaken, but I thought that you would realize what I was trying to do for you. Look around, Jaimah."

Jaimah cast a look about at the hearth and at the bowls that were on the stonework, which appeared the same as they always did. A thin trickle of sweat went down her left side. "What am I to see? I don't understand what I am looking for," she said.

"Knowledge, Jaimah," he said. "Learning, understanding. It can be yours if you want it. You don't need to be sitting in a dark corner while others do the doing. You, too, can learn if you will. All you have to do is ask; just ask and it can be yours."

Cold went through her. Encheon had said the same thing time and time again. *Knowledge is freedom*, he had said to her. *Knowledge is a weapon, and without it there is nothing. For you, only servitude unless you learn* . . . And then he had said of Corwyn, *Learn from him. He is one of your kind. He can teach you.*

Suddenly, inside her, a wanting began to stir. The possibilities could be exciting. Yes . . . Maybe . . .

She looked at the green liquid, now much thinner than the paste it had started out to be, then looked at the bowls scattered behind where Corwyn was standing. Something was missing or out of place there, but she couldn't see what it was.

"I don't know," Jaimah said at last. "Shayna wouldn't like it."

She pushed the bowl of green liquid away with a sigh and stood. She was unable to meet Corwyn's eyes at first, looking instead at the floor, at his black boots, and at the black breeches he wore. But Corwyn didn't say anything and she was compelled, finally, to raise her eyes and meet his, which were gazing steadily at her. There was no anger or disappointment, only measuring assessment. She wanted to say that she was sorry, but the words were stopped before they even began.

She forced herself to look away and consider why Corwyn would offer to teach her things that Shayna would not. Perhaps it was another deception, perhaps it was a calculated move to confuse her. Or perhaps it had nothing to do with any hidden plan at all, but was just as it appeared, a genuine offer to teach her the things that she wanted to know. Whatever his motive, it was out of place. Only Shayna could make that kind of offer, not her apprentice.

Her gaze once again fell on the bowls behind Corwyn, and she frowned. Something was not right there—something was changed, or moved, or was missing, but she just couldn't figure out what it was.

Chapter Nine

IT WAS FINISHED.

Jaimah stood and watched Corwyn pour the potion into a skin container and stop up the spout. She still didn't know what the liquid was, nor what he planned to do with it, because she refused to ask.

She should ask, she knew. At least she'd know what to tell Shayna when she finally got to talk to her. Shayna would want to know what Corwyn had made and what it was for, but Jaimah just couldn't bring herself to ask. She didn't want to know, because she was afraid to know.

Corwyn left the bulging skin bag on the counter while he gathered up the bowls and put them in the water basin. As he pumped water into the basin, Jaimah stared at the empty counter. The gray stone gleamed softly in the flickering firelight from the hearth. The bowl with the pollen was gone. Where . . . ? Corwyn drew a small bowl out of the water, green with brown mottling, set it dripping on the counter—the bowl she had eaten from—the bowl that had contained the loveroot pollen. She tore her eyes from it to Corwyn. He turned and looked at her, the expression on his face unreadable.

She stared back at him. A sob caught at her throat. "No," she choked. She shook her head. "No."

Corwyn frowned. "Jaimah, what's the matter?" He started toward her.

"Stay away!" Jaimah cried. "Don't come near me!" With

that, she turned and fled, stumbling up the stairs away from him. She couldn't believe what he had done, but she should have known—should have known—should have known!

Shayna wasn't where she expected to find her. Jaimah ran up more stairs and found her in Corwyn's new room, looking at the pile of herbs on the table. "Shayna," she gasped in relief, and sudden apprehension as she hesitated at the door. Shayna looked up at her. A marshwart plant was in her hand.

And rage in her eyes.

Jaimah bit at her lip, her heart quickening, for she did not want to face Shayna's anger, not when she needed her help and needed it quickly before the pollen began to take effect, if it hadn't started to already. She clasped her hands tightly together and came forward, hoping desperately that this would be resolved quickly, whatever Shayna was angry about.

"Shayna," she said. "You found the herbs before I could prepare them for you. I'm sorry that it has taken so long. Please forgive me."

There was a long pause.

"Forgiven," Shayna answered, and paused again as she turned the marshwart over in her hand. "Jaimah," came her voice, deadly, quiet. "Why has this room been unlocked?"

A chill of foreboding went through her. "Corwyn opened it. He needed a place to sleep."

"I have forbidden that these rooms ever be opened again. Have you forgotten that, Jaimah?"

"No . . ."

"And you allowed Corwyn to unlock the door anyway? To move in where he has no business being? To let the light of the sun come in here again? Jaimah, who are you serving here?"

Now was her chance, she saw. "Corwyn is not as he seems, Shayna. He frightens me; he is a danger."

"Is he?" Shayna said drily.

There was a long silence. Jaimah waited, watching Shayna. The Lady finally put the marshwart on the table and sat down.

She clasped her hands in her lap and fixed Jaimah with her black eyes.

"All right, Jaimah. Why don't you tell me what you are talking about."

Jaimah swallowed nervously. "I don't know where to begin." She looked at Shayna sitting there, a familiar figure that represented security. A sudden shudder shook her, and she went and knelt at Shayna's feet. "Help me. Help me before it's too late!"

Again Shayna did not answer. A chill sense of something utterly amiss was over Jaimah now; something was afoot that she didn't know anything about. Perhaps Shayna was just waiting for her to explain.

At the beginning, from the very moment she saw him—that was where she had to start.

And Corwyn would come. He had to now. She reckoned in her mind what would happen when he arrived down that corridor and came to where she and Shayna now were. He might wait to do some other thing that she had no knowledge of; he might not wait at all. It was too much to hope that he would not come, not when Shayna could possibly undo what he had done.

She began to talk quickly, disjointedly, and told Shayna everything that she could remember . . . but wasn't there something that she had known before? . . . strange how the events in the ravine seemed so unclear . . . She knew that she could lose Shayna's trust forever, because she had not told the truth before.

And as she finished telling her story, she looked up at Shayna's impassive face, trying to find a hint of softness there that would tell her how Shayna was receiving what she heard.

What Jaimah saw there did not reassure her. For a fleeting moment, Shayna seemed to believe her and looked at her with concern, then terror seemed to close her face, followed by uncertainty and indecision. Then, as if the fear was too much to face, Shayna seemed to make up her mind. Jaimah watched Shayna's face change and realized that the Lady, whom she had served all of her life, to whom she turned now for help, could not—would not—believe her.

She drew back, panicked.

"Jaimah, girl," came Shayna's voice at last. "Clearly you are imagining things. This is all impossible."

Jaimah shook her head, her hands clenched. "I would not be making this up Shayna, truly. Everything that I have said to you is true. It happened exactly as I have told you."

Shayna regarded her silently, but there was no sign of belief anywhere on her face. None.

"Please, Shayna," Jaimah pleaded.

Again Shayna did not reply. She stood, brushing past Jaimah, and went to the window where she was silhouetted against the light.

Jaimah waited until she finally turned. "I tested Corwyn. I should know if he has the capabilities that you speak of. You've either imagined it or you are making it up."

"No, Shayna."

The Lady silenced her with a look. She took a deep breath. "I really don't think that you need to worry about the loveroot pollen, either. Only the purified oils from the crushed blossoms can do what you're afraid of, and you should know that if you had been paying any attention when you helped."

"He can do it with the pollen," Jaimah said, trying to make Shayna understand. He *could* do it with the pollen—he knew how!

"Impossible!" Shayna's eyes flashed with emotion, angry and unreasonable. "Enough of this, Jaimah! I won't hear any more!"

"But, Shayna . . ." Jaimah pleaded, desperate that the Lady believe her. She did not see the frightened, furious look in Shayna's eyes.

"Enough!" Shayna shouted, and spun around.

It hit Jaimah at the pit of the stomach—pain . . . terrible, searing, burning, consuming. *The ring!* She held on to the chair while the whole of her body screamed at once; walls flowed like water, forms seemed to twist inside out, forming a space into which she was plunged; pain was more terrible than anything she had felt before.

And then . . . blackness . . .

No, no, no! Shayna raged at Jaimah in her mind, shaking with the strain that the sudden pull of strength from the ring caused. She had spun in a blinding heat of rage, and in an action both impulsive and deliberate, struck the girl with the entire power of the ring. The girl probably would not survive. She wrenched her hand back, cutting the force off. Jaimah slumped to the floor.

Shayna reached for the table, finding vertigo in every movement she made, reeling with the impression that she was about to fall into a deep abyss. She slumped into the chair and fought against the emotional upheaval that threatened her. She bowed her head into her arms and tried to take her breath again, her muscles shaking with rage and reaction. For a moment she could do nothing else; and then, fingers still shaking convulsively, she tugged at the ring, trying to pull it off. She yanked it off, almost dropping it, then closed her hand over it.

Warmth spread through her, a sense of tranquility, a feeling of rightness and her, mind cleared so she could think again. Sometimes the ring was more than she could manage.

She looked at Jaimah, lying on the floor, and wondered at what she had done. She had probably killed the girl, injured her certainly, if she wasn't dead. Anger, fury, fear had all attacked her at once, but it was Jaimah who lay on the floor. It was Jaimah who had suffered because she could not hear that Corwyn had deceived her and did not want to know that he had deceived her.

She was calm in thinking these things. She wondered whether the exhaustion of the past few days was to blame for what she had done. Had she been in the right? After all, the girl had defied her, hiding what she had seen all this time. Or maybe . . . but it was a lie . . . a clever little plot to . . . to do what? She tried to sort out all the questions, but only came up with more questions that had no answers. She looked again at Jaimah. If the girl was still alive, she might yet be able to get the answers from her.

She pushed herself away from the table, her senses still sending her confused sensations, even though taking the ring off had calmed her. She felt Jaimah's pulse; it was weak. With the help of the ring she might be able to bring Jaimah out of the place into which she had been thrown. Jaimah would be able to answer questions—just barely—if she could be kept conscious long enough.

A figure appeared in the door, paused there a moment, and then entered the room.

She drew back. Corwyn came wordlessly, as he usually did, face unreadable. He walked across the room as Shayna stood up, and his midnight-blue eyes swept the place and centered on Jaimah, who lay crumpled at her feet. He went to the girl, ignoring Shayna, and touched her throat, kneeling on one knee—touched her as if to ascertain whether she was alive or not.

Then he straightened. His dark eyes sought Shayna's, shadowed and piercingly direct.

"What happened here?" he asked, his voice low, not demanding and yet somehow so.

Shayna carefully considered her words, wondering why she should feel the need for caution. She stood straight, a steadying hand on the table, and for a moment she felt fear. But it passed and she let go the table to clasp her hands together.

She looked steadily at him. In her hazed senses she saw him as another—not as apprentice as she knew him to be, but as some other identity that she did not recognize. She wondered if she saw right, saw him as he really was. He was gazing at her directly. Behind him she saw the room where she had once faced another like him. But this was not the same—for then *she* had been the apprentice.

"Shayna," Corwyn said softly. "What has been going on here?"

She remembered that it was this same question that *he* had asked so long ago; things were different now. She was no longer apprentice.

"The disciplining of my servant," she answered with a shrug.

"What has she done?" Corwyn asked, and an anxious frown came over his face, confusing Shayna. She had thought that she had been looking at the man that Jaimah had described, but now . . . ?

"You don't know?" she asked him.

"Should I?"

She shook her head. "No. But I thought perhaps . . . She spoke of you. Things that she'd seen."

Corwyn's face became like a mask, as unreadable as it had been a moment before. "What did she say? Things that you did not believe? What had she seen that you could not hear?"

He trod on questions too close, as if he had known what had been in her mind. She fought her thoughts clear, feeling danger, but Corwyn put out a hand to her.

"Sit, sit down," he bade her, insisting, and there was nothing to do but to comply. "You are very pale. You are not yet strong enough to be about." His voice was veiled, but sounded truly concerned.

She leaned back, trying to appear at ease, but her senses were alert. She watched Corwyn closely, trying to see behind his eyes, but could not penetrate their shadowed gaze. She grew afraid, and saw that Corwyn knew it, sensed it somehow. She repressed the fear, and Corwyn relaxed.

"May I do something for her?" Corwyn asked, the tone of his voice filled with concern for the girl on the floor. "Is there something that can be done?" He knelt beside Jaimah and lifted her head so that he could see her face.

Shayna frowned, perplexed. This was not the man that Jaimah had described, with secret abilities and secret plots that would destroy her. Had he been, he would have known what to do for Jaimah. He was just as he seemed, one with minimal talent that would never amount to anything.

"You may try," she said. "But I fear that there is little that can be done. The ring does not leave much behind when its full power has been used. I had not meant to use so much . . . but . . ." Then she shrugged. What was, was—and nothing could be done.

He was silent a moment. Shayna looked at him and found nothing to reassure her. She was not sure what she saw, but suspected that he was angry. He turned to Jaimah and spoke a monosyllable, a word she did not know and felt suddenly that she should know. She sensed that it was important.

"Does Jaimah have reason to hate you?" she asked. "Enough that she should lie so about you, Corwyn?"

A troubled frown grew upon Corwyn's face as he gazed at Jaimah. "I cannot think of any reason," he confessed. "I do not know what she has said, nor why. I do not think that I have given her cause."

"Jealousy," Shayna surmised in a low voice. "Perhaps she thought that you were a threat to her position."

"I do not know," Corwyn said. "I was not aware that she had position."

She had none, that was true, but Corwyn's *position* acquired demeaning force, and Shayna felt the sting of it. There was danger in it. Her fingers tightened into a fist and she steadied the sudden tremor that shook her.

"You do not know," said Shayna then, "what it was that had caused Jaimah such concern? She did not say anything to you?"

"She was unsettled by my coming," he said.

"This is all? You did nothing to 'unsettle' her?"

"She has led a life of isolation, Shayna," Corwyn said, his eyes flashing angrily for an instant, but then it was gone. "I was a stranger who frightened her."

Jaimah moaned and began to stir. Shayna started to rise, but Corwyn's hand took her wrist, a pressure without strength, a restraining motion that was no threat. "No," he said and he looked at the girl, his eyes no longer hard. "Sh. Be quiet, Jaimah."

The girl's head turned as she caught the sound of Corwyn's voice. Her moans stopped abruptly, but she still breathed as if she were in pain. Her eyes fluttered open, and they were filled with alarm when she saw him, but after a moment she grew calm.

And quietly, in words that Shayna did not catch, Corwyn spoke to her—received an answer and spoke again, firmly, as if he were . . . what? Reassuring her? Instructing her? Shayna listened tensely but was able to catch only the words *mistaken*, *protect*, and *danger*. She could not even guess what he said to her.

Finally, picking the girl up, Corwyn rose, fixed Shayna's eyes with his own. Then, defying the Lady to stop him, he turned and carried Jaimah into the other room.

It had a chilling effect on Shayna for some reason. She gathered herself to her feet apprehensively and followed him. He placed the girl on the sleeping cot and covered her with a fur.

"She said," Corwyn said, "that she was trying to warn you, although she didn't tell me what was said. But I do know this—you have ill used her, Shayna. And that is not right."

She stared helplessly at Corwyn, and that helplessness served to fuel the anger that came quickly after. "I did not allow you into this tower to question me, Corwyn. Remember your place."

"I do not question you," Corwyn said.

It set her off balance. "Then I don't know what you want."

"It is not what I want that matters here."

Shayna remained still a moment, staring at him in a rising fury. "You are treading on dangerous ground, apprentice."

"Do not misunderstand me, my Lady. I only meant that I am here to serve you, to learn from you if I can. I will obey everything you say."

"And if I say to let the girl suffer the ring in punishment for her disloyalty, you would stand back and say nothing?"

"I hope it won't come to that."

His words did not register for a moment. Then she thought she understood with a sudden angry suspicion.

"You would stop me?" Shayna asked.

"I would stop you."

"Listen to me, apprentice," she said with derision, a tone

that she put there deliberately to hide her apprehension. "Perhaps you think that you have enough talent to stand in the way of the ring's power and thus protect this servant girl, but I assure you that you don't. Your talent is minimal, Corwyn, and you can't stand against the power that *I* have, let alone that of the ring. Forget it and turn your attention to learning. The life of this girl is of no consequence, not when there is something of much greater importance in the balance. Everything that must be done will be done to insure the success of this greater thing, even if it means the end of a servant girl. Do you understand this, Corwyn?"

"I understand, my Lady," His voice was carefully controlled so that she could not read it.

A memory crowded her, cold and real, filled with emotion. Shayna felt a numbness and sensed, almost, a transference in time, seeing a remembered face that had long been forgotten, a quiet voice that had long ago been silenced. She edged back to the door of the sleeping room, fighting down a sudden rise in panic. These things from the past were not welcome. Long she had feared that the opening of these rooms would cause the memories to return. Strange that it was an apprentice that had opened them.

"Just remember," she said, "what your place is in all of this."

Corwyn frowned. "It is not necessary to remind me. I know perfectly where I stand here."

The panic of the moment before was receding and the coldness that was left in her lent a harshness to Corwyn's words. She heard what he said, and it twisted forebodingly in her mind. She looked at the sleeping girl and wondered if that was what Jaimah had heard in Corwyn's voice, that something that sounded like a threat. And yet, when she looked into his eyes, she could not see that threat. He had only the look of an apprentice.

"Come," Corwyn said, gesturing to the door. "You are not well enough yet to be standing. This I *do* know."

"And what of Jaimah?" she asked, unwilling to leave the girl without having the answers that she wanted, without asking the questions that she had not yet asked.

Corwyn's entire body stiffened; the frown reappeared. "Come," he said again. "Now is not the time for anything more. You must rest."

Maybe he was right. It would wait. After the girl recovered

and was strong again, then she would be more able to answer questions. Shayna decided that she must refrain from rashness and premature action. There would be another time.

And there was Corwyn.

Here was something that did not ring true. Something was hidden and buried beneath an exterior that did not reflect accurately. A peril to her maybe. She could not be certain. It was something she'd have to tend to before long. But this, too, would wait until a later time.

She yielded and let Corwyn take her into the other room where he helped her into a low reclining chair by the hearth. He left, and she heard the door to the sleeping room close behind her with a quiet click.

Chapter Ten

T HE APPRENTICE SLEPT.

Shayna, wrapped in a fur, sitting close to the fire, her mind filled with plans for the future, watched Corwyn in the half light of the evening's twilight, and willed herself to wait. She could have gone down to the rooms she now occupied and slept while Corwyn did. But she had slept enough and had grown impatient with the idleness that had been imposed on her. She now wanted to sit and watch Corwyn, to study him while he slept or, at least, while he seemed to sleep. Her instincts told her that she would have to tread carefully now. She had to discover what she wanted to know by small degrees. No rashness could be allowed here, not if what she suspected was true.

She opened her hand and looked at the ring that lay in her palm. It had served her once before, long before Jaimah had come to the tower. Perhaps now it would serve her again . . . if she was careful . . . very careful. She sighed and closed her fingers over the ring again and studied Corwyn's face.

This time it was going to be more difficult than it had been before. This time she would be walking a fine line of danger, and that danger was going to be Corwyn. She almost laughed at the irony of the thought that an apprentice could be a danger to her, just as she had once been a danger . . . She thrust her thoughts away from that direction.

Jaimah still slept in the adjoining room where Corwyn had

left her. Shayna's grip on the ring tightened as she pondered what was going on between them. There was something that she could not see, but could feel, a perplexing mixture of vibrations that she could not decipher. And they were passing between Corwyn and Jaimah.

It was a development that she had not expected when she agreed to take Corwyn on as apprentice.

The girl had cried out in dream once, not long after Corwyn had left her, and he went immediately back to her and remained for quite some time. Shayna had not looked in on them, allowing him to care for the girl. This once she'd allow him to do as he saw fit. There would be time later for putting him in his place. Besides, he was, after all, caring for the girl so that she would be better able to answer questions, whether he knew it or not. Shayna snorted to herself smugly. Let him think he was protecting the girl. He would soon find out differently when it was too late to do anything about it. She looked at the ring again and smiled. Yes, it would be too late for both of them. She took the ring and slipped it onto her finger again, letting the firelight reflect off it. It wouldn't ever fail her.

She closed her hand into a fist, feeling her finger strain against the encircling band. She stared into the fire as memory came back to her.

It had been this same hearth and this same room. But the figure that stood before her was not Corwyn. *He* was cloaked in black, and his black eyes looked fiercely at her. Shayna blinked and shook off the vision. A cold chill ran the full length of her spine and she pulled the fur tighter about her. But the effect of the vision stayed with her.

She hadn't thought about him for years.

He had been in the tower, had been there as long as anyone could remember—Naibus, the greatest to have lived in the tower. The awe that she had of him drove her from the plain to the mountain to seek him.

Against the admonition of her mother and ignoring the threats of her father, she had come. The tower held no terror for her. It was knowledge and power, and she was determined to see it for herself and, if she could, have it for herself. The hatred and fear that the plainspeople had for Naibus did not deter her. She was not going to languish in the imposed ignorance that seemed to be the only accepted way of life in the villages and the holds of the Warlords. Many times she had seen mobs hunt down and rend to pieces someone they sus-pected of having *the eye*. She had found little patience or tolerance for such mindless frenzy. And when she began to show some minute signs of having talent of her own, she had to escape a mob of villagers and flee to the mountain. Never would she try to prove her innocence of a crime that she felt was no crime, even though her father had threatened her with her very life.

So she went to the tower, seeking Naibus, never dreaming that, when she found him, he would take her in to apprentice, nor that she would love him. Nor that she'd destroy him.

Even the memory of it shook her and caused her pain, pain that she had learned to ignore many long years ago. She couldn't even remember how many years it had been—so many, so many. Absently she turned the ring on her finger, remembering the young girl she had been, about the same age as Jaimah was now when she climbed the trail to the tower. The isolation of it had frightened her and filled her with fore-boding when she first saw it standing at the edge of the preci-pice, surrounded on all sides by bare, rocky peaks. Almost, she turned and fled its shadow and returned back to the plain, where she would deny what she felt inside of her. But some-thing pulled at her. Some invisible force compelled her for-ward until she was knocking at the door, staring up in fear at the black tower.

He was an imposing figure, imperious, arrogant, and frightening. But he let her in. Shayna blinked hard as she stared into the fire, her eyes not seeing the flames but seeing Naibus as he had been that day. Had she known what was to come, she wouldn't have stepped through that door and let it close behind her. His eyes seemed to look into every fiber of her being, and from that moment she was his.

She stared into the dancing firelight and wondered if he had known beforehand that she was coming to the tower. And if he had, surely he would have known what she would do. And if he had known, why had he taken her in? She shook her head slowly. She had asked herself these same questions time and time again at first, trying to deal with what she had done. Finally she locked up his rooms and made herself forget.

But now she remembered.

He let her stay. Maybe he had planned it that way; she couldn't have left, even if he had sent her away. So he kept her, taught her, cared for her, until the hunger for more and more knowledge grew in her, becoming an obsession that left room for little else. She wanted it all—everything he knew, everything he could do, everything that he was. But no matter how she tried, he was always in the way of her ambition.

"Oh, Naibus," she thought bitterly. Perhaps by then he had known what was to come, even if he hadn't before. But still he didn't send her away. He could have banished her, but he didn't.

Then she had found it—in an obscure little cask hidden in a large chest—the ring. She kept it, not knowing what it was. Her hand unconsciously sought the ring and twisted it on her finger.

But one day she discovered what she had and what it could do.

She would never forget that moment. It was impressed upon her mind more clearly than any painting she had seen, more than any reality she had ever lived, for it was at that moment that all she wanted came within her grasp.

Understanding had opened before her, dizzying in perspective. More awaited her than she had ever contemplated . . . not only power equal to that which Naibus had, but even greater. She did not need to be content to be like him. She could remove him, replace him. She could have everything. She could *be* everything. She could be more than Naibus ever was, or ever would be.

It had happened in one of her moments of frustration and anger when the knowledge she sought had once again evaded her in the obscure words of a book that she had found. Unable to stand the frustration any longer she flung the book across the room and cursed it to the dust. At that instant, it exploded into flame and extinguished into nothing. Shayna had stared in shock. But that moment changed her life.

She learned how to use the ring.

And with it she confronted Naibus—and she destroyed him. Shayna raised a trembling hand and wiped away a tear that had fallen unbidden to her cheek. A short time after that she had taken in a girl child to hold back the loneliness.

Shayna stroked the fur that lay wrapped around her, running her hand up and down her arm, gazing at Corwyn, whose face was shadowed and lit in turn by the firelight. She marveled that he was able to sleep with her sitting so close by. She looked at him closely to see if he were indeed asleep. Her eyes then roamed over the room that had been closed and locked for so long, now warm with life, and she felt a shiver as a prescience of danger touched her. From where? Corwyn? She looked at him, troubled. Would this apprentice do to her what she had done to Naibus? Was that how succession was done?

Her instincts told her to get rid of him, send him away—the girl, too. But he had some talent. She had seen the evidence and it might make the difference in whether she accomplished her goal or not. With his added talent she might be able to do what she had not been able to do alone—bind Morgus to her, or destroy him altogether. As long as he was free, she could not become the supreme power.

But what had she let into the tower? Friend or foe? If she listened to Jaimah, she had taken an enemy into the heart of them.

Yet she remembered a long and terrible dream after her attempt at the spell, in which Corwyn had been a faithful presence—in which she had fought for her sanity along with her life, and Corwyn had stayed by her.

Waiting?

Perhaps, Shayna thought, he had hung by to see what the spell had done to her. Perhaps he had waited around to pick up the pieces when she expired.

But she hadn't passed out of this world. She had clung to the tendrils of her life, determined to live and try the spell again and again and again until she had what she wanted—Morgus at her feet.

Not for an apprentice, such a spell as she sought. And yet, if she were to accomplish what she set out to do, she had need of him. He was inextricably entangled in her plans—from the time that he had stood before the door and she had missed the chance to send him away.

Shayna, he has deceived you, Jaimah had said to her, *and if you let him stay, something terrible is going to happen.*

But what could he do against the ring? had been her reply. *No matter what you think he's capable of, he can't stand against the ring*.

Jaimah had frowned at that; the very thought was terrible. And at last she had turned her face away. *You have not seen what I have seen*, she said. *Can one who commands the clouds face the ring? You tried it on him the first night he came, and what happened?* She looked back and Shayna could see the fear that was in her eyes, infecting, disturbing.

What happened, Shayna? Did he feel pain, did he scream at your feet, did anything happen at all? Or was there nothing? Do something about him or someday some terrible thing will come upon us.

"Corwyn," Shayna said into the dark and saw Corwyn's face, lined with deep shadows, react. "Corwyn."

Eyes opened, wells of shadow in the orange light of the fire. He sat up and ran a hand through his hair. Then he turned on Shayna a stare that was far from sleep, no trace of drowsiness in them. Shayna fought back a shiver and pulled the fur tighter around her arms.

"The night has come," she said. "There are things to be done."

The apprentice nodded, glanced over to the herbs that were still on the table, and Shayna saw that he understood her meaning.

"Jaimah cannot do it," she said. "You will have to assist me." Then she added, "But that's what you've been wanting all along, isn't it, Corwyn."

"Yes," Corwyn said, a hint of something in his voice that brought her eyes sharply to him. But he only waited for her instructions and his spirits seemed to have lifted marginally, as if this moment was what he, as anxious apprentice, had been waiting for.

"But first, check on Jaimah."

Corwyn considered and nodded in consent. Shayna watched him closely for anything that would betray him as being other than what he claimed. But she could see nothing.

"I think that she is all right, but I will look in on her," he agreed.

"Do that," Shayna said. "Then bring food for us. We will be busy for most of the night. It is important that we are finished before the first light of dawn."

Shayna watched as the apprentice gathered himself up and wrapped a fur about him. She looked again for the man that Jaimah had described and again failed to find him. And yet . . . there was something. But she did not dwell on it, not now; there were other more important matters.

Shayna did not attempt to rise until Corwyn had left the room, for she knew that he would be watching her. Using the chair to steady herself, she rose to her feet and stood against it until her legs stopped trembling. Her strength was returning, but much more slowly than she would have liked. She was impatient with her weakness and forced herself to do the things that she should have waited to do; at least she should have waited until Corwyn could do them for her.

She moved slowly away from the hearth to the table in the center of the room.

If he is what you say, she had told Jaimah, *I will see it and I will deal with him, but not until then.*

Jaimah did not accept that. Shayna had been unsettled by that. She knew of a certainty that she herself would have seen it if Corwyn was other than what he portrayed himself to be. But Jaimah was insistent and would not be comforted. Shayna frowned at herself.

Someday, when Corwyn had given all that he had to give, he would not be capable of being a threat. This talent of his was needed and must be used, just as the herbs that had been brought up from the ravine. And then the man who frightened Jaimah would no longer exist.

Shayna thought to herself that, when that time came, she would miss the man that had come to learn from her. The very realization made her uneasy that someone should have become such a presence within the tower.

Jaimah had feared what she planned and had known without being told. She had spoken against it, desperately, pleadingly. But Jaimah did not know what she herself knew—that without Corwyn's added talent she could not control the spell that would destroy Morgus. This she had come to know within the past two days.

She went gingerly, on exhausted legs, around the table and looked at the herbs that were there. She noted the entire plant of hazel, broken neatly off at the root, just as it should have been. She puzzled why Corwyn would make anything out of the root. There were no properties in the root that would make it of any value.

If he had designs of his own, plans that were different from hers, it would be best to know it soon. It was one thing to use what he had and another to let him have free reign to become a danger that she could not control. Through the years, she had learned to be ruthless, to be pitiless in order to survive.

She gathered the herbs, separating them into different piles according to use, some of one kind in different places, and others of another kind all together. She worked quickly, knowing from long years of doing, exactly what went with what. She wanted to be finished before Corwyn came out of the sleeping room, suddenly feeling that, if he watched her combinations, he'd know exactly what she was doing. And this spell she would never let him learn. She covered them all with a fur.

When that was done, Shayna looked about her at the room, at the things that had belonged to Naibus and at the chair where he sat, and resolved on other things.

She gathered up what of Corwyn's belongings she could find and bore them to the door and thrust them out into the hall. She heard a movement behind her. She closed the door firmly and only then did she face Corwyn.

"I will take these rooms," she said to him.

Corwyn had changed his clothing; he had on the the doe-skin breeches and the brilliant red tunic that he had worn the day he arrived, the black of his boots catching a soft glow from the firelight. He carried in his hand the fur that he had taken with him. He turned and put it on the small chest by the wall.

"And what of Jaimah?" he asked in a low voice, and Shayna felt the sting of that—the accusation that had gone unvoiced, the words that had been left unspoken. It surprised her for she had supposed that he would not challenge. But she had not taken the girl into consideration when she resolved to take the rooms for herself.

"Take her with you," she said, moving around him, trying to hide her limping walk. "She can recover just as well in her own room as she can here."

"Yes, Shayna," he replied coldly. Shayna stiffened, set her face against his anger, and refused to be provoked.

"Understand," Shayna said, "that you are apprentice here. This is my domain, Corwyn. You will learn, if you remember this. I will not allow you or anyone else to usurp my power here, and I will teach you as I was taught. There can be no other way. If you cannot accept this, then your time here will come to an end. But understand that to apprentice is to follow, to obey . . . without question. And if you have it in you, you will survive. That is what my master once said to me, when I first came here. It is possible that you cannot become what I am. But if I hadn't been convinced that you have something, you would not be here. I would have never accepted you."

She turned to him. He was looking silently at her, and she suddenly felt uneasy. But Corwyn's face did not change. It remained unreadable, like a mask that could have covered anything.

"All right," he said. "But, Shayna, she should not be moved."

Tension. Shayna could feel it in the room.

And she was troubled after Corwyn had gone, bearing the girl easily in his arms, as to whether she had gone to the extreme. But now that she had been in the rooms that Naibus had once occupied, she could feel a place inside herself that she hadn't felt in many years and a power that hadn't been there before.

She couldn't leave it, any more than she could have left the tower that first day so long ago.

She had not done all that she had done, then or now, to step aside when she was so close to having what she wanted. Had she known that Naibus was not the master power, but that there was another who was greater, she would have left the tower and gone to him, taking her ring with her. But by the time she had made the discovery, she had already shown her hand. She had destroyed Naibus.

And by that time she had discovered that the silence in the tower had become very deep and very long.

Chapter Eleven

F IVE NIGHTS HAD PASSED.

Jaimah held them as a blur in her mind, a confusion out of which she remembered little of reason. A vague memory stirred, just out of reach, that she could not grasp hold of and bring into focus. A familiar voice spoke to her at times, and a face appeared over her off and on. She was more aware of the passage of time than anything else; she knew when night came and knew that with it came the dreams, five nights of terror. But that familiar voice always kept her from slipping away.

Jaimah wakened again, a great lethargy on her. Her eyes rested upon Corwyn, who was sitting on the edge of the cot. She grew confused and turned her head to see a bookcase and remembered cleaning it.

"I thought," she said to Corwyn, "that Shayna slept here now."

Corwyn shook his head. His hand touched her face. Jaimah tried to move away, and that effort was beyond her strength. "Don't go back to sleep," Corwyn told her. "Stay awake."

She tried, earnestly, striving to do as that voice insisted; but the heaviness in her head and eyes made focusing too difficult. Darkness began to slide back over her, and that was more comfortable, more welcome. She felt a hand touch her face, gentle, persistent, a touch that kept her from surrendering to the oblivion of sleep.

"Drink," she was told in a voice that was familiar. She felt herself lifted—Corwyn's arm, she remembered. A vessel's rim touched her lips, and she drank. Cool water slid to her stomach and sat there.

She was let back, but the weight beside her did not go away. Slowly and painfully, she opened her eyes and looked at Corwyn through the haze that restricted her vision. There was a light behind him that was a harsh glare and framed him so that she could not see his face. She blinked several times before she closed her eyes, abandoning her efforts.

But she had been pulled out of the darkness that had held her. It no longer threatened to consume her, and the pressure on her chest was gone; she could breathe easily now. When she became aware of her surroundings again, the weight on the cot was no longer there.

When morning came again, Corwyn returned, bringing some honey tea and a little cheese. Jaimah held back the questions she wanted to ask. She ate and watched him.

Corwyn's blue eyes swept her face; a long-fingered hand touched her jawline. "You remain here," he said, "until you are stronger. Do not get up without my help."

Jaimah drank the last of her tea and considered the matter.

But when Corwyn left, she set her hand on the cot to steady herself so that she could stand. Then she walked on weak, trembling legs to the other room. She rested a moment against the door frame to catch her breath before crossing the room. After looking out to ascertain that she was alone, she went out into the corridor and slowly navigated the stairs, going down to her own room.

By now she had remembered what had happened when she had gone to Shayna, although she didn't remember the attack itself.

And she remembered about the pollen.

Corwyn came looking for her shortly after that and found her huddled before the fire hearth. She was wrapped shivering in a fur. He looked at her, his face set in an expression that Jaimah did not want to read.

"This is not wise," he said.

"It is no concern of yours," Jaimah said with an edge of ice in her voice.

Corwyn came toward her slowly, dropping to his knees in front of her. "It is pointless, anyway," he said.

Jaimah frowned, considered saying something rude; but that he intimated he knew what she was doing brought her up short. She looked at him, holding the fur around her as the only barrier that she had.

She wondered if he was going to admit to what he had done.

She leaned back against the chair, her legs trembling visibly. She assumed carefully a calm mask so that he would not see the apprehension that filled her. Corwyn reached out and took her hand.

"You must rest," he said.

Jaimah flinched from his touch, startled. Corwyn frowned in puzzlement. Then his face became grim. Jaimah met his eyes with a determined show of bravado.

"Come with me," he said, drawing her to her feet as he stood.

Jaimah tried to pull her hand out of his, but his grasp tightened. "Jaimah," he said. "You cannot stay here in the cold."

"But I need not go with you," she said acidly. "I'll light a fire."

He looked at her for a moment. Then, cursing under his breath, he swept her up and bore her in his arms up the stairs to his rooms. There he deposited her on a low reclining chair. She cringed as he dropped down beside her and regarded her angrily for a long moment.

"Shayna's preparations are nearly complete," he said at last to her, "and soon she will try the spell again. You will have to be strong, Jaimah. You have to be. This is not going to be easy for any one of us, and to survive, we have to strong. It is important that you stay here and rest. Don't try to go anywhere. It's not going to help anyway. You will only succeed in making yourself ill."

Jaimah's heart skipped a beat. He spoke in veiled, general terms, never naming nor confirming what she suspected to be true, what she believed to be true. And he hinted . . . what? That what she feared would happen was inevitable, no matter what she did?

She drew in a painful breath. "If I do not rest," she asked. "What then? What happens then?"

Corwyn's gaze did not falter. "You will not survive," he said. "You will not live through the things that will come when Shayna works the spell again. This is why I insist, Jaimah." As he spoke, the tension that flowed freely between them seemed to ease somewhat. Jaimah found that the low reclining chair into which he made her sit was an extreme relief to her sore body.

"You must be strong enough to come through it all or you will not be able to. It's as simple as that. Nothing more—nothing less. You live or you die, that is all." His words fell from his lips with a heaviness that settled on her and filled her with a chill of foreboding that would not go away.

This was not what she expected him to say. She had assumed he would speak of the pollen—had hoped that he would. She was desperate that he would, so that she could demand that something be done to stop what she was afraid was already happening.

"You are still very weak," Corwyn said, "even though you have tried not to show it. Shayna will be asking for you soon, and, Jaimah, you must be ready. Don't let her hurt you again."

Jaimah blinked. Corwyn held up his hand, and the light within the room waned, fading to a dim twilight cast by a small fire in the hearth. Jaimah held her breath, dismayed anew at the ease with which he did it.

"Please rest now," Corwyn said then. "I will not leave until you do." He picked up a fur from another chair and laid it across her. Jaimah wondered where the new chairs had come from. She could see that besides the table and the new chairs that had been there before, there was the one on which she now lay, the one beside which Corwyn stood, a chest in the corner, and a stand of candles on the table. She knew that these things had not been stored anywhere in the tower.

"Corwyn," Jaimah said, making an inclusive gesture. "Where did all of this come from?"

Corwyn shrugged, an answer that was no answer.

Jaimah plucked at the fur on her lap, considering what she should do; all of a sudden Corwyn's hand stopped hers. She jerked it free and looked up at him, startled.

"Do not trouble yourself with all of these questions. Sleep awhile."

She considered refusing, but instead lay back, holding her tongue. Deciding not to press for an answer, she shut her eyes and forced herself to rest, hearing Corwyn go to the table and sit down.

And she slept, dreaming.

It was in her consciousness a subtle moment before panic took over.

"No!" she cried, trying to banish the dream.

Raw fear washed over her like a tide. Suddenly came the feeling of uncertainty, and she rippled and shredded, going into a place that didn't exist, a nothingness that was all-consuming. Her mind went through a kind of convulsion as all she knew vanished, but there remained an impression of inconceivable depth, of senses overstimulated. She clung to where she was, a structure that she could not see. The warping began again, rippling, stomach-wrenching like a fall to death. She screamed, lost her grip, and fell into the darkness.

There was solidity about her, touch, and sensations of light that were familiar, but in a disjointed, disassociated way. She cried out, and felt arms warm around her, solid and comforting.

They were her anchor. They held her, were one with her. She fled the dream to them and gave way to them for a time, with her arms around, clinging, receiving warmth and comfort until she began to realize who it was she clung to. With a choking cry she pushed him away and, in the cold of his absence, came to herself.

She hurled herself up and staggered to the door. Her legs failed as she reached for the handle, her fingers sliding helplessly from the metal and down the wood. Her stomach heaved and twisted into a painful knot, but she couldn't be sick, even though she desperately wanted to. For a moment, everything went black.

She had fallen and she realized it, although she had not been able to do anything to prevent it. She lay still, gasping for air.

Corwyn came to her—after how long she did not know. He knelt down and laid a gentle hand on her shoulder.

"Let me help you," he said after a moment. That much Jaimah could understand. And he said something further, but Jaimah's mind couldn't make out what the words meant, even though they were words she knew.

"Go away," Jaimah said, an effort that cost her. Corwyn shook his head. "Get away from me," she said.

But Corwyn replied nothing, gathered her up into his arms and took her back across the room to the chair.

Jaimah tried to sit up and protest. But the effort knotted her stomach and she had to fight the sickness down, leaving herself shaking and sweating. She could not move, even to turn her head for fear that nausea would become more than she could handle. She closed her eyes and concentrated on staying calm and taking slow, deep breaths to keep from jarring her stomach even that way.

Corwyn sat beside her and took her hand in his. Jaimah moved her limp fingers to pull away but couldn't. His touch was soothing, in spite of how she fought it, she felt a drowsiness come over her. There was nothing she could do to stop it. A brief flurry of panic took hold of her.

And again came the dream, the terror, and dissolution.

Jaimah cried out and began to gasp, unable to breathe, until something or someone snatched her and pulled her out of the hole into which she was falling. A force gripped her and shook her with bruising strength and she came out of the daze. After much effort, her eyes focused on Corwyn. She clung to him and wept while he held her close.

By evening she was better composed. The shaking and trembling had diminished somewhat. A dull ache was still in her head, but not such a pain as to prevent her from moving. She remembered with acute shame how she had clung to Corwyn, letting him hold her while tears ran hotly down her face, tears that came on their own, a silent weeping that she could not stop.

Now Corwyn watched her, his dark blue eyes sober, from where he sat at the table. The candles on the stand had been lit and the yellow flames stood tall and motionless, casting a golden glow over the tables and the books, and lit Corwyn's hair with the shine of polished metal. He turned over in his fingers a small blade. The red jewels in the thin handle caught and flashed in the candlelight. Over and over the knife turned while Corwyn looked at her thoughtfully. Jaimah looked into his eyes and met there a veiled secretiveness behind which there lurked something that she didn't recognize. It shook her.

He put the knife down on the table and said, "Tell me about the dreams."

"No," she said with such force that a brief look of surprise crossed Corwyn's face. He regarded her, frowning while he absently turned the small knife over on the table. Jaimah felt his gaze like a tangible force, and turned her head so that she looked out the window on the darkening sky and the silhouetted mountain peaks.

She heard him rise and walk toward her. She ignored him, closing her eyes, feigning sleep.

"Don't do this," Corwyn said to her finally, after standing and looking at her for a time.

Anger burned in his voice. He walked away, and the sudden panic of it gave Jaimah the strength to rise and fight her blurring senses. She tried to walk across the room and made it halfway. Her head reeled, and she grabbed frantically at the table. She leaned against it. Then shaking, she sat down—slowly, so that she wouldn't fall.

Corwyn stood watching. She had not seen him there. She had thought that he had left.

"You don't have to do this alone," Corwyn said then. "I can help you."

Jaimah searched for words to answer and found none. Corwyn came to her, pulling a chair with him and sat down beside her. Jaimah wanted to rise and go back to where she had been. This was too close to him. She could not. Corwyn's anger had disturbed her, although it seemed now to have disappeared. She clenched her fingers and reckoned where this new anxiety had come from and thought she knew.

"Corwyn," Jaimah ventured, speaking slowly and with effort. "Can you really help me?"

"Yes," said Corwyn quietly. "If you will let me."

She looked at him a moment, then down at her hands that she held tightly in her lap. "All right," she said at last.

Corwyn let out a soft breath that was much like a sigh of relief. He rose and took her arm, drew her to her feet, and helped her walk back to where she could lie down. She broke out in a clammy sweat, and the spinning in her head turned into a hissing buzz.

Corwyn sat next to her, took her hand in his, and traced a light design on her forehead. Then he gently stroked back her hair. The dull ache and the noise inside her head went away. A soothing coolness radiated from his fingers and sank into her, easing the nausea and the sickness and replacing the dizziness and weakness with calm and content. Jaimah felt muscles that were knotted with tension release and limbs that were tight against spasm relax. Breathing became easier. The clenched muscles of her face smoothed.

She opened her eyes and looked into his. She thought distantly of the loveroot pollen and dismissed it. It didn't matter.

And that thought brought fear to her. A sudden frown furrowed Corwyn's brow. He knew—he knew!

Corwyn gazed at her and silently estimated. Jaimah met that look directly and felt his touch leave her. He sat back. She felt suddenly alone in that movement, as if he had done more than just sit back and had withdrawn more than just his hands.

She almost wept, but managed not to.

Corwyn put out his hand and touched her face. It was a frightening gesture at that moment, for she had wanted it more than she had ever wanted anything.

And that night she lay with eyes open, troubled by a waking dream.

Chapter Twelve

WHEN SHE AWOKE IN THE LENGTHENING AFTERNOON, THERE was a strange dark cloud framing the jagged mountains in an ominous black rim. She stared at the contrast of white mountain peaks on blue-black cloud. Somehow she could tell that this cloud was different from any other cloud that she had ever seen. This one was not natural. It seemed to shimmer with some inner light that she had not noticed until she was turning away. She looked back again, staring in alarm, but did not see the light again.

A dread she couldn't explain fell over her.

As she stood at the window she felt a sudden awareness of eyes watching her, unseen eyes somewhere out there in the mountains, very much aware of her and waiting for her. She stared at the mountains under the shadow of that cloud, but could not see anything in the distance, other than cliffs and jagged peaks. The Watchers! Why they were focusing their attention on the tower and seemed to be drawing nearer to it she could not quite grasp.

But there was something in that sending that was new to her. She touched the window, holding her breath.

Yes . . . Yes! There was a change! There was a clarity to what she sensed now. It hadn't been there before. It was almost as if she could hear their thoughts—or feel their thoughts . . . or something . . .

She turned from the window and hurried across the room.

She had to find Shayna and tell her about this new thing.

Jaimah's steps slowed as she went up the stairs. She was compelled by some will other than her own to turn toward the fire-gutted rooms that once belonged to Shayna. She stopped when she saw a faint light coming through the door.

Silently, suddenly wary, she stood just a short step from being able to see into the room. The shadows about her were thick and dark; only the faint glow coming through the door held them back. Light that was even less than that of a candle flame.

And from the doorway appeared a blacker shadow, the hint of light glowing on blond hair. Corwyn!

The apprentice stood still, waiting. Jaimah hesitated, unsure. She found that she could think of nothing to say. No words came to her to explain why she had come to this dark place. Corwyn looked at her, and after deliberation, beckoned her to come.

She went forward into the light, which came, she saw, from dying coals in the brazier. A musky smell hung thick in this shadowed room, which had been cleaned and rehung with drapes, undeterminable of color in the darkness. Two chairs sat close to the heavy drapes, a small table behind them. The bookshelves and all else that she was accustomed to seeing here were gone.

"Go in," Corwyn's voice said softly at her back.

She felt the touch of Corwyn's hand between her shoulders, and went forward, not wishing to and feeling her skin contract at his touch. She came to a halt once she reached the brazier and could feel the heat that radiated from it. The coals were glowing red and yellow, a faint light that was about to die out. Jaimah wondered where Shayna was or if Corwyn had used the brazier on his own.

"I have been expecting you," Corwyn said in a low voice, so that the tremor inside her became intense. Jaimah looked part-way toward him, heart pounding unexpectedly. For a terrible moment, she thought that he was angry, but then saw that he was not.

"You knew that I was coming?" she asked hesitantly. She looked back to the brazier of dying embers, the faint glow becoming less even as she watched. And she made a guess. "Did you summon me, Corwyn?"

"Is that what you think?" he asked after a moment. Then he said, "You do me injustice, Jaimah."

There was a stillness in Corwyn's voice that chilled. Jaimah did not try to answer. She looked around the room that was in deep shadow, alien and unfamiliar.

It had no trace of Shayna left within its walls. Even the brazier, from which a faint fragrance rose, which Shayna had used countless times, seemed a thing strange in the emptiness. The room was no longer a place of familiarity, but was a place of mystery, hidden things, and whispered secrets.

"I have been waiting for you to come." Corwyn said, coming up close behind her. "It was only a matter of time."

Jaimah went around the brazier to escape his nearness and turned to look at him, a black figure only slightly illuminated by the fading embers. "Has Shayna been here?"

"Just a short time ago," he answered. "I waited here after she left."

"You waited for me?"

"I thought you might come."

She thought she saw him shrug. She turned away, disturbed, went to the window, and pulled aside the drape a fraction to look out. The sun had gone down behind the thick black cloud that framed the mountain peaks. It was as if it was lurking there. When it finally came . . . She shivered and did not complete the thought.

She looked over her shoulder at Corwyn, now more discernible in the added light of the twilight coming through the narrow opening in the drapes.

"You've seen it, too?" Corwyn asked.

"Yes," she said, looking at the cloud. She felt out for the presence of the Watchers, but they had gone. Corwyn's footsteps were soft as he came up behind her; her grip on the drape tightened.

His hand reached over her shoulder and pulled the drape aside more. After a moment, he asked. "Did the dream come again?"

Jaimah's heart sped. She looked warily up at him, standing so closely behind her. "No," she said, and wished herself out the door, for she had had a dream of a different kind.

"Good," he said. He still looked out at the ominous cloud that hung like an anvil in the sky. "It will be here soon." He let the drape fall back into place, and Jaimah shivered again.

Corwyn set his hand on her shoulder and moved her across the room to the hearth in which a small fire suddenly sprang. He sat down on the floor, and Jaimah sank down beside him.

The tiny flame burned among some wood, casting a soft light a short distance into the room.

There was silence. Jaimah slowly let go her breath, trying to control the pounding of her heart. A long time Corwyn looked into the fire, his face sober and thoughtful. Jaimah cast a glance at him, her eyes drawn to him in spite of herself.

"The dreams were caused by the ring," he said to her finally, turning his head slightly.

Jaimah's breath chilled in her lungs. She stared at him, her hands clasped tightly in her lap.

"They are a sort of memory of the place into which you had been thrown. A kind of oblivion. We were fortunate," he said, reaching out to move a piece of wood closer to the small flame on the hearth. "Shayna stopped just in time. A few more moments and nothing would have brought you back. It was difficult enough, as it was. And bringing you back whole was even more difficult. Having residual dreams was a natural consequence." He rubbed some ash off his hand onto his knee and looked at Jaimah.

It explained much.

"Shayna helped bring me back?" she asked.

Corwyn raised his hand and ran his fingers along her jawline, then let it fall back into his lap. "No."

A tremor ran through Jaimah at his touch, and she pulled back, looking at the fire that had not grown to consume the wood around it. The light it cast remained small, the circle of its illumination close, so that they were drawn together by its warm light, his knee touching hers. She crossed her arms tightly in front and strove to keep her breathing calm.

And in sudden and anxious attempt to find out about the loveroot pollen, but not quite brave enough to approach the subject directly, she asked, "What did you do with the mixture that you made?"

"It is aging."

Jaimah considered that. "What is it for?"

Corwyn shrugged. "Depends on what it is used for." Another answer that was no answer.

Jaimah then took a deep breath, hesitated, took another and abandoned all pretense. "What did you do with the pollen?"

She stared at him, not daring to turn her head to look away. Her heart was thundering against her ribs, a coldness settling on her.

Startlement passed over Corwyn's face, followed by an

amusement that lit his eyes, but then a soberness came and stayed. "Why do you ask, Jaimah?"

She swallowed nervously and shrugged, affecting complacency. "I didn't see what you did with it." Her fingers clasped her upper arms tightly, a pain that was welcome, for it kept her calm.

"I see," Corwyn said, looking down at the toe of his boot and rubbing it absently with his thumb. "What do you think I did with it?" His eyes raised back up to hers, dark with secretiveness. Jaimah found it suddenly difficult to breathe, the air caught with a gasp that was more surprise than fear. Her voice failed her in that same instant.

Corwyn laughed softly and leaned close so that his face was just inches from hers. "Don't you know what I did with it, Jaimah?" His voice was barely above a whisper.

Still unable to find her voice, Jaimah shook her head imperceptibly.

"But you have your own ideas?"

Jaimah strove to look away, but his eyes had a hypnotizing force, one that she could not fight. She seemed to be falling back into a bottomless void. Then he looked down and she was jerked back to herself.

"I didn't do anything with it," Corwyn said.

But Jaimah didn't believe him. She had seen the bowl and knew that it had been the same one that she had eaten from. The memory of his ladling stew into it was still strong in her mind. She bit her lip, weighed the consequences, and gave an answer.

"I don't believe you," she said.

Corwyn looked up sharply. He considered, then reached forward to take her hand and turned it over in his so that her palm was facing up. With the finger of his other hand he traced an intricate design lightly on her palm, sending shivers down the full length of her spine. And, she thought, if he could affect her so with just a touch, why would he need the use of loveroot pollen? Then, in the next instant, she realized where that thought had come from. She stared at Corwyn with fearful apprehension.

As if he were erasing what he had just drawn, he covered her hand with his, pulling it away in a slow, sensuous motion. The flesh on her palm tingled where he had touched it, and there was an unaccustomed flurry in her stomach, accompanied by a tightness in her lungs.

"Enough talk of pollen and potions," Corwyn said.

His fingers closed around Jaimah's hand to prevent her from pulling it away. Then he raised his other palm up, brought all of his fingers together to form a kind of hollow, conic pyramid. Turning his head slightly, he blew a small puff of air at his fingers and a three-inch flame sprang into being there.

Jaimah flinched.

"I have a question that needs to be answered," he said, bringing her hand up and transferring the flame to her palm. Jaimah winced but felt nothing—no heat, no pain, as if the flame didn't really exist.

"You told Shayna about the things you've seen me do." Corwyn's free hand closed around her other wrist, holding her captive. He gestured to the flame with his chin. "You cannot lie. I will know."

A chill, different fear crept over Jaimah as she stared at the flame, and despite what he had just told her, she said, "I didn't tell Shayna anything." To her horror the flame flickered and began to die.

Corwyn's grip on her wrist tightened. "Don't lie, Jaimah."

She swallowed as she stared, mesmerized, at the flame. It was going out, jumping and struggling as if it couldn't breathe.

"Jaimah." Corwyn's voice was quiet, insistent. She dragged her eyes away from the flame to his face.

"This is important," Corwyn said slowly. "A thing that I must know. The time approaches when Shayna will be able to use the spell. I must know what she knows of me. What did you tell her, Jaimah?"

Jaimah found no answer, for there was a tone in his voice that she had not heard before, a confession, almost. She searched his face for something to explain what he meant, for a hint to tell her what he confessed.

"Very well," she said, and was surprised at the relief that came over his face.

"What did you tell her, Jaimah?"

All of a sudden, Jaimah feared she was being led into a trap, one in which there would be no exit. She realized suddenly that she was truly being thrust in between Corwyn and Shayna, just as she had feared she would be.

Corwyn's slender fingers released her wrist and touched the flame; its convulsions were slowing as it struggled for life.

"The flame dies, Jaimah."

She hesitated.

"That is no good," Corwyn said. "If you wait, it dies."

Jaimah jerked her hand out of Corwyn's. The flame went out with a hiss. But Corwyn caught her hand again, gently closed his fingers. Another flame sprang into being.

Jaimah returned his gaze, feeling resentment and anger. But slowly the anger was replaced with uncertainty and confusion. What he asked was not such a hard thing to answer. It would hurt no one to tell him; he *did* tell her once that she could tell Shayna anything about him she cared to. There was no reason not to tell him what he wanted to know.

Jaimah hesitated in midthought and stared at Corwyn with a rising angry suspicion that he had put those thoughts into her mind.

"I told her everything," she said, tightly.

"I see." Corwyn took the flame from her hand and closed his fingers over it, extinguishing it. His thumb stroked her palm thoughtfully a moment before he let go.

"I have my loyalties to her, Corwyn."

The apprentice's midnight-blue eyes regarded her soberly, looking at her with that measuring assessment that he turned on her from time to time. "Of course you do." Corwyn rose, unbending upward with a single fluid motion. He stood looking into the fire burning on the hearth as if he could see something other than the flame. Then he made a small tossing move with his hand and the fire leaped up, becoming instantly brighter, filling the room with its light.

"Why did you do that to me?" she asked. "Force me to answer like that. Could you not have just asked?"

"Would you have answered?" He looked down on her expressionlessly, the firelight flickering softly on his face. She stared back and said nothing.

He turned to her. "Let me see your hand." He knelt and took her hand in his again, inspecting it in the firelight.

Jaimah frowned at his head. "What are you looking for?"

"Scorch marks."

"But there was no heat."

Corwyn regarded her soberly. "None that you could feel," he said finally.

Jaimah regarded him suspiciously.

Corwyn lifted a corner of his mouth apologetically. "I *did* tell you not to lie. But . . . you can see."

Jaimah looked and saw with surprise that there was an angry red circle on her palm where blisters were beginning to form. "But I don't feel anything," she exclaimed.

"You will."

Jaimah jerked her hand away and closed her fingers over the burn. Corwyn sighed and sat back on his heels. "How long are you going to fight me, Jaimah?"

It was several moments before Jaimah even attempted to think of an answer. The heat of embarrassment began to rise to her face. Reluctantly she held out her hand so that he could see it.

Jaimah watched him, finding it strange that after so long a time he had finally made a protest. She considered the amusement that lurked just behind the blue eyes, and reckoned that she had been tricked into extending her hand and that Corwyn found that humorous. But instead of bristling, she allowed the situation to make her smile.

"Tomorrow," Jaimah said, "I will apologize."

"Not today?"

She shook her head. "No. First you must do something about my hand."

Corwyn's face went sober, but there was pleasure in his gesture of assent. "All right." He touched her palm with his fingers and Jaimah watched in amazement as the blisters shrank and the red faded to a healthy pink.

Jaimah frowned, all humor suddenly gone, old suspicions aroused again. She drew her hand back, staring at it.

"How do you do that?" she asked. "Shayna could not do it so easily. Even with her herbs and her words of power she could not do it so easily. You just . . . touch." The last word came out almost with loathing. She looked up at his eyes that had become hard, like blue-black glass, and a sudden shiver took her.

Corwyn expelled a short breath and rose. He walked away, to stand staring out at the night, his hand lifting the drape. Jaimah felt the withdrawal of him like a pain. The surprise of it shook her. And in that frozen figure, she saw total disappointment in her. She drew a quavery breath, trying to hold down the sharpness of that pain. She thought of the pollen and felt a sadness that she could not explain.

"Corwyn."

The apprentice turned, eyes shadowed, veiled, and looked over at her.

"Why have you done this to me?"

"What have I done, Jaimah?"

"This . . ." She stopped to seek for the words. "You have . . ." She hesitated again, the words not right. Then she shrugged helplessly and looked down at her hand that no longer bore any sign of burn. She heard his soft footsteps come to her. But she did not look up.

"What do you think I've done?"

Jaimah shook her head and he knelt on one knee beside her. When she still did not answer he sat with legs crossed.

Jaimah looked at him, where he sat so close to her. The relief she felt was frightening, and she thought desperately that the pollen had at last taken hold. There was a tremor inside, and she had to look away.

"Jaimah . . ." Corwyn began and took her hand in his.

But Jaimah snatched her hand away, his touch a thing she could not bear. "Don't touch me," she choked, closing her eyes against another tremor. "Please."

When she opened her eyes again, she saw that Corwyn had gone. She stared at the empty room and wept in despair.

Chapter Thirteen

THE MORNING CAME QUIETLY, WITH ONLY THE SOUND OF THE wind blowing around the outside of the tower. Jaimah looked and saw that the black cloud still hung just beyond the mountain peaks. It seemed to be gathering its strength there, building in force until it would no longer be able to hold back. Then it would come down on them, bringing the full fury of winter with it.

The Watchers were back. Jaimah could feel them out there somewhere, their presence pressing on her mind like a physical hand. She shivered as she searched the lonely crags for them. They were waiting for something to happen; she could feel it. They were watching and waiting. But their intent did not manifest itself to her. She let the drape settle back into place.

She was stiff from sitting by the fire all night. Sleep had been driven from her, and she had spent the long hours with her mind going to dozens of places that she couldn't even remember. A numbness of limb and bone was all she retained from those empty hours. She put a hand to her face in an unconscious attempt to wipe away the fatigue.

The door opened, and she turned to find Shayna looking at her. The Lady's eyes showed surprise and something else that was slightly sinister.

"So you have recovered at last," she said, her voice matter-of-fact.

Jaimah nodded, suddenly unable to bring herself to answer aloud.

"Good," Shayna replied. "I have need of you."

A chill ran down Jaimah's back. "The spell is ready?"

Shayna closed the door and came to the brazier, her black robe whispering against her feet. "Today I bind Morgus," she said, running her fingers around the cold metal bowl. Her black eyes leveled on Jaimah's face. "By tonight he will be mine."

She threw a pinch of powder into the cold bowl; a red flame flared and pulsed as it died down to burn with radiating heartbeats.

"Go tell Corwyn to come," Shayna said at last.

Jaimah hesitated a moment, finding the mention of the apprentice's name unsettling, and her nerves were taut-strung at the thought of having to go down to his rooms.

Then, having no choice, she nodded in compliance to Shayna and went.

Corwyn was looking out his window at the mountain and the dark cloud beyond when Jaimah found him. He acknowledged her presence wordlessly, a glance that halted her uncertainly just within the door.

"She wants you to come," she said so hesitantly she was afraid her voice would not carry across the room.

Corwyn continued to stare out the window for a long moment, his profile veiled by a sober, unreadable expression. Jaimah felt her heart lurch at the distance that was on his face. He reached out a hand and touched the window with his fingertips. "Close the door," he said finally.

Jaimah pushed the door shut, then went slowly to the table. Her eyes fell on the open pages of a book, seeing a drawing of some kind. Beside the book was a stand of candles that had burned down to nothing—evidence that he, also, had not slept. She clasped her hands together, then let them fall to her side.

She heard the whisper of his tread as he came slowly across the remaining half of the room to her. Her hand sought a nearby chair back and gripped it.

No closer, she wished him for she was becoming increasingly disturbed as he drew nearer, and she knew it was the pollen working within her. He did not stop, and she had to hold herself with an iron will to keep from running out of the room. When at last he came to a stand, he was only a few inches from her. Jaimah attempted to step back, but could not, unable to move under his steady gaze.

"Do you want me to go upstairs?" he asked.

There was a long moment while his eyes held hers. Jaimah's heart thudded with strong, jarring strokes, and she could not have looked away had she even attempted to. A shivering thrill went through her, a lacy kind of excitement that frightened her.

"Yes," she whispered. "Please come." Then she fell silent, not knowing what else to say.

He turned his eyes away to look down at the book that lay open on the table. His fingers absently turned a page, the quiet sound unexpectedly loud in the silence.

"Last night you sent me away," he said. He looked up at her with a hardness that she had not seen on him before, an anger that surprised her. "Now you want me to come?" He snapped the book shut with an angry bang.

Jaimah flinched. All the breath seemed to leave her, and a cold shiver chilled her.

Corwyn breathed in a long breath and looked back down at the book. "You know why she wants me there, don't you, Jaimah?"

She nodded, her heart stilling. Shayna wanted his talent and was going to try to wrest it from him. "Yes," she answered in a whisper. "I know."

"And you still want me to come?"

She clasped her hands together, let them drop. She could think of nothing to say to him.

Corwyn pushed the book away, his eyes thoughtfully studying its cover, but when he looked back to Jaimah there was no sign of softening in his expression. His eyes leveled on her, and he studied her for a long moment. Then he sighed, and the hardness on his face yielded in surrender.

"All right, Jaimah. I will go with you."

Jaimah breathed in relief so acute it brought tears to her eyes. She gripped the chair beside her with a painful clasp and silently cursed the pollen and Corwyn for doing this to her.

Corwyn looked at her with a slight frown. Then he said, "Let's go." He walked past her to the door and waited for her to follow him. Together they went up the stairs to Shayna's rooms.

Jaimah sat in a chair beside the small table where she could see both Shayna's and Corwyn's faces. But before Shayna began the spell, as Jaimah had expected her to, the Lady brought out from someplace within her robe a skin container. Jaimah recognized it immediately as the one that contained the liquid that Corwyn had made. "Tell me about this," she said to Corwyn.

He looked from it to Shayna's face. "It is nothing. A harmless mixture of loveroot and hazelroot."

"What is it for?"

"It's properties are very small. A healing lotion, that is all."

Shayna shot a glance at Jaimah; she did not believe him. Jaimah held her breath trying not to betray anything on her face.

"You know," Shayna said, "that I have ways of finding the truth."

"I'm aware of that."

"You do not fear me?"

Corwyn did not answer. The question seemed to have no effect whatsoever on him. Jaimah, however, felt the words with a shock of fear.

"I have attempted," Shayna continued softly, a softness that had nothing to do with gentleness, "to discover what this liquid is, using methods that only I know, and I have not yet found the secret that it contains. But I *do* know, apprentice, that this is not a healing lotion. I also know that there is no value in the hazel root, and yet . . . you have used it and have created this that hides its purpose from me. And this makes me wonder about you and about the things that Jaimah has told me, which I did not believe. And when I wonder, I can become very ruthless. I use any method at my disposal to find out what I want to know."

There was heavy tension in the room, one that was almost tangible, like a thing to be seen. It was suffocating and made the moments seem like hours and the silence a thing to be heard loudly. Jaimah gripped the edge of the table in her fear.

Shayna would use the ring if desperate enough.

"Shayna," Jaimah protested. "Does it really matter?"

"It matters," Shayna answered harshly. "Tell me, Corwyn, if I asked you to . . . drink from this skin, would you?"

"I would do as you asked, Shayna. There is no harm in it."

The feeling in the air was like that before a storm, thick and close and unreal. Jaimah began to rise, to intercede, suddenly afraid.

"Stay there, Jaimah," Corwyn said, turning his head slightly to give her a look of warning. Jaimah sat back in surprise.

Shayna's eyes narrowed suddenly, and she looked from Corwyn to Jaimah. Furious comprehension came to her face as she finally saw the control that Corwyn had over her servant. Jaimah was already moving when she cried out in a rage, her ring blazing. The power struck Corwyn hard, hurling him to the draped window where he sprawled at the impact.

"No!" Jaimah cried at Shayna. "Don't!" She grabbed Shayna's arm and dragged it down, wincing at the fury in Shayna's eyes when the Lady pulled her arm free. Jaimah flung herself to Corwyn's side, knowing that Shayna would probably use the ring on her as well.

Corwyn was on his knees, holding his arm against his body, shuddering convulsively. His face was white and beaded with sweat. Jaimah touched him, aching painfully inside because his arrogance and command could be crushed so easily.

But that was the power of the ring.

"Let me help you," Jaimah said to him, holding him, trying to ease the shuddering that shook him. She was not sure what she could do, but felt an urgency to be doing something. Shayna came with a silent movement of robes, bent down, and laid a hand on his head seeming to judge how badly he was hurt.

"You did not need to do this," Jaimah said to her without thinking.

"He has deceived me," Shayna said. "And he has lied to me; you told me yourself, Jaimah. It could not go on. He needed to be put in his place."

"But there was no reason for this," said Jaimah. "He was going to do whatever you asked him to. You did not need to do this."

"You forget yourself!"

Jaimah looked up into Shayna's angry eyes, then quelled suddenly and lowered her gaze fearfully. "Yes. I'm sorry," she murmured.

"And you forget to whom you are servant."

"I'm sorry," Jaimah repeated, pulling Corwyn close to her, her arms going around him. "Please, Shayna. He's hurt."

Shayna said nothing, but stood silently staring at them. Then she turned away. "Get him ready." Her voice was tight with anger.

Jaimah stared after her in disbelief. There was absolutely no compassion in her, no remorse or guilt at all for what she had done.

Another tremor shook Corwyn and she turned to shelter him against the window, easing him down so that his head lay in her lap. "Corwyn," she whispered anxiously. "What can I do? Is there anything?" Her hand trembled as she touched him. His skin was damp with sweat. Jaimah wiped it from his brow, brushed his hair away from his face. "Tell me what to do."

He stirred slightly. "There is no need," he said softly, startling her. His voice was strong, even though quiet. He sat up slightly, leaning partly on her and partly on the window. He looked at her with eyes that seethed with anger. "I am quite all right."

Jaimah began to sit back in confusion. His hand stopped her, so that she still appeared to be ministering to him. "I don't understand," she whispered shakily. "I thought . . ."

"I am all right."

"You should be . . ." She faltered, unable to say the next few words.

"I don't think Shayna will again use that much power on me," he said.

"Why not?"

"Because she needs me."

"She is afraid," Jaimah said, not knowing exactly how she knew that.

His lips tightened grimly; his hand took hers. "You tried to stop her," he said. "That was a dangerous thing to do."

"I couldn't let her use the ring on you again."

"It was unnecessary," he said. And then, with an edge of utter bitterness. "Or was it because you could not help yourself?"

Corwyn's words caught her off guard. She did not know what manner of accusation he was making. "I thought that she was going to kill you."

"You wanted me gone yourself once."

It was the truth. She tried to find some kind of softness on Corwyn's face; she could only see closed anger, held and controlled, and something else that she could not define or put a name to. She did not know how to answer him. "I no longer do."

"Yes, I know." he said finally, after considering her.

"I saw the things that you did and saw how easily you did them, and I was afraid. I knew you weren't what you said you were. I thought you were dangerous."

"And what think you now?"

"I don't know. I still don't know who you are."

Corwyn turned his head to look out the window. "You suspect me of other things, also, Jaimah."

Her breathing caught in her throat. She knew he was talking about the pollen. "Tell me I'm wrong."

"Would it really matter, one way or the other?" he asked her.

Jaimah hesitated, unsure suddenly that they *were* talking about the same thing.

"Does it really make that much difference?"

And again there was that in his voice that sounded like confession. Jaimah's heart skipped a beat. Corwyn looked at her soberly, waiting for an answer that she did not have to give. And he extended a hand to touch her cheek. "There is really no point in asking now, is there?"

Jaimah stared at him, her breath caught in her throat. She wondered wildly if he meant that it was too late, that it was already done and nothing could undo it. Her hand clenched his tightly in horror.

Corwyn moved his thumb gently over her fingers and looked out the window to the cloud that waited beyond the mountain. His thoughts clearly turned there. His eyes began smoldering with anger and held such a look of determination as Jaimah had never seen.

"It is time," he said, as if speaking to the cloud rather than to her. "The waiting is over."

"What are you going to do?" Jaimah felt her blood go chill.

"It is already done."

Jaimah followed his eyes and saw with dread that the cloud was suddenly higher in the sky and that it now churned with a seething motion.

"It is growing," she said, dismayed by its glowering appearance. There was a flash of lightning within the depths, a shower of sparks that fizzled here and there, blue, green, and white, until they died into nothingness.

"What was that?" Jaimah whispered in fear, alarmed, never having seen anything like it before.

"It is nothing," Corwyn said.

Jaimah watched in horror as the clouds moved up to cover

the entire western sky. Churning and swirling within itself, the edges against the blue sky seeming to boil and foam, swiftly shrouding the mountain with its turbulence. There was something malevolent in its depths, a familiar kind of watching that reminded her of the Watchers. But the bursting flares and shimmering sparks that flickered and glistened as the storm swept toward the tower were more reminiscent of Encheon. Yet this had none of the benevolence that she had come to know as Encheon. This was demonic power as she had never imagined.

"What is it going to do?" she asked in a strangled voice.

Corwyn looked from the storm to her. "Don't worry," he said, lifting his hand to touch her face. "Nothing will harm you."

"No?"

He shook his head slightly. "No."

"What of Shayna?" Jaimah pressed.

The air he expelled through his nostrils was not a sigh, but was from the determination that still lurked behind his eyes. "That depends on what she does. Go tell her that I'm ready now."

Jaimah gathered herself to her knees and cast an anxious look at Shayna, whose face was drawn and weary. She did not yet know about the storm.

"Are you sure?"

"Yes, Jaimah. Go tell her. And tell her that when the storm comes, the potion I have made could be of use to her, if she has the skill to use it."

"I can't tell her that!"

Corwyn's eyes lifted suddenly to hers, dark with repressed anger; his hand closed tightly around hers. "Yes, you can. And you will." He leaned closer. "Do not be afraid of her."

"She will not like it."

He sat back, his fingers tracing a light design on her hand. "I know."

Jaimah rested unmoving, panic stirring in her. The touch of his fingers was cold, like ice, and burned because of it. She stared at their hands together like that, unable to look away. One hand held hers in a strong grasp, while the other hovered over it. She thought how much like those hands Corwyn and she had become, entwined together from the first day, painful like the cold fire of ice.

She slowly pulled her hand from his grasp, expecting and

finding strangeness in the absence of his touch. "I will try to tell her," she said, rising to her feet and avoiding his sober eyes.

Shayna met Corwyn's message with stony silence. Her eyes took in, for the first time, the storm that was descending on them in a frightening detail of sparking lights and flashing fizzles. High winds reached the tower and blew furiously around it with a howling roar that reminded Jaimah once again of the Watchers. She shivered and thought she could feel their presence out there somewhere, pressing on her awareness.

She waited for Shayna to do something—anything; but the Lady said nothing for a long moment. Then she finally turned from the storm.

"Yes. I think there is power there to aid me. Go get Corwyn."

Jaimah went quietly across the room and knelt down beside Corwyn where she could look into his face. He was looking out the window, leaning back against the curved wall, resting. The room had become dark, even though the drapes were open so that the storm could be seen easily. The only light was coming from the dim twilight of the flashes that came through the window. It chilled her to see that he was so unconcerned about the storm that it was easy for him to rest.

"Corwyn. She says to come."

He turned to look at her, his eyes shadowed. "Yes. I thought she might."

He sat up and wiped his hands on his knees. For a moment Jaimah feared he was going to reach for her. His face was sober, lit by turns of green, blue, and white; in between, the dark was so thick she could not see him at all. He moved to get up. "Let's go."

Suddenly Jaimah hesitated, clasping her arms tightly in front of herself, feeling very, very small.

Corwyn studied her with a frown. "Are you really afraid?"

"Yes," she said shakily. "A little."

He shook his head grimly and, leaning forward, kissed her on the cheek. "You don't need to be afraid anymore. Don't you feel something familiar about the storm?"

She stared at him stunned. She had felt it, a familiarity that she had tried not to acknowledge. Encheon. How did he know about Encheon? Or was he talking about the Watchers?

He leaned back a little, lifted his hand, and ran two fingers lightly over her lips and around under her chin. "Nothing in the storm is going to harm you." He looked up into her eyes. A smoldering fire darkened his gaze. "I guess," he said very quietly, "that it makes no difference, after all."

And Jaimah was suddenly thinking of the pollen. She pulled back away from him.

He smiled humourlessly. "Come," he said, taking her hand in his and standing. "Shayna waits."

Jaimah went with him, reluctantly.

Shayna stepped aside and let Corwyn go around the brazier to where he had stood before.

"Go sit down, Jaimah," Shayna ordered and then paid her no further heed. She began to mutter her words, throwing powder on the glowing brazier. One after another, colors flashed and lit the room, taking on images that wavered and disappeared in smoke.

Jaimah expected trouble right from the very beginning. But there was nothing. No engulfing fires, nor rumblings of earthquakes. She slunk back into the corner and sank to the floor, hugging her knees to her chest. She couldn't help comparing Shayna's awkward formulas to the ease with which Corwyn accomplished the same things. Suddenly, Shayna did not seem so all-knowing, but appeared childish and pathetic instead, playing at something she knew nothing about.

Jaimah heard it first, after she had been lulled into thinking that nothing was going to happen—the sound of rushing wind coming from the curled smoke over the brazier. The red glow in the bowl boiled, lights and plumes of steam rose, and the sound grew. A burst of fire leaping up to the ceiling lit their faces and spatted them with burning sparks. Jaimah cried out and smothered it. A sick dread gathered in her stomach.

The room was suddenly lit in flames of white and red, swirling in mists, steam, smoke, and clouds of vapors. The brazier splashed and bubbled.

An explosion heaved the tower, numbed the senses, and drove Jaimah against the wall.

And hard upon that, a white light lit the room. It grew, eating everything, a pressure that was unbearable. Jaimah heard Shayna crying, *Give me your hand, give me your hand.* The white burst over her, then it was red.

The wind came upon them in force, making the red swirl, sullen and angry, the wind coming from the brazier, a demon wind that howled and screamed until Jaimah's ears ached.

Jaimah gathered herself up and saw the fires blazing, sending smoke boiling aloft. This was what must have happened the first time. And Corwyn stood unshaken, while Shayna struggled within a flame, clawed fingers reaching, mouth in a scream that was drowned out by the wind.

Corwyn turned, grabbed the skin bag from the table where Shayna had left it, ripped it open, and threw the contents on Shayna, over the brazier and on the floor. The Lady crumbled, the flame going out instantly. The brazier flared in new light, hung suspended and then crumbled down into ashes of metal, an orange glow still coming from it.

Jaimah watched, wishing to turn her face from it, knowing already what was to come next. *The Peak.*

She knew with a foreknowledge just as surely as she knew that the Watchers were out there waiting for her to come. Shayna would take them to the Peak now. She shuddered.

She crept to Corwyn, a great knot swelling in her throat, and her body cold and numb. She reached for him and he put his arms around her, holding her tightly so that her face was hidden against him. She shut her eyes and let the shaking inside her calm, Corwyn's arms a security to cling to and a protection.

Then he said words that surprised her, the unexpectedness of them startling. "You see," he said, "it depends on what it's used for." The amusement in his voice so alien in what had just happened she looked up at him in astonishment.

"Come," he said. "We must see to Shayna."

Jaimah let him go and stood gravely by as he knelt on one knee beside Shayna. He lifted her by the shoulders and shook her gently. He spoke her name and turned her head from side to side, trying to rouse her.

"Is she all right?" asked Jaimah.

Corwyn looked toward her, then back again. "She's going to be fine. She's not really hurt." He rubbed her arms and cheeks. A moan came from her, and her brow knotted in a frown. Corwyn sat back with a satisfied sigh. "She'll come around now."

He offered that quietly and slowly rose, still looking at Shayna. "She's failed again," he said then. "Even with the power in the storm—she couldn't do it."

"You're wrong," said Shayna hoarsely, opening her eyes, startling Jaimah. She gathered herself up, a little stiffly, but otherwise okay. "There is no power in that storm!" she said harshly. "Just as there is no power in you! I searched, I reached, and there was nothing! Nothing!"

Corwyn's back stiffened. Jaimah saw it, but Shayna did not. "Are you certain?" he asked. "Or do you just lack the skill to take what is mine?"

Shayna looked on him with shock in her face, an impotent rage. She did not answer, and Jaimah felt a chill creeping over her skin in the Lady's silence.

"Did you think to find out what kind of power may be in the storm?" he continued, tightly. "Or did you just go ahead without considering what could happen?"

"You forget to whom you speak, apprentice!"

"Do you know what is in the storm?"

"There is *nothing* in the storm!" Shayna's hands clenched, and Jaimah started, thinking that Shayna was about to use the ring on him again. But this time, when she did it, it would be with its full power to smite him to that place beyond which there would be no return. She looked to him to warn him, but his eyes were on Shayna, smoldering in anger that was barely under control.

"Is nothing not a power?" Corwyn's voice was deathly quiet.

Jaimah looked from the window to the storm and its strange lightning still playing around the tower. Nothing—emptiness. She suddenly understood.

"Leave!" Shayna said. "Leave me! Jaimah, take him back downstairs."

Jaimah hesitated, looking to Corwyn questioningly. He swept his gaze from Shayna to her, the blaze in his eyes still burning. Again she hesitated until he said, "It's all right. I'll go."

Jaimah glanced at Shayna uncertainly, then stepped back in sudden fear at the rage in the Lady's eyes.

"No!" Shayna screamed at Jaimah. "It is *my* word you obey, not this usurper's!" Her hand came up, and the ring blazed. Jaimah stepped back again in panic.

Corwyn caught Shayna's arm, one handed, and held it so that she could not move. "I will go. There is no need for this." His voice was low.

Shayna returned his gaze furiously and, after a long moment, said, "All right. But you remember your place or she dies."

"I'll remember." He let go of her and looked to Jaimah.

Then, turning on his heel, he walked out, striding rapidly down the corridor. His steps echoed down the stairs, and after a moment a door closed.

Jaimah stared at Shayna. Her skin was pale, her eyes dilated: never had she looked so haggard, and never had Jaimah been so afraid of her.

Chapter Fourteen

"**W**HAT'S GOING ON BETWEEN YOU TWO!" SHAYNA'S VOICE was edged, cruel, a blow that stunned. She grabbed Jaimah by the arm, her fingers digging into the flesh.

Jaimah gasped at the pain. "I don't know what you mean."

"This . . . thing between you and Corwyn." Shayna's eyes were dark with fury, and her fingers tightened.

Jaimah winced. "There is nothing between us."

"You spend all your time with him."

"You send me to him," Jaimah's voice rose in protest.

Shayna snorted in derision, dismissing that with an angry shake of her head. "What is he up to? What is he planning?"

"I don't know."

"Is he out to destroy me?"

Jaimah cringed at the tightening grasp on her arm. "I don't know."

"Are you in league with him?"

"No!"

"Then how do you fit into all of this?" Shayna punctuated her words with furious shakes on Jaimah's arm.

"I don't know," Jaimah cried. Then suddenly she was in tears.

Shayna regarded her a moment with contempt. A glare of white light flashed through the window, followed by blue sparks that fell like scintillating rain against the glass.

"I don't know what you want to know," Jaimah sobbed. "Only Corwyn can tell you."

"Stop sniveling!" Shayna drew in a breath of exasperation. "Come with me." She dragged Jaimah to the door. "The spell will have to be done again." Her voice was edged. "We will have to go to the Peak."

Jaimah's heart struck with fearful foreboding. She had known it would come to this. She had known it when Corwyn had thrown the contents of the skin bag over Shayna and the spell failed. She would take them to the Peak, the place of the ultimate power, of summoning. It was the only place left where the spell might work.

Shayna dragged her up the dark stairs. "There is much to be done before we go."

Jaimah stifled an outcry as she stumbled and caught herself with a hand against the cold stone wall. Hard fingers hauled her mercilessly up to her feet.

"There are things that I will need. Corwyn's potion for one, and . . ."

"It is gone," Jaimah choked.

"Gone?" Shayna halted at the top of the stairs, her hand still on Jaimah's arm.

"Corwyn used it to put out the fire."

Shayna's face was dark in the shadows, but Jaimah could still feel her hard stare. "This is what he made it for? To put out fires? Water could do as much."

"I don't know. When I asked him what it was for, he said that it depended on what it was used for. Perhaps it could do many things, if you knew how."

Shayna was silent for a long, tense moment. Then she said, "Come on," with a wrenching pull on Jaimah's arm that tore a cry from her. She was dragged down the dark hall to the rooms that Corwyn had unlocked.

Shayna released her at the table with a suddenness that staggered her. The Lady strode about the room, gathering the things that she wanted to take: bottles, vials, boxes, putting them on the table. Jaimah watched her, seeing her as she had never seen her before, seeing for the first time how mad she was—how dangerous she was.

"I want you to put all these herbs in something that can be carried to the peak," Shayna said. "Make sure it's something strong, because we'll be going through the storm."

Jaimah looked from the bottled and vialed herbs on the

table to Shayna; she had not considered the storm. "Should we not wait?" she asked.

Shayna looked over at her, her shadowed face set and determined. "You do not approve, Jaimah?" Her voice was harsh, hard.

Jaimah crossed her arms in front of her, an unconscious attempt to protect herself. She raised her head to look at Shayna more directly, trying not to shrink in fear before that angry gaze. Her instincts screamed at her to choose her words carefully.

"It is not my place to approve or disapprove, just to obey."

That seemed to mollify Shayna; she became less angry. "And that's something that you seem to have forgotten."

"I did not mean to show disrespect."

Shayna crossed her arms, clenched her long fingers and strode over to the chairs and table. She sat down, looking suddenly very tired. Her hand that lay on the table seemed too thin. Then she sighed.

"I once came to this tower, long ago, seeking to learn, wanting to know things that few others knew. And I defied my family, my village, even the Warlord that held our lands to come here. I wanted to be an apprentice, and I became just that—apprentice." She stopped and smiled sadly to herself. "You should have seen him, Jaimah. My master. He was beautiful. And powerful. He knew everything. He was supreme." Shayna's laugh was filled with pain. "At least I thought he was. But he wasn't because I destroyed him. I found the ring and destroyed him."

Jaimah found herself trembling, the horror of Shayna's words settling on her like a weight. She spoke of things she had never spoken of before, revealed secrets that Jaimah did not want to know. She opened up a part of herself that Jaimah did not want to see.

Jaimah shivered as shadows tore away between herself and the past. She saw Shayna alone, torn between grief and ambition, never being able to reconcile the two. The grief could not be undone, nor could the ambition that had caused that grief; even though it had become a hated thing, it was also coveted.

Jaimah knew that the Lady saw in Corwyn a threat, for she saw in him herself—ambitious, ruthless, using whatever he could to undermine her so that he could take over the tower, just as she had once done. And in her fear, Shayna determined to eliminate that threat, to do away with anything that he might use against her. In this case, it was the servant girl.

The vision came to her, clear in the moment between one breath and the next. Jaimah yanked herself out of it and clenched her arms across her chest, gripping flesh to keep from shuddering. She was trapped and she knew it. She feared it, was weighed down by it, but could find no way out of it.

And Corwyn was in it with her.

Jaimah felt shame because of it. He had put himself between Shayna and her. The danger to himself could not be avoided now without bringing Shayna's vengeance on her servant. Jaimah had not expected it of him and grew cold inside as she realized that he might let Shayna strip him of everything he had because of her.

She swallowed the sudden ache in her throat and looked miserably at the room they had opened together. It had not changed overly much since Shayna had taken over occupancy. But the feeling of Corwyn's presence was gone, and she was surprised at that. She had never realized before that she could always feel when he was in a room.

"When I try to reach his talents, I find nothing," Shayna was saying. "And yet I think he is out to destroy me. And I see *you* look to him for *permission* to obey me!" Her voice lost the sad tone and became angry. "You, whom I have taken in as a daughter!" Her eyes flashed with the reflection of a sudden glare of white light from the window. "I know he has found a way to threaten me. But I will stop him! And I will stop you."

Jaimah stared at her as the light from the storm flickered blue on her face. The black of her eyes was impenetrable. Jaimah ceased even to tremble. "What will you do?"

"Much, my dear, much. But you would like to know, wouldn't you, so that you could tell him? Yes, I see that you would. But I'll not tell you. I've said too much already."

That shook Jaimah, and the fear that she had tried to hold away was on her strongly. She was afraid for herself, but she feared more for Corwyn. Weighing Shayna's determined obsession against his skills, she reckoned that Shayna could and would destroy him. That thought caused her more distress than she liked. It was because of the pollen, she knew, but she could not shake it. All she could do was try to hide it, for Shayna was watching her intently.

And she knew that Shayna was going to destroy them both.

This stilled her heart with a foreboding that almost took her strength away.

Shayna stirred and rose to her feet. "Get these things together. Then go get Corwyn. We leave immediately."

"Yes, Shayna," she murmured and she turned to find a fur that was large and strong and had lacings with which to tie it.

The door to Corwyn's room was ajar and she entered, her steps quiet on the stone.

"Corwyn," she called, suddenly loath to enter farther and search for him in the other room. She folded her arms against the cold and drew in a long breath. Expelling it slowly she stared at the skirling clouds just outside the window, feeling the pressing awareness of the Watchers that were crowding closer around the tower. She shivered at that silent waiting and tried to turn her mind from it.

A light step sounded behind her. Jaimah turned and faced the ghostlike figure in the hall, dark-clothed and silent. She could not see his face, and she was not sure whether she was welcome or not. But it didn't really matter.

What she had to tell him did not depend on welcome, but only that he listen and, in the end, come with her to Shayna. And in her heart she would carry the hope that he was indeed something more than an apprentice.

Corwyn was an enigma, appearing reserved and obedient, save for now and again when he would look at her, speak to her, or stand in a certain way. Corwyn had a silent secretiveness about him, watchful, guarded, and challenging, seeming out of place in his role of apprentice, and yet never admitting that he was something else. He had hinted at it—once. *I am only an apprentice. Nothing more. For now—nothing more.*

For now—nothing more.

Jaimah had not caught on to that until last night as she sat alone, staring into the fire. It was a confession, and yet it was not. He seemed to be telling her that he was restraining himself in a silent watchful waiting, concealed, veiled, and disguised.

And in that restraint lay a tenuous thread of safety, a small hope that there was indeed something more than an apprentice, and that she had seen true behind the guarded dark blue eyes.

Neither she nor Shayna, Jaimah reflected with sudden grim humor, wanted to see beyond the grave self-control he kept.

"Why are you here?" he asked, his soft voice seeming loud in the silence.

"Shayna sent me."

He answered nothing for a moment, only regarded her as if he waited for something further.

She felt the anger that was in the stiffness of his shoulders.

Then, as she studied him, she came to a decision, knowing, she thought, what it was that she chose. And she trembled.

"Shayna has decided," she said, "to try the spell one last time, at the Peak."

She saw his back stiffen. "And I am to go with her." His words were quietly angry.

Dismay came on her; she smothered it and sought to put reason into her words and persuasion into her voice. "Corwyn," she said softly. "You have to go."

An image came to her of last night, of a small flame in her hand, and of dark eyes. Jaimah pushed it aside, but it came back again, a recollection of a dominion that did not waver, that did not loose its hold until she sent him away. He would not have gone otherwise.

He stepped forward, pushing the door closed behind him. Jaimah took an unconscious step backward under his steady gaze.

"She is waiting for you to come," she said. "If you do not, I do not doubt that she will destroy the both of us."

A frown creased Corwyn's brow. "Did she tell you this?"

"No. But other things she told me. Of how she came here to apprentice, once, long ago, and destroyed her master."

For a moment Corwyn said nothing. Then he nodded. "Yes. Naibus."

Corwyn still had the power to surprise her. She stared at him in confusion, momentarily without words. "You know of this?"

"It is not a thing unknown." He moved around her and sat on the corner of the table.

She turned to face him. "Then you know that she may do it again. She thinks that it is what you are here to do," Jaimah said. "She will destroy us if you don't come. But . . ." She hesitated.

"Go on."

She ran her tongue across dry lips. "I know Shayna; I can tell when she is planning something, and . . . I do not think she will let either one of us come back from the Peak. When this day is over, there is going to be only one survivor and that will be Shayna. The fact that she is taking us there in the first place says that there is something wrong. The Peak is a forbidden place. No one may go there but Shayna. I have never been there."

"Yet, this time, she takes the both of us."

Jaimah swallowed and laid a hand on the table for support. "I am to go so that you will . . . cooperate."

His long hand reached over, slipped her fingers into his. "What do you want me to do, Jaimah?"

Breath failed her an instant. It did not matter one way or the other; it would all end the same. But she had made her choice and the question stood. After that, there would be no going back.

"Come," she said, and the word almost failed of sound.

Corwyn looked at her in quiet, grazed her mouth with his glance, and returned to her eyes. "Do you betray me?"

She pulled back in shock; Corwyn held her hand tightly.

"No," she whispered.

"No," he agreed. "I think not." His sureness disturbed her. She thought again in panic of the pollen, but knew trembling in the knowledge, that there was no other choice.

For her there was no other choice.

If it came to what she feared, and Shayna turned on them, if there was to be any hope at all . . . All she could do was plan to survive—any way that she could, even if it meant making that one choice.

It was all Jaimah could do, for there was nothing else, save yield to Shayna. Jaimah reckoned what it would mean to yield, to surrender to Shayna's mad obsession, one that she hadn't even known existed until Corwyn.

Slowly, slowly she came to terms with what she had to do and looked at Corwyn, afraid.

"Shayna is waiting," she finally said.

She expected refusal, that after what she told him he'd refuse, even though the end of it all would be the same. She hoped desperately that he would not.

Corwyn's eyes lowered and he soothed her hand with his, the other wrapped loosely about her fingers. Then he nodded and said, "I'll go." His gaze brushed her face and swung over to the window.

And Jaimah realized suddenly that he had never meant to

refuse, that he had always intended to go. It was for this purpose that he had come. She stared at him and wondered how it was that she knew this. Then she recalled of a sudden that just moments ago she had known something else that she hadn't before. Last night, when Corwyn had put the small flame in her hand, he would not have left her if she hadn't sent him away. It chilled her as she thought about how she knew these things.

"Shayna intends to go through the storm?" Corwyn asked.

Jaimah's eyes followed his to the window where the storm pressed at the panes, flashing with glowing lights within its depths. She tried to imagine what it would be like climbing the mountain to the Peak with it all around them.

She found it strange that the only sound she could hear was a rushing wind—no thunder, no rain, just the wind. And she also found it strange that she wasn't afraid of it as she had been when watching it descend on them. But when she thought about stepping out of the tower to be engulfed by it, that was different.

She pulled her hand from his and crossed her arms, feeling the cold again, and wished she had a fur to wrap around herself. She looked up and found Corwyn looking at her. There was a touch of something in his gaze that caught at her breath and held it checked a moment.

She looked quickly back to the window and thought about Shayna upstairs waiting, knowing that each moment that passed without their return would increase the Lady's anxiety and send her looking for them. But she was unable to turn and suggest that they go.

Corwyn rose easily from the table. "Stay here," he said. "I'll get the things that we're going to be needing."

She was about to protest when he stopped her. "I'll be right back." His eyes held her, painfully intense. She swallowed, unable to look away. Then he turned and left.

The storm raged, a harsh enemy against the walls of the tower. The winds blew it hard against the window where it sizzled and flashed in scintillating colors that fell bursting and sparkling to die out and start again. Jaimah shivered. The Watchers were still out there, edging closer and closer, their presence weighing on her like a physical force. Almost, it felt as if they were willing her to come to the window and look out into the storm. And suddenly she knew that, if she did, she would be able to see them there, ranging around the tower with restless anticipation.

Jaimah stepped back into the deeper shadows of the room, staring at the window. A sweat broke out on her skin as she stood in the gloom. Then she ran to pull the drapes together, not wanting to look out any longer.

As the drapes fell together her stare was drawn down to a solitary hulk that was pacing back and forth before the tower. It raised its head and looked at her just as the drapes closed. She shuddered and clutched the heavy fabric in white-knuckled hands, as if to keep it from coming open again.

Chapter Fifteen

IT WAS DONE.

Shayna stood and watched Jaimah leave, knowing that soon Corwyn must come, having no choice if he was to protect the girl.

That was the way of it, now that Corwyn had stepped in and made the girl's welfare his concern. It was a weakness that Shayna had seized on and quickly turned to her advantage. She was smugly pleased that he had provided her with the unexpected leverage, although it had infuriated her to see how much he had undermined her control over the girl. But she'd deal with that very soon.

Jaimah had not understood what she had done; that did not surprise Shayna. The girl was a hopeless dolt, inept beyond comprehension. She found it impossible, at times, even to tolerate the girl. Why her apprentice would want to protect such a simpleton was more than she could fathom. But it didn't really matter, because it had given her something with which to hold him. She had him in her grasp with no way to escape. No matter what he did, it was the end of him. But first, she'd have to make sure that he did what she wanted him to, and she now had the leverage to insure that.

She found herself with a curious lack of fear for the thing that she was going to do. She had felt fear when watching the storm come over the mountains, not knowing what it was. She had not recognized the power that she could feel coming from it. It was new to her, and she had been unable to grasp it when she tried to use it. But now all the fear was gone and only deadness remained.

There was still a good chance that the spell would turn on her and kill her. She had known that from the beginning, but it was not a thing that would stop her. If it was going to happen, it would happen. The risk, whether to herself or anyone else, was one that she didn't even stop to consider.

It was long past time for regrets or recriminations. What she had done, she had done. There was little time left now for thought, and since *he* was gone, no one else mattered. She crossed her arms and ran a hand up to her shoulder, noticing absently that it was cold in the room. Irritably, she dismissed it and thought of the mountain peak.

She moved about the room, gathering up the furs, wondering how to use them against the storm, and recalled then that Hagoth, the merchant, had brought fur coats with him this trip. There wouldn't be enough for all three of them; someone was going to have to make do with the furs that were left. She'd send Jaimah for them as soon as she returned with Corwyn. She put the furs on the table and looked impatiently to the door, then turned again to face the window.

She watched the storm surging and rolling around the tower, the lights within it flashing and flickering, blue, green, and white. It was all soundless, except for the wind that blew furiously at the tower. In the storm she could feel—a something that watched.

Her breath died in her throat. There was a terrible menace in that watching. She did not dare turn her back on the window and the storm. If she did, she knew that that presence would be at the window and into the tower.

She bit at her lip, her heart pounding fearfully, unable to turn her head or even to look away.

"Whatever you are," she said to the storm, her fingers moving in a dispelling formula, "you are not welcome here and are forbidden to approach any closer. Leave at once. Your death awaits you here."

Shayna waited, watching the storm, reaching out with her senses. A malevolent will pushed back at her with violent force. She staggered back against the table. "Be gone," she gasped and repeated the undoing.

Something struck the window like a fist slamming against the glass. A beating of unseen wings attacked the window, and the battering increased with a frenzy that threatened to break it. Shayna cried out in terror. "Go away!" She flung the power of the ring at the storm. The blue flash shattered against the glass and disintegrated into nothing, having no effect on the tempest outside.

This was Corwyn's work. It came to her, despite her assertions that he had no talent. The thought hit her hard. *He has come to destroy me*, she thought in panic. She was shaking with terror, staring into the storm.

Then suddenly the thrashing at the window was gone. The assault broke off and seemed to flutter back into the swirling lights.

Too late, she realized that there had been something familiar about that presence. It was an entity that she had only known at the Peak. But there had been a threatening malice in its intent at the window that she had not encountered before, and she had failed to recognize it until too late.

"Encheon," she cried, running to the window. "Come back. I didn't mean to use the ring."

She pressed her hand to the glass and searched the churning clouds for the being that always before had been there to do her bidding.

But the power that had been there, the presence that had been there, was gone.

"No!" she cried aloud in frustrated rage and slammed her fist against the window. A hairline crack ran up and down from the blow.

Shayna stepped back blindly, fighting down the fury that had come over her. Her hands gripped a chair to smash it through the window, but she forced her fingers to open while she stood shaking and staring at the storm that was now empty.

She pushed herself away from the chair, her senses still reaching out in frantic hopes of finding Encheon. There was nothing—just an empty storm that covered the entire mountain.

She leaned on the table for support and closed her eyes, trying to clear her thinking.

The door opened, and she looked up to see Corwyn.

She drew back. Corwyn came into the room, and his dark eyes swept the place, took in the crack in the window, and centered on the fur pack Jaimah had made, now resting on the table. He went to it, not yet looking at Shayna, and tugged briefly at the knots with one hand as if to test the strength of what Jaimah had done. He fingered the pelt of the fur thoughtfully.

Then he turned. His blue eyes sought Shayna's, shadowed and impossible to read.

"I am here," he said, his voice quiet; and Shayna carefully laced her fingers together in front of her and composed her face to reveal nothing. She stood up straight to face him directly and forced her shaken confidence to the back of her mind, reminding herself of her control over him. It was only a matter of time until she had what she sought, because now he was hers. A sense of satisfaction came over her, as she contemplated him. She would be the conqueror. No one would be able to stop her and all those who tried would be no more. She felt a new confidence that she hadn't felt a few minutes before when she had faced the presence outside the window.

Shayna looked at him. In her new confidence she saw him under the control of her ring, at her mercy. She gazed at him directly and saw then, for the first time, that Jaimah had not come with him. She wondered angrily if he had thought to leave her behind and thus eliminate the leverage.

"We will be ready to go shortly," Corwyn said.

She remembered the anger in his eyes when she had tried to use the ring on Jaimah and the unspoken anger in his eyes the time that she *did* use the ring on the girl. But things were different now. No longer would she tolerate interference from him, and Corwyn knew it.

"Where is Jaimah?" she asked, as much to throw him off balance as to find out where the girl was.

"She waits downstairs."

"She is to go," Shayna told him. "She'll not remain behind."

"This we know, Shayna. I just have to go get her."

Shayna frowned. *We?*

Corwyn's eyes slid past her to the window and the storm beyond, then came back to her. "Why do we go now? Might it not be wiser to wait until another time?"

Shayna heard the disapproval in his voice and chose to ignore it. Before the morning, it would not matter anyway. She reached out and pulled the pack closer, wondering why he had tested the knots. She looked up at him.

Corwyn's gaze rested on her, steady and unmoving. She

felt a fear stirring inside and forced it away. "We go now. Go get the girl," she said.

Corwyn turned to the door and stopped, looking at her over his shoulder. "We may not reach the Peak," he said—then, after looking at the storm again, "I hope it is worth it."

"Never you mind about that, Corwyn. Go get Jaimah."

He studied her, silent, assessing. "Yes, ma'am," he finally said. Then he left, leaving the door open behind him.

Shayna went slowly to the door, shaking inside for a reason that she could not determine. Pushing it closed, she was glad that it fell shut without sound. She felt safer with it closed and was disturbed because of it.

Corwyn had to be eliminated. He could not come down from the mountain. But first she had to take his talents—all of them. And she began to reckon what that might entail, for Corwyn was something that she had not expected. He was far more than she had supposed, and taking what was his was not going to be easy.

Now that the door was closed, Shayna began, methodically, to go over again in her mind the spell and how it worked and the things that she needed to do. She went to the fur pack and untied it, checking again the herbs and powders, wondering frantically what it was that she was missing. She went over everything a second time, looking for something that was not right, anything that was not as it should be. For a while she stared helplessly at the bottles and vials and little boxes. There was nothing that she had not used before in one way or another. She thought of Corwyn's mixture that he had used as common water, wondering if it was something that could have helped her if she had just known what it was.

Finally, she put all of the things back on the fur, changed her mind, took everything off again and combined the contents of two vials, judging carefully the difference it would make on the spell. She hoped that it would be an improvement, but was unsure suddenly that any herb or powder could do what she wanted.

She tied the bundle up and stared at the chair where Naibus used to sit. Always the memory of him was in the room, even after all these years. She would have to lock up the rooms again, once she returned from the mountain. She would have to try to forget again.

It was strange that the pain had never ceased—that even after all this time it still had not gone.

And now that his rooms had been opened it was more acute than ever.

Shayna knew in that instant that she would never be free of the memory and the regret. She realized it as she took in the entire room and could see Naibus in every part of it. She could remember the moments, the details, the places where she sat, how he had been, sitting exactly so, across the room, looking into the fire that day. It had been an unusual thing for him to be doing, but Shayna had thought since that day that he had been waiting for her, knowing why she had come.

Naibus' face had been intent, the fingers of his left hand tapping absently on the arm of the chair. His hands that had known so many skills had never been aimless before. It had taken her years to learn the half of what he had known, to uncover what he had left beyond in his books.

He was not an arrogant man, Naibus—prideful, perhaps, but he never vaunted his abilities . . . save now and again when she practiced the skills that he had taught her. Then he sometimes moved, perhaps from mischief, so fast the eye could not follow it, changing the spell into something else, a change in the finger-weaving perhaps, so tiny and deft and subtle that Shayna never caught it.

Patterns—they governed the whole of the spell.

And Naibus' patterns made magic where there was none, extending the power beyond the fire and the words and the herbs and extending the strength of the spell beyond what she could do.

There was nothing she could do, Shayna reflected with sudden realization, that Naibus couldn't have done better, neither then nor now, even though she had learned much over the years.

She still wasn't as powerful as he had been, despite the ring.

He doesn't use herbs nor words, Jaimah had said of Corwyn.

She spoke of power that didn't need these things. And she had not said anything about finger-weaving, which meant that Corwyn had not even done *that*.

Shayna searched her memory, seeing the things that Naibus had done with new eyes. She realized with a sick feeling that she may have been too hasty in using the ring.

Sudden, sickening understanding came over her.

There were several levels of power, a thing that she had not known. Horror ran through her.

She was still at the most elementary level.

She sat down weakly, realizing that she had only tested Corwyn with that elementary knowledge. That thought circled through her mind endlessly. She stared helplessly at the pack on the table, filled with the herbs and powders she had thought were so powerful, but now realized were just toys.

But there had been no mention of this from Naibus; and Corwyn, having come to the tower, had said nothing. Jaimah had seen it, but Shayna had not. She had not even suspected, even after the girl had told her what she had seen.

She had chosen, ignorantly, to ignore what Jaimah had brought her, to ask no further, to do nothing. Corwyn remained in the tower, watching her, learning about her in a way that she did not know of him. And he cultivated the skills that he had.

There were three levels of power. She saw this clearly now.

Spells that relied on herbs and words were crutches. Then came spells that were produced by finger-weaving, as Naibus did. And the most powerful was power that was controlled and produced by the will.

Corwyn could do the latter.

An image came to her of how she had tried the spell. She saw the fire that resulted and recalled Corwyn's anger. Shayna pushed it aside and brought it back again. Did she know what he had? She remembered the words he had said, *Do you lack the skill to take what is mine?* Had he known? Had he guessed? Or had he just been angry?

Spells!

Shayna felt the taint of the word and scorn for that which she had been trying to master. She hated whatever in her had been too blind to see.

She had been deceived and deprived. It had come to that. She had been left thinking that the spell was the most powerful skill to be mastered.

Naibus had not planned to teach her more, knowing what she would do with it. He knew what she was doing with what he had already given her.

Shayna saw this now.

Too late, too late, forever too late, unless she succeeded at the Peak.

It was the only way, as she thought about it, that she could see to undo what Naibus had done. Shayna reckoned the difficulty of what she must do—try to strip Corwyn of a power that was beyond anything she had ever seen, beyond anything she had even known existed.

And if Corwyn knew what he had, she was done. He would destroy her.

But he didn't seem to know, at least not that he showed.

Shayna rested back in the chair, her arm on the table, and bit at her lip, disturbed at what she could see now as Naibus' deliberate undermining of her ambitions. Anger stirred in the back of her mind. But she held it off because she knew she wouldn't be able to think and plan if it consumed her. Yet the thought worried at her and would not let her go—that Corwyn was not ignorant of all this and that he had plans of his own, she could only guess at.

But, the one thing that gave her a little courage was the knowledge that she still had the ring, and there was Jaimah as leverage.

She tried to imagine how it was done, this power that came from the mind only; and all that she could imagine was the power of the ring on her hand, doing something similar, but not the same. She wondered desperately how she was going to find the method, the secret of this new power. She thought of asking Corwyn to teach her but tossed that thought away. She would never be apprenticed again.

There were other means of learning these things. She had ways, her own ways.

Slowly the shattered bits of her confidence came together, along with a new plan. She would win at this yet.

She pulled the pack that she had rearranged toward her, considered it a moment, then took it apart, discarding everything except a small box that fit into the palm of her hand. She closed her hand over it and smiled to herself.

Corwyn did not know she had this.

Carefully, she put it into the hidden pocket of her robe. Then she went downstairs to find Corwyn and Jaimah.

Chapter Sixteen

JAIMAH BECAME AWARE OF A PULSATING GLOW THAT HAD NOT been there before.

She looked about her and saw, standing close to the wall, where the open drapes had concealed it, a large globe on a stand of four thin ornate legs that were inlaid with colors and intricate sculpting. The globe glowed with a soft light that grew and dimmed slowly by turn, alternating between gold and pink. Next to it stood the chair with the large bulbous legs.

Jaimah's mind ran back to the day when she had first brought Corwyn to this room. These chambers had been empty, except for a cot, a bookcase, a table, and dust. He had insisted on helping her clean the rooms that day. And since then, every now and then, something new had appeared until the rooms were no longer bare and empty. But this globe of pulsating light was different. In an eerie, subtle way, it was very much like the orange fire that they had seen Shayna with the day that she had first tried the spell. It was not at all what she would have expected in Corwyn's rooms.

Drawn by the color on the shining surface and reflecting off the drapes, Jaimah moved close enough to look into its depths and was surprised to see moving shapes within it. She leaned closer.

It occurred to her, belatedly, that this was maybe something she should not do, and she paused. Corwyn might not allow her to come so close if he were there. But she leaned forward, drawn to it by some unknown force that she could not fight against.

Jaimah looked into the soft glow of golden light, a great attraction pulling on her. Her eyes tried to discern the moving shapes within the center of the globe and her brain became confused, disturbed by a vague dizziness.

She reached forth a hand, laid it on the smooth glassy surface just as the gold faded into pink. She tried to pull her eyes away but that effort was beyond her.

"Kojo, what have you seen?" a voice asked within the globe.

Jaimah gasped and tried desperately to pull away from the globe; but the lure closed over her until she was within it. She felt a warmth that did not come from the tower, but from another place within the globe. It was a warmth that she had never known, a heat that did not come from the mountain but from . . . a desert. It reminded her of something. It was perplexing.

"What has happened?" she heard—a voice that she knew. She felt herself go closer, and she recognized the voice of Corwyn. The glowing light around her seemed to fade in intensity and become darker until it was no longer a light but was a place, a room into which she could see.

It was a room of dark colors: browns, reds, blacks, and blues; and walls covered with more books than she had ever seen before, large and leather-bound, of different colors. There were big windows covered with heavy drapes, a massive table with massive sculpted legs, high-backed chairs of rich wood, arms inlaid with various tones of red. The floor itself was covered with a handmade carpet, having intricate patterns of browns and reds woven into it. It was a room in which to go, to find relief from the harsh cold and spartan atmosphere of the tower. Jaimah was drawn to it as she had never been drawn to any place.

Then her attention was directed to a glow in one end of the room away from the windows and the books. A globe—the same as the one into which she stared—glowed softly with a pink that faded to orange and back again.

She drifted for a time and came back, to find that the light in the room was darker, the glow from the globe a faint red. She was still outside the room, looking down on it as an observer, but felt warmth upon her skin. She saw a movement, looked, and saw to her surprise that a small, withered man sat staring into the globe.

A door opened, and Corwyn entered—dressed as she had first seen him, a gray cloak with hood thrown back and high black boots of leather pulled over doeskin breeches: she noticed this first. Then saw, when he took off the cloak, that his tunic was the same red that he had worn that day. A chill came over her; this was important—she knew it but did not understand it.

Corwyn went to the shrunken man, laying the cloak on the table as he strode past it. "Kojo, what have you seen?"

Disturbed, the small man raised his dark head, his eyes filled with a troubled alertness.

"What has happened?" Corwyn asked again. "Why did you send for me?" He put a hand on the globe and leaned over it, the red reflecting off his face, turning his hair bronze.

"The Lady has found the spell," a papery voice answered.

Corwyn looked up and studied the face of the man beside him. "I see." He straightened up. "Has she tried it?"

"No. She doesn't know what she has."

"It'll only be a matter of time." He turned, went to the table, and picked up his cloak absently, his brow lined with deep thought.

The shrunken man, Kojo, lifted his eyes from the globe again, rose, and limped to Corwyn.

"Master," he said in his thin voice. "You knew she'd find it."

"Yes, I knew." He sighed, turned the cloak over in his hand, and laid it on the table again. "Something will have to be done." Then he asked, "What of the girl?"

"She knows nothing."

Corwyn nodded. "That is good."

This was incredible; Jaimah could not believe what she was seeing and hearing. She tried to pull away and stop the images. But she was caught, trapped, an observer of something she didn't want to see. Yet she was drawn to it with an incredible curiosity. Without knowing it, she sat down in the chair, looking deeper into the globe, oblivious of anything else.

The room returned after a dark space; and in it was Corwyn, alone. He was sitting at the globe, but leaning back with his feet propped up, not looking into the glow. His elbows rested on the ornate arms of the chair; his fingers were steepled together and pressed to his lips. His eyes stared unseeing at the wall, lost in thought. A slight frown was on his face.

Kojo came into the room, limped to a chair, sat, and waited silently until Corwyn's eyes focused and turned to him. He took his hands down and rested them on the arms of the chair. He did not move to rise; there was a question on his face. "What troubles you, Kojo?"

The little man coughed nervously and cleared his throat. "Forgive me, I don't mean to pry . . ."

"What is it?"

"It's the girl . . ."

It was a moment before Corwyn answered, "Yes?"

Kojo hesitated and Corwyn repeated, "Yes?"

Corwyn sat up, putting his feet down. "Come, old friend. You can speak plainly. What is it that you want to know?"

The dark head bobbed, the old eyes trying to take on confidence, and the old mouth worked, trying to form words.

Elsewhere, Jaimah sat breathless also, waiting for him to speak, the pounding of her heart shaking her with each thunderous stroke.

Kojo cleared his throat again and shifted nervously in his seat. "All these years," he finally said, "I have watched the tower for you. This is what you asked of me. And I have watched, day and night, all of these years. But . . ." he stopped, looking decidedly uncomfortable.

"Go on," Corwyn said.

Kojo glanced aside unhappily. "It occurs to me, after all this time, that it has not been the Lady that we have been watching, but the girl." He flinched visibly as his eyes flickered over to Corwyn and back again.

Corwyn's eyes were, Jaimah saw, shadowed with weariness, as if he had gone long without sleep. His mouth frowned. But the frown eased, and he expelled a breath. "And this surprises you?"

"Should we not be more concerned with the Lady? Isn't she the one who possesses the threat?"

Corwyn said nothing, only studied the old man's face, entwining his fingers together, his elbows on the arms of the chairs, his thumbs idly pushing each other up and down.

"I don't wish to offend," Kojo said after a moment.

"You could never give offense, Kojo," Corwyn said. He

raised a hand and scratched his chin thoughtfully. "And you are right, in part. We should be watching Shayna. But you've been doing that have you not?"

"I have done my best."

"Well, then?"

Kojo sat back in confusion, questions running in rapid succession over his face. "I don't understand."

"What's not to understand?"

Kojo frowned, perplexed. "Why are you so concerned with the girl?"

"Why should I not be?"

"Because it is much more important to concern ourselves with the Lady."

Corwyn shrugged. "I think the girl important."

The confusion on Kojo's face grew and his frown deepened.

Corwyn laughed good-naturedly at his bewilderment. "I had not thought that you had grown so old you could not remember these things," he said. "Has it been so long?"

The old man stared at Corwyn, greatly distressed at first that he had been laughed at. Then understanding came, and after a moment the color began to rise in his face and an embarrassed grin crept across his mouth.

"So you see . . ." Corwyn didn't finish, but shrugged again. He rose to his feet and slid his hand over the globe. The glow died and he stood a moment looking into its depths. Then he said, "I'll have to go get her."

Kojo looked up from where he had been staring at the globe. "And bring her here?"

"Yes."

"What about the Lady?"

"She'll have to be stopped."

"But . . ." Kojo hesitated, a new frown creasing the lines of his face into darker shadows.

"What is it, Kojo?" Corwyn had turned and was watching him.

"If you care for this girl . . ."

"Jaimah," Corwyn reminded him.

"Jaimah," Kojo acknowledged. "If you care for her . . . why have you left her with Shayna all of these years? Why have you not gone to take her out of there instead of letting the Lady . . ."

"Grind her into dust?" Corwyn's voice was bitter. "Ah,

Kojo." He turned and looked into the darkened globe and his shoulders bent as with the weight of those accusing words. "You have named that which has caused me much torment since the moment she set foot on that mountain."

"I don't understand."

Corwyn slid his hand over the globe. "It was a promise made to an old friend of mine, who had an affection for his apprentice."

"Naibus?"

"Yes," Corwyn nodded. "He had taken a viper into the very center of his stronghold. But the foolish old heart could not send her away. It was unwise, he knew. She would destroy him. This he also knew. But he sought to protect her, nonetheless. So he extracted a promise from me. He created a spell. One that would attract her and lead her into my hands, for he knew that someday it would come. Her destruction had to come. But until then, he wanted my pledge that I would not set foot on the mountain until she found the spell. He made me swear my oath that I would not go against her until that time. I swore the oath. He set the trap. And in the spell were traps to slow her down." Corwyn drew in a breath.

"That was before the girl. He did not know, nor did I know, that there would be the girl . . . Jaimah," he said softly, and it was with profound sadness that he murmured her name. He drew in another bitter breath.

"She was the first-born child of Bel' Shanzar, Lord of the Warlords, but she was a daughter and not a son, and he was displeased. Then, as she grew into a young girl, it became evident that she had the *curse*." Corwyn's voice became angry. "Such a daughter could not be tolerated. But before the Lord could kill her, his wife secreted her away and took her to Shayna. A brave woman—and rare. The Warlord was going to kill his daughter, but instead settled for killing his wife, for he reasoned that the taint had come through her!"

Corwyn clenched his hand into a fist and stood staring at the globe. And in the tower, Jaimah sat stunned at what she was hearing, unable to move or breathe as Corwyn turned to look at Kojo.

"Shayna does not yet know what she has with her in the tower. She took the girl to rape her of her talents, but I sent Encheon to protect her, and Shayna found nothing. Then I waited. I waited until I thought I would go mad with waiting. I could do nothing until Shayna found the spell. I was bound, and there was no way to undo that binding. All I could do was send Encheon to protect her—and set you to watch her. How I have repented of that pledge I made!"

He strode to the table where he had placed his cloak. "I must go get her. Her talents are beginning to awaken again. Encheon will not be able to hold them back this time. They are too strong. And once Shayna learns what Jaimah has, she'll destroy her."

"But won't the girl be able to . . ." Kojo began.

Corwyn shook his head. "She'll be weak and unskilled. She won't even know what she has. She will not be able to withstand Shayna and that demon ring. I can't wait." He threw the cloak over his shoulders, covering the red tunic.

Jaimah realized suddenly as she watched that he must have come straight away without even stopping to change his clothing.

Kojo limped to the table so that he was in front of Corwyn. "I will go with you."

"No, my friend," Corwyn said, laying a hand on his shoulder. "This I must do alone."

A hand passed over the globe, cutting off the images, and Jaimah looked up with a startled cry.

Corwyn.

He stood still, waiting. Jaimah rose to her feet to face him, heart racing in fear and legs weak. "How long have you been there?"

"Long enough."

She felt the touch of his hand on her arm and she stepped back, feeling herself tremble. She fought it down and stared into his eyes, which were dark and shadowed.

And there was silence for some few moments.

"Did you see anything of interest?" Corwyn asked in a low voice, so that the prickling of her skin became intense. Jaimah looked toward the globe, heart pounding as she recalled what she had seen and had heard there. For a moment, she thought Corwyn did not know, but then realized he knew exactly what she had listened to.

"I'm sorry," she said, her voice shaky. "I didn't know what it was."

"You could have asked me."

There was a stillness in Corwyn's voice that chilled. Jaimah did not try to answer. She looked away to where there were heavy fur coats and boots on the table.

She remembered where Corwyn had gone.

His hand closed over her arm, and she looked into his dark eyes. "This is why you came?" she finally asked.

"Is it so hard to believe?"

Jaimah's heart sped. She looked warily at him. "No," she said, suddenly believing him; she wished herself out the door.

She pulled back, attempting to break his hold on her, but his grip tightened, and she found herself with the drapes at her back and no way of getting around him.

There was silence. Jaimah slowly let go her breath, understanding finally that there was no threat. "This is why you gave me the loveroot pollen? So I would go with you?"

He shook his head. "There was no pollen. There never was."

A chill fear crept over her as she searched his eyes for something to tell her that he was lying—not panic-fear, but a cold reckoning that things had gone beyond what even she had thought they would. She considered the frankness on his face and the cold settled on her in an ominous forewarning. Despite herself, she believed him.

"I thought you had," she said, almost in protest.

"I know."

She looked at his face and sought some trace of humor there, but found none.

"I could have," Corwyn said slowly. "But I didn't want it that way, even though I was afraid I was going to have to, to get you away from here. But I didn't."

Jaimah found no answer, for there was in his voice that which begged for her to believe him.

"I am sorry," she said, and found it pathetically little.

His free hand came up and his fingers traced her jawline, his thumb moving slowly over her lips. "It doesn't matter now," he said. His dark gaze brushed over her mouth and then looked up.

Jaimah blinked, dismayed, the strength running out of her as she realized what he was going to do.

"No, Corwyn," she pleaded, her voice failing her. She tried to pull back out of his reach, but he stepped closer, pressing her against the window, imprisoning her there.

"It's time, Jaimah," he said, the curled backs of his fingertips brushed lightly over her cheek, went around her head, and pulled her slowly to him.

"Please don't." Raw fear rose in her.

"Yes," he said as he bent his head and his lips firmly covered hers. A shock tore through her—ripping, shredding, wrenching the last of her strength away.

Her mind begged him to stop as a gulf opened and she fell into it, spinning, reeling, unable to breathe. The room dissolved, the walls, floor, and time twisted and slipped until everything was gone, except the fire of his lips on hers, caressing until she could no longer fight him. She let him pull her tight against him, his arms going around her with a force that startled her.

Then the walls rippled back into solidity, as his mouth left hers. Jaimah clung where she was, wishing to run away but unable to do so. His cheek touched hers. "You see." The flutter of his breath was warm against her ear. "I was right."

Jaimah fought against the emotional upheaval that stormed inside her and tried to calm her breathing. Her body was shaking with reaction. For a moment she could do nothing else; then, still trembling, she pulled back, and found herself already against the window with nowhere to go.

Corwyn's head came back. His midnight-blue eyes sought hers, shadowed and piercingly direct.

"What is it?" he asked.

Jaimah fought her mind clear, gathering excuses so that he'd turn her loose. But she knew that he would not free her and knew herself to be trapped. She grew afraid, and Corwyn saw it. A troubled frown grew upon his face as he gazed into her eyes.

"What is it, Jaimah?"

"Shayna . . ." she began, seizing the closest thought that would bring it all to an end.

"Cannot stop this," he said.

Jaimah stared helplessly at him. What he had done and what she had felt terrified her. She closed her eyes to shut it all out, but the warmth of his body against hers was impossible to ignore.

"Corwyn," she ventured, and was appalled that her voice was no more than a whisper. She looked up at him and felt an unexpected tremor go through her when she met his eyes. "Please, let me go." It took all the strength she had to get the words out, and she was certain that if he did let go of her she'd not be able to stand. But the assault of his nearness was more than she could bear.

But instead of turning her loose, Corwyn slid a hand up her back to the nape of her neck, strengthening his hold on her. "Not yet, Jaimah." His dark eyes were on her with an intensity that made her tremble. He drew her irresistibly closer until his mouth hovered close to hers and his breath warmed her lips.

The unyielding strength of his arms frightened her, and she fought for control over the quavering inside her. "Corwyn, please," she said breathlessly. "Please don't."

"Be quiet, Jaimah," he said, and his mouth came over hers and she could do nothing but yield to him, give way to him for a time, until she clearly realized what she surrendered to him and cried out. She pushed him away and became aware of herself again.

She stared at him in dazed fear, trembling, thinking what this all meant. She turned and fled out of the room and ended up in the cooking area. Desperate to hide where he wouldn't find her, she fumbled with the hidden door until she found the latch, opened the door, and closed it again, plunging herself into total darkness.

Chapter Seventeen

THE TUNNEL WAS DARK, ABSOLUTE, COMPLETE, A RELIEF where she huddled against the wall. The icy cold from outside reached to her through the rock of the mountain, laying its chilling fingers around her like a hand. She shivered and wiped a cold tear from her face, then clutched her arms about herself, trying to stop the shudders that convulsed her body.

The voices resounded in her head, echoing over and over again, their words assaulting her like a physical force. *The first-born child of Bel' Shanzar, Lord of the Warlords . . . she had the curse . . . took her to Shayna . . . first-born child of Bel' Shanzar . . . had the curse . . . took her to Shayna . . . had the curse . . . had the curse.*

Why did she not remember?

And there was what Corwyn had done. She trembled at that memory, the feel of his touch still on her. It would never go away, because it had been burned into her skin forever.

She curled tighter, wanting to disappear, and closed her eyes to shut out the blackness of the tunnel. Instead, she saw the glowing globe and the images she had seen within it. Again she heard Corwyn say, *I must go get her,* felt again the window at her back, his hand on her arm, the touch of his breath. She forced it all away. Round and round it whirled in her head with dizzying speed.

He was not apprentice. The globe had shown that he had no need for training. He had not come to the tower to learn,

170

but to stop Shayna and take the servant girl away with him.

She pressed her head into her arms, trying to stop the flow of thoughts that raced around inside her. Her body was trembling in a way that it had never done before. For a moment, she could not stop the tremor, could only flow with it, as she had done when Corwyn had . . . She thrust that thought away angrily.

Then her mind was whirling back over the days since he had come, perceiving the things he had done and the things he had said in a different light. There was a strangeness in the knowledge that he had come for her, and she could not understand it.

How long has this been going on? Shayna had asked her. *This between you and Corwyn?* Even Shayna had seen it.

She wished now desperately that Shayna had sent Corwyn away that first day, but knew it would have made no difference if she had. He would have gotten into the tower anyway. Of this she was certain.

The picture came to her, as real as anything that she had seen him do, of Corwyn walking through a shattered door that had been closed to deny him entrance and of a clash between Shayna and him. Jaimah did not doubt that he would have torn the door out of the walls of the tower if Shayna had refused to take him in.

And it was this that she had chosen, she thought wildly, because she had thought that he'd given her the pollen and had no other choice. And because she had feared Shayna more than her apprentice.

She had made her choice, knowing that whatever happened to the one she allied herself with would happen to her also . . . life or death.

She had chosen Corwyn. What other choice was there?

It had the portent of death, a sign of what was to come. She did not think Corwyn was going to win, and she was numbed by the realization. Her hand trembled as it wiped at the moisture that was cold on her cheek.

She had made her decision, had committed herself. There was no turning back. It shook her, what she had chosen; she feared it now that she saw it. She had chosen to die with him if it came to that.

Not if—when!

Not that another choice, a choice of Shayna instead, would have made a difference. The outcome was going to be the same either way. Only she would not be standing next to Shayna when it came, but would be standing with Corwyn.

She closed her eyes tightly and shivered in the memory of his arms going around her.

A step sounded in the corridor to her right. She turned with a gasp, frightened by the green glow that surrounded her, and knew he had come after her.

His boots crunched on loose rock when he came to a stop in front of her. He stood looking down on her a moment, his hand holding the fur coats and boots he had brought with him.

"Are you all right?" he asked of her.

Jaimah folded her arms between her chest and drawn-up knees, her heart fluttering in a way to take all of her strength from her. She nodded.

"Good," he said. He looked at her long, the expression in his eyes sober. Then he held out his hand. "Come. We must go."

Her skin chilled, and she thought suddenly of Shayna and the impending trip to the Peak. She remembered that she had been hoping that Corwyn would be something more than the apprentice he had claimed to be. In fact, she had been gambling on it. Now she knew that he was. But she didn't know *what* he was.

"You'll have to trust me," he said, as if he could read her thoughts. "We will go with Shayna to the mountain and give her what she wants, although maybe not quite the way she wants it." He paused, his eyes on her, probing, assessing. "Can you trust me, Jaimah?"

She considered, uncertain about him, not knowing whom she could trust. "I don't know," she whispered.

She looked at him in the glow of the green light, her eyes drawn to his, saw the searching there, then looked to his mouth and could not stop the memory of it on hers, seeking and possessing.

She tore her stare away, drew in a tremulous breath, and strove to calm the quavering inside. She glanced back to him. His attention was on her, his eyes watchful, alert, waiting.

She shrugged slightly and repeated, "I don't know." Her gaze faltered before his.

She heard him settle to his heels, so close that she could feel the warmth that came from him. She clenched her hands to stop the sudden trembling that shook her and raised her eyes to his fearfully. The warmth of a flush touched her face under his close study.

"Who are you?" she asked of him at last.

There was a moment before he answered, and he gathered the furs into his lap, his arms folded lightly over them. "Just the one you see, Jaimah."

Always the same answer, she thought. It did not say anything. The green light rested on his face eerily; his eyes were shadowed, black instead of blue. For a brief moment she wanted to reach out and touch him. But she did not and was dismayed that the compulsion had come at all. She knew now that it could not be attributed to the pollen anymore, for there had never been any.

A slight frown brushed Corwyn's face and she wondered if the constraint had come from him. She foreknew that he was going to change things for her forever; and she could not stop him from doing it. She realized then that it didn't matter what choices she made, whom to trust, whom not to trust, whom to stand with, whom not to stand with. Corwyn had already decided and would always decide. Their lives had become inextricably entwined, impossible to pull apart. And she saw that Corwyn knew it. He had set out to make it so.

Suddenly she felt that he was going to plunder her innermost self and rob her of her soul. He was going to strip her of everything she was. She shivered from the cold and the turmoil inside her and looked away in agitation.

"Is it so hard," Corwyn asked, "to trust me?"

"I don't know," Jaimah answered, her voice barely above a whisper. It was the only answer she had to give him. She looked at him cautiously, expecting and finding his eyes on her, dark with hidden flame. Her breath stilled in her throat.

She looked at him, frightened.

Corwyn touched her then, trailing his fingers along her cheekbone and down to her mouth. She closed her eyes in fear, trembling, shrinking inwardly from him, willing him not to do anything more. And yet she was afraid that he would not, suddenly wanting him to go on. She pulled back, her eyes flying open, the tumult inside threatening to overwhelm her.

"Don't," she choked, ignoring his frown. She reached up to push his hand away, but his fingers easily took hers and pulled her hand down.

"You don't need to be afraid," he said. "I will not hurt you."

She stared at him wordlessly, afraid in spite of his reassurance, afraid to move, afraid to speak, afraid to breathe.

Corwyn's fingers caressed the back of her hand several moments while he contemplated her, his other hand holding her captive. Then he lifted her hand unexpectedly and touched his lips to her fingers, lightly, no more than a soft graze. He turned her hand over in his and pressed a kiss into her palm.

Jaimah stared at him, a tightness constricting her lungs, and she found it difficult to breathe. When he looked up at her, his eyes were smoldering, and she flinched.

Corwyn sighed. "Why," he asked, raising his hand to her face, his thumb moving slowly across her lower lip. "Why are you afraid of me?"

The question struck her with confusion; it demanded an answer, one she did not have. The warmth of his hand on her cold skin was distracting, and she wanted suddenly to turn her cheek into his palm, to rest there a time. She searched his eyes uneasily, fearfully, trying to think of something to say to him, but could not. She could only answer what she had said before. "I don't know."

A shadow crossed his face, but was quickly gone.

"Have I given you cause?" His hand fell away. "I hope that I have not."

Jaimah stared at him without answering. He shook his head and began to disentangle the furs in his lap. Reaching forward he draped the coat around her shoulders. He turned his eyes back to her, looking at her with lingering possessiveness. Jaimah quelled inside, but she met his gaze steadily.

"We must go," he said at last. "Shayna is going to be looking for us." He stood, pulling her to her feet.

Reluctantly she went with him out of the tunnel and up the stairs, clutching the coat closed at her throat. She felt out of place and strange knowing things would never be the same again, and she walked beside him silently, hoping that there would not be a confrontation because of her.

"Shayna," she heard Corwyn say softly when they reached the entrance door, and she turned and saw the Lady standing within the receiving hall. Jaimah felt an impulse to run; perhaps she had even involuntarily withdrawn a step, for Corwyn put his arm around her. She felt his warmth near her, felt the lean strength of him. She looked at Shayna and found anger in the Lady's eyes. She realized suddenly that the anger was directed at her.

"I'm sorry that I took so long," she said.

"Save your apologies," Shayna snapped. "You have turned against me, Jaimah, and that cannot be forgiven."

Shock coursed through Jaimah and with it the realization that Shayna somehow knew what had passed between Corwyn and herself.

Shayna turned to Corwyn. "Are you ready?"

"Yes, my Lady."

Shayna nodded curtly. She turned her eyes on Jaimah again. "Stay close to him, girl. And pray that he'll be able to save you."

Jaimah stared at her, chilled to the bone.

Then Shayna turned, pulled her furs tightly around her, and walked to the door.

Chapter Eighteen

JAIMAH WAS UNPREPARED FOR THE FIERCENESS OF THE WIND and the hard-driven ice particles that tore her breath away and threw her against Corwyn. It was as if her lungs had been sliced mercilessly by a frozen knife. She gasped at air that did not want to come and faltered as the wind battered her with demon strength. Corwyn took her arm, steadied her, and guided her through the gathering snow as they followed the obscured figure of Shayna through the swirling clouds and flashing shards of light. Jaimah fought back a paralyzing panic, stifling a cry as a shaft of lightning split the air in front of them, crackling against the ground in a million splinters of color.

"Lean on me," Corwyn said, his voice hoarse and blown quickly away.

Jaimah did not answer. An emotion was coming at her from somewhere out in the storm, a watchful anticipation that scared her. She tried to ignore it and let Corwyn take some of her weight. But the watching was close behind them, and she felt the skin on her back contract as if she were being attacked.

"We . . . go along a ledge," Corwyn said. "A cut in the side of a cliff." His voice was ragged in the wind. "Stay with me. Stay with me."

"All right," Jaimah said, a sound that did not leave her throat as the ice struck her in the face.

A dark cliff loomed up on the right, rising up past sight in the blinding lights. They entered the trail itself and passed under the towering cliff. Snow had filled here, blowing in on the howling wind. A thick blanket lay knee-deep in the cut, half burying rock that had once stood clear.

Suddenly, the snow swirling away from the cliff opened up the view to a terrible vista of bottomless depth. Jaimah faltered, giddy even to contemplate that fall. She breathed an exclamation, a choked sound.

Corwyn reached out, flung an arm around her, and guided her as they came down along the edge of the cliff. The snow had begun to build up in great drifts, covering most of the ledge. The footing was treacherous. The snow seemed about to slide loose from the ledge and plunge them into that bottomless chasm as it fell away from the wall.

She and Corwyn struggled along the edge of the cliff, Shayna barely discernible in front of them, the gray of her furs blending into the storm at times. When they could they hugged the cliff, shouldering against the rock, fighting through the drifts and ice.

They reached a place where the ledge widened, the cliff falling back into a side canyon that wound away, hidden behind the seething storm. Beyond that, the snow swirled in crazy eddies, and crackling colors of blue and green ran along the ground. Snow was blowing off the top of the cliff, which was once again looming above them. They continued on under the wild snowfall, snow from the sky and snow from the top of the cliff, whirling and whipping together until even the wall next to them couldn't be seen. They crossed under a ledge and back and back into another canyon, away from the chasm.

Corwyn took Jaimah's arm and hurried her, though she stumbled at times and plunged into deep snow. He only pulled her out again, and they went well into the upper reaches of the canyon, where she became hopelessly lost in her direction. She'd never be able to find her way out alone.

Gasping, coughing, and having to lean heavily on Corwyn, her strength was almost at its end. And she began to despair of even seeing the Peak. Visions of being buried alive in the deepening snow filled her imagination. When a large spear of lightning split the air in front of them, shattering into great shards of light, she cried out in terror that brought Corwyn's arm tightly around her. She clung to him for safety and stumbled blindly where he led her.

Finally they reached the place where the trail, completely obscured now, went across the canyon to the other side. There it climbed up into the mountains even higher, and Corwyn followed it unerringly, seeming to know where the trail lay and where it was going, his quiet voice next to her ear urging her on and telling her what next lay in their way. Jaimah reasoned that Corwyn must have given him an extensive description of the trail, and she wondered with a numb surprise at it.

"Now," Corwyn was saying, "we cross here. Quickly. There is danger of avalanche."

Jaimah looked for Shayna but could not see her and wondered if they still were following her. Corwyn seized her by the arm. Together they ran, Jaimah struggling in the drifts. Corwyn pulling her through. Her strength flagged, and she fought to keep her feet moving. Rocks loomed before them. Jaimah stumbled and caught herself against them, then moved when Corwyn pulled her, putting his arm around her, guiding her on up into the tangle of rocks and piling snow. Jaimah clambered beside him, up and up, above the danger of snow-slide.

And behind them, there was something following.

She kept looking over her shoulder; it was there, unseen, but felt. Not close, but there nonetheless.

A light-laden gust of wind rocked her, stinging her face and hands with ice. She let the long sleeves fall over and past her hands as they were designed to do. Corwyn tugged at her arm, and she leaned into the wind, the gusts making her stagger. After a time, she was no longer sure where they were. The way they went was uneven and dipped and rose, making it difficult to continue in a straight path.

She turned her head yet again and looked over her shoulder, half-blinded by the crystalized lights of blue and white. And behind, there was a figure on the west horizon, silver and gray. A cloud of mist swirled around it, obscuring it, then cleared; the figure was gone. She stared, wondering if it had been real.

Panic tugged at her, but she leaned against Corwyn and forced it away. She glanced back, apprehensive now of every part of the horizon, and saw nothing but featureless snow and a lowering sky, which suddenly split with a shaft of lightning that fizzled into sparks of blue and green. Still behind, she could feel the something that followed. So strong was the feeling that it was as if a part of her had come out of a deep sleep.

She struggled on, fighting to keep her balance as Corwyn's arm came around her again. She slipped suddenly, crusts of snow peeling under her feet. She hit soft snow underneath and caught her balance, trying to retreat back to rock. Corwyn's arm was gone and she flailed as she struggled for footing. She couldn't see in the blinding swirl and instantly lost her direction. She threw back the hood to see better. It was a mistake. She pulled it up again. The wind had chilled her to the bone in that instant.

She couldn't see, was out in open snow, and, of a sudden, was very much afraid.

"Corwyn," she cried. Her voice was torn away, ragged on the wind. "Corwyn, where are you!" She swung about, shivering violently. She did not know where to go and could not see where she had been. Then she felt an invading presence somewhere off to her right, and she forced herself through the knee-deep snow away from it, driving herself away from that pursuing threat.

There was menace in that searching, a sullen warning that terrified her. The wind sounded like a demon, howling around her, drowning out all other sound. She thought she heard someone calling her name.

"Corwyn!" she cried in answer, but it was ripped from her and flung into the storm.

And suddenly a shadow came at her, a towering shadow that stood up on its hind legs, silver-gray, a massive, furred wall that stood over her. She cried out in terror and flung herself backward. The monstrous shape crashed down where she had been standing. She caught a brief glimpse of flashing claws before hot, foul breath enveloped her and a deafening roar stunned her senses. She struggled back again, staring into reddened black eyes. The thing lunged at her, a massive, slope-shouldered shadow in the blowing snow. She screamed and flung herself to the side out of the path of its fury.

The snow bank gave way and she fell, amidst a wall of sliding snow, over and over and over, landing hard as she was buried under a boiling avalanche of heavy white powder, suffocating and crushing. She tried to move her hands, but could not. She could not even breathe. She fought to move, knowing that she had to. If she didn't . . . Her hand and arm jerked, her fingers scraping at the snow, but it was pathetically little. Her lungs felt they were going to burst, and her fingers pushed harder at a tiny hole. There was fresh air. Her heart leaped, then she feared suddenly that the creature would be there waiting for her.

She pushed with her hand and tore the hole wider. Pulling herself out of the snow, she slid helplessly down a small hill and lay still, looking up at the cliff she had fallen over. The creature was up there, standing at the edge. It rose up on its hind legs, a towering shadow, threatening her. But it couldn't get to her.

Slowly, very slowly, she got to her feet. Stumbling forward, she fought the impulse to run, knowing that she could not, because she did not have the strength. The feeling of something following her sawed at her nerves, raw and frightening. It was chilling knowledge. The Watchers were stalking her, wanting her. And she was hopelessly lost.

She pushed forward. Time had no meaning. Only pain and weariness meant anything, except for the awareness that another pursuer joined the Watchers behind her and was even more relentless in the chase than the beasts. This new pursuer never stopped, even when she did.

She paused where a ridge of stone offered a moment's shelter from the wind, lowering her head into her coat out of the cold. Coughing racked her body. Her head ached, and she shook from exhaustion. She ate a handful of snow, for her mouth was so dry it hurt. Then she closed her eyes and found that sleep was not far away. She forced herself to her feet and forward.

Something else grew into reality, a tall shadow that stretched up higher than she could see and to each side, a dark barrier. She went to it, dreading what she already knew. The shadow took on substance.

A sheer cliff stretched up and out to either side, blocking her way. She touched the cold rock, felt the ice and snow that was crusted on it. She had hoped to find that it had been a mirage born of exhaustion. It was real, too real. She leaned against it, unable to think, unable to decide which way to go. She wanted only to sit, to sleep, to die, to have the nightmare over.

Again, suddenly, she received something from her senses which slammed panic into her.

She moved, the beast sense loping behind her. Terror blinded her, paralyzing her thinking, and made her a target for the beast.

She stopped and faced about, blind in the blowing, her

breath ragged in the wind. She felt out with her senses to find what waited for her. It had stopped running when she had and waited now, as she waited. She could not tell if this was the same creature she had encountered before, nor if it might have been the new presence that had started following her later. But it waited now for her to make the first move; this much she knew.

She swallowed great gulps of air and searched the area round about, seeing nothing through the snow. The creature hovered close by. A rumble arose from its throat that came to her more as a feeling than a sound. She willed it to go away, flexing the cold numbness of her fingers.

The beast shied to the left. She faced that way, heart pounding, as the heavy shadow materialized out of the shimmering lights, silver-gray.

"Go away," she whimpered.

The beast rumbled a warning that froze her where she was, her fingers clenched in fear. She tried to project her will to it to make it go away. There was a moment's silence. The creature backed up a step, rumbling threats. She tried again. *Go away. Leave me alone.* She started to shiver in the cold. She had to be moving soon or she would not be able to. *Go away! Go away!* She took a trembling step sideways, her back to the cliff. *Go away!*

The beast roared and rushed. Pain hit her arm even as she screamed and lunged aside.

"No!" she shouted as the beast spun again to strike. If that heavy paw hit her again she was dead. The creature did not strike, backed up in uncertainty.

Jaimah reached to the numb place on her arm and drew away her hand, red with sticky moisture.

Shuddering, she got to her feet and faced the beast that had begun to weave back and forth in front of her.

She didn't try to send her will to it; she knew that it would not tolerate such a touch again.

She gasped for breath, thinking, desperately thinking, trying to figure a way out of this.

She slid an inch to the right, her back to the stone. The beast stayed with her. She froze. The animal stopped.

She did not take her eyes off it and took another slow side step. The cold was biting into her arm, the pain coming in throbs now. Another step. Another.

The creature did not come closer, but it still weaved back

and forth, its intentions obscured by anger and threat.

A warm stickiness oozed down her arm to her fingers. She did not dare look.

Another step.

The beast sat down, swinging its head from side to side, rumbling angrily. Jaimah's heart stilled, hoping beyond hope that it would let her go. She inched away slowly, until she could not see it any longer in the pelting snow. She reached out hesitantly with her senses.

The beast had not moved.

She turned and ran, fearing that it would suddenly come after her.

She cried at the pain that tore through her lungs, her legs, and her arm. She sucked in snow with the air, coughed a racking cough, and finally slowed when she could no longer keep going.

The beast's awareness prickled at her; it knew where she was.

She held her arm to her, running a little, walking when she could not run, the sticky flow from her arm slowing and finally stopping.

The land began to rise, a climb that she would not have chosen. Her breath came hard and her lungs ached; and every few paces of altitude gained made breathing that much more difficult.

Finally she leaned against the cliff, her hand pressed to her aching arm, as she tried to bring her breathing to normal.

Then she felt the beast presence join the second one that had been tracking her. The beast radiated occasional impulses of anger and confusion, and it was driven to follow.

Jaimah pushed herself forward again, stumbling, and stepped into yielding snow. She floundered, struggled for balance, and stumbled on her way, half running a few steps in the effort.

They were closing in on her. She could feel distinctly the two separate entities, one sending surges of confusion, the other only searching.

She pushed forward, tried to go faster for a time, and gave it up when the pain in her body was more than she could bear. She leaned against the cliff again, slow throbs biting into her arm, her breathing heavy in a tight chest. Blue and green sparkles struck the rock over her head.

Suddenly she got a strong, clear warning, an apprehension

like a chill wind behind her. Her trail had been found. They were close enough that the wind had not yet erased where she had gone. She started to move again.

It was madness to run blindly in a place that the beasts knew better than she. It was better sense to turn and face them; but she didn't want to die. She gasped breath and tried to maintain a steady pace.

Abruptly the awareness deserted her, leaving her more than blind.

Panic breathed at her shoulders; she turned to face it, backing up the incline, where she stumbled over a ledge. Backing up it, and not daring to take her eyes from where she had come, she felt a wildness surge into her brain. And suddenly it hit from all sides, beast senses all around her, too many of them.

They had come, following the second presence that had come after her.

She was trapped. A terror settled into her bones.

A beast roared in front of her. Its body parted the veil of snow, higher than her head.

Jaimah choked on a cry, and scrambled backward, up over a series of small ledges that were covered with crusted ice and snow.

The silver-gray beast came down, uttering a deep, guttural growl, hostile and agitated. A gaping maw, fanged and foul-smelling, passed close by her face.

The small black eyes glittered at her. She stared back, afraid to turn and run. She backed up the ledges, bent over to keep her balance, her breath coming in tight little sobs.

Her heel struck the edge of a ledge, taller than the rest had been, and she slipped, throwing her off balance. She slid feet first toward the beast.

Her fingers clutched frantically at the rock for a hold.

A claw grabbed at her foot. She cried out in terror and kicked it away.

She flung herself backward, crablike, up the ledge, her frozen fingers searching through the snow for each new level, her feet pushing her upward.

The beast lunged with a roar that tore at her ears.

She screamed, sucked at breath that entered painfully into her chest, and flung herself to the side, the heavy feet of the beast landing just inches away from her.

Rolling, she got to her knees and backed away. The beast

seemed to be confused. It couldn't see her and shuffled in the opposite direction. She rose shakily to her feet and inched up the incline, keeping her eyes on the disappearing hulk of the shaggy animal.

Another shape rose to her right, below her, yet standing taller than her head. A deafening roar echoed off the cliffs.

She threw herself upward and tried to run on the narrow, ice-covered ledge, with a cliff at her feet. She slipped and fell through the air, landing hard.

A low sound was the the first thing she was aware of. Then pain, hot and in pulses.

The sound became distinguishable and was coming from her own throat, a groan or a moan that was born of pain.

She pushed herself to her knees with a ragged sob, clutching her arm to her side.

An angry rumble and snuffling came to her from overhead. The beast was pacing back and forth on the ledge, which was not as high as she had thought it. If it had been, the fall would have surely killed her, for she had not landed on soft snow.

The beast stopped and stared at her, growling. Her breath stilled. It gathered its feet together to jump.

Jaimah dived for the base of the cliff, wincing at the pain that tore through her. She hugged the rock and took in her surroundings desperately. There was an undercut a few feet away. She ran to it, slid back into it, and heard the wuff of the beast as it landed and the shuffling through the snow as it searched.

A silver-gray shadow came across the opening and reached in for her.

She cried out hysterically and kicked at it, trying to pull herself back into the undercut farther, sobbing uncontrollably. She kicked again and again.

A hard hand seized her and held her tight against the rock.

Corwyn!

Jaimah gasped and stared into his dark eyes, her mind struggling for balance. She said his name with a sob and was pulled to him, his arms going around her. She closed her eyes, feeling the warmth of him and the strength of his arms. Silent tears of relief slid down her face.

After a moment, she felt the pain in her arm, a hot searing that told her it had been torn open again. She pulled back and raised her hand to the tear in her sleeve.

Corwyn frowned and looked to her hand. "What is it?"

"My . . . arm . . ." She took her hand away, fresh blood on it, her head spinning.

The last thing she saw before darkness came over her was the look of shocked anger on Corwyn's face.

Then nothing.

Chapter Nineteen

A FUZZY MIST HUNG IN HER MIND BEFORE SHE OPENED HER
eyes. Then she could see only darkness. She lifted her head,
but still could see only darkness. She shivered. It was bitterly
cold. A weight stirred next to her.

"Jaimah?" Corwyn's low voice came to her, his arm that
had been across her pulled back. His hand touched her face.

"Corwyn," she said. "It's really you. I thought I dreamed
it." She laid her head back, her eyes a dead weight.

"You didn't," he said.

Jaimah did not answer; the strength beyond her. She shivered violently.

"You're cold," Corwyn said, his hand traveling down her
arm to her fingers, and up again, feeling the shudders she
could not stop.

She drifted a moment and felt a movement next to her, a
stirring her numbed mind could not interpret.

"Come here," Corwyn said, pulling her close, and she felt
her cheek against his fever warmth. His fur coat went tightly
around her, the fabric of his tunic smooth against her face. His
hand came around her and undid the length of her coat,
opened it so that he could pull her next to him. He wrapped
his arms around her, furs and all, the heat of his body gradually stopping the tremors that shook her. The steady rise and
fall of his breathing was soothing to her, and she slept.

When she opened her eyes again, it was still dark, but was

a different dark because she could see a dim light coming from somewhere. She felt the even rhythm of Corwyn's breathing against her cheek and could hear his heart. She lay still a long time listening. The double layer of furs kept their combined heat close, and she shut her eyes and knew she was caught.

She tried to raise her hand to touch him, wincing at the painful stiffness of her arm.

Corwyn pulled back to look at her, the furs coming apart as he did, and the light of the storm flooded over them, dim in the undercut where they were. His eyes searched her face, clear and wakeful, and Jaimah realized that he had not been sleeping, but had been lying still to let her sleep. A shiver touched her at that.

He moved the fur aside and examined her arm in the flickering light from outside. His lips were grim, but he seemed to be satisfied with what he saw. There were two angry scars, jagged and long, down her arm, looking black in the blue and green flashes from the storm. And although her arm was stiff and ached when she moved it, it was almost completely healed.

"It's going to be all right," Corwyn said, and his eyes flashed a brief blaze of anger.

Jaimah did not understand what the anger was for. She sat up and pulled the fur around her in the sudden cold, disturbed, knowing that something was wrong.

Corwyn sat up, looked at her, and said, "They were to find you, not hurt you."

Jaimah lowered her eyes, unable to meet his, and took his meaning. She closed her eyes against the anger that she could feel coming from him. "The beasts," she whispered, shuddering at the memory of them.

"Yes."

"You sent them after me."

"Yes. After we became separated."

Disturbance went through her, coming from him, and she pressed a hand to her heart. This bombardment of emotion was something that she had never felt before. The tumultuous blending and mixing of her own confusion with that which came from him was an overstimulating of senses that was hard to contain.

"Where are they now?"

"Gone."

She opened her eyes and did up her coat slowly, her fingers stiff, trying to calm the surging emotion inside. She knew his eyes were on her and did not dare look up.

"I didn't know it was you following me. I thought it was something else." She felt the shock that went through him and held her breath until it was gone. She raised her eyes to his uncertainly and was surprised at the look on his face.

A burst of white light fell against the rock outside.

"You could feel that I was there?" He didn't need to ask; she could tell that he didn't need to ask. He had known all along what would come to her. He had been waiting for it to happen so that he could . . .

He cut the thought off before she could hear it.

He drew in a breath and expelled it, and tied the laces on his coat slowly, painstakingly, one at a time. He looked up at her, his eyes dark with an inner flame.

And Jaimah almost cried out at what he sent to her, so intense was the emotion of it. She gasped for breath in the suddenness of it. Then she was left reeling when he turned his eyes away, stopping that sending with the same suddenness with which it had come. She trembled in the emptiness that was left.

He reached up and touched her face. "I'm sorry," he said. "I should have prepared you for that." His fingers left her cheek with a slow, caressing movement. Jaimah shivered.

He smiled. "Come. Let me show you." His eyes were dark in the glitter of the blue and green lights from outside. He extended his hand.

She said nothing, but simply took the hand he held out to her, and her vision centered on them as his fingers enclosed hers. An unexpected thrill shivered through her that was almost like a shudder. When she forced herself to look up at him, his face was quiet. He was even smiling a little.

"It's not so difficult," he said, taking her other hand from where it lay in her lap. He held it gently, his eyes searching hers. "Do you trust me, Jaimah. Can you?"

It was a moment before she could nod. "Yes," she murmured, and was surprised that she did.

"Good." He gave her fingers a reassuring squeeze.

Then she felt an inward flow from his hands, a warmth which spread along her hands, her wrists, and up her arms. From that flow, a vibrant force throbbed between them, an almost visible pulsing of power that brightened and darkened spasmodically. Corwyn's figure was blurred as she looked through that surging of power, as if he were behind a shimmering veil. But his eyes were sharply in focus, seeming to bore into her, and she could not look away.

She felt the outreach of his mind slip into hers, a melding of thought and identity that took her by surprise, so that she almost cried out.

"Do not be afraid," he whispered.

And she heard that dually, both with her ears and inside her head.

It was as if he had put his arms around her, so all enveloping was the awareness of him in her. But she could see with her eyes that he had not. Yet, the complete unity of it was so intimate that the fact he only touched her hands practically had no meaning. She understood then how he had influenced her thoughts so many times and how he had so often seemed to know what she was thinking.

"Now—" The right hand of Corwyn rose, and his fingertips touched her forehead, held so for the space of several heartbeats. Then they slid down over her closed eyelids and again held so, before going on to her lips. The touch withdrew.

From each of those touches there issued an inflowing of strength, so that her breathing quickened. This inflow of energy made her flesh tingle alive in a way she had never experienced. It was as if something tight and hurting inside her had suddenly exploded apart. And there was a longing in her, a strange longing—for what she did not know. But she gasped in the overwhelming strength of it and clutched at Corwyn for support. She felt herself gathered to him and held tightly.

"What was done is now undone."

His voice was tranquil and remote; it fell on her ears like cool water as they sat thus. Buoyed by it, she was able to let herself become part of the flow, not even noting when the voice merged with the new perceptions of awareness in her mind and finally stopped altogether.

She could feel the force of Corwyn surrounding her, so strong and intense she swayed under its weight. His fingers touched her, and his arms held her tightly.

How long she sat so wedded to him, she never knew. Except that there came a moment when her hands fell, as if too heavily burdened for her to raise.

His mind gently pulled away from hers. At that moment all

was gone. She whirled away in a dizzy, giddy retreat. And before she dropped her heavy head, she saw that Corwyn was looking at her anxiously. She could no longer see through him; yet the consciousness of him, how he sat, what he did, was so much with her that it was as if she physically watched him.

Slowly, the warmth of his possession receded, and she shivered in its absence. But she was aware that there had come a change within her. Doors had opened and would never close again. She found tears on her cheeks, but whether they were from regret because of this new change in her or from gladness because she was at last free, she did not know.

She pulled away from him, turning so that she could look at him. "Who are you?" She had to wet her lips with her tongue before she could shape those words. "What are you?"

Fainter still came the voice of Corwyn. "What I have just done, you also can do."

She stared at him a moment, the implications of what he was saying sinking into her. Then unaccountably, fear seized her. "No—I cannot." She began to rise, but he caught her hands.

"Jaimah, you can. It is for this which your father sought your life."

She winced at that.

"Forgive me that," he said quickly, his eyes catching instantly the pain that had gone through her. "I would not willingly bring you any unhappiness, but I want you to see what it is that has been yours all along. It is this that Encheon hid from you and from Shayna. But it is yours nonetheless. It is your birthright. You cannot deny it."

His words fell on her like pronouncements of doom. Because doomed she was if she indeed could do this that Shayna wanted for herself. She shivered with fright, as she stared at him.

His eyes became wells into which she sank and became a part of. Not a mind slipping into mind as before, but an opening into which she entered, seemingly on her own. And she saw—saw enough to make her flinch. She shut her eyes, held them firmly shut, and then, after a few deep breaths to dissipate the fierce power she had encountered in him, she opened them again. She looked into those eyes that were regarding her but she held herself away from them. A faint smile touched his lips.

He reached down and slipped his fingers around her hand, his flesh warm against the cold of her skin.

"I want you to try," he said. "I want you to find the center of the storm."

She did not stir. "I cannot!" she whispered. Yet her fingers remained curled in his hand.

"Yes." His hold on her tightened. "You can." Lightning flickered and glimmered through the air. This time there was that in his voice which compelled her.

The lightning that flared and darkened showed his features in stark relief.

Turning from him she looked out into the storm. She did not know how to begin. She could feel the power out there, the almost elusive magical energy that one just had to reach out and tap.

Deliberately, she tried to close out the mountain world about her, shut her ears to the howl of the wind. Self-doubt held her and she felt naked in this which she did not know. She tried to feel how Corwyn had slipped so easily into her mind. But she could not duplicate it.

Her thoughts did not seem to go beyond the inside of her head. She concentrated, and nothing happened. It had seemed so effortless and natural when Corwyn had done it. But now . . . She could not reach outside of herself. And the harder she tried, the more imprisoning her body seemed to be. Her fingers bit deeply into Corwyn's hand as she pushed harder to get outside of herself. But there was a barrier.

She came upon it suddenly.

It was a solid blackness that she struck, as if she had run full force into a stone wall, and it struck back with a violent blow. She jerked back and did not know if she had cried out.

Shivering, spent, she opened her eyes. Corwyn's hand was still around hers, patient but insistent.

"I can't do it. There is something . . . a blackness . . ."

He was silent a moment, his thumb moving slowly across her fingers. Then he withdrew his hand.

"It's not as difficult as you make it," he said. "You don't really have to fight your way in. It's more like a whisper. Like a breath of air. You don't really have to think about it at all."

With that he lifted his hand a little and moved his fingers, a very subtle gesture. A flickering green light sprang up around them; another move deepened the light to a steady radiance with no apparent source. "It takes no more thought than it does to close your hand." His fingers curled into a loose fist.

"Just open your mind." His voice stroked her like a caressing hand. "Once you find it, it is yours forever."

"How? I could not get through. There is something stopping me."

"Search inside. You knew it once. You can remember it again."

"But I *don't* remember!" she whispered desperately. "I don't remember any of it."

His hand touched hers. "You will remember what you need to."

She stared at him a long moment, hearing the absolute certainty in his voice.

"All right," she said. "I will try."

His fingers closed tightly over hers and he smiled. "Just take your time and don't force it."

Jaimah nodded and drew a breath, closing her eyes. Corwyn's hand was warm over hers, and for a moment that was the center of her thoughts. She forced it away and once more her sight turned inward, using her sense of perception, groping, seeking for what it was that would open this power to her. Sound and touch faded.

Then out of nowhere came that area of darkness, a great smothering, as of a cloak folding about her so tightly she could not even struggle. She gasped for air that wasn't there, cried out in a voice that had no sound. She struggled, fought that darkness, and thought she was going to die. Hands pulled away the folds of the cloak at last. The air she drew desperately into her lungs was icy, like the blade of a knife. Her fingers reached out for Corwyn and clung to him.

But the barrier was gone.

She opened her eyes to a world that at once was the same and somehow altered. A crackling and sputtering of sparks outside drew her attention, a tittering of laughter that came from the sparks themselves. She looked at them in astonishment, and they laughed again in merriment, dancing away into the storm. She stared at the storm as she realized that it had an essence to it that was almost alive. It pulsed and breathed and moved, enshrouding the mountain with a definite purpose.

And it was Corwyn's purpose! She found *him* there in the center of the storm.

Then suddenly, in the wake of her disturbances, a wind swept up over the peaks and rushed down the mountain slopes toward the rocks where she and Corwyn sat. It came at them, a howling maelstrom that threatened to destroy the entire mountaintop. She watched it with a rising panic because this she knew she would not be able to control. It tore down the slopes, ripping the snow from the rocks and whipping it into a violently boiling cloud that surged down on them like a wall.

"Corwyn!" she cried and clutched at him.

"Do not try to control it," he said, knowing what was in her mind. "That is not your talent." His hands touched her face, drawing her eyes to his. "But you can find your way. Think. What is it that you can do? What has been awakening in you? Think, Jaimah. Think."

She stared at him. Then she forced her thoughts away from the wind. She tried to think.

"I can't," she protested in rising panic.

"No. Stop." His hands held her when she would have risen to run. "Think. How did you know I was following you? How did you know?"

She stared at him uncomprehending, trying to pull out of his grasp. They were going to die, and he was asking her stupid questions. But the look on his face stopped her. This was important. She blinked, trying to focus her thoughts.

"How . . ."

"How did you know, Jaimah?"

"I could feel you."

"Exactly. You can feel. You can become a part of things, the way you can become a part of me."

His mind slid into hers easily. The touch was intimate, as if his whole body had slid into hers and filled her and caressed her everywhere at once inside and out. It only lasted between one breath and the next, and then he was gone. Jaimah moaned in the intensity of it.

"Make it a part of you," his voice said, and her mind was instantly aware of the wind tearing toward them. "Become one with it. Feel its life, its energy. This is what you are able to do. Slide into it. Make its mind yours."

She did as he instructed and reached out to touch the swiftly advancing wind. It roiled over her in all its strength. It was like being torn into a million pieces, a pain that was so exquisite she thought she screamed. Arms were around her, holding her, buoying her, feeding her strength.

Then the pain was gone. And she was in the wind, was a part of it, the eddies and vortices surrounding her and lifting her in the force of its violence. There was something there, a kind of awareness, a quickening of animation that sprang into being just because she touched it. It was as if she had been blind all of her life and suddenly was now able to see.

Then she saw she could pull the power from it and she let the wind whip from her, willing it into nothingness until all was quiet. She sagged. Corwyn drew her closer to him. She let herself lean against him, the aura of power quite gone from her.

"Corwyn, what is that storm supposed to be?"

His answer did not come right away. "Do you fear something in it?"

"I don't know,"she said. "But you are at the center of it." She looked up at him; he was watching her. "I felt you there and something else . . ."

"I know." His voice was quiet.

Jaimah put a hand on his chest. The fur was cold. "I could not find its purpose. Is it to destroy Shayna or the mountain?"

He shook his head. "No."

She breathed a faint sigh. "Good."

His eyes still did not leave her face, as if he were coming to a kind of decision that he had not intended on making, and had no wish to make. But now he considered it because of her. His mouth was pressed into a resolute line when he lifted his face and stared into the storm.

For half a breath Jaimah stared at him and then she knew what he was going to do. In the next instant another thought flashed into her mind—that without the storm, Shayna would not have at the Peak what she hoped to have.

"Corwyn," she said quickly, taking a hold of his arm to stop him. "Don't."

He looked at her, a frown in his eyes."Why not?"

"Shayna . . ."

"She doesn't know how to use what's out there."

"She thinks she can."

"She's already tried. She failed."

Jaimah drew in her breath, wiped her free hand on the fur, and let the breath go again. She looked up into his eyes and held down the apprehension she felt. She turned her face aside and stared into the storm and the lights that flashed and burst into shimmers and glimmers and died, only to be replaced by more.

She could hear wind in great force skirling away the clouds

and mist, making the dark blue-gray swirl across the ground.

And all about the mountain was darkness, sullen and gray.

Even as she watched, the gray lightened, and in the light, snow fell, whirling, blowing faster and faster, thick and blinding.

Jaimah watched her body shuddering under her. She had known it all along; Corwyn did control the storm. She felt the confirmation of her belief an unexpected burden. She reached out to find the rock to give her support, found instead Corwyn's hand and held onto it while he drew the power out of the storm.

She watched the snow come down, whipped into a blizzard by the hard wind. She wondered what Shayna's reaction would be when she saw that the magic storm was gone and whether she would guess at what had been done. She would be angry, Jaimah knew, would see it as a great chance gone. But she would not be detered and would go to the Peak anyway, despite the change in the storm.

Jaimah watched as the flying snow, powdered and icy, quickly began to grow thin. The swirls slowed, the flakes grew larger and fewer and the light became brighter until the sun was touching the snow outside the cavity with brilliant light. She stared at glints of ice that reflected sunlight. The storm had gone, leaving a bright world of white. She moved her numbed limbs and felt where a rock had been pressing against her leg.

"We must go," Corwyn said. "Shayna will be anxious about us." He moved out of the small cave into the snow, drawing her after him, and held her up until she could stand.

The world lay in a white hush, and Jaimah looked at the mountain peaks and cliffs and wondered that she hadn't fallen off one of those precipices.

Through a cleft in the rock puffed a gentle wind. She lifted her face to it as it tugged at her hair. On it was the smell of ice and snow, and a chill that did not yet pierce through the fur coat she pulled tightly around her.

Corwyn's hand moved up to her shoulder, turning her attention to him. Under his gentle urging she moved along the face of the short cliff away from the cave where they had been. The sun off the snow was a dazzle of sparks. The sweep of tundra away from the cliff to the right was a featureless expanse of white that glittered with broken bits of light as if someone had flung shattered glass across the unmarred snow.

In her new state of heightened awareness, she was stunned not only by the beauty of it to the eye, but also by the impact upon her inner senses. She stared at it bedazzled, barely aware of the nearness of Corwyn beside her.

Then she was suddenly aware of another presence—no, more than one—approaching, a mental pressure that preceded something physical. What came toward them moved in over the open tundra that lay between the cliff on their left and the distant broken crags before them.

Jaimah found herself trembling in the strength of its sending and more than a little frightened. Then, after a moment, she recognized that presence. It was one that she had felt many times before.

She caught hold of Corwyn's arm, stopping him.

"The Watchers," she breathed. "They come!"

There were four of them, large, slope-shouldered, wading through belly-deep snow. Foremost was the largest beast, dragging a mountain stag by the neck.

"No!" Corwyn said angrily as it drew closer.

The beast shied and lifted a paw in threat, then dropped it. It stood rocking to and fro as it eyed them. Jaimah could feel a general attitude of uncertainty emanating from the Watchers, though foremost was a begrudged desire for reconciliation. This was from the beast with the stag.

All watched Corwyn until he gave sign of relenting, a shift of shoulders that was almost a shrug. Jaimah sighed in relief, although she did not know why. His hand traveled down her back and fell away.

The beast edged forward again, head slightly averted, uncertainty in its movements and strong in the air. But by degrees it came closer, dragging the carcass with it until it had worked its way to Corwyn's feet. There it dropped the animal. The massive head thrust at his knee. With a sigh, the beast sat down.

Jaimah could smell the damp fur on his coat and feel his solid body, though he wasn't touching her. Its coat was a silvery gray-white with a faint mottling of darker silver along the back and haunches. Its black eyes looked down at the ground, its head hanging until its muzzle was almost in the snow. The wuffs of air from its nostrils turned the snow at its forepaws to slush that quickly froze in the cold wind.

The other three did not approach close, but hung back, weaving uncertainly back and forth among themselves until finally settling down in the snow, their black eyes on Corwyn and Jaimah.

Corwyn stood looking down at the beast that had settled and was waiting, almost as if for a deathblow. Then he sighed. He dropped to his heels beside the beast and put his arm up around the fat neck. There was a rumble, not a threatening sound, but a pleasure sound.

"Okay," Corwyn said softly. "You're forgiven." His hand stroked the massive silver-gray head. "But I'm not the one you attacked."

He looked up at Jaimah. She stepped back involuntarily, knowing instantly what he wanted her to do, her heart going chill. But as she looked at the creature and into its black eyes, the chill drained from her. Its eyes bored into hers and held her, and she sensed an intelligence that she had not expected.

She went to Corwyn and knelt beside him. Within her, there was a new excitement, for something told her that this was a moment of importance in her life.

She reached out to touch the animal, compelled by a desire to read him as she had read the wind and the storm. The Watcher's hair stiffened along his spine, and he no longer lay at ease, but drew his limbs under him as if he prepared to spring. His lips wrinkled but his snarl did not sound aloud.

"Don't move!" Corwyn warned.

Jaimah froze at his words.

An instant later she gasped with shock. A strong mental force burst through her mind. She felt as if she had been caught in a hostile hand, raised to the level of unfriendly eyes which surveyed her outwardly and inwardly. Jaimah swayed, shaken by the nonphysical touch. Again came that hostile sensation of being examined and weighed, but this was from the other beasts that had hung back. She sat motionless under it.

Then those minds swiftly pulled away. But she could feel that the strength of that probe had left a tenuous thread of linkage between herself and the animal before her, even though he had withdrawn. In her was the sharpness of his hunger.

She became aware then of Corwyn, so close to her that their shoulders touched.

"He will not hurt you," he said. "And he brought a peace offering."

Jaimah looked at the dead stag and felt the hunger that was a pain in her. And she wondered what this beast was that it felt the need to make peace with Corwyn when it so hungered. What was Corwyn that this beast brought contrition to him, for it was to Corwyn that the stag had been given? What was the beast that it had such powers of the mind?

But she asked none of this aloud. The link with the beast was still there, and again she hesitantly put out her hand to him. He did not move as she touched him, her fingers sinking into a pelt of fur so thick it was like putting a hand into soft snow. For an instant, she wondered if she would ever feel one with this creature as she had with Corwyn.

Never.

From the creature under her fingers came that knowledge. Wonder started in her that she had been able to sense so clearly his thoughts. And he hers.

She felt his mind touch hers in condescension as he gave her confirmation of her thoughts. It frightened her that this creature could be so strong.

She turned and saw that Corwyn was watching her. A faint smile crossed his lips, touched briefly the corners of his eyes. He had read her thoughts as clearly as the beast had. The rush of embarrassment rose swiftly to her face as she recalled the intimacy with which she had remembered that brief moment when he had so easily entered her mind, how much like a caress it had been and how it had turned her limbs to fire.

She opened her mouth to say something, but he shook his head slightly, forestalling her. He reached up and took her hand.

"Learn all you can, Jaimah," he said quickly. "Learn what you can do and what you cannot."

She returned his gaze for a moment until she found herself trembling. Then, on impulse, wondering how he saw her, she laid a light hand on his wrist. With a moment of vision, she caught a brief glimpse of the enormity of his feelings for her. Its magnitude was so great it seemed to fill the whole universe and to infuse into every particle of matter in existence. The power and intensity of it rushed over her like a colossal wave, disorienting her with its fierceness.

She gasped and snatched her hand away, rubbing her fingers together as if they'd been burned. She looked up at him and saw that he had not turned his eyes away and was still watching her with an unreadable expression. And she knew then that she'd never be able to read anything of him that he did not want her to. He was greater even in this and ever would be. She sat staring at him, lost in his gaze until he took her hand and pressed a kiss into it.

"Jaimah," he said. "We must go. Shayna is waiting where I left her and she must be impatient by now, and angry. You have yet much to learn, but it will have to wait until a later time because we cannot stay here. I will not go without you, and I must go." His face was grim.

She looked at him with foreboding, a prescience telling her that ill was yet going to come between him and Shayna. But she nodded.

"All right, Corwyn. Where you go, I will go." Turning her eyes away from him she hesitantly put out her hand for the beast at her side to nuzzle, knowing he would only if he chose to.

Chapter Twenty

THEY CLIMBED. HAD BEEN CLIMBING FOR A LONG TIME.

Corwyn guided her faltering steps, his hand grasping her arm and pulling at the fur of her coat by turns. She struggled upward, determined to keep his pace even though she felt her strength flagging. Her feet fought for purchase among the broken rocks of the slope, and she scrambled to keep from falling as Corwyn pulled her to the next level. At last they reached the upper rocks where they were shrouded in deep snow.

Beyond that, Jaimah knew only a seemingly endless time of struggling upward and onward, over rocks that sometimes turned under her feet, often through knee-deep snow, and with the sun a constant glare off the whiteness before her. The short stops for rest were too brief, and the grueling efforts between were too long. But Corwyn urged her on, and somehow she kept going.

Then there was another presence, a feeling that they were not alone. Jaimah searched the blinding snow with squinting eyes, looking for the one she sensed so close to them.

"She's waiting," Corwyn said. "Can you feel it?"

"Yes." Her voice was only a whisper. "I can."

Corwyn put his arm around her. "Come. She is not going to be pleased that we have delayed so long."

Nor will she be pleased about the magic storm being gone, Jaimah thought. But she was too tired to say so. Wearily she searched the landscape for Shayna as they pushed through the snow. Rounded domes of snow stood here and there, knobs of snow over stone, smooth and satiny, sometimes hollowed into bowls and drifted by the wind. A swirl of powder snow ran along the lip of a half-moon drift, a wind that was for once at their backs, cold and biting, but not torturing their faces.

They drew near a shape that seemed suddenly to acquire more substance than the blazing white around it. It was a stone that didn't have the feel of stone. Jaimah eyed it warily. The shape straightened, fur clad, and Corwyn stopped.

"Shayna," he murmured.

"I thought you were not coming back." Her voice, though quiet, had a whiplash to it.

"I gave you my oath that I would return."

"Sometimes a man's word has no more substance than the wind," she bit back.

"I honor my word, my Lady."

"So I see."

Jaimah made a faltering step and sat down, unable to stand unless she was moving forward. Impetus was her only strength now; with it gone, every muscle in her body sagged and cried out for rest. Shayna spared her a cold glance, and Corwyn moved to stand beside her.

"I was certain you'd find her dead," and when he didn't reply, she said, "I would have come after you."

"I know." His voice was tight.

Jaimah bowed her head, too weary to wonder what was going to happen next. The old feeling returned, that tautness of stomach muscles whenever Shayna and Corwyn faced each other.

"Get her to her feet," Shayna said.

Jaimah heard or felt Corwyn kneel down beside her. His hand came gently against her face and stroked her hair under the fur hood. "Come, Jaimah," he said. "Can you?"

She moved and tried. Corwyn rose and took her arm, lifting her up. He slipped an arm about her and started in the direction that Shayna had already taken. Shayna hung back, walking slowly until they caught up to her, then she increased her pace, not breaking stride. Nor did she break the silence that had descended among them.

The trail led up and up. As they climbed, clouds began to gather, lowering until they hid the peaks and the sun. Gradually the view became covered with mist, where the trail curved upward against a sharp rock cliff, to a notch between two towering crags.

It was very silent, even their boots sounded muffled underfoot, and snow began to fall, slowly at first, but gradually increasing as they climbed. The trail ran along an edge that fell away to a deep drop on the right where the snowflakes drifted and swirled on the wind as it carried the veiling flakes below them.

Corwyn came up behind her and put his arm around her. She gripped him tightly as a dizzy *other* feeling from outside washed over her. Then she felt radiating from Corwyn's body a strength that flowed from him to her. The other feeling ebbed and she stopped trembling.

"There is someone—something—out there," she was at last able to say.

Corwyn's arm tightened around her. She knew that he, too, had felt it.

"Over there," he said.

She looked up at him, then followed his gaze across the wide ravine through the obscuring snowflakes.

At first she saw nothing more than the towering rise of the broken, rough slope on the other side, topped with massive cliffs. Then in the deeply recessed shadows she felt rather than saw a faint movement, as if the Watcher stirred, for Watcher it had to be. She stared for a long moment, not certain, for she could get no clear feeling from it. Then the Watcher moved. She saw a shadow pass across a streak of featureless white; then it was gone, the snowfall veiling any more sighting of him.

If she hadn't known that he was there she wouldn't have seen him at all.

"They follow us."

"Yes."

"Why?"

"They are masters unto themselves, Jaimah. Their reasons are their own."

A Watcher beast roared suddenly and others joined him, the keening echoing back and forth the full length of the ravine.

Shayna spun, staring startled across the ravine, her face white with shock and fear. Corwyn urged Jaimah forward on the trail before Shayna glanced nervously at them over her shoulder. She turned and stared again across the ravine. Then she turned and started past one of the many outcroppings of rock rising from the snow.

She led them into a narrow canyon, following a path that Jaimah found difficult to see. Deep in the shadow of the cliffs, they came to the end of the canyon, and Jaimah wondered if this was the place where Shayna had intended to come. It was not the peak she had seen in the distance, nor was it anything like what she had pictured the place of power to be.

Shayna turned and pushed through the snow to a trail that Jaimah had not seen until that moment. Nor could it have been seen until then, for it was well hidden by a wall of rock, leading up and up into more rock, covered with ice and snow, barely seen through the falling flakes.

Jaimah was uneasy at the thought of entering that steep, narrow way, with Shayna ahead of them where she could easily turn and send both apprentice and servant to their deaths. She shivered at that thought and shook the snow from her hood.

Suddenly Shayna was looking at her, and she shrank next to Corwyn. Her fingers sought for support, entangling in the fur of his coat, as she tried in panic to cover her thoughts. Somehow, she suspected Shayna had felt what she had been thinking. And she wondered wildly if she had sent her thoughts out inadvertently. The idea terrified her.

"Come," Shayna said shortly. "We climb now." Her eyes rested on Jaimah a breath without further words, her eyes filled with contempt, then she turned and began to climb the narrow trail.

Jaimah took Corwyn's fingers wondering why they were even bothering. They could have run, disappearing into the mountain never to be found again. But instead, Corwyn had led her here, where together they were struggling up a narrow cut in the cliffs of the mountain following Shayna to her Peak. It was suicide. But she let him pull her up. The entwining of their lives was too intricate to undo. She had no other choice but to go with him . . . and die with him.

Suddenly she felt regret at that eventuality, for she was just coming alive as if being awakened from a deep sleep. And it was Corwyn who had brought about that awakening. To lose it so soon . . .

She felt the strength of Corwyn's fingers around hers, flesh on flesh, as he pulled her effortlessly up next to him, and she felt sharp grief that she would not get to know him, would not have time to take this thing between them into a deeper kind of knowing.

She met his somber gaze and knew that he was very aware of her thoughts. For a moment she hesitated, caught in an instant of intimacy that both warmed her and wrenched at her heart that this was going to come to an end. Then she turned to follow Shayna.

They came at last, into sunlight, among an unlikely landscape of tall spires of rock, flowing mists, and dark, fantastic shapes looming beyond. In this place the wind had scoured the rock and ice.

Jaimah stopped and turned so that she was half-facing outward—into a world of astonishing space and light. It was flat in one direction. Beyond that flatness were mountains, peaks, cliffs, rugged bare rock, and snow glimmering with a dull blue light, reflecting the sky. In the other direction the land fell away into a faded haze, misted with silver white. It was no mere valley, and there was no glimpse of a plain beyond, but a gap into breathtaking depths so great the bottom was lost in terraces, slopes, shelves, and reaching arms of cliffs that were blue-white in shadow and purple where the shadows were deepest on the winter snow. Jaimah thought that she was looking at the very edge of the world and stared at it in awe. Momentarily, she forgot why she was there and that she was extremely tired.

Corwyn came up behind her and took hold of her arm over the fur. The sun went down, thrusting pinnacles, minarets, and balanced rocks up through the haze as if they had no foundation. Mountains leaped into being that had not been visible before, and the land grew back and back, extending to the horizon and blending into the sky.

Jaimah leaned back against Corwyn, feeling a sudden pang of loneliness, a sense of being nothing in such vastness. The solid strength behind her had become natural to be there. But the tiredness and the aching of her body was suddenly the only thing she could concentrate on.

The pink and purple blaze of the sunset flung a twilight at them that was bright and yet was muted with pastels. The great space was a limbo of blues and purples and grays, with spires upthrust through the haze. Corwyn stood still while she rested against him, the keen cold of the wind biting at her face.

The great chasm was developing new limits with the sun

behind the hills. On the end of a long out-thrust stood a causeway, stretching out from the peak on their left, a fingerlike ridge of rock pointing out from the falling slope of the mountain. And there at the end of that causeway rose three slender spires together, only a shade darker than the mauve of the sky.

"There!" Shayna breathed, looking on those pillars with barely concealed anticipation and triumph. Jaimah gazed with reluctance and loathing at that miragelike place that hung before them. It remained distinct only for a few moments, and then faded into shadow as dusk came upon them, the pinks in the sky turning to maroon, the purples darkening to black.

"Where we must go," Corwyn said quietly.

"Something is alive there," Jaimah murmured.

"Yes."

Jaimah did not answer because she could feel something coming from that place that was somehow familiar. But that familiarity eluded her when she tried to focus on it, and she could not name it. That it was something that she should know shook her, and she suddenly didn't want to face it.

Darkness closed in on them, slow and steady, but not yet total. The bitter cold became even more harsh with the setting of the sun. Corwyn put his arm around her and guided her to where Shayna broke through the snow as she pushed forward toward the distant finger of rock.

Chapter Twenty-one

THE WIND SWELLED AGAIN, KICKING UP THE SNOW IN A SWIRL-
ing cloud that was difficult to push through. Jaimah's eyes
burned in the cold. She kept her hood pulled low over her face
and went where Corwyn's hand guided her.

She worried about going out onto that narrow stretch of
rock, covered with snow and ice, and thought that prudence
dictated they wait until the wind died. But Shayna led them
relentlessly forward toward those spires.

Snow flowed in rivers over the ice and bare rock at their
feet. They went like ghosts onto the causeway, and their tracks
vanished behind them as they walked. Spires towered in front
of them, indistinct beyond the swirling eddies of ice crystals,
save where outlined by the moon that occasionally pierced
white through the storm. The wind howled with a demon
voice around them.

Spires spanned by arches that they had not seen earlier
made the causeway a world unreal. Jaimah looked up at them
through squinted eyes and found nothing to reassure her. She
felt eyes on them, watching and waiting, always hidden, but
never far away. Fear settled over her that was a deep depres-
sion of soul.

For a time they had to rest, sheltered against the base of a
great spire out of the wind. Jaimah sat with her head bowed
against her knees, weak and hungry. She did not speak of the
Watchers that were out there somewhere, but saw Corwyn

looking out into the blowing snow as if he had seen something.

They rested, and then Shayna led them again farther out onto that finger of rock. That presence that was other than the Watchers became stronger. Jaimah looked about and could see nothing, though she could feel its touch. Corwyn turned a hooded face in the same direction, stood still a moment, then looked at Jaimah, his eyes seeing that she, too, had felt it. He pressed her arm, a brief smile touching his face.

The spires thinned, and they came upon a large flat space.

There stood the three towering fingers of stone that had appeared in the sunset's glow, now in moonlight, veiled with glittering ice crystals that fell through the suddenly still air. It was an awesome mass of stone reaching up into the sky, three spires at the very edge of the ridge. And below, just steps away, was an empty space.

Jaimah's breath stilled to see that emptiness.

She looked down into the frozen and trackless waste of rock more closely now at the pattern that leaped at her, the sawtooth pattern that was the fabric of that gaping hole. She looked at its huge, alternating bands of cliff and hanging terrace that reached down, repeating over and over until lost in the mists below. She looked north and south as far as her eyes could strain in the dim moonlight, until cliff and terrace faded away into hazy distances. It was mysterious and terrible—and beckoning.

"Come," Shayna urged them.

They followed her until she stopped a short distance from the center spire of rock.

"Guard your eyes," she said.

Jaimah turned, saw her throw her hands up, herb powder flying. Light blazed, cold and sudden. Even through blinding tears Jaimah saw black writings on the spires that soared over them—markings that were of an age far older than anything she had ever seen. She wiped the tears from her face and stared up at them. A prickling stirred the nape of her neck, a warning sense, a recognition of power.

"Come," Shayna said. She spoke in a low tone, and her voice echoed off the stone and down to the reaches below. "Corwyn, here. Jaimah, here."

She indicated places that were on either side of her, separating them—to increase her advantage, Jaimah thought, and went reluctantly, suddenly afraid to leave Corwyn's side. It

came to her that if Shayna should turn on her, Corwyn would
be unable to stop it. She looked to him helplessly, but his face
was hidden in his hood as he watched Shayna. Jaimah's eyes
turned to the drop that was a short distance away. One quick
push would be the end of anyone. She wondered if she would
feel that emptiness about her and the rush of wind against her
during the fall.

Jaimah pulled her hood closer to repress a shudder and
peered uneasily at Shayna. She stood with her back to them,
her hood pulled over her head; she was only a figure against
the snow. She stood thus for several moments before turning
an imperious look on Jaimah.

"Come here!" she ordered. Jaimah cringed inwardly at that
tone and then was angry at herself for it. Her chin came up,
and her jaw set stubbornly. Forward she went, forcing herself
to walk with confidence, though she was wary. She didn't
know what Shayna wanted, nor why she was called and not
Corwyn. But she wasn't going to show fear anymore and
clenched her hand to reenforce that resolve.

She deliberately raised her eyes, straight into that play of
curbed light that was the slowly fading remnants of the herb
fire that Shayna had sent aloft.

Abruptly Jaimah sensed that they were no longer alone.
Somewhere at the pillars in front of them was another intelligence, a measuring power. Not one of the Watchers, but another who had waited—that which she had sensed before,
now concentrated here at what seemed to be the source of its
power.

Shayna moved, raised her arms, and breathed forth a word.
It had no meaning that Jaimah knew. There was no recogniz-
able syllable to it. But even though it had been whispered, the
sound rang like a thunderclap into that long silence.

It was then that Jaimah realized that Shayna had come
without any more herbs. She looked at Shayna fearfully, feeling alarm that she was planning something without her herbs,
knowing that she could do nothing except use her ring.

Shayna's lips were slightly parted, and Jaimah caught the
faintest whisper of sound issuing from them. Jaimah watched
the procedure intently with increasing uncertainty.

Then Jaimah turned to look at the pillars with rising alarm.
There was a stirring there in the center of where the pillars
stood in a wide triangle, the tallest standing at the very edge of

the precipice and the other two widening out like beckoning arms toward where they watched.

Her skin tingled. The air about them was charged with energy. Jaimah knew a growing hunger, as of a yearning for something that was lost—for what, she could not have told. This new sensation frightened her, for she could not put a name to it or sense where it came from. Beside her, Shayna seemed carved out of marble, so still she was. The very night seemed gathered into that stillness. There was no sound other than Shayna's whispering, no motion, and Jaimah could feel the furious pounding of her heart. She closed her eyes as the warmth of that increasing longing suffused through her, almost bringing tears behind her lids.

She felt a tingle at the base of her head, and the sensation dissipated, but not for long. It came again in another surge of energy. The tingle in her head became a tightening of the scalp. And Jaimah became increasingly aware of the presence in the center of the pillars. It was coiled, waiting, Jaimah sensed, as if within the pulse of her blood there was a vibration pitched just too high for her ears to hear.

By now she was breathing as fast as if she had run a long distance.

She knew that they were caught in a vast wave of some energizing force drawn from the rock and mountain under their feet and from the pillars before them, something that she thought had gone from her forever, which had come instantly awake and aware. But this was much stronger than what she had ever experienced.

Something clenched in the pit of her stomach. She tried not to show her fear, desperately clinging to her resolve to appear unaffected.

Then Corwyn was beside her. Without even knowing it, she closed a hand on his arm, her fingers gripping into the fur to help her to contain the cry of anguish which was rising to her lips. His other hand came over hers, squeezing it lightly, as both warning and comfort.

From the ring on Shayna's finger, a spear point of light struck upon the tallest of those toothstones, the center pillar at the very end of the causeway, and from that juncture of beam and rock spread a curling mist which thickened into an impenetrable fog, blanketing out the pillars and the drop behind.

"Corwyn," Shayna's voice cut through the quiet. "Stand beside me."

He turned his head to look at Jaimah. He removed her hand gently from his arm, his eyes enjoining her to silence. She stared at him, powerless to do anything else. He moved to stand close to Shayna.

As if his presence beside her were a signal, the mist before them began to take on visible form, curdling in the center. It began to glow, azure light growing upward before them, shimmering in the air. The power that had been throbbing around them coalescing there. It began to resonate along Jaimah's body, making her throat ache.

The power centered between the rocks, suspended like a web between the pillars. It flickered, becoming more definite as Jaimah backed away, suddenly frightened.

This shouldn't be here. This was not of the mountain, but was of a small room in the tower. This was something dearer to her than anything had ever been. This was not for Shayna!

There came a swirling within the area of the stone pillars, a melting that was too familiar. Then up from that oval shone a brighter glow, a shaft of flame. The light appeared to drip from the rock of the pillars, until it held her eyes, made her dizzy.

Then words tolled in some deep voice, as if the mountain itself gave tongue.

"What would you?"

"Encheon," Shayna addressed the fire presence, and the very rock seemed to vibrate with the power of that name.

And it was like a dagger through the heart to hear the sound of it on Shayna's tongue. Jaimah closed her eyes to fight back the aching that was suddenly about to overwhelm her. When she opened her eyes, the swirling of fire had grown high overhead. It had the feeling of condescending indulgence, as if it were answering a bothersome child.

"Encheon, I require your services."

A bright flare leaped almost as high as the pillars. Jaimah stared. This was not Encheon as she knew him; this was a being of such power her heart shuddered to see it.

"What is your command?" the voice asked.

Shayna drew a deep breath and stood still for several moments in which Jaimah did not dare to move. "Encheon," she said then, "there is a spell that I am unable to control. The secret of its working eludes me. And I have need of it."

"What is this spell?"

"It is the spell of binding."

There was agitation within the flame, and Jaimah was reminded of the small one that Corwyn had put in her hand. There was a flurry of sparks, a crackling sound, and the light intensified. Jaimah suddenly realized that she was looking at a smaller version of the magical storm that had covered the mountain. A shower of blue and green sparks fell the full length of the fire presence to the ground. There appeared to be no heat in the flames, only blinding light, a quicksilver cobweb of light that sparked, white and green. And Jaimah remembered that veiled center of the storm where the will of Corwyn had been, the feeling of recognition that she couldn't quite place and understood now.

She took a step forward. Corwyn stopped her with a quick glance.

"Whom do you wish to bind?" asked that deep voice.

"Morgus."

The fire pulsed, an angry increase in activity and for long moments the voice did not speak. Jaimah could feel the anger from him, a shuddering of heat that went through her and left her trembling. The wind sang eerily among the pillars, tugging at her fur coat, pressing it against her body. She glanced at Corwyn. He was watching Shayna steadily, without any sign of emotion.

"There are others with you," the voice said.

"They are here because I require them."

"Their presence is forbidden."

"I require their assistance."

The pulse of the fire quickened, then slowed as the brightness of the flames dimmed slightly.

"I have a question," the soulless voice said, the anger that Jaimah could still feel from the flame was strangely missing.

"Ask."

"Why do you want to bind the Master? This is a dangerous thing."

"My reasons are my own. Just know that he is a threat to me, a threat that cannot be allowed to stand, one that I must deal with."

"And these who have come with you?"

"My servant and my apprentice."

There was a brief contemplative surge in light, then the flame seemed to pause for a brief moment. "Apprentice?" A tendril reached out toward Corwyn, slow, almost uncertain. Shayna turned her head to stare at him. Jaimah held her breath. The tendril of flame touched him, then instantly withdrew, a recoiling that was almost like fear. But Jaimah knew it was not fear, but only recognition, because these two had known each other long. It had been Corwyn that had sent Encheon to her from the very first. This she had seen in the globe in Corwyn's room.

"Why are you here?" the flame asked.

"Because Shayna insisted."

The fire wavered, seemed confused. "What is it that you want?"

"I am Shayna's apprentice. What she commands, I do."

"I do not understand."

"I assist Shayna."

"You would do this, assist with this binding spell?"

"Yes, Encheon."

The flame fell quiet for a long time. Jaimah held her breath again, and slipped her hands into the opposite sleeve ends, clasping her arms against the chill that came from inside her as well as out. She could feel the uncertainty in Encheon, and it unsettled her.

Finally, the flame that was Encheon spoke. "Very well, Shayna. I will show you what you want to know."

The answer struck. It went uncomprehended for several heartbeats, for Jaimah had not expected it.

"Corwyn," Jaimah exclaimed, and tears stung her eyes. She stood still then, berating herself for her outburst, and tried not to think that he had betrayed her. The spell would be their death. He had told her that from the very beginning. She had known it would be this way, but had hoped he'd fight against it. Then she recalled his words, *We will go with Shayna to the mountain and give her what she wants, although maybe not quite the way she wants it.*

She looked up at him and found his eyes on her. A shiver went through her for it was not a look of betrayal, but was something else that left her weak.

Shame touched her that she had thought of him so, even briefly; he had asked her to trust him, and she had doubted. And she felt deep shame because of it. Perhaps Corwyn sensed it. He lifted his hand for her, and she went to him.

Shayna had moved forward. Her face shone with triumph, and she said to the fire presence, "Then let us begin."

"You asked, Shayna. Remember this." Those words seemed to have come from the very core of the earth.

Jaimah shuddered at its tone.

Then the flame came forward and engulfed Shayna in a swirling vortex of blue-white light that surged to the sky, illuminating the clouds until the whole causeway was awash in light. Faster and faster the whirlwind spun, until Shayna was just a figure of shadow within its depths, and the power pulsed from the center stronger and stronger until the very stone underfoot throbbed with it.

Jaimah clutched at Corwyn for strength to stand as she stared into that whirlwind. The surging power enfused itself into her, the strength of it tearing at her soul and straining at her heart. The air was alive with electricity; she could feel it crawl along her skin like ghostly fingers. But all else was closed to her. What was being shown to Shayna was not shown to her, and she felt an unaccustomed sense of resentment.

The flame fell back away from Shayna after a time, leaving her face as white as the snow on which she stood. The light died, the flame extinguished with a sudden hiss. No! Jaimah stifled that cry of dismay. He couldn't go without saying something to her. He couldn't. Corwyn's hands tightened around hers, silencing her.

And then something exploded into motion in the center of the pillars. A spinning form, whirling too fast for the eye to follow. The surge of energy nearly knocked her to her knees. This was not flame. This was nothing that Jaimah had ever seen before. The flash seemed to dim her sight. Tears ran down her cheeks as she fought to see.

Violet trails uncoiled and crawled within that web of spinning power, coalescing, then stretching upward, moving into a tangible form. Unbelieving, she watched it slow, so that it finally halted, suspended in air above the stone before Shayna. Jaimah saw that it had the form of a man. He was tall, at least nine feet or more, and shadowed, wrapped in mist as in a shroud, half-incarnated in the half light of star and stone. Shayna stood before him as if made of stone. His eyes rested on her, shadowed and dark.

"Encheon?" Jaimah whispered, unable to believe what she saw. Involuntarily she stretched out her hand toward him.

He turned eyes that became the color of gentle flames in her direction. "Jaimah." His voice was the sound of flame. "Favored One." His eyes seemed to look into her soul and read everything that was there. "You have at last come into your own." He sounded pleased. "It was as I taught you then?"

"Yes, Encheon." And then she could say no more. Emotion made it impossible to speak. Then, fighting the frozen aching in her marrow, Jaimah stepped toward him.

"Come no closer, Beloved One. I am in my full power here on this mountain. To touch me is to find death." His voice was gentle but was that of warning. Crossing his arms upon his breast, he began to spin again. But somehow, as Jaimah watched, his eyes were locked on hers all the time, even as he whirled so fast that the snow began to roil in clouds beneath him.

And fearing that he was going to vanish from her again, Jaimah thrust out desperately with her touch, and meshed with the life of him, pulling herself violently into the vortex of his whirling. It grew in leaps, howling around her and inside of her in sparkling spirals, until it was at last almost unendurable, and she would have to shout or die . . .

"Jaimah," the voice of Encheon said. "I have called you Beloved, and Favored. But I have named you thus for that is what *he* thought of you. All that I taught you, all that was shown to you was at his command. Every word that was spoken to you by my mouth was his. All this that you attribute to me was his. Look not to me for what is not mine to give, for I have nothing. All of it, every moment of it, every nuance of it was his. Turn to him for what you seek, for the ache which is in your heart is his, for I only spoke his words. You will find none of it here. I am steward of this mountain, and obedient servant to him who sent me to you. And this only will I ever be. Do not make more of me than what I am."

It was as if the fiery end of a burning splinter touched to her bare flesh! From it her mind flinched as if she felt the actual pain of a burn. She tore her mind from his, not understanding what he had said, only knowing that he was turning away from her as if she was nothing to him.

She was breathing hard and fast as if she had fled some danger. She turned and stumbled away, avoiding the eyes of Corwyn and Shayna. There was nothing else for her to do. He had clearly turned her away. She forced her feet to move. Each step took her farther from Encheon, and she twisted with the pain of that separation. Too bereft to cry, too stunned to resist, she fell to her knees at the edge of the clearing. Her hands trembled, and from her eyes the tears began to come.

She was wounded as if her soul had been torn from her. She felt she was going to die.

And she could feel him still, so cold, so remote, filled with power that burned to the center of her bones.

"Jaimah?" Someone touched her. It was Shayna, breaking her awesome communion with Encheon.

There was a sharp agony of light flashing between them, like a small fireball. The force jolted between them, knocking Shayna back, sizzling up Jaimah's arm and almost shocking her off her knees. Shayna tottered and grabbed at a large boulder. Shuddering, she stared at Jaimah.

"What happened? What was that?"

Perhaps it was the tone of her voice; perhaps it was the power in the air compelling something within Jaimah. It might have been that she saw that Encheon was truly gone and only darkness was left in the center of the pillars. But she answered directly with the truth.

"It was the life force of Encheon, what of it was left in me. But it is gone now, never to return, just as he is gone never to return. As he told me." Her voice broke and she had to stop.

Shayna's wild expression hardened into disbelief at her answer.

"You've seen him before?" It was an accusation.

Jaimah nodded. "He came to me often in the tower."

Shayna's face contorted with shock and new hatred. "Impossible! He is the power of the mountain. He is found only here at the Peak."

"Not true. He was my friend. The only friend I had. He came to the tower many times."

"Shut up!" Shayna ordered, grabbing Jaimah's arm.

Jaimah felt a flicker of amusement through the shreds of her grief. Shayna was afraid. And she reached out her mind and touched Shayna's to see that it was true. Shayna's eyes widened at that touch, and she stared at Jaimah as if she had never seen her before.

"How long have you been able to do that?" she gasped. Was that an accusation or triumphant recognition?

"Encheon hid the truth of it from us both so that you would not take it from me." Her voice was defiant, and she met Shayna's stare unflinchingly.

The light in Shayna's black eyes was inhuman, and the ring on her hand blazed like a glaring and malevolent star. Her hand lifted as if, in spite of herself, she was about to strike

Jaimah. Instead, she diverted its direction and reclaimed possession of Jaimah's arm. She was pale now and in complete control.

She dragged Jaimah to her feet. "Stand up."

"Let her be, Shayna!" That was Corwyn.

Shayna turned to face him, her hand pulling Jaimah closer. "Let her go."

"You overstep your bounds, apprentice."

"Perhaps."

"Take care, then."

Corwyn's eyes swung to Jaimah. "Come here."

"No!" Shayna's hand tightened on Jaimah's arm.

Corwyn became very still, and Jaimah, seeing it, also became still. On his face was the arrogance and authority that had been there from the beginning, but this time it was for Shayna to see. His eyes were dark and smoldering, his stance unyielding. And in her mind's eye she saw him superimposed over the memory of Encheon, standing in her room at the tower, speaking to her when Echeon spoke, saying the words that Encheon had said, comforting her as Encheon had done. Stunned, she began to see what the mountain spirit had wanted her to see. He had only been the messenger for the care and concern of Corwyn. And her anguish over Encheon fled, melting frost in the warming sun, to be replaced by awe and wonder at what Corwyn had done for her.

His eyes flickered to her. And there was that in his brief glance that stole the strength from her and set her trembling. Was she so open to him? Did he know everything that ever went on inside her? Was he that fine-tuned to her? She trembled at that possibility.

Then she heard at last his voice, "I said, let her go."

Shayna replied with a shouted sentence that made Jaimah wince. Her words, incomprehensible to Jaimah, were taken up by the wind, aided by the ring on Shayna's finger held high over head, echoed from the sides of the pillars and reechoed down into the vast void beyond the causeway.

Suddenly, from all around came the sound of incredibly loud thunder, and a sudden wind whipped up over the edge of the out-thrust. Thunder rattled behind the black clouds, rolling with gathering speed behind the force of the sudden gale that was blowing up in increasing ferocity. Jaimah gasped for air in that sudden tempest, only to have it torn from her. She staggered in its force and came up against the stone behind her.

She was stunned at this power coming from Shayna without her herbs. But there had been the words and the ring. And she heard Shayna call again.

Pulling away, she wrenched her arm out of Shayna's grasp and cowered by the rock but was unable to hide her face away from what was happening.

The first flakes of snow began to whip against the rock, striking her in the face. A crack of thunder made the pillars bow and sway threateningly at the end of the causeway. Lightning flared above them; thunder snapped the air apart in a tremendous crashing. And through it all, Corwyn stood unmoved.

Then he raised his hand with a half-dismissing wave.

A web of white lightning flickered over the surface of the three pillars, running the full length from their bases to their tops and flamed out from the rocks to the sky. It split the clouds so that there was a large rent overhead and the stars and moon shone through. Another vivid bolt of lightning split the sky, just above the pinnacles. A tremor in the rock under them began to echo the thud of the thunderbolts. The power he used was deeper, stronger, seeming to come from the very roots of the earth.

Jaimah struggled up to her feet and looked at Shayna. Her head was thrown back now, her hands raised high. The whole causeway was enveloped in reddish murk and fitful with lightning. Thunder rattled at the pillars again. It was like a horrible dream come true. Somehow it had to be stopped—somehow she had to stop it!

She thrust out with her mind toward Shayna, not sure what she could do. She thought to compel Shayna to turn away and desist.

Her mind entered into Shayna's with uncertainty, and the Lady was instantly aware of her.

"No!" Shayna turned to her in outrage. She darted forward and grabbed Jaimah, with the ring blazing into a hot blue light. Jaimah pulled back in panic. "Stand, girl!" Her hand raised to strike.

"Shayna." Corwyn's voice was frozen steel.

Shayna stopped. Her head went up; her eyes no longer strove to cower Jaimah.

Jaimah looked to Corwyn, longed to run to him and feel safe in his arms. It was thundering again. But this thunder was different. This thunder sounded to come from the bowels of the mountain. Shayna became very still. Her attitude was one of listening, and Jaimah knew that this thunder was not of her doing. This new gathering storm was of Corwyn.

"What . . ." Shayna broke off, then looked confused and a little frightened. At that moment Jaimah realized that Shayna hadn't seen the lightning that Corwyn had caused to lace up the pillars and stab to the sky. She had been so wrapped in the power of her ring that she had been completely unaware of what Corwyn had done. She only now realized that something untoward was happening.

The thunder rolled again, causing the ground to shake underneath them. Rocks broke from the distant cliffs and tumbled down in loud crashes to the slopes below.

Shayna turned to Jaimah and spoke in a frightened voice. "Let me draw upon your powers, Jaimah."

Jaimah stared at her. Ice seemed to form around her heart. Her mouth was desert in the instant. It was a request that even in her wildest imaginings Jaimah hadn't expected to hear from Shayna's lips. All these years Shayna had thought that she had nothing and was worthless. But now . . . Shayna pushed forward, searching with eager eyes. And there was that in those eyes which made Jaimah recoil.

"Quickly, Jaimah, or else we will die here this night. Why do you hesitate?" she whispered anxiously. "We must stop him now, before he can bring his power to bear." She grabbed Jaimah's wrist in a painful grasp. "Stand with me, girl. We will defeat him together."

Her words were like splinters of ice tearing into Jaimah's flesh. And she did not doubt that Shayna would use her in the next moment whether she agreed or not. Her entire life with Shayna spun before her eyes. This woman had raised her, had almost been a mother . . .

It was an effort to wrench her eyes from that contact.

Along the arch of the sky flashed a jagged sword of purple lightning. Shayna turned to face Corwyn in panic.

It was then that Jaimah caught a trace of something, like a faint scent on the wind. She turned, frowning, to quest after it. It had been there only a moment, but it raised the hair on the back of her neck; then it was gone, as if she had only imagined it.

"Whatever powers you may have hidden from me," Shayna was saying to Corwyn, "will not prevail against my ring. This paltry show of lights will do you no good." There was fear behind her words. Jaimah could feel it like an illness from her. It was a fear born of horror at Corwyn's strength, a fear that Shayna obviously was fighting to control. Jaimah watched for only a moment.

The scent came again—not an odor but a pulling on her mind, compelling and impossible to ignore, though she tried to push it away.

Shayna was saying something to her, but she did not hear it. The compelling pull from the mountain behind her grew quickly to become constant, an insistance call, striving to force her to return back along that pillar-edged causeway. She looked into the darkness, where the mountain rose to the sky.

It was as if she could see a shadow drifting down the slope toward her, but that sight came not through her eyes but from that other sense. The pull was a screaming ache in her, and she felt sweat start out on her forehead. Unknowingly she moved a few paces toward it.

Then she was aware of Corwyn. She turned to look back at him, her attention half divided between him and the pulling. Someone had called her name, but somehow she knew it hadn't been Corwyn. She could feel his stare laid across her face, like a cold hand in the night.

He knew. And he was letting her go.

There came a trace of thought! Jaimah turned back to the mountain and poured all her strength into touching that shadow, wrapping about it, finding its source.

She fled over the ice-covered rock, sliding and leaping, blind and deaf. Lightning and thunder cracked around her. The wind rose, battering at her. Great drops of rain spatted down. She fled over the causeway, back the way they had come, her eyes blind and mind numb to everything but that pulling and the dark shadow somewhere out in the night.

It was hard to catch her breath in that fierce, unslaking rush of air and rain. After a time she turned aside to shelter in a small recess cut into the stone.

Then lightning came almost continuously, and an odd, sharp thunder cracked like breaking boulders directly overhead and was immediately silenced, short, sharp, and ominous in its abruptness.

Chapter Twenty-two

JAIMAH WAITED IN THE SILENCE.

Loose rocks rattled a short distance away, and Jaimah turned to face the sound and thought she saw a silent form moving away in the darkness.

Then came a stirring, a quiet rythmic sound from somewhere ahead of her—a dragging, scraping sound that slowly grew louder and at last she realized it was coming closer.

"Who is it!" she cried aloud, straining to look forward through the night, panic touching her, settling in her stomach. Her voice echoed off the spires and back again, and she scrambled to her feet, terrified to stay where she was, terrified not to.

The sound stopped. There was silence. She went to the spire of rock, put her hand on it, nerving herself to go beyond. But she could not. She waited, shivering.

She felt a presence come toward her and sit down facing her. "Go away!" she rebuked it softly. It settled, there to stay.

And from across the flat appeared another presence, a black shadow that she could only feel.

Then there was a loud clap of thunder behind her out on the end of the causeway. Shayna! She looked over her shoulder for just a moment, for with that thunder she felt a presence brush against her face, a mental flutter that at once took hold of her and yanked.

For an instant she fought against it. But then she was being drawn forward. Then came a touch on the back of her hand, so light and fleeting she was not even sure she had really felt it. There was a movement beside her, a shuffling through the snow. Again there was a touch on her hand, but this time it lingered. Jaimah made no attempt to grasp, though she tried to read through that contact. She met a void that startled her. The touch left, and the shuffling seemed to veer away, leaving her alone.

Lightning burned the images of four Watchers out of the darkness. It had been Watchers who had been walking beside her. Now they followed alongside, but at a distance.

Lightning flashed again showing an open area of flat unmarred snow, and across that space stood a cluster of large boulders. It was here where the compelling took her.

The Watchers dropped behind, as if this place was one they dared not enter. They drew behind her as she faced that cluster of stones. She could tell they had amassed between her and her exit. Forward she went, slower and slower still. Lightning flashed over head again and again, giving her a stark, sharp-edged vision of what lay before her.

The Watchers had not left her. Turning, she saw the beasts at the edge of her vision. From those Watchers she believed she picked up an answering sensation of uncertainty. They were not looking at her, but at the rocks behind her. She stared, frightened by a presence that was at once one of the Watchers and yet was something far different. This was far older, and far stronger. She waited breathlessly, fearfully.

Then she tensed, for from between a snow shrouded rock and that next to it, moved a heavy figure. A great Watcher pushed into the open. Its head swung about deliberately, then paused as it looked in her direction. Jaimah stepped back, bravado deserting her in the face of such a manifestation. She was horribly aware of its cold, impassive scrutiny. It was still too deeply immersed in shadow for any feature to be clearly visible. Yet she could tell that there was sinuous strength to him, a sheathed intimation of very great power.

She stood absolutely motionless under the animal's cool, almost amused regard; there seemed to be a human intelligence behind those black eyes. A magnificent male he was, with thick, shaggy fur brindled in bars of gray and white, and Jaimah estimated uneasily that he would stand over ten feet tall on his hind legs.

There was no hatred in his look, only a cold, merciless

will. Hate she could have understood; what she saw was worse. She could feel the threat behind that mind as if a whip had been snapped in her direction and flaked a scrap of skin from her cheek. And the pull from him was unmistakable, imperative, terrifying. Looming in night shadow, he reached out for her, his eyes, unnaturally distinct, boring into hers.

Then somehow her hand was touching his fur, sinking into its warm depths. His mind reached into hers, a shaft of strength that pierced into the center of her.

"No—" Her voice, broke out in an involuntary protest. But now—she was linked with the Watcher, was one with him and could not extricate herself. She felt a bubbling in her blood; her face was hot and tight in spite of the chill in the air blowing against it; she was breathing fast. Everything about her expanded. She heard, smelled, tasted the air far more intensely, read the shifts of the wind as if she had always known them, and most of all saw with dreamlike clarity everything about her, saw the night as if it was a fine black-and-white etching, detailed to the smallest particle.

There was movement behind her. The Watchers were now moving in again, as if they were no longer reluctant to come forward. The large Watcher came around her and trotted silently across the flat of snow to the pack. He turned and waited for her. So strong was his compelling that Jaimah found herself pushing away from the rock, getting to her feet, and running, matching her stride to his. And when they came to a slope she did not remember climbing earlier she began to work her way along the crest, hunting for a path down.

She slid from the rock as the Watchers bounded down to the causeway. Shayna was out there, threatening the mountain's existence. And the Watchers could not let her go on. She must be stopped.

But when Jaimah reached the bottom of the slope and would have gone on, the large Watcher slipped in between her and the rocks of the causeway, snarling. She did not understand and moved to go around him. The beast pushed against her knees making her stumble backward. Then she knew. The time was not yet. They had to wait.

She settled to her heels beside him, and he sank to a waiting crouch. Leaning against his shoulder, her head bent to his, Jaimah squinted to see through the thin strands of mist that hung among the numerous pillars of the causeway. And she waited with him as the other Watchers milled about them in restless impatience.

There were only a few snowflakes drifting down from the clouds. The light, through which Jaimah could see with the clarity of the beast beside her, grew red for a moment, like that from a fire. Shayna was working her ring. Was she using it against Corwyn? Jaimah wondered.

She looked at the horizon. The clouds stretched unbroken as far as she could see. Strands of mist were hanging among the stones and pillars and crawling over the edge of the causeway, to fall in tattered curtains to the depths below. Absentmindedly, she scooped up snow and drew with it, a slow trickling from her hand. She didn't even feel the cold of it on her fingers, nor the ice in the air.

For a moment she battled the control the beast had over her, but to no avail. There would be no retreat. He was too strong for her.

Suddenly a light came in the sky, and there was a noise of thunder. She rose to her feet, urged on by the beast as he sprang forward. She rushed quickly through the snow, hearing the scrape of claw and the whoosh of mighty breathing. She raced down the causeway right to the edge of the clearing and she would have plunged into its openness to face Shayna before the three towering pillars save that the beast had stopped in front of her and would not move and she had no room to push past his bulk. The Watcher snarled, bared fangs, so she remained where she was.

Lowering herself beside the animal, she peered around the small pillar into the clearing. She thought she could dimly guess a cloaked shape in the mist in the center of the clearing. The animal sense that coursed through her told her that this was Shayna. The size, even though hidden by the concealing furs, was too slight to be Corwyn. The mist parted enough for her to see Corwyn a short distance from Shayna looking at her with an expressionless face. And although her hearing had been accentuated by the beast, she still had to strain to hear what Shayna was saying.

"You have deceived me, Corwyn. You led me to believe you wanted my guidance. You came into my tower under false pretenses. You misled me, asked me to teach you, and all along you were hiding from me the truth about your abilities. And I wonder to myself, why has he come to me if his powers are so great? And I think—perhaps he is out to destroy me and my tower.

"You will not succeed. It is mine and I will not give it up. I have the right and I have Encheon and I am yet able to destroy you. I can and I will destroy you."

Corwyn remained silent all through her speech, but his dark blue eyes had never left her black ones.

"And you could be mistaken," he said.

His tone was so alien to anything Jaimah had ever heard she felt her heart constrict with unease. The voice had sounded barely human.

"Do you think you can take the tower away from me?" Shayna asked that question savagely, as if she would eliminate him with just her words.

"Actually, yes, if you put it that way." There was mockery in Corwyn's tone. His gaze crossed hers, steel cold. "Are you going to fight me over it, Shayna?"

"I could kill you, apprentice," Shayna grated.

He smiled again, but not with his eyes. "Then try, but I'll tell you now, you will fail."

Some inflection in his voice made Jaimah's blood run cold. But she could feel that Shayna had not heard that menacing slant to his voice.

"And if you test it . . ." He let his voice trail off meaningfully.

His voice was quiet, and yet Shayna had understood the intent of his words, even if she had not caught that undercurrent, for a shadow of fear passed through her. But she did not flinch.

"You think you've got the skill to stop me?" Shayna's question was a challenge.

"Of course."

Jaimah saw naked fear wipe Shayna's face clear of triumph, and Jaimah watched her get herself under control. A malevolent sneer replaced surprise at his assertion. Did she think his defiance was empty? After what she had seen him do while they sat under a rock on the mountain, Jaimah did not doubt he could do anything that he said he could. She shifted uneasily against the rock she leaned against, raised a hand to bury her fingers in the thick pelt of the Watcher beside her.

"So!" The wariness had gone from Shayna's voice. "Show me. I'd like to see just how good you are. I'd like to see how you would handle a spell with words. Perhaps you could create a drawing spell. Bring that servant girl back here. Or call *me* to you. This I would like to see." She made of that challenge the whistle of a whiplash. Jaimah winced against the animal.

Corwyn's eyes flashed dangerously. "Would you indeed, Lady?" he asked. "Then I shall oblige you."

Shayna, her face changing rapidly from surprise to triumph, turned to face him squarely.

An odd shadow flickered across his face, one that made Jaimah shudder. It was strangely mischievous, as if he were about to turn things on Shayna. She watched him with an uneasy foreboding as he straightened up and seemed suddenly to grow taller.

Throwing back his coat, he began to chant. His words were soft and unintelligible. But Jaimah could take no clue from that. Shayna's own chanting was often incomprehensible, so she was unable to guess what it was that he was going to do. It sounded very much the same as Shayna's had sounded in all those years of weaving spells.

But in its way, Corwyn's chanting wove a spell far different from Shayna's, for it began to change thought images and to evoke another kind of response. Jaimah realized it for what it was and what it could do. Already it was beginning to work upon her. She covered her ears with her hands to shut out that sultry heat which seeped from words in the air to the racing blood in her body.

The sounds set up a vibration that ran down the bones behind her ear to her spine. The noise rang through her skull, despite her defending hands. It was all she could do to keep from jumping up and running to him to be encompassed by his arms and his embrace. Against the mental and physical strength of him, she felt like a bird crashing itself in a gale against the granite hardness of a rock. It was only the hold the Watcher had on her that kept her still.

And she had once believed that he needed pollen to draw her to him? She almost laughed at the absurdity.

She saw Shayna take a step nearer to him, and then another and another until she almost touched him. Suddenly Shayna pulled away, looking into his face wildly, terror growing in her.

"Stop!" she cried. "Don't do this to me . . ."

Corwyn fell silent and smiled, and the tingling in the air began to ebb.

"What was that?" She gasped angrily.

"A drawing spell."

"That was no drawing spell!"

"Certainly it was." He smiled again. "Could you not feel its drawing power?"

She stared at him, alive with hate and rising panic. But then she snapped out of her trance in an instant and was all command.

"Insufferable." Her voice was a whisper. "You take too much upon yourself, apprentice. Do not forget that I now have the spell of binding. I could bind you to me with no effort at all."

"Yes, I know." Corwyn said. "But wasn't that part of the purpose of coming here? To use my talents for yourself?"

Suddenly, without knowing it, Jaimah was rising to her feet, the strength of pent-up fury filling her mind and body, the will of the beast sending her forward. He drew aside to let her pass, and power pulsed from him through her. The world about her seemed to turn crimson. She arose to her full height, moving away from the rock behind which she had taken cover and stepped out into the mist. She did not even look at Corwyn, her eyes—the beast's eyes—were on Shayna.

Shayna turned to see her and smiled angrily. "So you did draw her." She threw Corwyn a malevolent glare and moved into Jaimah's path.

Close upon Jaimah's heels came the Watchers. They all converged in a loose semicircle around her. Shayna stopped and eyed them warily. The large one sat next to Jaimah. He wrinkled an upper lip; but if he meant a warning, it was a soundless one.

Shayna looked at the beasts uneasily. Then she faced Jaimah. "So you came back. You surprise me," she said tersely.

"Why, Shayna?" Jaimah found herself asking. "You forget who I am and what I am. I may surprise you still." It was the beast's anger that gave her voice, though it was she who felt the truth of what she was saying.

But, to her consternation, Shayna laughed. "You cannot change the way you are, girl. A worthless dolt with no spine. You are only here in answer to Corwyn's very interesting summoning. As I suppose are even these creatures."

"These have not—" Jaimah got out no more than those words when Shayna interupted her.

"Stay out of this, Jaimah. It is not your concern."

"I cannot stay out of it, Shayna." Her hand, of its own will, dropped to fondle the ears of the beast. "We have come to stop you."

"We?" Shayna stared at her with scorn.

"I believe that she is speaking for the beasts," Corwyn said from where he stood. "It was they who brought her here, not I."

Jaimah remained where she was, watching Shayna. The control of the Watcher was on her and she could not turn her head, but she knew that Corwyn was as aware of her as she of him. Enough of his spell still hung in her blood to make her heart race at the nearness of him. There was a heady excitement in this centering upon him.

A swift mind touch came then from him, although she knew his eyes never wavered from Shayna's face.

"What are you talking about?" Shayna demanded.

"It is the nature of her skill, to be able to mold with the life of what's around her and take that power and augment it. Although, in this case, it seems to be the beast who has taken her power to himself."

"What nonsense!"

She looked speculatively at Jaimah for a moment. Then she approached her, holding out her hand. The Watchers stirred with agitation, but Shayna did not look to them.

"Jaimah. You can see how this is. If you do hold somewhat of power, I will need your strength to fight him."

"I can do nothing to help you."

Shayna shook her head. "We both know that is not true. If what he says is true, then within you resides power. Do not keep it buried from me. It is the only way! But it must be quick."

Jaimah was at last able to turn her head to look at Corwyn. There was a glitter in his eyes which warned her.

"I will not help you, Shayna," she said, unable to take her eyes off of Corwyn. "Not ever."

There was silence from Shayna for a long space. Then she said in a low voice. "Girl, it seems that I have been right about you all along. I had hoped that I was wrong. You are a spineless little—"

The cold menace in those words brought no fear, but a growing anger to Jaimah. And to her surprise she heard herself interrupt the Lady. "No, Shayna. You have always under-rated me. And now it's too late."

"Too late?" Shayna asked, mouth twisted in sarcasm. "Too late for what?"

But Jaimah was not to hear her words, for ringing into her mind came a challenge, so clear and sharp that she reeled and saw that even Shayna had caught that mental assault. Jaimah felt from her a weak panic, a fear which seemed to wipe away all the Lady's strength. And Jaimah stood trembling, for there was nothing she could do.

"Now, we destroy her." The words from the beast was hardly more than a whisper in her mind. But the force of the emotion behind it shook her, as well as Shayna.

"Jaimah, what is this you do?" Shayna cried, frightened.

But it was not Jaimah's doing, and she could not stop it.

She was suddenly rocked back by a wave of rage; the thought strength of the Watcher was gathering to blast Shayna. "No," Jaimah cried, but she did not know if she cried it aloud. What answered her then was no mind words, rather a blast of uncontrolled fury. She swayed under that mental blow, but she did not fall.

Always, she had known anger as a hot and burning thing, the way Shayna's flared and died and flared again. But the wave of emotion which washed from the Watcher to her now was cold and deadly. Jaimah's whole body quivered with it. And there flowed into her mind such power as she would not have believed she could hold—nor did she try to contain it. Instead she was forced to direct it outward.

"Shayna—" she whispered and raised her hand. Of their own accord, her fingers moved in the air, as if gathering threads of mist and rolling them into a ball. She made a tossing motion, as if what she had pulled out of invisibility had indeed been substance. Shayna, startled into movement, shrank back against the stone of the pillar. And her hand raised to meet that invisible assault, the ring on her finger flaring into a white-hot blue.

In the netherparts of her mind, Jaimah knew what that meant, and she struck back, her new-found strength centering upon the countenance of Shayna.

In and in Jaimah aimed her power, that power that was of her and the Watcher, boring deep to reach the soul behind the eyes. The power went deeper and deeper to the very source of life that was Shayna.

"No!" Jaimah cried when she saw what was to happen. "Stop it." She flung both hands up before her face, palms out, hands crossed, fingers spread. But it didn't stop. And she could only change the direction of the attack.

Bright yellow sparks seemed to fly from her fingers and reach out before her, narrowly missing Shayna and centering upon the tallest pillar. She could see through the Watcher's eyes that the stone of the causeway blazed in the light. Lightning tore from the ground to the sky. Thunder followed immediately, a deafening crack that shocked the senses. Over the thunder's noise came a deep rumble that rose to a screaming roar. Above their heads, the central pillar glowed briefly red, then blinding white, then it burst apart in an explosion that shook the causeway to its very roots. Huge chunks of pillar crashed to the ground, thudding against each other with bone-jarring force. Loose rubble rattled and bounced to a stop while sand rained through dust-laden air.

The power finally ebbed, but it had been too great a burden on Jaimah's mind. She slipped into unconsciousness, and time passed. Finally consciousness returned. She found herself pressed against and supported by the Watcher. The beast was rumbling softly. Slowly she became aware that something— some spell—was in progress. Then raw fear washed over her as she realized what it was. Shayna had begun the spell for the binding of Corwyn!

Even yet Shayna was still going on with her obsession. And Jaimah found that she was held from acting by the beast's will on her. She had thwarted him in the destruction of Shayna; now he would prevent her from helping Corwyn.

Through the senses of the Watcher, Jaimah saw that there was a light as of a fire, but there was no fire. Neither was there any chanting. Shayna had learned to do it without chanting. Encheon had taught her. She looked to Shayna in sudden fear. She was doing it without herbs, without words, and this time she could succeed.

Suddenly the ridge shook underneath them. It groaned and settled, heaved again, and in the dim gray of the dawn that had just begun to show in the distance, Jaimah saw the spires of the causeway shudder, a slow leaning to the left and then to the right. A howl came from the rock underneath them, like some huge animal. The Watchers began milling uncertainly around the clutter of rubble from the pillar. Jaimah could feel their agitation growing to a dangerous pitch.

"Something's wrong!" Shayna cried. Jaimah saw the look

on Shayna's face—such fear as she never thought ever to see there before this day.

The shaking began again, rippling, wrenching, threatening to break up the ridge and throw them into the depths of the gulf below them. Jaimah knelt where she was, wanting to run, but remaining because there was the Watcher. The howling went on and on, the stone and rock of the world screaming against each other, straining with stresses that threatened to tear them apart.

Shayna fumbled in her furs, brought out a small box, and held it up in the palm of her hand. "What is this, Corwyn?" she cried. "Your potion! What is it? Can it help me?" She reached up to open the box.

"Be warned, Lady. You don't know what you're doing!"

Shayna laughed. The Watchers suddenly were growling dangerously and were surging toward her.

She opened the box and a pulsing light sprang from it, and fell on Corwyn. Light bathed him, white, growing until it blazed blue-white. The sound of a rushing wind came, but there was no stir of air around them. The earth shook, groaned, and settled. The Watcher tore himself out of Jaimah's grasp and leaped forward. Light seemed to erupt in a second, lesser flash before the scene was plunged into stunning darkness as the Watcher slammed down Jaimah's sight of what happened next.

But the darkness was laced with an emotion close to hysteria.

Jaimah's sight returned in time to see Shayna flee from the pillars. She looked to the Watcher, but abruptly the beast turned away. With that movement, an invisible but tangible barrier seemed to descend between them. The flood of power that had taken her over totally was gone, leaving her empty and without support. The Watcher bounded after Shayna, a silver streak, weaving a path back among the spires and arches of the causeway where the Lady had already vanished.

Jaimah rose unsteadily to her feet, very aware of the loss of mental pressure from the animal. She stepped up to the ice-covered stone and looked, scanning the desolate expanse of snow and rock, toward the openness and the pillars. There was something wrong, a gap in the silhouette, a vacancy where a pillar had stood. Vaguely she remembered it exploding.

She stumbled back against a large block of rubble, weakness in her legs, her arms hanging heavily by her sides; she had neither the will nor the strength now to raise them. With her back against the rough stone she began to slip downward, the ruins rising around her like a protective shield. A wave of nauseous darkness rose, ebbed, and rose again, stronger this time; she felt her legs giving way.

She sank forward, feeling the drift of the snow over her. She was so tired, so very tired.

Then Corwyn was beside her, unbound and unharmed. Hands caught and held her; muscular arms gathered her near, and a soft voice spoke her name in triumph.

Jaimah could only repeat his name in a witless fashion, letting him take the weight of her worn-out and aching body.

"Corwyn! Corwyn!"

"It's all right." He held her steady, letting the very fact that he was there seep into her mind.

She was trembling uncontrollably now, and he took her face between his hands, speaking with quiet urgency, his voice low. The words she could not understand. She felt his mind in hers like a caress pouring strength into her.

"Jaimah," he said. "Can you stand?"

She looked at him in incomprehension. She was too tired to move. Why should she stand?

"Shayna has gone back to the tower. We must follow her."

It took a moment for that to sink in. Then she caught his urgency, and it drove her wavering to her feet. She staggered and came against the stone. She pushed away and limped a few steps, sweat beading her forehead, teeth clamped on her lower lip.

"Lean on me." Corwyn slid his arm around her waist.

She clutched at the strong arms that held her.

"Why did you let the Watcher use me like that?" she managed to ask, for she did not doubt that he could have stopped it.

"The beasts are their own masters, as I have told you."

"But they obey you. I've seen it."

"Yes. At times they will give a grudging obedience. But mostly they do what they will." Then he said, "Shayna had to be shown that there were other powers that she had no knowledge of and could not fight against."

She was about to ask why it must be shown and why it was his to show her these things. But then she became aware that somewhere, far away she thought, someone was running, footsteps scrabbling and stumbling as someone fled.

In the silence that followed this, Jaimah became conscious of the ring of Watchers surrounding them. They just sat there on their haunches, watching and waiting.

Waiting for her, she sensed.

Jaimah regarded them in puzzlement, not knowing what they were waiting for. She glanced at Corwyn, who nodded encouragement. Then she knew. Turning back to the beasts she sent her mind out to them.

Chapter Twenty-three

BEAST MIND, BEAST SENSE WARNED AND HUNTED.

Shayna inhaled the cold air and staggered as she came down the steep slope, slipping and regaining her feet with a struggle. When she reached the bottom she rested, leaning against a boulder as she settled to the cold snow and let fatigue flow from her joints. She drew her hand across the cold of her cheek to warm it with her palm.

It was madness, she thought, shuddering in the memory of the attack of the Watcher beasts. Never had she known them to attack, not in all the long years of her coming to the mountain.

And Corwyn had been able to stop them. This was a thing that chilled her blood. She shook, and it was from anger as much as from fear. She had run . . . from the beasts, from Corwyn. There was no choice. The ferocity in the attack upon her had been like nothing she had ever felt before, murderous, hateful, all-consuming, a vengeance for what had happened to Corwyn. And she could feel it even now, coming from the mountain that had never before denied her anything.

They had stopped at Corwyn's word.

They had stopped dead at his command and retreated in total, complete, instant obedience.

And when he turned to look at her, his eyes leveling on her, she ran, a panic on her that she had never felt before.

She gathered herself and began walking again, staggering

in the strong wind that kicked up suddenly, stirring the snow into a ground storm. She blinked in the cloud that swirled around her and saw that it did not settle when the wind did, but hung shimmering in the early dawn. The gust of wind came again, stronger this time, and became a steady blowing that picked up the snow from the ground in a boiling and swirling that obscured the trail. But that did not hinder her. She knew this trail better than any other.

She pulled the hood lower over her face and trudged forward. She felt exposed in what she had seen Corwyn do, felt acutely her lack of skill. She could not have done what she had seen him do, move in that imprisoning light that should have been the death of him. She could tell that much from the light that had fallen on him. Had it fallen on her, it would have been her death.

Shayna! he had said, his voice sounding weirdly through the light, pulling her attention from Jaimah, who was cringing beside that monstrous beast amongst the ruins of the pillar, and the spell of binding that she was aiming at her.

Startled by Corwyn's tone, she looked at him—and saw the iron hardness in his dark blue eyes. He had no need to harm her physically. He could destroy her sanity with a flick of his fingers if he chose to, and they both knew it. She struggled with her panic, knowing she was defeated, but striving not to show weakness.

The Watchers descended on her in that moment.

She screamed in terror at the vicious hatred that had assaulted her.

Corwyn reached out, gathered the imprisoning light into his hand and flung it away, spinning. A second bolt followed, from his left hand.

He stood free.

Shayna panicked in the murderous emotions that flooded over her. A new presence added itself in a thunderous onslaught of anger. Encheon, who had never before been her enemy.

She saw Corwyn standing untouched by the attack and terror seized her, unreasonable and insane, and she threw the power of the ring at him.

Corwyn held up his hand, easily received the bolt, sweeping it effortlessly from the air. Shayna blinked, dismayed at the skill of him.

But that had not frightened her half so much as hearing him command the beasts and Encheon to stop and then seeing him obeyed.

It was that, she thought, which sent her running, disgracefully, but desperately for the tower and the things of power that she had left there. He would follow her, of that she was certain. He had been found out, and he knew it; perhaps he had even planned it. Perhaps not . . . But now a confrontation between them was inevitable. If he did not come to her, she would hunt him down, relentlessly until she had him.

The great rift in the world came into view when the wind abated a brief moment, the only other place on the mountain than at the Peak where it could be seen. She looked away into that hazy depth where snow trailed off in streamers over the edge. She lost her sense of height and depth in that brief moment, but the wind picked up again and veiled the view with a skirl of ice crystals.

She kept moving, her stomach knotting in hunger, remembering now that in her haste to reach the Peak she had forgotten about food. The ache in her side became a constant throbbing.

Hunt!

She felt it and looked up expecting to see a dark figure in the hazing mists. There was none, neither man nor beast.

Yet the hunt feeling was there.

She put it down. It was a thing that she did not care for, a feeling out with the senses, a hindrance to clear thinking. She put it away, slammed her mind against it, and did not let it touch her again.

She scanned those horizons she could see. There was nothing. It had been illusion, then.

She took the way that was so familiar to her that even in the storm she could find it. She was footsore but pushed herself relentlessly. Time was precious—life to her now because she was afraid that she was about to run out of it. A prickling at the nape of her neck pushed her faster, the suspicion of enemies behind.

A brief surge of strength came to her. She grasped it thankfully, not questioning its source, only knowing that it would get her closer to the tower and the herbs she had left there.

It had been foolishness to attempt what she did not yet

understand. She should never have left her powders and potions behind. She should have known that she would never be able to face Corwyn without them. Not yet.

She walked steadily and did not falter, even when the brief surge of strength left her and exhaustion took over. She stopped when she could go no farther and curled up in a sheltered recess until she could regain her strength. Inadvertently, she slept.

She came awake with a jolt.

At that moment there sounded, through the afternoon, a call that brought her to her feet. Only once before had she heard such a sound. And that had been when she was climbing the path to the Peak with Corwyn and Jaimah. The beasts! She had thought she had outrun them. For a long while after she had fled the causeway they had kept doggedly on her trail. Then they seemed to have vanished into the mountain, fading away like phantom shadows into the wintry reaches of the cliffs and ravines.

That unearthly sound, echoing back and forth between the peaks, inspired new panic in her. She ran, mindless of the snow she floundered through, heedless of anything except the sense of the hunt that was behind her. Then she stumbled out on firm ground, the tenseness of her body leading to pain in her back and shoulders, a warning tremble in her legs.

Her head jerked around. There was a sound behind. The beasts might have been questing before, but at last they had the trail. Like Jaimah, she could sense the rage and malice that drove them. She shivered. Never before had emotions other than her own been fed to her in this way. The alienness of this was frightening. And she could not stop it from reaching out to her and seeping into her like the cold.

But there was no time to hesitate. She must reach the tower.

She pinched her lips together, her mind closing in on itself like fingers into a fist. Onward she pressed.

Eventually she had to rest. She sank down to a rock against a cliff wall, her arms clutched about her, her head back against the wall . . . she leaped up again, spying a white movement among the rocks on the opposite ridge.

She turned and stopped, shock-still, staring at the motionless pack. There were at least ten—or more—between her and the trail. Their black eyes glittered in the hazy afternoon light that came through a thin layer of clouds.

She whirled, face-to-face with a creature, and cried out.

It wasn't only the size that told her this was the creature that had been with Jaimah. There was a menacing air about him that was rooted in a hate-filled intelligence that struck terror into her. She found herself captured by the beast's black eyes. His will beat on her, forcing her back against the cliff wall. Her world spiraled down to his eyes, black, glittering, malevolent. She felt the heat of fire surge through her, strong enough to snuff her life out.

Her hand moved involuntarily over a stone; the biting cold of the snow and ice was painful and shocking. Desperately her fingers grasped the rock and pulled it free of the cliff wall. The creature saw her intentions on her face and in that same instant she saw his.

She bolted, ducking just beneath the sweep of his paw. With unbelievable reflexes, he reached out and caught her a blow, just above the ankle.

She stumbled, almost fell. But she caught herself and turned on him again. Her hand raised to strike him with the large rock if he came near.

For long, terrible minutes they stared at each other. Hate radiated from the beast so strongly Shayna felt she was being battered by it.

Then, incredibly, the beast stepped backward, clearing the trail in a single move.

Shayna eyed him uncertainly. He just stood there looking at her. The others sat motionless on their haunches, watching and waiting.

She dropped the rock and her other hand went to her ring. But it was not the moment to risk her life with the beasts—far from it; she began to walk slowly, cautiously through them. They let her go. When she looked back, they were no longer there. But still, she could only walk away slowly, her body unable to respond to her panic reaction.

When she was finally able to break away and flee to the next ravine, she was near hysteria. She held her trembling hands up where she could see them. The ring on her finger gleamed in the pale light, her power and her burden. There was a taste in her mouth like ashes of grief.

She sped from the mountain toward the tower, her mind seething with frustration.

So close! So close! How could she have come so close and yet fail? All the preparations, the arduous years, flew by her in a brilliant flash. And it was then, for the first time, that she truly understood just how bad things had become for her. She felt mortified, hating herself for having had to admit her own failing.

She wished desperately that she had not been so rash in the use of her ring so many long years ago. Had she applied herself with more zeal to the studies that Naibus had given her, she would know what was likely to happen now.

The wind shifted, and the light, muted as it had been, began to wane in the approach of evening. Shayna tucked her furs in around herself and hurried ahead.

It had become imperative to know things that were beyond her. Her survival depended on it, and she almost ran with the desperateness of it. Hate followed her heels, hate for Corwyn, hate for Morgus, and hate for herself. Then she was running, no longer able to hold herself back.

She hesitated at a turn, for she had not been watching and suddenly found herself staring at the dark shadow of the tower a distance away. The wind was letting up and she could see farther than she had been able to up until now. Finally, after staring for a long moment, she began to stalk toward the tower.

Climbing the stairs, she entered the rooms that had once been her own, but were now fire-gutted and ravaged. She lit the brazier, waited until it burned down to a dark glow, then faced the window as the last of the sun's rays faded from the sky.

From where she stood, she could see the dark slash across the cliff face that was the trail to the Peak. He would come along that path to her. She didn't know how soon, but he would come. She almost reveled in that knowledge.

With an impatient gesture, she pushed back strands of her long black hair and ran her fingers across her face.

She drew two deep breaths and raised her arms above her head, joining her palms together, then closed her eyes and summoned all her power, pulling the words of the spell as if out of the air and the very stone of the tower. Finally her

hanting came to an end. As the sparkling vortex began to
uild around her, she smiled, for nothing could stop it now.

"Corwyn," she whispered. "You are undone." And the evil
adiance began to stream outward from her hands—the bind-
ng spell.

Let him come. She was ready.

Chapter Twenty-four

JAIMAH HAD NOT EXPECTED TO BE RETURNING TO THE TOWER ever. She had thought that she and Corwyn had gone to the Peak to die. Not in her wildest imaginings had she thought to have survived the mountain, let alone be returning to the tower to find Shayna. But here she was, pulling herself through the snow and trying to keep to Corwyn's pace. Shayna would have reached the tower by now and could be setting up any kind of trap or ambush to meet them. Jaimah wanted to forget the whole thing and leave the mountain forever and let Shayna to her own designs. But Corwyn would not, and because of him, Jaimah could not.

The light was dying over the western peaks now, the sun having gone behind the mountain, and she caught her breath as they went from shadow to shadow. She knew that they were coming near the tower and went reluctantly where Corwyn led her. She wanted to go back the way they had come and become lost on the mountain where no one would ever be able to find them. But she knew that it was not to be.

They reached where the trail cut across the face of the cliff and she could see the tower like a dark finger in the distance, ominous and threatening in its isolation. A small light shone in one of the windows. Shayna was there, waiting.

Jaimah was gasping for air when Corwyn took her hand and pulled her quickly along the trail through old drifts and along the ice-covered ledge. For a time they were perilously

lose to the yawning gulf that stretched out like a black void at
heir feet. Jaimah clung desperately to his hand as she tried
ot to look out into that emptiness. Then she realized that he
was trying to reach the other side before it got dark.

She tried to catch her breath and had to smother a cough
hat was brought on by gasping at the bitter cold. She kept her
aze turned away from the depth that opened up away from
he cliff—not the terrible void that fell away from the Peak,
ut no small depth either. She concentrated on going where
Corwyn wanted her.

When they reached a place of safety and stopped, she
agged against the cliff, pressing a hand to her aching side. As
he fought to bring her breathing back to normal, she looked
head to the light in the tower, brighter now that dusk was
eepening. The welcome there was going to be less than
varm, although, more likely than not, they were expected.
aimah frowned at the light, a small beacon from near the top
f the tower, a summons for them, should they come within
ight of it. She knew Shayna well enough to know that that
vas her intent. And she would be waiting, should they come
o that summoning.

Corwyn came to her and steadied her.

"Perhaps I should stay here," she said. "Then she couldn't
se me against you."

Corwyn looked at her. "No," he said.

And in the darkening of the night on the mountain, the
ght in the tower shone brighter.

"Come," Corwyn said softly, his fingers grasping hers,
hen moving lightly up her arm to pull her along, close beside
im.

But Jaimah could not find the strength to move. She drew
erself straight with effort. "Go—I'll follow," she told him.
Iad she said that aloud, or had he read it in her mind? She
vas not sure.

But Corwyn's arm was about her and he was striding to-
vard the tower, bearing her with him. Together they found the
nassive entrance door standing open, like a yawning gate
eckoning to them.

"When this is over," Corwyn murmured, his fingers lightly
rushing over hers, "you and I have much to talk about. Much
o learn."

Jaimah blushed for the implied intimacy of the statement.
he felt uncomfortably shy all of a sudden. She stared down at

her feet, then up again at Corwyn, unable to see his face in the darkness.

The door at her back slammed shut with a noise that jarred her to the bone. She whirled to face the sound.

"Shayna," Corwyn said. His shadowed figure moved around Jaimah to the door. In the dark lit with just a few stars in the gradually clearing sky, a faint light gleamed, as if a child blade had been unsheathed. There was a blow, soft but heavy, and the door shuddered. At a second blow the door fell open with timbers about the lock burst and lock broken.

Jaimah followed him into the entrance hall and waited while he pushed the door closed again.

Nothing could be seen in the darkness and there was not a sound in the still air. Then elsewhere in the tower a door closed. In the sudden silence, Jaimah moved closer to Corwyn.

"Now it begins," she said, her voice almost a whisper. This was the thing that she had been most afraid of—Corwyn and Shayna confronting each other in a last dreadful vying for power.

"Yes," Corwyn said then. "Stay behind me."

Shivering and telling herself it was no more than the chill of the tower, she went up the stairs after him. But there was a spell in the air. Jaimah sensed it with instant alarm. She recognized the feel of this spell immediately. This had the feel of Encheon's binding spell. She felt it pressing in on the air with suffocating force; with her heightened senses she felt it a hundredfold and she staggered against a step, gasping for breath.

Then Corwyn seemed to part it with the ease of a knife slicing through air, his hand taking hold of her arm and pulling her up next to him. With her hand on the wall, she felt her way along the cold stone as if the tower was a strange place. The nightmare was beginning again. But she held down her fear when they entered Shayna's room at the very top of the tower. The spell was stronger here; but at Corwyn's entrance it seemed to dissipate and fade away.

Shayna turned from the window at their entrance. A stand of candles there on the low sill was the only light in the room besides the fire in the hearth.

"On the plain," Corwyn said quietly to her, "a candle in the window speaks of welcome. Is that your meaning here, Lady?"

Shayna came forward and paused at the table; Jaimah felt

e Lady's eyes on her, coldly assessing her presence. Shayna as not pleased she was here; Jaimah felt it in that too-close crutiny.

"You brought her with you?" the Lady asked Corwyn, and ere was mockery in her voice. "Is this not a foolish extravagance?"

Corwyn said nothing.

Shayna's eyes shifted from Corwyn to Jaimah again, then ent back to him. "You have brought your death with you. Whatever you are, you have brought the means by which I ill destroy you. You are foolish to come here with her."

"It was for her that I came," Corwyn said.

There was silence from Shayna. She was perturbed; it did ot take a feeling out with the senses to know the disquiet ehind her eyes as she puzzled out Corwyn's words.

"Her service to you is at an end," Corwyn said.

"You are going to take her?" Shayna asked. Her lips retched into a scornful smile, and she struck Jaimah with ords.

"After all that I've done for you! After all that I've sacrificed for you! You can do this to me?" She had moved closer. With a soft expulsion of air, not even a sigh, she slapped Jaimah hard across the face, hard enough to send her stumbling against Corwyn. "You traitorous harlot! Get out of my ower! Get out!"

Jaimah took a step backward, feeling a rush of blood to her ace. She had experienced this kind of thing many times before, but this time there was embarrassment, and the embarrassment became rage.

Shayna raised her hand to strike again, but Corwyn caught er wrist and gazed steadily into her eyes. She was rigid with ury. Her eyes burned into those of Corwyn, who endured the ook without expression.

She was long quiet. Finally she said, in a near whisper, "Turn my hand loose."

Corwyn let go, and Jaimah felt his mind touch hers, cautioning her to silence.

Shayna's face was white and set, but triumphant contempt anced in her eyes. "So you came back to tell me that you are king her with you. Why? You could have gone without returning here."

"There is one thing yet that needs to be done."

Shayna hesitated, then put a hand on the table, a slight

betrayal of uncertainty. She was dressed as Jaimah had alway[s] seen her, in a long flowing robe, long in the sleeves, high i[n] the collar, a blackness that seemed even more so in the candle[-] light that came from behind her. She studied Corwyn in th[e] candlelight.

"And what is it that has yet to be done?"

"The stopping of you, Shayna."

There was a moment of stunned silence. Shayna's eye[s] went to Jaimah, worry in them about the part she might pla[y,] wondering why she was important to this. But the fear th[at] Jaimah saw briefly in her eyes was quickly covered with a[n] arrogant smile.

Shayna suddenly laughed in derision, turned her back i[n] defiance of him, went to the window, and picked up the stan[d] of candles.

Corwyn took off his coat of fur and laid it on a chest by th[e] wall, turning as he did so to look at Jaimah. "Do not sa[y] anything unless I bid you to." he said in a low voice.

Jaimah said nothing, but stared into his eyes, fear stirrin[g] in her at what she saw there. She wondered that this was th[e] same man that had forgiven a wild beast with gentleness fo[r] yielding to its natural instincts. There was a hardness in h[is] eyes now that set her heart to trembling.

A tread disturbed the silence; she looked from him t[o] Shayna, then back again.

He was a figure of awe between them. Jaimah did n[ot] know what he had come here to do—but knew suddenly th[at] it boded ill for Shayna. She had thought, until that momen[t,] that Shayna would be the end of the both of them. Now sh[e] knew that that was not to be.

Shayna sneered at Corwyn's approach. "I know what yo[u] think of me, but you are being insolent, apprentice. Yo[u] would do well to speak carefully."

"How do you know," he said softly, "what I think of you?[”]

Subtly and with the faintest hint of insult in those unspa[r-] ing eyes, he reduced her from mistress of the tower to th[e] vilest of creatures. He projected an aura of such disdain th[at] Jaimah cringed inwardly.

"This mountain," Corwyn said, "is a mountain that ha[s] long known my tread. Its beasts know my voice. It is mine."

Her short laugh was harsh.

This time he caught her hand in his, holding the wrist s[o] that he could inspect the ring.

"Such a fancy little trinket and so much destruction you ave caused because of it. You really should be rid of it."

Shayna shot him a startled look and snatched her hand back om him.

"Why should I?"

His face froze. "Why should you, indeed?" he asked. Only because with it you will destroy everything?"

Now Shayna swung farther around. "Do you not under-and?" Her tone held the hiss of an adder warning one away. er eyes were as fierce as those of an untamed hawk. Jaimah w that she gripped the candle stand so tightly her knuckles ood out in pallid knobs.

"The tower is mine," she said in a tense, low voice. "I will eep it."

"At all costs?"

"At all costs."

"Then I have come to stop you."

Again that hawk fierceness shone in Shayna's eyes as she ised her head to look at him.

"Do you think you can?"

"I know I can."

Shayna stared at him angrily, uncertainty lurking behind er eyes. She paled, as if a new thought occurred to her. She egan to believe him.

"Go away from here," she said, as if she were suddenly ath to do anything but beg him to leave. "Go unharmed. here will be no challenge."

"I will not go. There is much that needs to be answered r."

Shayna's lips trembled. Her face was lined with dark adow from the candles that flickered from her agitated reathing. Her eyes searched Corwyn, and the tremor per-sted.

"You are mad. You are more than mad. Do you know what u are claiming? No one can claim such and live. *He* would ot let you live."

"Yet, I do claim."

Shayna's eyes flickered over his face, to Jaimah, back gain, and her hand clenched. "Go from here, Corwyn, while u yet live. Take the girl with you if you must, but go. I will ot stop you."

"Shayna, you know that I will not go." His tone was al-ost kindly, and much more frightening because of it.

The Lady withdrew to the window without answering. No one moved. No one spoke. A misery crept into Jaimah's tau muscles, a chill that grew to a numbness. Shayna stood still while looking out into the night with her hands tucked into the wide sleeves of her robes.

"Go away," she said softly then. "I ask you to go away an take the girl with you. I will not give you the tower."

"I did not come for the tower."

There was a pause. At last Shayna turned and looked di rectly at him.

"You came here begging apprenticeship to me, hiding from me the talents that you have, biding your time until you coul take all of this from me. I can see your plan. I can see throug it. I know every part of it, because once it was my plan. But will not let you succeed. I will stop you."

"I did not come for the tower," he repeated.

Shayna glared at him, then stabbed a finger at Jaimah "You came for this? This pathetic little child? She is devoid o any worth or value. If this is what you want, then your amb tions are not very high, and I am amazed beyond words."

Corwyn folded his arms. "All of this is pointless, Shayna And I have not found Jaimah to be without value. She ha talents yet to be discovered, some already awakening. Bu they will not be yours to use. I have come to see to that."

"There is no doubt the girl has power, and some sma innate talent for using it. That's why I took her in to protec her."

"Protection?" Corwyn asked. "Or restriction?"

Shayna glared at him. "Take her and go!"

"I will not go. I have told you this."

Shayna made a helpless gesture. "You will not go; you d not want the tower. Why, then, are you here?"

"To do what Naibus could not bring himself to do."

"Naibus?" She stared at him, suddenly striken, pain an grief coming to her face. "You know of this?"

"There is much I know, Shayna."

Tears came to Shayna's eyes. She looked on Jaimah, an on Corwyn again. The tears in her eyes astounded Jaimah a much as if one of the walls had wept.

"Who are you to speak the name of Naibus to me?"

"One who knew Naibus better than any other. One wh watched as he became trapped in a web that he saw too late

ut such was his affection for his apprentice that he would not
ve stopped it had he discovered it sooner."

"You will not speak of Naibus to me, apprentice!"

Anger fired briefly in his eyes, but by the time he replied it
as gone.

"And you will not address me as apprentice, Shayna."

She stared at him, then smiled mockingly. "And what do I
ll you?"

Corwyn gave her a long measuring stare before he spoke.
Corwyn," he said. "It is my name," and the sting of the cool
tle rebuke cracked across the room.

She turned from him to set the candle stand on the table.
er robe swept the floor with a faint rustling sound and she
asped the back of a chair with an angry grip. "Your inso-
nce is intolerable."

"Naibus was my friend. And he was your protector. He
usted you."

"He didn't trust me enough to tell me the truth!"

"What truth?"

"The truth about the real power. These spells are nothing!"
he hit a small bottle of powder in anger. It scuttled across the
ble and came to a stop against an open book. "He did not
ust me enough to teach me where the real magic lies."

"He would have, had you not taken it upon yourself to take
e tower from him. He would have taught you everything that
u wanted to know, despite advice to the contrary. But you
ere greedy and dangerous with that greed, and you struck
o soon. In your obsession for power you destroyed the very
ing that you wanted."

Shayna listened to him with bent head; only her fingers,
xing and unflexing on the back of the chair, gave evidence
' her anger. But now she looked up at Corwyn, and her eyes
azed black in a white face.

"Then upon my head be it," she said softly, in a voice that
illed Jaimah. "And upon you a curse, for you will never
ve this tower. You will never rule from its rooms. And the
wer you sought here you will never possess, for it is mine.
nd the only thing you will take from these walls is that
thetic child."

Corwyn lifted his head and bent upon her a stare of such
ger as caused Jaimah to step back from him.

"And in return, Shayna, I set this doom upon you," he
id, his voice deadly soft. "What curse you lay upon me I lay

upon you. This tower will be taken from you. You will neve
rule from its rooms. And the power that you sought here yo
will never possess, *for it is mine!*" His words slapped acros
the room in terrible implication.

"I am not like Naibus, Shayna. I came as soon as yo
started tampering with things that are not yours to meddl
with. And I—will—stop—you."

Shayna stared at him, the fear that had come on her mir
utes before, suddenly plain on her face, final disbelief turnin
to belief, stunned and terrified.

"You!" she choked, as she recognized him and was horr
fied in that recognition. "Morgus!"

Into the screaming silence he spoke. "Yes."

Beside him on the table, amid a clutter of books and manu
scripts that Shayna had gleaned from the rest of the towe
stood a sconce containing a single, partly burned candle. Co
wyn moved his left hand over it and a pale, nacreous gree
flame sprang into being. Holding his fingers in the flame, h
coaxed it, drawing it upward and outward. Then, closing h
hand around it, it extinguished with a hiss. He raised dar
eyes to hers.

Shayna's head went back. Her glistening eyes closed an
shed tears. "I should have known. But I was too blind!" The
was a note of self-pity in her voice. She looked at him agai
fear fighting with something else unidentifiable in her. Sh
took a step back, looked at the door, stopped in her retrea
glanced at Jaimah, and turned her eyes on Corwyn again.

The room had grown very quiet.

Jaimah stood frozen at what she had just heard, the poun
ing of her heart a weight inside her.

Suddenly a smile came to Shayna's lips, and the black
her eyes glinted hard. "I have you!" And she turned to Ja
mah, the ring on her finger suddenly ablaze.

In blind instinct Jaimah whirled away. She saw the blu
white light leave Shayna's hand and flung up her arm to shie
her eyes as she fled, hesitating only a moment before runnir
to the stairs. She hesitated again, looking down the dark we
of stairs. Her stunned thought was becoming clear at last.

Corwyn was Morgus!

She looked back to Shayna's door in astonishment and sa
a movement there, shadows on the wall. She turned an
leaped down the stairs, taking them two at a time. A wild fe
was in her, that Shayna now had more cause to destroy them

Corwyn was Morgus!

She heard steps above her. Shayna must be running, trying to overtake her.

Jaimah struggled with the heavy entrance door, wedged through the opening before it was wide enough for her, and ran out into the snow, the cold of the air tearing at her lungs.

She was in the open now, looked wildly about her.

There was the slide to the ravine on her left, the cliff that rose behind the tower on the right, the trail to the Peak behind, and the trail to the plain around the tower on the other side. And there was a stand of boulders and rocks between that trail and the ravine—the only place to hide, unless she hid in the tunnel.

She turned and saw Shayna squeeze through the door, a black figure running toward her across the snow.

She ran, floundering clumsily in the knee-deep drifts, and rounded the tower, her breath coming in sobs.

Even if she hid, Shayna would have her eventually. Shayna knew the area around the tower as well as she did.

She ran, fell, scrambled up, and raced for the rocks, the snow tearing at her feet and fur coat, the cold air burning in her lungs, and her throat raw with the effort.

She darted into the rocks and scrambled for cover.

"Jaimah!" Shayna cried. "Come back here!"

Jaimah ran low among the rocks that bordered the trail from the plain, staying as far away from the ravine as she could.

"You owe me, Jaimah!" Shayna's voice came to her. She ducked and found a place where she could hide, sheltered, with her back against a boulder, wrapped her arms around her knees, hid her face in the fur and tried to breath slowly and silently, a thing that was almost impossible.

"I took you in. I raised you," Shayna's voice sounded. "Jaimah."

Jaimah remained still.

"I kept you, gave you a place, took you in when your own parents did not want you, raised you as my own."

Jaimah closed her eyes, a sudden heartache constricting her breath. It was a pain that she did not know that she had, an emptiness that had no mother, nor father. Shayna was using that loneliness to bring her out, to find her hiding place. She saw the trap and did not move, dared not even breathe. She did not look up, and her ears for a few moments heard no sound, but her new sense picked up Shayna's increased tension. Then the Lady called again.

"Jaimah, you owe me. I will not hurt you. Where are you?"

Jaimah pressed her face deeper into the fur.

Suddenly there was a sound, a muffled explosion.

A burst of fire lit the rocks around her and spattered her with snow and shards of torn boulder.

Jaimah fought to move, to bring herself to her feet.

Another flash of fire tore up the rocks where she hid, and she staggered as rock exploded and tore her leg, bringing a warm flow of blood.

"I will find you, girl!"

Jaimah could not see clearly, and the pain in her leg was a sudden hot torture. She forced herself to move, crept between the boulders, some of which burned with the impossible flame of herb fires.

She moved toward Shayna slowly, shaking. She hoped that the Lady thought that she was at the far end of the rocks. Then Shayna was beside her, seizing her with fingers that dug painfully through the furs and into the muscles of her arm.

"Stand up, girl!" she ordered.

She hauled Jaimah to her feet and dragged her away from the rocks. Struggling for purchase in the snow, Jaimah floundered through the deep drifts. Then beyond Shayna's shoulder there was a movement.

The Watchers!

Jaimah saw them first. Their hatred hit her like a sledge.

She gasped and cried out, stumbling back, pulling on Shayna's grasp. They were using that hatred as a weapon, beating at Shayna; and the hurtful blows of it made her sway, sick and spirit-wounded. Behind them came a score of others, closing in, their eyes avid with a lust of hatred such as she had never met before. And she saw all of this through the eyes of the largest Watcher who sat to one side, his link with her partially restored.

Shayna stared at the beasts, her hand on Jaimah's arm tightening into an agonizing grip. But she could only have seen the animals as indistinct shapes in the dark, because she did not see through the beast as Jaimah did. The Watcher began to rumble in his throat, his eyes following Shayna's every move.

"You've got to help me, Jaimah," Shayna whispered. "I an't defeat these animals and Corwyn, too."

Jaimah shook her head. "No." Her voice seemed to come rom another.

Shayna's fingers tightened, whether in fear or anger Jaimah ould not tell.

"You've got to understand what's happened here—what Corwyn has done. What he is! These creatures are his!"

Jaimah flung her head up to meet those darkly condemning yes with her own stare.

"I know what he is," she said. "But do you? He is Morgus. nd he came here because he knew what you were doing. Do ou understand that? He *knew* what you were doing. You were side the sanctity of your tower and he still knew. You can't efeat him!"

"You pathetic child! What do you know of these things? He an't stand against our power combined."

Jaimah lifted her head a degree higher. "I'm not in your rvice any longer, Shayna."

The Lady glared at her. "Are you really so stupid after all?"

But Jaimah was prevented from replying.

There was a sound from the tower, the opening of the door nd its striking the stone wall with a resounding thud. Jaimah ood still; in her heart was a wild, sudden hope.

Shayna whirled, sprang forward, and dragged Jaimah in ont of her. She whispered fiercely in her ear. "You move, ou say anything, and he is dead!" Her arm tightened around aimah's throat with a painful jerk. "Do you hear me, Jaimah? e dies at even a flinch from you. I have the ring and he on't strike with you in the way. Do you understand?"

Jaimah nodded and Shayna pulled her stumbling away om the rocks. The Watchers moved restlessly, angrily, weav-g back and forth, rumbling threateningly deep in their roats.

There was a movement by the tower, a shadow in the dark nd the crunch of even steps in the snow. He came toward em, his lean body making a blackness against the stars, his othes shimmering like frost; he seemed to gather the dark-ss about him and pour it forth again.

"Girl!" Shayna whispered, then switched to a conciliatory ne. "Daughter. Give me your strength." There was pleading her words.

"I'll never help you!"

There was a snap of fingers in the silence, and a green light winked into being high above them, lending an eerie glow to the whole area.

The Watchers shifted restlessly in the new light. Corwyn stopped several feet away.

"No closer!" Shayna warned, her fingers vengefully tight on Jaimah's arm, her other arm still tight around Jaimah's throat. "I have her now and if you want her to live, you will do as I say."

He gave no answer, and there was something about his silence that chilled.

"When one has enemies, one can not afford to have vulnerabilities," Shayna taunted. "It will be your downfall, just as it was the downfall of Naibus. You should never have loved, Morgus." His name fell from her lips with scorn and contempt.

"Don't do this," he said. "The game will destroy you."

Shayna laughed. "I don't think so." Her grip on Jaimah tightened. Jaimah winced.

"Let her go, Shayna." The aura of his power was palpable, seeming to glimmer around him at every movement.

"No."

"Let her go."

"She has betrayed me and now she is my hold on you. I think it's fitting that she be the means of your death. Don't you think so, Jaimah?"

Her fingers tightened even more on Jaimah's arm, and Jaimah clenched her teeth to keep from crying out.

Shayna laughed. "Do you see how obedient she is?"

"Shayna, I'll not tell you again to let her go."

Shayna just laughed.

Corwyn's hand came up.

A bolt of light whizzed past Jaimah's head; she cried out as she was flung to the side.

Shayna landed in the snow, but quickly came to her feet.

For half a breath they faced each other, Shayna and Corwyn, mistress and apprentice.

No—Shayna and Morgus.

Indecision was on Shayna's face. She looked at Jaimah just beyond her reach.

Corwyn gave a low whistle and the Watcher slipped into place between them.

"They have a mind of their own, but they're useful creatures at times." He smiled at Shayna's glare.

Then she chose retreat and whirled and ran, with the Watchers surging after her.

Corwyn strode to Jaimah and pulled her to her feet. "Are you all right?"

"Yes," she said, omitting to tell him about her wounded leg. Blood was still oozing down into her boot.

"Good," he said. His eyes rested on hers, searching, then he turned his head to look out in the direction that Shayna had taken. The green light on his hair was like glowing moss. "Get back," he bade Jaimah. "Where I won't worry about you." His hand on her arm gently put her from him.

Jaimah hesitated, then turned to him. "Corwyn?"

He did not protest her hestitation; nor did he turn his head from the darkness he was watching. "Go, Jaimah," he said. "We will talk later."

"I will stay," she said.

He turned dark eyes on her, then took hold of her arm.

She grasped his intent immediately. "Corwyn, I will not—" she tried to loosen his grip. This was her battle as well.

"Jaimah," he said, his voice deep and quiet and carrying a tremendous authority. Jaimah felt the stare of those night-blue eyes pierce her heart with an indefinable pain.

"I will not leave you," she said.

"You must. You are not ready for this. You still have too much to learn." He held her close a moment with a final fierceness, then flung her from him so violently that, entangled in her cloak, she overbalanced and fell.

There was movement. Hands caught her, pulled her erect, steadied her for an instant against a firm body. "Forgive me." Then both body and hands were gone. "Stay here."

She felt the resistance against her bone and flesh increase as she made to follow him. She felt also his searching thought, though it was not aimed at her.

Corwyn, turning from her, gave an order to the beasts. "Keep her here." The absolute command in his voice startled her for a moment.

She plunged forward. At the same moment there leaped from among the rocks to her right a gray-white body, bowling her over so that, in a moment, she lay flat, the heavy forepaws of the Watcher planted on her, pinning her to the ground, while its long fangs were very near her throat. She fought against the weight, but the beast held her helpless. Yet it did not follow up that leaping attack with any swoop of those jaws to tear out her throat. She smelled the strong breath of the beast and heard the rumble of a growl, so low it was more a vibration through its body than an actual sound.

Out of the air sounded a command, a word perhaps, but none she could understand. The beast wrinkled lips in a silent warning snarl. Then it raised the bulk of its weight from her, though it did not back away. Instead, it crouched as if well ready to pull her down a second time, should she move forward again.

She felt bruised and sore from being flattened so against the stone and was slow in drawing to her knees. Her legs throbbed with pain.

Corwyn turned and moved away without looking back at her. She limped back to the rocks where she huddled behind a boulder, her brow on her trembling arm, her eyes on his profile.

He stood still, waiting while time passed and the silence continued, a target in the green light. Icy and chill, a slight breeze stirred, the early warning of another storm on its way. Corwyn did not move, though he was without fur or coat; the fur boots still on his feet reached only to his knees.

A voice from atop the tower broke the stillness; it's owner well hidden in the darkness. "You cannot win. I will have you before the night is over." There was a flying hiss and a flame streaked to Corwyn's feet, fizzled out in the snow. More herb fire.

"You remember I know the spell now. Your doing I think, Morgus. Encheon gave it to me by your permission, it would seem. For this I am grateful."

Corwyn turned and swept fire in that direction. Shayna laughed before the night sky erupted in a crown of light, cutting her off. Jaimah lifted her head and squinted as lightning cracked the sky. She grimaced as a roar sounded, to be swallowed almost immediately by a thunder crash. She looked and saw Shayna on the tower. Her hands were held high as her fingers wove patterns in the air. Jaimah saw, too, that her lips moved, but she could hear none of the words. The evil radiance began to stream outward from her.

Jaimah gasped, for this was the spell that had been waiting

or Corwyn in the tower—the spell of binding. She cried out
Corwyn and rose to her feet in alarm.

Corwyn did not appear to have heard her, but she knew that
e had. His left hand moved slightly. Jaimah was just able to
limpse his face before his form was blurred by a dark aura
at seemed to flow out from within him, swallowing even the
rim, green night.

The air turned bitterly cold as Shayna raised her hand
igher, holding it, palm outward, toward Corwyn. A sneering
oice rang through the air.

"You know nothing, Morgus. You are a fool!" Shayna's
lack hair blew in her eyes, and her robes fluttered around
er. She began chanting again, this time loud enough to be
eard.

Like spiders, the words crawled over Jaimah's body. The
hanting of the words grew louder and louder, Shayna's voice
ronger and stronger. Silver light flared, then vanished. A
gged flash of lightning blinded Jaimah, and the vicious crack
f thunder immediately following made her cover her face
ith her hands. When she looked up, the largest of the
Vatchers was standing a few feet from her.

His eyes bored into hers, black and glittering. Jaimah
asped. A terrible ache in her chest caused her throat to close,
nd for a moment she could not draw a breath. Sharp, tingling
ins jabbed her fingertips, and a chill convulsed her body.
nconsciously, she shrank back against the rock, her hands
lenching and her nails digging into her numb flesh. She could
ot move. His gaze held her, and she wondered in panic if he
ad cast a spell upon her.

Sharp as a blade, his gaze pierced her soul. She found
erself rising, moving forward, his will moving her instead of
er own. She faltered as his nearness smothered her and stole
er breath. She stumbled, nearly falling. She felt weak and
izzy.

Shivering, she hastened the last couple of steps and had
ised her hand to the beast, when the sky suddenly sizzled
ith a blue-white flash of lightning. The simultaneous explo-
on of thunder knocked Jaimah against the Watcher. She
rew her arms about him, pressed her face against his
oulder, and let herself sink into the darkness of his mind.
he beast at last gave a sigh and blinked.

The same feeling of duality that Jaimah had experienced in
e mountain came over her again, many times stronger, al-

most buckling her knees with the strength of power it brough
to her. She saw with a clarity that startled her, so much
sharper was her vision than the last time they had shared
minds. But this time it was not just the Watcher that controlle
what was seen and heard. Jaimah added her own will in
strange but exhilarating kind of partnership. This time th
beast welcomed the merging. And this time Jaimah wanted i
as well.

With the Watcher's eyes, she saw a lone figure tread softl
toward the fading light that surrounded the tower. Walking
unheard, his footfalls were sucked into the vast darkness al
around him. Unconsciously, Jaimah held her breath. At firs
she could discern no features of him, only a shadow of dark
ness in the dim light, as if night itself had taken form an
shape there. The shadow was lit by a shimmer of warmth.

Then he spoke.

"It will do you no good, Shayna. Naibus created the spell
and it will not work. Even if it did, I would not let it work
Why do you think I let Encheon give it to you?"

Shayna's chanting voice broke off enough to shout
"You're a liar, Morgus. Naibus would not do that to me."

"He knew you better than you know yourself. He set it t
tempt you and to give me time to stop you."

"Lies! I'm not afraid of you!"

"You would be wise to be afraid, Shayna." Corwyn's voic
sank into the night. "But no matter how much you would fear
you would not fear enough."

Jaimah shuddered. The words had a portent of doom i
them, and she gripped the beast tighter, knowing that som
terrible thing was going to happen.

Shayna's voice could be heard chanting again, loudly, i
taunting tones. A flash of lightning and a shattering cras
made Jaimah cringe. Opal color flickered up from the top c
the tower, an ominous darkness howled overhead, and wind
came, shrieking. Shayna stood in the storm, a clear figur
looking down. Lights flashed across the sky and across th
cliff behind Corwyn. For a spell that didn't work, Shayna wa
creating havoc with it.

And Corwyn stood, a terrible figure in the tempest.

Raising his arms, the darkness shimmering about him a
the lightning flared and the thunder roared, he spoke a singl
word.

Black lightning streaked across the sky and crashed into th

iffs. Black fire rushed down the rocks toward the tower, ering and uncontrollable. The full fury of the storm raged abated.

Corwyn raised his hand and a black flame roared from it. It ruck the wall of the tower with an explosion that burned on e stone. Brilliant, jagged light forked down in answer, a ark contrast to the black flames that burned on the frozen ow.

A second black flame was cast.

Another streak of light answered, this from Shayna's ring, riking Corwyn. He was engulfed in blue-white flame.

Jaimah cried out. Stuggling against the beast's hold on her, e sought to free herself.

"Look!" the beast's thoughts centered on her unmercifully, inging her sharply into control. "The flames do not touch m!"

Gasping in the tightness of the Watcher's possession of her, e saw that he spoke the truth. Corwyn was not affected by e white blaze that danced around him. He stood, a black gure in the writhing tongues of wildfire, untouched and un-athed. Jaimah caught her breath.

From the first moment she had ever seen him, she had felt e forceful magnetism of him. She had also felt the glint of anger behind his unwavering gaze and had been terrified of a unseen energy that she could feel but not identify. Now she w him in the authority of his power. There was in his stance e absolute knowledge of who he was and what he was capa-e of doing. In him was a power that was beyond compre-ension, totally and completely unparalleled in anything she d ever seen. He was superior in his strength, extremely owerful, unequaled and unrivaled by anyone or anything. He tally and utterly eclipsed Shayna.

Now she knew why he was called the Master.

The Watcher spoke in her mind, his thoughts soft and thal. "Watch," he whispered exultantly.

And as she did so, a curtain of blackness smashed down on e area between the cliffs and the ravine. A single, titanic ack, so deafening that it went beyond the threshold of hear-g, hammered out of nowhere, and the blast of it hurled the o of them off balance and threw them with bone-jarring rce to the ground. As the incredible noise roiled away, Jai-ah tried to get to her feet, her head spinning and the link

with the Watcher shattered. She felt sick, and her limb
wouldn't obey her.

The world was suddenly filled with a profound silence, a
if poised.

Jaimah felt the first tremors and, for a moment, thought
was her imagination. Then a sudden heaving of the groun
sent her to her hands and knees. Light erupted. The roc
under her cracked. The foundations of the tower buckled. Sh
struggled to her feet only to be thrown off balance again.

As she fell, she heard words of magic, and they mingle
with the singing of her blood and the singing of the stone c
the tower. His voice . . . Corwyn's voice . . . entered her like
stabbing rapier. She seemed to be spinning around an
around, caught up in the incredible power of his words an
whirling away with him into the blackness of the night.

In the nethermost parts of her mind, she realized with as
tonishment that he was using words. But before she coul
discern why he was doing so, she perceived, as if in a drea
from another time and place, Shayna shriek in blind anguis
and pitch forward, writhing.

A hand caught at her, pulling her up from the snow.

"Away!" This voice belonged to Corwyn, not to the beas
"Away—the tower falls!"

There were crashing sounds and a rumbling. She came o
of her dream and cringed as a huge block landed nearby. Co
wyn had her hand and was pulling her away through the u
yielding snow. The tower flared, engulfed in a sudden flame
and then crumbled, the sound of its going a rumbling shoc
the sky alive with it. The whole ledge hung suspended an
crumbled down the slide into ruin at the bottom of the ravin
And through it all came one discordant note—a harsh, hear
broken moan.

There was a sudden sweep of wind, sword-sharp with colc
whirling out Jaimah's clothing and raising snow to blind he
eyes. Somewhere from within that icy haze came hands, arm
and a body that steadied her. Was it the wailing of the win
which carried that strange chorus of grunting cries? Then sh
knew there were Watchers all around them, triumphant in th
fall of the tower.

She could barely keep to her feet. A moment later, Corwy
caught her up and carried her out of the whirlwind of nois
and ice, back toward the cliff. She summoned strength t

tand and pulled away from him, facing the swirling fires that oiled from the ravine to the sky.

She thought that she cried out, so great was her horror, and hut her eyes only to open them again. She tried to see hrough the flame; sobs that she could not stop were tearing at ier. She stood rigid, breathing heavily and having to exert all ier self-control to prevent her legs from buckling under her as he power of Corwyn in the air and the stone of the mountain lrained away.

All she could think about was Shayna down in the ravine mong the shattered walls of the tower and lying within the lames that ate the rocks and leaped to the sky. It seemed to urn forever, bright, hot, and cold.

Then, at last, it was over; the fire was gone, and Jaimah, iow slumped to the ground, felt as if that energy which had illed the air and her blood seeped away little by little, leaking ut of her until it was completely gone. The mountain was leathly silent, and she was conscious of the Watcher flanking ier. The air was void and empty, cold gray again. Only a faint race of ozone lingered. She bowed her head and hid her face n her hands.

For a long time she wept, unable to move, unable to think, nd unable to stop.

And then, when there was nothing left, she looked up to vhere Corwyn had withdrawn and was watching her with a evel contemplation.

She stared at him, almost angrily, now that he was Morgus.

The beast lay at ease on the other side of Corwyn-Morgus, .is eyes near closed, though he licked now and then at one aw. And Jaimah knew in that moment that these two, animal nd man, had known each other long. For many years they ad walked the mountain trails together. Many times they had .unted together and had eaten together. And often they had hared the same cave at night. Although the Watcher had been n the mountain and Corwyn had been in his fortress, they ad watched the tower together.

In that watching, they had watched her.

She looked up as Corwyn came with his almost silent read. Even if she could not hear his footfall on the rock and :e, she could sense his coming. He was like an invisible force listurbing the air.

Her reaction was to stiffen with anger.

"You killed her," Jaimah's voice was tight with accusation.

He stopped and stood stone-still, looking at her. The dar
of his eyes was no more than a shadow in the aftermath of th
blaze that was lingering in reflected light off the snow and th
cliffs.

"It could be no other way," he said.

"But to kill her?"

"She would never have stopped—you know that, Jaimah
She would have destroyed everything in the attempt of wha
she was doing. She had to be stopped."

"But to kill her?"

"It had to be done."

"Who are you to decide such things?" Jaimah said angrily
"Shayna was all I had. She was the only life I have eve
known. She took me in when others did not want me. Sh
gave me a place to be. She gave me a place that was safe."

"But its only safety was Encheon."

"So *you* say. How can you make such judgments?"

"She was stepping beyond her bounds. It is my responsib
lity to see such things and to take measures."

"Measures?"

"I do not like the way that this turned out, either. Shayn
had talent. She had real possibilities. What she could hav
learned," he said, "beyond the simple knowledge that she had
if she had only been . . ." His words trailed off, and he didn
finish what he was saying.

Jaimah thought that she heard regret in his voice. But ther
was nothing on his face to indicate that he felt anything lik
remorse. She studied him for some other clue to give meanin
to his words, but she found nothing, and the faint, narrowin
of his eyes told her he knew she had failed. He was closed t
her, and she felt an unexpected regret that he had drawn bac
from her.

"Is it so hard knowing who I am?" he asked, his eye
unwavering on her.

For a moment she could think of nothing to say. The ques
tion could have been a plea for understanding, could hav
been an apology, or could have been wistful. But it was no
And his eyes remained steady on her, taking in every reactior

"You never told me who you were. Even though I aske
again and again." She realized then that it had hurt her. H
was Morgus and had never told her—in fact, had gone t
great lengths to keep it from her.

"I could not tell you," he said. "I could not let you know who I was. You were not so certain that you could trust me. You were not so certain that you *wanted* to trust me."

"And can I? Trust you?"

He sighed.

"Can I?"

"You will always be able to trust me, Jaimah," he said wearily, "if you will only let yourself believe it."

"How can I be certain? How can I know what you are, who you are? After this, how can I ever know?"

"Does a name change so much?"

She stared at him for a moment, then her gaze faltered before his penetrating one.

"It makes a difference who I am?"

"Yes," she said. "You are Morgus!" Her voice failed, and his name passed her lips in an angry whisper.

"And you cannot trust Morgus."

"No!"

She looked up at him in defiance.

He narrowed his eyes again, turning his head to one side as he squinted at her.

He drew in a long, slow breath.

"Very well, Jaimah," he said.

Suddenly her heart was thudding hard against her ribs, and she met his gaze as steadily as she could. She foreknew that he was going to change things, turn them upside-down. Things would never be the same for her again.

"You are free," he said, bringing her attention back to him with a jolt. "You are free from Shayna and now from me. I will take you anywhere you want to go."

She felt her heart constrict in violent reaction.

"Or, if you prefer, I will leave you here and you can go where you will on your own."

She stared at him, stunned.

He turned to face her directly, his eyes resting on her with a curious appraisal. He asked her quietly. "Do you want me to go?"

He stood there without any expression on his face, waiting for her to answer him. She had the horrible suspicion that he already knew what her answer would be and was just waiting for her to say it. But try as she might, she could not keep it from her lips.

"No," she answered hoarsely. Her voice trembled; she would have backed away, but his eyes did not release her; she felt the tremor in her muscles. "No." Her heart was laboring, his words burning like a knife in her flesh.

She remembered with startling vividness how it had felt to have his lips on hers; she remembered how it felt to be pressed against him with his arms tight about her. She thought of what it would be to have him gone, and she knew that her heart would wither up and die.

"You want me to stay?"

"Yes."

"You could come to terms with how I am?"

"I have no liking for the name Morgus," she said.

His lips quirked grimly. "What is in a name?"

He was unyielding. There was no compromise on his face. He would not deny that part of him, nor would he change it. If she went with him, it would be on his terms. She would have to accept him as he was.

She looked at him, so silent and unswerving, and knew that that was how it was going to be.

Then it came to her—that even as Corwyn, he had been as she saw him now. He had kept only his true identity from her. He had never kept the truth of his abilities from her. He had never hidden his nature. Morgus would be no different than Corwyn had been.

But could she ever forget what he had done here? She looked to the ravine where the tower lay in ruin.

Could she forgive him?

"Jaimah?" His voice broke softly into her reflections.

She turned back to him, her eyes drawn to his. Then she knew it did not matter. Whatever he was, whoever he was, whatever he had done, it did not matter. He had come for her. He had left his fortress at the edge of the desert and had come to the mountain to take her away with him. That was all that was important. Now he was talking about leaving her and the decision was hers. But she couldn't let him go.

She began to move, slowly at first, then quicker, until his arms came up around her, drawing her close.

"Take me with you. Take me with you." In her own hearing her voice was very thin and hoarse. "Do not go without me."

His eyes swept hers with an intense search. "You are certain? You can accept me for what I am?"

And Jaimah heard herself say, "Yes," and realized that the
:ision had been made long ago. She whispered. "But where
you taking me?"

His chuckle was vibrant and the sound seemed to travel
ough his fingers and down her arms. Jaimah felt a little
gle of exultation. A moment later she felt herself lifted,
ortlessly, and wrapped in an embrace so encompassing she
t, on that lonely elevation, as if she had come home after a
g voyaging.

He took her mouth with a hunger she could feel through
:ry sense. His mind reached into hers with a fire so deep it
iddered through her like molten lava. She clung to him
ible to take in the flame of that sending all at once. She felt
if she had vertigo, her head spinning dizzily, and clutched
his shoulders to stop herself from falling. Finally, she was
are of the touch of his lips on hers, the strength of him
iinst her, and the thrill that went through her as his kiss
essed her.

His mouth left her parted lips and softly brushed over her
:ek to her throat. She pulled back a little and met his eyes,
 heartbeat erratic. But he looked at her calmly, a slow smile
 his mouth. Heat rose to her face, conscious that he knew
 as no other and that it would be that way forever.

His arms tightened around her almost convulsively, and a
id reached up to stroke her hair, soothingly, comfortingly.

"Jaimah, my dear, What do you know of the desert?"

"Nothing," she answered. "Only what Encheon showed
."

"Oh, yes." He looked down on her. "The time he brought
i to my fortress and you ran away. Well, then. I will have to
e you there again . . . But this time, you'll not get away."

The beast arose from where he lay beside Corwyn, threw
 his head, and gave such a roar as made her head ring. She
ught at first it was an echo of his cry she heard, until it was
eated from afar. Then she could not mistake the ring of it
 it sounded a second time. She had heard such before but
 /er as full-toned and holding the notes so strongly.

Out in that blackest of the night there was another now—
 he sent forth his challenge.

About the Author

DEBORAH TALMADGE-BICKMORE is a native of Western Colorado and makes her home there with her three children and two cats. Giving up a column in a local newspaper to concentrate solely on her creative work, she writes the kind of novels that she wants to read but has difficulty finding. Now she spends much of her time exploring and hiking in the desert canyons of the Western Slope and eastern Utah where she writes on index cards that she carries in her pocket. The rest of the time she spends with her children.

Julia or Lisa? Life or death? . . .

"Why?" Julia whispered. "What are you doing this for? I never saw you before in my life—"

"Sitting in that car," he said, "waiting for him. I knew then, he'd always take you from me."

He's crazy, Julia thought, *absolutely crazy. But Fox will get me out of this; Fox won't let him hurt me.* She felt a great numbing unreality, a conviction that this was not really happening. But it *was* happening—to her.

He held the Mercedes to a steady 55 m.p.h. They swept through the tunnel, then he braked sharply and pulled into a turn out, reaching for her brutally as she flung herself at the door. Paralyzed with fear now, she did not resist when he dug into the glove compartment for a length of white cord, and bound her wrists together. He said in a neutral voice, "Can't have you jumping out at the first stop light, can we?" He examined his work critically, checking the knots. Then he sat back and stared at her.

"I'd sure like to stop and play with you right now, Lisa," he said with regret, "but we'd better push on. But there'll be plenty of time, Lisa. I'm going to play with you real good. Not like you played with me—"

"Oh God, God," Julia cried. "I'm not Lisa. My name is Julia Naughton. I don't know what you're talking about. Please! Take me back!"

"I can't go back," he said reasonably. "I killed Jack."

Julia cried: "And who in hell is Jack? D'you mean Fox? *You killed Fox?* . . ."

Also by Mary-Rose Hayes
from Pinnacle Books:

The Neighbors